MW01592459

SUBURBAN BOY

SUBURBAN BOY

Peter Doobinin

iUniverse, Inc.
New York Lincoln Shanghai

Suburban Boy

Copyright © 2005 by Peter Doobinin

All rights reserved. No part of this book may be used or reproduced by any means, graphic, electronic, or mechanical, including photocopying, recording, taping or by any information storage retrieval system without the written permission of the publisher except in the case of brief quotations embodied in critical articles and reviews.

iUniverse books may be ordered through booksellers or by contacting:

iUniverse
2021 Pine Lake Road, Suite 100
Lincoln, NE 68512
www.iuniverse.com
1-800-Authors (1-800-288-4677)

ISBN-13: 978-0-595-36597-5 (pbk)
ISBN-13: 978-0-595-81026-0 (ebk)
ISBN-10: 0-595-36597-3 (pbk)
ISBN-10: 0-595-81026-8 (ebk)

Printed in the United States of America

1

When I left the shack, where I had spent three months trying to write and failing categorically, I was besieged by a number of difficult feelings, including anger and resentment, frustration, fear, anxiety, disillusionment, disappointment, and despair, but beyond these feelings, much deeper, much further in, lay something else. It was not something I would call a feeling. It was a hunger. A hunger for answers.

As I pushed my battered Toyota down the New York State Thruway, I didn't have a clear idea about where I was going to go. I thought I might try to find a place to live in Queens, in one of those grimy districts across the East River from Manhattan, in Astoria or Woodside or Jackson Heights. I thought perhaps I'd try to find a small dingy apartment, a place I could rent cheaply, a place where I could hole up and write, where I could crank out a book, a novel.

But I wasn't enthralled with the idea of locating myself in Queens. I wasn't moved. I wasn't inspired.

But then, as I approached the Triborough Bridge, I had an insight. An inspiration. Suddenly everything was clear, as clear as the bridge making its pattern against the blue-grey November sky. Suddenly I knew precisely what I was going to do: I was going to sail over the Triborough, and through Queens, eschewing Elmhurst and Flushing and Ridgewood, all those gloomy brickridden

1

enclaves, and I was going to head east, into the vast sprawl of sub-urbs, into Long Island. I was going to go to Bayview.

I was going to go to Bayview.

The thing was, I had to go to Bayview. I had to go to Bayview, because that was where the answers were.

I pressed the accelerator.

I was going to go to Bayview, to the town where I had lived when I was a boy. I was going to encamp myself there, at least for awhile. And I was going to study the landscape. I was going to investigate. I was going to excavate. I was going to dig. Like an archaeologist. Except that I wasn't going to dig for crumbled arti-facts, for bits of pottery or arrowheads. I was going to dig for answers.

2

I got off the Southern State Parkway at the Jerusalem Avenue exit, headed down Jerusalem into the heart of Bayview. I drove past an asynchronous assemblage of strip malls, fastfood restaurants, used car lots, gas stations. Then I drove into the neighborhood where I had lived when I was a kid, the grid of long straight streets studded with small nearly-identical boxshaped houses.

I drove down Massachusetts Avenue, a long straight street that intersected at right angles with long straight streets with presidents' names. Van Buren. Fillmore. Cleveland. Grant. I drove slowly, examined the flat terrain, the boxshaped houses, the tiny rectangular yards, the driveways cluttered with cars sitting in the late afternoon gloam, the trees, branches hanging, filled with colored leaves.

Right from the start, the reader should not be mistaken. This was nothing like those upscale martini-sipping wife-swapping suburbs depicted in the books by Updike and Cheever and other chroniclers of so-called suburban life. No. This was a fiercely middleclass suburb. A blatantly suburban suburb. This was a place notable, more than anything else, for its unrelenting, unrepentant ordinariness. It was a place notable for almost nothing, other than its ordinariness.

I turned onto Jefferson Street, the street that I had lived on, drove past the strangely familiar houses, the strangely familiar yards.

I pulled to the curb in front of number 57, the house where I had resided for the better part of my youth.

I stared through the windshield, studied the house.

I was thrown. I was taken aback by what I saw, by the way the house looked. It didn't look at all like the house where I had passed my growing-up years. It had been almost completely transformed. The house's exterior, which had been covered with green shingles when I was a boy, was now encased in dull white aluminum siding. An addition had been built above the garage; a screened-in porch had been attached to the side of the house. The lawn, perpetually yellow and crabgrass-stricken during my early years, comprised a healthy-looking cape of greenish blades. The driveway, formerly a crooked strip of loose gravel, owned a sleek blacktop surface. The tree next to the driveway, a mere sapling during my childhood, was an impressively tall specimen, with long reaching branches inundated with yellow and gold leaves.

I stared at the house. I stared hard. I tightened my focus. I squinted, contracted the muscles around my eyes, manufactured a strict tunnelvision. I tried to see something. I tried to see something I couldn't yet see. I tried to see beyond the changed surfaces, beyond the superficial realities, the aluminum siding, the shiny driveway. I tried to ascertain a certain non-physical understanding of the place, a deep charged truth that I was sure was lingering, somewhere, here.

I got out of the car. I stood in the middle of the street. Stuffed my hands in the pockets of my jeans. The November breeze rearranged my hair, infiltrated my leatherjacket.

I bent my head down, looked at the street. I stared at the street, the bare pavement. I inspected it, carefully, noting every detail, the different grey shades, the black specks, white specks, smudges, the coarse textures, subtle bumps, ridges, cracks, folds.

The thing was, I knew that this street held answers.

I had always believed that the best times of my life had transpired on this street, on this piece of grey road. They were the times, the perfect timeless times, when I was seven, eight, nine years old, when I had played on this street with my friends, Chris Adelkravitich, Willy Smithberger, Kevin Anderson, Louie Plunkett. They were the times we had spent playing in that exuberant way that kids play, the times we had spent riding our bikes up and down the street, the times we'd spent playing all sorts of games. And, specifically, and most significantly, they were the times, these times I considered the best times I had known, they were the times we had spent playing baseball.

I had never known the same happiness I had known back then, during those times I had spent playing baseball on this street with my boyhood friends. I had never experienced, during the course of my thirty-nine years, anything close to that sort of joy, that sort of clean, untarnished joy.

I lifted my gaze. I looked toward the part of the street where my friends and I had staged those memorable baseball games. I studied the sacred terrain, the site of that ancient ballfield, the narrow length of pavement, the spot where we had chalked home plate, the big tree that had served as first base, still there, bending, if haggardly, over Jefferson Street. I stared. I riveted my eyes to this segment of the street. I stood there for a couple of minutes, and I concentrated on the street, I stared intensely.

The thing of it was, I wanted to see something.

I wanted a vision.

I wanted a specific vision: I wanted to see the street the way, the exact same way, it had looked on a July afternoon in the summer of 1963 or 1964. The sun slanting down, across the street. My friends and me playing baseball. Positioned on the sunsplashed pavement, our thin bodies leaning forward expectantly, infused with joy.

Chris Adelkravitich, blonde hair plastered down, at the plate, holding a bat against his bony shoulder.

Willy Smithberger standing at first base, touching the tree, yelling, "Cmon Chris, bring me in!"

Kevin Anderson, the pitcher, holding up his ragged brown mitt.

And me. Perched at shortstop, my crewcut glistening. Gripping the baseball, bending my arm, throwing the ball.

The ball flying through the summer air.

3

I decided to check into the South Shore Motel.

When I was a kid, the motel had been a Howard Johnson Motor Lodge. I remembered it as a bright, nearly sparkling establishment, a place that had exemplified Bayview's hopeful, forward-looking attitude. But the motel building had not withstood the passage of time with much style or grace. The two-story edifice was in terrible condition. It had a wasted look. It looked, now, decades later, in the 1990s, as if it was in the throes of a terminal illness. At some point the brick exterior had been painted white, but the paintjob, which obviously hadn't been applied with alot of expertise, had faded, had turned drab grey, the color of cigarette ash. The plastic motel sign was dented, the "h" in South was lying on its side. The parking lot, which, to my surprise, was about half filled, was buckled, riddled with craters. Scraps of litter, hunks of newspaper, blew about.

As I pulled into the lot I noticed a sign in the registration office window indicating that the South Shore offered "X-Rated Videos" and "Mirrored Rooms" and I quickly realized that the motel no longer catered to the same clientele, the travelling salesmen and visiting relatives, that it had during my younger days. It seemed quite obvious that the South Shore was focussed on serving the needs of a very specific population, namely horny couples, men and women who wanted to rent a room for a few hours, a room where they could attempt to fulfill their most basic, and urgent, and perhaps illicit, carnal desires, a room where they could fornicate, where they could perform any variety of sexual maneuvers in an uninhibited, unhinged manner, a room they could enter quietly, surreptitiously, and then exit from, after wiping their sullied body parts with the motel's inevitably coarse towels, in an equally surreptitious fashion.

I went into the registration office, stepped to the plywood counter. A scrawny baldheaded guy wearing a white tee shirt was sitting behind the counter, watching a miniature color TV.

"I need a room," I said.

"Short stay?" the clerk asked.

"No," I said. Having visited motels of this ilk on more than one occasion, I knew that he was asking if I wanted to rent a room for just a brief length of time, perhaps four hours, enough time to engage in some form of sexual activity. "I'm not sure how long I'm going to stay," I said. "Maybe a couple of days."

The clerk wriggled his lips, gave me a querulous look. He probably hardly ever encountered customers who wanted to remain as guests at the motel for more than a few hours. He probably, undoubtedly, thought that I was a dubious sort.

He gave me a key to a room on the second floor. Number 23.

I went back out to the Toyota, got my suitcase. Went up a flight of corroded wooden steps, then along a corroded wooden veranda.

I found number 23. Went inside.

Standing inside the door, I surveyed the accommodations. As I might've guessed, the room was a dismal affair. A kingsized bed dominated the space. The big bed monopolized the limited square footage with a kind of weary spite, like an old, demented beast asserting its domain. The bed had a flimsy plywood headboard, a thin sunken-in mattress. It was covered with a brown bedspread, a piece of fabric that'd undoubtedly been subjected to a long sordid history of battering, pummelling, pounding, flopping, grating, seeping, splotching. The other furnishings, the night table, dresser, easychair, were terrifically dilapidated, they were the sort of items you might find at an especially down-and-out goodwill store or a garage sale in a less privileged section of town. The TV was an ancient model; you knew, even before you turned it on, that the picture would be fuzzy, erratic. The carpeting, which was a dull brown color, was matted, squashed down. The walls, also a brownish hue, were afflicted with different streaks, stains, blots, discolorations. The walls were bare but for a single painting, a watercolor rendering of a brokendown rowboat that looked like it might've been the work of a seventh grader at Bayview Junior High.

I stepped to the bed, inhaled the room's not-exactly-pleasant odor. A thick fetid smell stuck rather stubbornly to the atmosphere. This smell, I knew, was not uncommon to these kinds of rooms. It was a smell, it was my fairly educated guess, that resulted from the clash of odors emitted by men and women participating in strenuous, no-holds-barred sexual exploits and the accumulating, long-festering odors that emanated from various mildews and bacteria that the less-than-diligent cleaning staff had neither the skill nor inclination to eliminate.

I dropped my suitcase on the bed.

I could hear, coming from both of the rooms adjacent to my room, the sounds, the impossible to misinterpret sounds, of couples having sex, probably fucking. In one of the rooms, a woman was screeching like some kind of tropical tree dwelling creature. In the other room, both participants, the man and the woman, were groaning desperately, as though they were trying to relate some important life-and-death news, but had lost the ability to communicate using their normal English-language vocabularies.

I stepped away from the bed, stepped across the room, my sneakers sliding against the sodden, mashed-down carpeting. I wasn't all that concerned, I wasn't all that put off by the deplorable conditions, the unappealing bed, the downtrodden furniture, the smell, the noise. I figured that I wasn't going to stay at the South Shore for very long, for more than a few nights. I couldn't. Even if I wanted to, I couldn't. Ironically enough, I couldn't afford to stay more than three or four nights. I couldn't afford the $45 per night that the motel charged.

I stepped to the window, pulled apart the moldy brown drapes, pushed open the window. I figured I'd let in some fresh cold air.

I stood in front of the window. I looked out, beyond the wood-plank veranda, beyond the parking lot, toward Sunrise Highway, the six-lane thoroughfare that slashed past the motel. The road was glutted with rush hour traffic, crammed with cars moving east and west. It was growing dark and most of the cars had their headlights turned on. And I stood there, and I watched the cars, moving slowly forward, the headlights burning. There was something about the whole scene. The cars lunging ahead, the lights prodding the increasing dark, the gradual movement in, the ceaseless urging, toward home. There was a poetry to it. An undeniable, exquisite poetry.

What can I say? I was, and always would be, a suburban boy, and I found stuff like this as beautiful as anything.

I sat on the bed, against the wobbly headboard, with a notebook and a pen, and I wrote down the names of some of the friends I'd had when I was growing up in Bayview, some of the friends with whom I had shared a close, meaningful bond. If I was able to connect with one, or more, of these old friends, I thought, I might get answers, I might get the sort of answers I was looking for.

I jotted down these names:

Chris Adelkravitich
Willy Smithberger
Kevin Anderson
Louie Plunkett
Mark Carroway
Mickey Fitzland
Andy Lerman
Kenny Pelligrini
Bob Filch
Steve Longeran
Rich Zoolman

I grabbed the phone book, and I attempted to look up each of these onetime friends. I flipped through the thick book, carefully, scrupulously, utilizing my knowledge of alphabetical order, acquired during my tenure as a student at Furley Elementary School. I wasn't sure if I'd find a listing for any of these boys, now obviously turned men. I sort of thought I might not. I sort of thought that most, if not all, of the friends I'd had when I'd lived in Bayview had probably long since departed this suburb, had probably long since left, in search of greener pastures. But in the end I did find one listing that I thought might belong to somebody whose name I had written down. It read:

William J. Smithberger.... 96 Willow St., North Bayview.... 523-4563

After thumbing through the phone book, after trying to find each of my former comrades, I went back to this listing. I studied the nearly mystical appellation. William J. Smithberger. I scribbled the address and phone number in my notebook.

I was rather confident that this William J. Smithberger was the William Smithberger, better known as Willy, that I had been friends with when I was a youngster. I doubted that there was another person bearing this unusual name, residing in this part of Long Island, just a short distance, it seemed, from the neighborhood where my boyhood companion, Willy Smithberger, had lived. No. I couldn't imagine that there was another William Smithberger navigating these long straight suburban streets.

The fact that this William Smithberger owned the middle initial "J" strengthened my conviction, helped to convince me that this Smithberger was the Smithberger I had known. I remembered, or at least seemed to remember, that Willy Smithberger's middle name was Jerome. I remembered Willy telling me this, we were five, six years old, we were sitting on the steps in front of his house, the grey house on Adams Street, I remembered him telling me that he'd been bestowed with this middle name, Jerome, because it'd been his grandfather's, or perhaps great-grandfather's, name.

All in all, I was rather confident that this William J. Smithberger was Willy Smithberger, the Willy Smithberger I had been friends with when I was a kid.

It had to be him.

I stretched across the squalid bedspread, listened, with a modicum of interest, to the sounds piercing the wall beyond my left shoulder. The sounds of a man and a woman fucking. The man was groaning like a moose that'd just been shot in the hindquarters. And the woman was talking, jabbering, in rapidfire style, like a play-by-play announcer describing the action in a fastpaced NHL hockey match.

I thought about Willy Smithberger.

I couldn't help but think about Willy Smithberger.

I was sure that the Smithberger I'd found in the telephone book was my boyhood friend, Willy Smithberger. I knew it was. *I knew it*. I could sense it. I could feel it. It was as if I could feel Willy, it was as if I could feel his presence, his middleaged vibration, it was as if I could feel him lurking, not that far from the motel, just a few miles from where I lay.

I was sure that this Smithberger was the Smithberger I had grown up with. And I knew that if I was able to get in touch with Smithberger, call him, and meet with him, that there was a good chance I might discover something, I might get answers.

I knew, however, that I probably wouldn't try to call him.

The truth, I knew, was that I had been deluding myself when I had taken the phone book off the night table, when I had tried to look up my old friends with the idea that I might attempt to contact somebody.

The truth was, I liked to think that I could do it, that I could effect a reunion with somebody like Willy Smithberger. But I knew I couldn't.

I knew myself. I knew that there were certain things I couldn't do, and I knew that this was something I couldn't do.

The truth, I knew, was that I didn't have the ability, I didn't have the ability to call somebody like Willy Smithberger. I hadn't seen Willy, hadn't spoken to him, hadn't had any sort of contact with him, in twenty-five years. And, I knew, I didn't have the ability to suddenly pick up the phone and call him, to bridge this wide expanse of time. I didn't have the ability to make such a bold leap.

I just wasn't the sort of person who could act in such a bold, uninhibited manner. I had never been that sort of person. I had never, for instance, been the sort of person who could walk up to a woman I didn't know, an attractive woman, in a grocery store, or at a bus stop, and, just like that, start a conversation with her, engage her in a stimulating dialog, and then ask her for a date. The fact of the matter was, I wasn't capable of acting in that sort of extroverted fashion.

And, I knew, I wasn't capable of calling Willy Smithberger, reaching out to him, after all the years, the long swath of time, the twenty-five years, that'd passed. I wasn't capable of it. I just wasn't.

I lay on the bed, on the flaccid mattress.

I thought about some of the times that my friends and I had played baseball on Jefferson Street.

I thought about a summer day when I was nine years old. It was a day when we played all day long. We started in the morning, and although we must've taken a break at some point to get something to eat, I couldn't remember that, I could only remember that we played through the afternoon, into the early evening. It was a boiling hot day, but as the day wore on we didn't tire, but, to the contrary, we seemed to gain strength, and as the afternoon progressed we fell into a rhythm, a deep groove, and every move we made, every throw, every swing of the bat, every stride of our thin legs, seemed synchronized, nearly elegant. And as the afternoon segued into evening everything became suffused with an irrevocable happiness, a resolute joy.

And then, during the last inning we played, I made what was probably the greatest catch I ever made.

I was playing shortstop. Louie Plunkett was the batter. Louie, who batted lefthanded, was a tall, strong boy. He wasn't an especially adept hitter, but every once in awhile he got hold of a pitch and crushed the ball.

This was one of those occasions.

Swinging as hard as he could, Louie hit a wicked line drive. The ball screamed past the big tree that served as first base, veered sharply toward the lawn that belonged to Mr. and Mrs. Shaw, the elderly couple that lived across the street.

I started running as soon as Louie swung. I ran over the curb and dove across the sidewalk. Or should I say, I flew. Because for a long radiant moment, I flew. I hung above the concrete. Then I skidded onto the Shaws' lawn. And I stretched out my arm and stuck out my glove, and somehow the ball landed in the webbing.

My friends ran toward me, cheering. Willy Smithberger and Kevin Anderson picked me up. They lifted me onto their shoulders....

They wavered, not strong enough, they kept me aloft for just a few seconds....

But, as I looked back, I couldn't remember them putting me down, I could only remember them holding me in their skinny arms, holding me up....

I lay on the bed, half-listening to the sounds coming through the waferthin motel room walls. In the room to my right, a woman was laughing, and, at the same time, crying. And lying there, and vaguely listening to her, I had a sudden realization. I had an insight.

I realized that I had to call Willy Smithberger.

I had to call Willy Smithberger.

I had to do the very thing I didn't think I could do.

I had to call Willy Smithberger.

I had arrived, it seemed, at a critical point. I'd come to a branch point, a point at which the road divided into two drastically different directions, and, it seemed, my life, the rest of my life, might very well depend on the direction, the path, I decided to take. And so, it didn't seem like I had any choice. I had to take the bold, unprecedented course.

I had to call Willy Smithberger.

The insight electrified me.

A new energy rippled through my reclined carcass. And, as often happens during moments of such insight, I suddenly perceived things, everything, with an enhanced clarity. I perceived everything through a highpowered lens. My surroundings, the motel room, suddenly seemed intensely bright. The bedspread seemed extraordinarily lovely, like something you'd find displayed in Bloomingdale's. The walls appeared to have just been painted. The picture of the rowboat seemed inordinately gorgeous, like something you'd see hanging in the Whitney or the Guggenheim.

I jumped off the bed.

I jogged across the carpeting. I went to the window, looked out at the cars, the lights drilling holes in the suburban night.

I saw everything clearly, more clearly, it seemed, than I'd ever seen anything.

I saw, clearly, what I had to do.

I had to call Willy Smithberger.

4

I left the motel room.

I drove to Main Street, to the Big Burger. When I was a kid, Main Street had been a calm two-lane road lined with stores and stretches of trees and scraggly brush. Now, two and a half decades later, it was a congested four-lane track overrun with strip malls, chain stores, office buildings, condominium apartments. The roadside had been altered significantly. Almost nothing that'd been there when I was a youth was still there. A notable exception was the Big Burger. The hamburger joint was still standing. And, remarkably enough, it looked the same. The flimsy sheet metal structure, painted white. The enormous red, white and blue hamburger hanging above the plate glass. The fuzzy light coming through the glass. It was as though the town fathers had decided to preserve the place, as though it was an historic landmark. And, in the scheme of things in a place like Bayview, perhaps it was.

I parked the Toyota. Went into the narrow glass-encased enclosure where you placed your order. A middleaged guy, a guy probably around my age, as a matter of fact, was standing at the counter. His kids, his son and daughter, were standing alongside him, they were both young, grade-school age, probably not even ten. A tall skinny pimply adolescent male wearing a ridiculous white hat was manning the counter, and behind him three or four similar, similarly behatted adolescents were preparing burgers,

17

dropping baskets of fries into vats of sizzling oil, pouring soft drinks. I stepped to the counter, told the pimplefaced kid what I wanted. Three burgers, two bags of fries, a medium coke. The same thing I'd always ordered whenever I'd gone to the Big Burger.

I received my food, went back to the car. The Big Burger was strictly a take-out place. There was no dining area, there were no ketchup-smeared plastic tables and chairs. You ate your meal in your car, the way you were supposed to when you came to a venue such as this.

I spread out my repast on the passenger seat, gobbled the greasy, but inarguably tasty, burgers and fries. I stared at Main Street, the vehicles coursing to and fro, and I thought about the times I went to the Big Burger when I was a boy…I thought about the times I went to the venerable hamburger stand with my family, my parents, my brother, Eddie, and my sister, Denise…I remembered a specific time, when I was eleven or twelve…we were all crammed into the light blue Chevy station wagon…and my mother and my father were fighting….

"David…," my mother said. She gave my father a pained look. "You dropped a french fry…."

"So what," my father said.

"You dropped a french fry," she said.

"What the hell do you want me to do about it," my father growled.

"Find it."

"Why don't you leave me alone."

"It went down the seat."

"That's too damn bad."

Sitting on the flat metal floor in the back of the station wagon, where I always situated myself when the whole family piled into the car, I looked, cautiously, toward my father. His massive, 6'2",

240 pound body was throbbing, rubbing, pushing against the pale-blue vinyl seat. His navy blue sportsjacket was twisted, bunched-up. The cheaply made jacket looked like it might rip, tear apart.

"It went down the seat," my mother said, in a thin distraught voice.

"I don't give a damn!" my father screamed.

"I want to keep the car clean."

"I don't give a damn what you want!"

"David...don't yell...."

"Fuck you!" my father said, and then he grabbed a bag of french fries and screamed, "Fuck you! You fucking cunt!" and he threw the fries into the back of the car. Fries flew everywhere, splattered the windows, the seats. Some of the limp oily fries hit my brother and my sister and me.

"David!" my mother shrieked.

"Fuck you!" my father screamed. He picked up a hamburger, squeezed it in his big fist, mashed it against the windshield. "You fucking bitch!"

He slammed the demolished burger against the dashboard.

"I've fucking had it," he said. "I've had it with your shit. I've had it, Maryanne. I can't take it anymore. It's the same goddam shit all the fucking time. It's the same goddam shit. I've had it."

He pushed open the car door.

"I can't take it," he said.

He got out of the car. He walked across the Big Burger parking lot....

I remembered watching him, hunched in his crummy blazer, walking across the lot, then walking down Main Street, down the sidewalk, into the developing twilight....

✤   ✤   ✤

I also remembered other, more pleasant times when I went to the Big Burger.

I remembered the first time that my friends and I rode our bicycles to the revered fastfood emporium. Chris Adelkravitich, Willy Smithberger, and me. We were probably about six years old. We pedalled through our neighborhood, Chris on his Schwinn with the basket attached to the handlebars, Willy on his hand-me-down that he'd painted black, and me on the Raleigh that I'd nicknamed "The Red Rocket." We left our neighborhood and pedalled down several unfamiliar streets, long straight streets that we'd never before bicycled on. Then we rode along Main Street, on the sidewalk, we pedalled down a stretch of Main that until then we had never biked on.

We were like pioneers, pushing forward into new territories, extending the frontier of our young lives.

We got to the Big Burger.

We sat on the concrete, against the building, consumed the spoils of our journey, burgers, fries, cokes.

We talked, laughed.

And sitting there, with my friends, I knew, I knew that life was inherently joyful, and that everything was open to me, anything was possible....

I left the Big Burger.

I drove down Main Street, then down Park Blvd, toward the South Shore Motel. I'd go back to the motel, I figured, and I'd see how I felt, and if I felt ready, if I felt strong, if I felt confident, I'd call Willy Smithberger.

I headed down Park, past the monotony of houses, windows awash with artificial light. I neared Sunrise Highway. But then, when I was about fifty yards from Sunrise, I slowed down, and I pulled to the curb. I waited for some cars to pass. Then executed a U-turn.

I drove back down Park.

I wasn't ready, I didn't think, to call Willy Smithberger.

I turned onto Main Street. I'd find a bar, I figured. I'd suck down three, or four, or five beers, and then I'd go back to the motel, and I'd analyze my condition, and if I felt like I was ready, then perhaps I'd call Smithberger.

And if I didn't feel quite ready, that would be alright, I told myself. I'd call Smithberger the next day, or the day after. I didn't have to call him right away, I told myself. I didn't have to call him immediately, on my first night in Bayview, on the first night of my prodigal's return.

I drove down Main Street.

I spotted a bar, a place called Bigley's, an unassuming tavern squeezed in between an array of stores, all closed for the night, in a beatendown strip mall.

I pulled into the lot.

Went in.

The place was typical. Dingy. Badly lit. Smoky. The long wooden bar was, of course, the main attraction. A handful of men and women, run-of-the-mill suburbans, were sitting on stools, leaning against the rail, clutching beers and mixed drinks, gabbing nonsensically. Toward the back there were tables, but nobody was sitting at any of them. There was a pool table, and a couple of burly blue-collar types were hovering over the felt, wielding cues. The jukebox blasted Sinatra. "My Way."

I sat on a stool, toward the end of the bar, the end furthest from the door. I beckoned the bartender. He waddled over. He was a big pulpy kid, probably just a few years removed from playing second string offensive tackle for the Bayview Beacons. I asked him for a Michelob.

He put a cold dripping Michelob on the bar.

I knocked down the bottle.

Then I knocked down another bottle.

Then I knocked down another.

Then I went into the john.

I pissed.

On my way back to the bar, I stopped in front of the jukebox. I studied the selections, thinking I would play something if I could find something I wanted to hear. I was hoping I might find something that would inspire me. I was hoping, specifically, that I might find a Beatles song, an early Beatles song, a song from, say, 1964, from that time when the Fab Four hit the scene, when they first came to America, first appeared on *The Ed Sullivan Show*. I was hoping I'd find a song like "She Loves You" or "All My Loving" or "A Hard Day's Night."

In 1964, when I was nine years old, I was thoroughly inspired by those Beatles songs.

I remembered the times when Willy Smithberger and I listened to his sister's Beatles records. Willy's sister, Louise, who was about five years older than us, had a phonograph and a goodsized stack of Beatles 45s, and when she wasn't around Willy and I would sneak into her room and play those 45s, we'd play them over and over, we'd sing, we'd dance, we'd strum imaginary guitars, pretend we were John and Paul....

And I remembered the times when Willy and I rode our bikes through the neighborhood, singing those Beatles songs. We'd pedal up and down the long streets, past the boxshaped houses, the nubby trees, the scruffy lawns, and we'd sing, we'd sing "I Saw

Her Standing There" and "I Want To Hold Your Hand" and "I Should Have Known Better"....

I examined the jukebox. I checked the selections carefully. But I didn't find any Beatles songs. I did find a McCartney tune, "My Love," but I didn't have any interest in playing it. I was only interested in playing one of those Beatles songs from 1964 or 1965....

I polished off my sixth, or seventh, beer, looked at the clock on the wall behind the bar. It was almost 10pm.

I had to decide if I was going to try to call Willy Smithberger.

If I was, I was going to have to leave the bar within the next few minutes.

I didn't think that I should try to call Smithberger after 10:30pm.

I assumed that Smithberger was an archetypal family man, that he had a wife and an assortment of kids, and I assumed that by 10:30 or so Willy and his clan of latter-day Smithbergers would be wedging their way into the evening's more subdued creases. They wouldn't want to be disrupted, jolted by a phone call from somebody like me. I didn't want to disturb Smithberger by calling him at an inappropriate hour. I didn't want him to have an adverse reaction, didn't want him to develop a negative opinion of me, didn't want him to think that I was a heedless lout, an inconsiderate jerk.

If I was going to go back to the motel and call him, I was going to have to leave Bigley's almost immediately, I figured.

I glanced at the clock.

I pondered my empty beer bottle.

Then I summoned the bartender.

I wasn't ready, I realized.

I would call Smithberger tomorrow, I told myself.

The bartender placed a fresh bottle in front of me. I picked up the bottle, guzzled a substantial amount of the ice-cold beer, the frothy liquid splashing down my throat like rainwater down the gutter on somebody's boxshaped house.

I would call Smithberger tomorrow, I told myself. I'd be better off, I told myself. It would be Saturday. It would be a better day to call. Smithberger probably grinded away at some unbearable nine-to-five job, in some unbearable office. He probably took the Long Island Railroad back and forth every day, to and from the city. By this time on a Friday night he was probably spent. He probably wouldn't be able to engage in any sort of enthusiastic dialog, I figured. But by tomorrow he'd be distanced some, physically and emotionally, from his undoubtedly stress-ridden work situation. He'd be more relaxed, I figured. More approachable. More able to converse in a spirited fashion.

I swilled my beer, acknowledged my dim visage in the mirror behind the bar. I would call him tomorrow, I told myself. I would call sometime in the afternoon. I would catch Willy in a relatively laid back, becalmed posture, perhaps sitting, slumped, against a big overstuffed easychair, watching a college football game, his feet, shoes removed, propped on the fucking hassock, the remote control glued to one hand, a bottle of his favorite domestic ale fixed to the other.

I would call him tomorrow.

I would *definitely* call him tomorrow, I told myself.

I knocked down my fifteenth, or sixteenth, beer. It was 3:30am. Bigley's had all but emptied out. There was only one person, besides myself, sitting at the bar. A guy with an unkempt ponytail wearing a Cincinnati Reds tee shirt; this guy'd been leaning against the wood for hours, in the same position, locked in a pose, like an animal in one of those displays at the Museum of Natural History.

I rested my empty bottle on the bar.

The bartender came over.

"Wanta nother?"

"Nah, thanks," I said.

"How bouta nother shot?"

"Sure," I said.

He poured a shot of sambuca, the seventh, or eighth, shot he'd poured me, at no charge, during the course of the evening.

I threw back the shot.

I dropped a five dollar bill, a tip for the barkeep, on the scuffed brown wood.

Then I left.

I walked, staggered, across the parking lot. I stepped in a hole, turned my ankle, almost fell down. The breeze slapped my face, my chest.

I reached the Toyota.

I realized, however, as I dug into my pocket for my keys, that I needed to piss.

I walked to the side of the strip mall. Stood, facing the blank concrete wall, unhooked my jeans, grabbed my dick, pissed. I squirted a long arching stream against the wall.

I got in the Toyota. I rolled down the window, all the way, thinking that the cold night air would keep me awake, alert. It was a strategy I'd employed many, many times, in similar circumstances.

I pulled out of the lot.

I headed down Main Street, through the blurred suburban night, the rheumy streetlamp light, the silent cold November wind that predicted everything.

5

I didn't get out of bed the next day until sometime after 2pm.

I rolled, I fell, off the kingsized bed, like a dilapidated suitcase, an archaic defaced Samsonite, falling off an airport conveyor belt.

I felt lousy, I felt like shit, as was to be expected, given the large quantities of beer and sambuca that I'd poured into my body the previous night.

I showered. I stood in the mildew-streaked stall, the water pelting me, a flurry of metal pellets, bruising, dinging my sensitive flesh.

I downed a couple of Tylenol.

I put on a black sweatshirt, jeans, my sneakers. I donned my black leatherjacket. Left the motel room.

It was a cold afternoon. The sky was thick, layered with grey, black clouds.

I drove down Sunrise, found a diner, the Flamingo Diner, a gaudy spectacle emblazoned with fake chrome and pink neon.

Inside, I sat in a pink booth, amidst other pink booths and pink tables. About half of the booths and tables were occupied, held down by textbook suburbans, chalk-faced, unimaginatively attired characters gripping forks, staring at heaps of food.

I wolfed down a plate of scrambled eggs, home fries, toast.

I glugged several cups of coffee. The waitress, a plump young blonde, kept bringing the pot and I kept pushing my cup toward her.

"Thanks alot," I said, after she filled my cup for the fourth, or fifth, time.

"No problem," she said.

"I appreciate it," I said, applying my friendliest tone of voice. I looked directly at her. And I smiled.

She smiled.

She wasn't notably attractive. And she was certainly overweight. But I nevertheless found her appealing. I found her rather appealing.

I studied her as she left my booth, I studied her clunky shoulders, her tits, her hefty ass projecting into her pink waitress's uniform. I watched her scud through the maze of pink tables, clutching the coffee pot. And I couldn't help but think that I wouldn't mind fucking her. I couldn't help but think about what it would be like, couldn't help but envision it, taking her to the South Shore Motel, peeling off her foodsplotched uniform, steering her onto the big kingsized bed, sliding my prick into her wet snatch....

I finished off what was left on my plate, the last particles of burnt potatoes, the crusts of dried-out bread, then I went to the cash register and picked up a copy of *Newsday*. I went back to my booth, opened the paper to the classifieds, and looked through the columns that listed apartments and rooms for rent. I wasn't sure how long I was going to stay in Bayview, but I knew that no matter how long I stayed I wasn't going to be able to quarter myself at the South Shore Motel for more than a few nights. I simply couldn't afford to stay at the motel. I couldn't squander my money, my limited funds, on $45 motel rooms. I just couldn't.

I'd had a fair sum of money in the bank when I had quit my job and left my apartment. And I still had a good portion of that money. I still had about $10,500. But this $10,500 had to last me.

I had no interest in getting a job.

I certainly had no interest in going back to my old job, working as a sales rep for L.G. Buchanan School Supplies.

I'd had that job for seventeen years. I'd spent seventeen years selling school supplies, scissors, paper clips, hole punchers, construction paper, etc., to elementary schools, junior highs and high schools in New York City.

I'd done what I'd done for too long, way too long.

I had killed myself for seventeen years.

Killed myself.

And I was finished with it.

I wasn't going back.

And I had no interest in finding some other job, another similar job, another job in which I'd be forced to trudge the mind-numbing heart-annihilating path of American worklife.

No.

The fact of the matter was, I had no interest in finding any kind of job.

I wanted to write.

I wanted to write a novel.

I realized that the $10,500 in my savings account wasn't enough money to sustain me for the length of time it was going to take to complete a novel. But I figured that this money would subsidize my efforts while I wrote a first draft. At least a first draft.

I'd stay in Bayview for as long as I had to, I figured. I'd perform the required archaeology. I'd call Willy Smithberger. I'd get together with Smithberger. I'd cull answers. I'd garner inspiration. And riding the fast currents of this inspiration, I'd begin work on a first draft, a draft that I might finish while I was still encamped in Bayview, or perhaps after I had moved on, had curtailed my visit to this suburb, but a draft, in any case, that would evolve, with a little work, a little striving, into a transcendent fiction, a luminous book, a book that would establish me as an author to be reckoned with, a book that would effect my transition into a new life, a writer's life.

I scanned the listings, came across several ads that described places that seemed to meet my criteria. They had affordable rents. They were furnished. They were located in Bayview or near Bayview.

I tore out the page the ads were printed on, folded it, stuffed it in my back pocket.

I would call a few, if not all, of these places tomorrow.

I wasn't going to be able to make any calls this afternoon. I wasn't going to be able to interact with potential landlords, yammer on the phone in an upbeat manner, present myself in a convincing way. I didn't feel well enough. I was, simply, too hungover. I didn't have the strength, the energy, the clarity, that I was going to need.

I would make some calls tomorrow, I told myself. I would try to arrange to look at some apartments, and if I was able to look at a few places, and if I saw something that I thought was suitable, I would take the place, I wouldn't hesitate, I would put down a deposit, and I would make plans to move in as soon as I could.

I drove through the grid of long straight streets, past the houses, the trees, the colored leaves. I drove down Jefferson Street, past my old house.

I drove down the block, past the house that Louie Plunkett had lived in, the house that Kevin Anderson had lived in.

I went around the corner, drove slowly down Adams Street, stopped in front of the house where Willy Smithberger had lived.

It had occurred to me that Willy's parents might still be living in Bayview, that, in fact, they might still be living in this boxshaped house. I hadn't seen a listing for Mr. and Mrs. Smithberger in the phone book, but I'd recalled that they'd kept an unlisted number. However, as I settled the Toyota near the curb, I saw sure signs that Warren and Edna Smithberger no longer resided here. A portable basketball hoop was standing next to the driveway. A purple girl's bicycle was lying on the blacktop. It was obvious that whoever lived in the house had young kids. It was obvious that the Smithbergers had moved, had moved on.

I stared at the house, this house that Mr. and Mrs. Smithberger, and Willy's older brother, Mark, and his sister, Louise, and Willy had once inhabited.

Like the house where I'd grown up, the house where Willy Smithberger had spent his youth was covered with dull off-white aluminum siding. Almost all of the houses in the neighborhood were covered with this kind of siding. As far as I was concerned, it was depressing stuff. Encased like this, the houses resembled teeth that'd been fitted with bad caps, the sort of caps that left no doubt that they were indeed caps, the sort of caps that forced you to believe that beneath their obvious guise something was rotting, was dying, was perhaps already dead.

I stared at the house, tried to see through, past, past the crude physical facts, the drab siding.

I remembered playing with Willy, playing inside the house, in the tiny family room with knotty pine walls. I remembered playing board games. Chutes and Ladders. Go to the Head of the Class. Candyland. Uncle Wiggly. I remembered sitting on the floor in front of the TV, the clumsy box with massive dials, watching the black-and-white screen, watching *Bozo the Clown* and *Officer Joe Bolton and the Three Stooges* and *The Sandy Becker Show.*

I remembered Willy and me playing in the backyard. I remembered playing in the corroded wooden boat that Mr. Smithberger had bequeathed to Willy, pretending we were PT boat commanders engaged in heroic battle with Japanese ships. And I remembered playing catch, Willy and me standing at opposite ends of the small rectangular yard, throwing a baseball back and forth.

I remembered Willy's father. I remembered him working on the boat, the seventeen-foot outboard that he kept on a trailer on the length of grass beside the driveway. I pictured him, leaning over the fiberglass hull, his roastbeef forearms lined with grease. This was the clearest picture I had of Warren Smithberger. In fact, it was the only clear picture I had of him.

He was a steamfitter, a scary-looking man, with a big pink head, a few wisps of hair, and a huge gut that protruded into his grime-streaked tee shirt like a Tupperware bowl.

He almost never spoke to me. And I couldn't recall him ever playing with Willy and me and our other friends, throwing a baseball, or kicking a football, or something, the way Bob Adelkravitich and Frank Anderson and even my own father sometimes did.

As a kid, I'd never quite been able to figure out if his reticence was the result of a general coldness or a discomfort, a lack of affinity for children. Probably, I guess, it was a little of both.

Sometimes he would summon Willy and me, usually when we were playing in the front yard, making a racket, creating more of a disturbance than he cared to endure. He'd disengage himself from the boat, call us over, give us some money, a few coins, and he'd tell us to go to Tony's Candystore and buy ourselves something.

And we'd ride our bikes to Tony's, where we'd sit at the long polished counter, swivel on the tall padded stools, sip cokes. Or perhaps we'd buy candybars. Or we'd buy baseball cards.

During the summer months, when my friends and I went to Tony's, we'd spend most of our money on baseball cards. We'd buy one or two packs—they cost just a nickel in those days—and we'd sit on the sidewalk in front of the store, and we'd tear open the packs of cards, and we'd examine the cards. There were certain cards that we coveted, usually the cards that depicted players from our favorite teams, and when we got those cards we exulted. We were truly happy.

I remembered a particular summer afternoon when Willy and I went to Tony's Candystore. I bought two packs of cards, and when I opened the first pack I discovered a Mickey Mantle card. I was an ardent Yankee fan, and Mantle was my favorite player, by far. He was a hero to me. When I saw that I'd acquired his card, I rejoiced. I emitted a triumphant whoop. I danced on the sidewalk. I flailed my arms and legs. Eventually, I sat down. And I opened the second pack. And I found another Mantle card. And I went crazy. I jumped to my feet and I performed another manic, unbalanced dance routine. And then I started laughing. And Willy started laughing. And for the next five or ten minutes, Willy and I couldn't stop laughing, we lay on the sidewalk, we rolled on the concrete, and we laughed....

I drove down Jerusalem Avenue. Stopped at a deli. Bought a six-pack. Budweiser cans. Sat in the car. Opened a can. Slugged down about half of it.

I headed back into my old neighborhood. I'd drive around for awhile, I figured. I'd drink the beers. I'd study the landscape. I'd try to absorb whatever vibrations, whatever psychic remnants from my childhood might be filtering through the late afternoon air. I wasn't going to be able to do much else. I wasn't going to be able to look for a place to live. And I certainly wasn't going to be able to call Willy Smithberger.

I would call Smithberger tomorrow, I vowed, as I motored through the grey light, past the bland houses.

I envisioned the call.

Sitting on the motel room bed, I'd pick up the phone. I'd punch out the numbers.

Willy would answer, his voice weary, but imbued with a touch, at least a touch, of his familiar boyish anticipation.

"Hello," he'd say.

And I'd say, "Hello. I'd like to speak to Willy Smithberger…."

And he'd say, "Yeah, this is Willy…."

And I'd continue with, "Willy, you're probably going to find this hard to believe…but…."

I traversed the local streets for a couple of hours. I drove slowly, my left hand gripping the steering wheel, my right hand wrapped around a can of beer. I held the beer between my legs, lifted it quickly, but casually, to my mouth, every minute or so.

I drove past Furley Elementary School, where I'd gone from kindergarten through the sixth grade.

I drove past Bayview Junior High School, the school I'd attended as a seventh and eighth grader.

And I drove past Bayview High School, where I'd been a student for just a couple of months.

I tooled past Cotter Park, where my mother had taken my brother and me when we were very young.

I cruised past the Bayview municipal pools, where I'd learned to swim and had spent quite a few summer days.

I drove past the Richard Place Little League field.

I went past the Bayview Multiplex, a monstrous sixteen-theater structure that stood on the piece of land that the Bayview Theater had once occupied. Chris Adelkravitich, Willy Smithberger, Kevin Anderson, and my brother, Eddie, and I had seen *A Hard Day's Night* at the Bayview Theater in the summer of 1964. We had stood on top of our seats and had screamed and had sung as loud as we could for the entire length of the movie. It'd been one of the most joyful, most ecstatic moments of my life. Without a doubt.

I drove to the place where Tony's Candystore had stood. The narrow brick building had been destroyed and replaced with a strip mall, a set of bedraggled stores burdened with a dirty plastic facade.

I drove around until I drained the last Budweiser. By then the afternoon had dissolved. The sky, grey to start with, had turned a much darker grey, and everything hung in the greyness, wavering, like somebody getting ready to leave a place they didn't quite want to leave.

I slid the final empty beer can into the plastic bag under the front seat.

Then I drove to Main Street.

I found a bar, a place called The Goalpost.

I parked on the street.

Scuttled in.

The Goalpost was crowded. The place was inundated with young chattering drinkhoisting suburbans. The reason why this unexceptional wateringhole was this heavily populated wasn't hard to figure. The Goalpost was in the midst of its Saturday evening Happy Hour. During this Happy Hour, which actually lasted three hours, male customers paid half price for their drinks, and females paid nothing, they didn't have to open their purses, they didn't have to put down a shiny nickel for their screwdrivers and white russians.

I weaved through the bodies, claimed a spot at the end of the bar, the end furthest from the door. This was always my preferred roost when I drank in a place like The Goalpost.

I held my position at the long, thickly peopled bar. I sucked down a number of Michelobs. And I scrutinized the women. The girls.

The Goalpost was teeming with young female bodies. Girls lined the bar, clamoring for drinks. They stood in clots, sipping from short glasses, smoking, jabbering. They leaned against the dingy walls. They grouped at the tables in the rear section of the dark tavern. These girls, as a rule, were prototypical suburban girls. They were possessed of an underdeveloped prettiness, devoid of alot of makeup, attired in mall-bought clothes. They were schoolteachers, legal secretaries, administrative assistants. Their vision, no doubt, was limited, the majority of them probably couldn't see past Long Island's flat landscapes, probably didn't have dreams that went very far beyond the prescribed suburban dream, the house, the rooms stuffed with recently acquired furniture, the oft trimmed lawn, the kids, the dog, the Pontiac sitting in the driveway, shining like a jewel.

They weren't the kind of girls that I was normally attracted to, they weren't the kind that I typically yearned to create an involvement with…but as I stood at the bar, and drank, I felt an increasing desire to connect with one of these young, unflinchingly suburban girls.

I suppose that part of the reason why I felt this desire had to do with the fact that these girls were so thoroughly, so incontrovertibly suburban. Their suburban-ness was very nearly erotic, provocative in a crude, if not quite smarmy, way. Any liaison I might have with one of these girls would, it seemed, have a verboten quality. It was as if their normality made them, to me, abnormal, and perversely desirable.

Of course, the main reason why I felt such a distinct urge to connect with somebody was that I was, simply, in need. I was in need of female companionship. I was in need of female touch.

Standing at the bar, staring into the maelstrom of female bodies, I was reminded, powerfully, of my loneliness, of the lack of connection in my life, the lack of connection with a woman. It was a lack I had suffered for an inordinately long time.

I hadn't had a girlfriend in three and a half years, not since Karen and I had broken up. I hadn't, in fact, had any kind of relationship with a woman in three and a half years. I hadn't had a boyfriend-girlfriend relationship, an affair, an interlude, a short-lived romance. I hadn't had any sort of involvement, not an inconsequential fling, with anybody in three and a half years.

Now I wanted to make contact with somebody. I wanted to initiate a dialog with somebody. But, for quite awhile, I didn't attempt to talk to anybody. I stood at the bar, I stared at the girls, but I didn't say anything to anybody.

Then I met Lorna.

I was leaning against the bar, slugging a Michelob, when she materialized, suddenly, like an insight. She wedged her way to the bar, pressed herself to the wood railing, directly next to me. She brushed me, inadvertently, her hip rubbed my leg.

I glimpsed her.

She wasn't exceptionally attractive. But she was attractive enough. She was young, probably twelve, fifteen years younger than me. She had shoulderlength blondish-brown hair, a slightly pudgy pale white face. She was on the chunky side, but she wasn't off-puttingly chunky. And, to her everlasting credit, she had a pair of big round cantaloupe-like tits.

She waved at the bartender, wriggling her stubby fingers.

The bartender approached—he was a huge weightlifter type who bore an uncanny resemblance to Arnold Schwarzenegger—and she asked him, in a voice marred by a Long Island accent, for a "spritza."

Schwarzenegger unscrewed a large bottle of white wine, poured some wine into a glass. And, as he poured the wine, she glanced at me. Her head turned, incrementally, and her eyes grazed my form. It was just a glance, but as far as I was concerned, it said everything, it said everything that needed to be said. It said that she knew that I existed. It said that she wasn't entirely opposed to the idea of interacting with me.

Schwarzenegger rested her drink on the bar.

She put her hand on the glass. Then she turned. And she glanced at me again. And she smiled, showing a partly crooked front tooth.

I knew that I had to say something.

"How you doing?" I said.

"Alright," she said.

She put the glass to her mouth.

"Having a good time?" I asked, finding an amiable voice.

"Yeah, not bad," she said.

"You come to this Happy Hour on a regular basis?"

"I come sometimes," she said.

"It's a bargain, huh?"

"Yeah, it is."

"The place is crowded, huh?"

"Yeah."

"My name is Peter, by the way," I said.

"I'm Lorna," she said.

"Lorna?" I couldn't quite hear her; the bar was noisy, everybody blathering on at a fierce drunken velocity, the jukebox pounding "I Will Survive" by Gloria Gaynor.

"Yeah," she said. "Lorna."

"It's nice to meet you, Lorna," I said.

"Nice to meet you," she said.

I continued forward. I asked her about herself. Largely because I didn't want to have to talk about myself.

Lorna, who was probably naturally talkative, and probably a bit drunk, didn't seem to mind carrying the conversational load.

She provided me with a full range of biographical facts. She lived, she said, in Lindenhurst. She lived with her parents, in the house that she'd grown up in. She'd gone to college on Long Island, at Adelphi, and she'd graduated with a degree in Elementary Education. At the present, she was teaching first grade at a school in the reaches of Suffolk County.

She spoke at length about her job. She went on and on. She described various facets of her work situation, her teacher's life, in great detail, editorializing here and there, making pointed commentaries, going off on tangents. She hardly paused, except to bring her glass to her mouth, sip her drink. It seemed like she could go on indefinitely, singing the praises of her best student, Lydia Guberman, complaining about the class troublemaker, Timothy McDermott, explaining the plotline of the story about a family of convivial bears in the first grade primer, explicating the different methods for teaching the short a. But finally, perhaps realizing that I'd told her nothing about myself, she asked me,

"What do *you* do?"

"What do you mean?" I said.

"What do you do?"

"For work?"

"Yeah."

I slugged my beer, tried to decide how I should reply.

Finally I said, "I'm a writer."

"Really?" she said.

"Yeah."

"That's cool," she said.

"Yeah," I said. I felt like a liar, telling her that I was a writer. I felt like a fraud. The way I saw it, I didn't have the right to say that I was a writer. The way I saw it, you couldn't say you were a writer until you had published some things, preferably a number of things. And I hadn't. I definitely hadn't. I'd had one short story published, when I was eighteen years old, when I was in high school. And that had been it. Although I'd been writing, although I'd been trying to write, trying to write a novel, for the past decade or two, although I'd been hammering away for the better part of my adult life, I hadn't finished anything, hadn't submitted anything, I hadn't had anything published. I hadn't had anything published since that goddam short story, since I was eighteen years old. I hadn't had anything published, not one story, not one goddam newspaper article, in more than twenty years.

To my way of seeing things, I couldn't, and shouldn't, say that I was a writer.

"What kind of writing do you do?" Lorna asked.

"I write fiction, for the most part," I said.

"Fiction?"

"Yeah."

She nodded. She wanted to know more.

"I'm working on a novel right now," I said. I slugged my beer. I held the bottle to my mouth, then placed the bottle on the bar, and stared down the stretch of brown wood at the myriad glasses, bottles, piles of wrinkled bills, buttclogged ashtrays.

"What's the novel about?" she asked.

I picked up my bottle.

"It's kind of hard to describe...," I said.

"Yeah?"

"Yeah, it sort of is...."

"Well, just give me an idea." She scanned my face, sympathetically, with her big glazed eyes. She put down her glass, and her knockers moved, swayed, against her sweater.

"It's always hard for me to describe...," I said. I was speaking fairly loudly, trying to make myself clear above the consistent din, the clash of voices, laughter, the jukebox thudding "Satisfaction" by the Rolling Stones. "It's the kind of thing, I think, that's hard to describe when you're working on it...I think because you're too close to it, you don't have enough perspective...."

Lorna nodded.

"I could give you a rough idea...," I said.

"You don't have to, if you don't want to," she said.

"No, it's okay...," I said. I quaffed my beer, and said, "I guess you could say it's autobiographical...."

She nodded.

"I write about my experiences...I write about what I know about...."

She nodded.

"Let's put it this way," I said. "I take my experiences, I take things that've happened to me, and I draw on them...I take bits and pieces of things, of things that've happened, and I push them, to the edge, to some sort of extreme...I extrapolate...."

"Uh huh."

"You know what I mean?"

"Yeah, I think so." She had an idea what I was talking about. But she didn't completely understand.

"I actually write alot about the suburbs," I said. There was truth to this. The novel I had tried to write during my twenties and thirties was to a large extent about the suburbs. And so was the novel I had tried to write when I was upstate, living in the shack. And I suspected that the novel I was going to attempt to write in the coming months would also have quite a bit to do with the suburbs.

"I write alot about places like Bayview," I said.

"Yeah?" Lorna said.

"Yeah."

"That's weird."

"You think?"

"Yeah."

"Why do you say that?"

"It just seems like it would be hard to write about Bayview," she said.

"Why?"

"I don't know…it's just kind of a boring place…."

"It is," I said, and then, with an added passion, I said, "That's the point. That's exactly the point."

"You like to write about boring stuff?"

"In a way."

"Huh."

"I write about the way things are," I said. "In places like Bayview. In this culture. In this country…and the fact of the matter is, things are pretty boring, pretty lifeless…and that's what I write about…the boring nature of things…the dullness…the loss of spirit…."

Lorna nodded, buying it, at least to some degree.

"I write about the loss of joy," I said, vigorously. I was feeling more comfortable, more confident. "To me, that's the most prevalent condition, the thing I see the most…the loss of joy…."

Lorna nodded.

"That's what I want to bring to light," I said. "I just don't see people living joyfully…I just don't see it…."

"I guess you're right," she said.

I trained my vision on her pudgy, but not unpretty face.

"I think we've lost the ability to live joyfully," I said.

After talking to Lorna for ten, fifteen minutes, I began to think that I might have a chance of making some progress with her.

I figured I'd ask her if she wanted to leave The Goalpost. I figured I'd ask her if she wanted to get something to eat. I figured that, if she said yes, I would take her to a nice restaurant, someplace cozy, a place where we might enjoy an excellent, if not overly expensive meal. And, during the course of the evening, I would try to make a more intimate connection with her.

I was enthused. I was inspired by the thought that Lorna and I might forge some sort of alliance.

If Lorna and I left the bar, and if we got along, if we clicked, I thought, I wouldn't be opposed to the idea of becoming more involved with her, I wouldn't be opposed to the idea of entering into something akin to a boyfriend-girlfriend relationship with her. I hadn't thought, before coming to The Goalpost, about trying to procure a girlfriend while I was staying in Bayview, but as I stood there, next to her, in such close proximity to her young, amply curved body, I began to think that it might not be such a bad idea, I began to think that I might significantly enhance the days and hours that I spent in these suburbs if I had somebody, somebody like her, to consort with, to cavort with.

Standing there, talking to her, I pictured the romance we might enact, Lorna and me hanging out, visiting the traditional suburban venues, the bars, the Italian restaurants, the Big Burger, the enormous movie theater complexes, the malls. I saw us, pretty damn clearly, buzzing along the local roads in my beatup Toyota, walking on the windy late autumn beaches, fucking relentlessly on the narrow single bed in the tiny apartment I would rent somewhere in the Bayview area.

Finally I made a move. I tried to coax her into leaving The Goalpost.

"I'm getting pretty tired of this place," I told her.

"Yeah?" she said.

"I'm not getting tired of you...."

"That's good."

"I'm just getting tired of this place. It's crowded. It's noisy."

"That's true," she said.

"I was wondering if maybe you wanted to get out of here," I said.

"Not really," she said.

"It's kind of hard to talk…," I said. "I was thinking that maybe we could go someplace…someplace quiet…someplace where we could talk…."

She didn't respond.

"I was thinking that maybe we could get something to eat…," I said.

She picked up her glass, sipped from it.

"Do you want to go someplace and get something to eat?"

"I don't think so," she said.

"Did you have dinner yet?"

"No," she said.

"Then let's get something to eat," I said.

"I can't," she said.

"No?"

"No." She shook her head. Her hair flounced against her shoulders.

"Are you sure?"

"Yeah."

"I think we'd have a good time," I said.

"We probably would," she said.

"Then let's do it."

"I can't," she said.

"I'd really like to get to know you better," I said.

"I can't," she said.

"Do you have other plans?"

"I came here with my girlfriend," she said, fingering her glass.

"Where is she?"

"I don't know," Lorna said. "She's around here somewhere."

"I guess you don't want to ditch her."

"No."

"I can understand that."

I glugged the last of the beer in my bottle. Looked down the bar. One of the bartenders—a guy with dark hair and a mustache who looked like Burt Reynolds in his heyday—was lighting a cigarette for a goodlooking blonde. Schwarzenegger was pouring shots, mouthing the words to the song pumping from the jukebox, Elton John's "Crocodile Rock."

Lorna moved her glass absently in small circles against the bar. She stared, expressionlessly, into the bowels of The Goalpost, the merge of bodies, the jerky noise, the cigarette smoke.

I looked, rather directly, at her.

"I really would like to get to know you better," I said.

She glanced at me, smiled dispassionately, showing, for just a second, her crooked tooth.

Catching sight of Schwarzenegger stepping toward me, I waved my empty beer bottle.

"Let me get another Michelob," I said.

Then, returning to Lorna, I said, "I'd really like to get together with you sometime…if not tonight, then definitely sometime…."

Schwarzenegger dropped a Michelob on the bar. I picked up the cold bottle, took a swig.

"Let's get together sometime," I said.

"I don't think I can," she said.

"You don't want to give me your number?"

"I really can't."

I swigged my beer.

"I really would like to go out with you," I said.

"I can't," she said.

"Why don't you at least give me your number," I said.

"I'm sorry," she said, "but I can't…."

"Give me your number…," I said. "I'll give you a call…and we can take it from there…."

"I can't," she said.

"Cmon…," I said.

"I can't."

"Cmon…."

I realized that I was pleading, that I was beginning to sound desperate. But I couldn't help it.

"Give me your number…," I said.

"I can't," she said.

"Why not?"

"I can't."

"Do you have a boyfriend?"

"Yeah. Sort of."

"Sort of?"

"Sort of."

"You don't sound too convinced."

"I have a boyfriend," she said firmly.

"You sure?"

"Yes."

I slugged my beer, and I said, "I really don't care if you've got a boyfriend…."

"I can't go out with you," she said. She was getting annoyed.

"It really doesn't matter to me if you've got a boyfriend…," I said. "I'd still like to hang out with you…."

She frowned. Her mouth twisted, burdensomely.

"I still think we'd have a good time…," I said.

"I should try to find my friend," she said. She'd had enough. She wanted to get away from me.

"I wish you'd reconsider," I said. "I'd really like to go out with you…."

"I definitely can't," she said.

"I guess I can't talk you into it…," I said.

"No."

"That's too bad…I think it could've been alot of fun…it could've been really cool…."

I slugged my beer.

"I just think you're a great girl…," I said.

"I'm going to look for my friend," she said.

She pushed away from the bar.

"Take care," she said, weakly.

"Take care," I said.

I shuffled through the thickets of flesh, the babbling, gesticulating carcasses. I went into the john.

Both urinals were being used. A guy wearing a Jets parka and a tall reedlike kid crowded the porcelain, hands on their dicks.

I went into a stall.

Pissed.

And then I just stood there. I stood in front of the bowl, amid the urine stink. And I stared at the graffiti-marred wall.

I felt like crying.

I felt like crying because I'd lost the opportunity to connect with Lorna. And because I'd lost the opportunity to connect with almost every woman I'd ever tried to connect with.

I felt like crying, simply, because I was alone. And because I'd been alone for most of my life. And because it seemed like I'd always be alone.

I hadn't cried in years, in decades. I couldn't remember the last time I had cried. But right now I wanted to sob. I wanted the tears to fall torrentially, to roll down my face, onto the grubby floor. I wanted to cry so hard that puddles would form on the floor near my feet, puddles that would grow wider and deeper and then turn into streams that would turn into rivers, long thick rivers of tears that would run for miles, over the glutted roads, through the flat wilting grids, to the goddam Great South Bay.

I wanted to cry profusely.

But nothing happened.

No tears came.

I couldn't cry.

6

I drove down Main Street, through the suburban night, the synthetic light, streetlamp light, overlit signs, neon, headlight glow.

I spotted a Citibank, pulled to the curb.

I went into the compartment lined with ATM machines. Withdrew $200 from my savings account.

I drove a little further down Main, parked in front of a deli, picked up a turkey breast sandwich, a six-pack of Budweiser, a large bag of corn chips.

Then I headed back to the motel.

Back in my room, I grabbed the Yellow Pages, and I looked through the ads for escort services. I perused the ads—there were dozens, hundreds of them—for a few minutes, finally decided to call a place by the name of Fantastic Escorts.

I telephoned Fantastic Escorts, arranged to have a girl, a hooker, sent to my room.

About an hour after I called the escort service, I heard a sequence of light timid knocks on the motel room door.

I went to the door, opened it.

The hooker from Fantastic Escorts stood before me, bedecked in a ratty purple skijacket.

I gave her quick inspection.

I was pleased. I had felt a degree of trepidation as I'd waited for her to arrive. I had realized, having had experience with places like Fantastic Escorts, that there was a possibility I'd be disappointed, perhaps terrifically disappointed, when I opened the door and put my eyes on the girl in front of me. But I wasn't disappointed. No.

This prostitute was just what I had hoped for.

I had told the woman I'd spoken to on the phone—the woman who dispatched the hookers—that I preferred a girl who was "somewhat young" and this prostitute was indeed young. She was very young. She probably wasn't much older than eighteen or nineteen, probably wasn't more than a year or two removed from her high school career, from the undoubtedly miserable days she'd spent slinking through grey corridors, sitting in Algebra class and staring out the window, smoking cigarettes in the woods behind the school cafeteria. She was young, and she was undebateably goodlooking, with long brown hair that fell carelessly against her shoulders, large eyes surrounded by smudgy mascara, a pouty red mouth. I could tell, despite the fact that she was wearing the bulky jacket, that she had goodsized breasts. Her knockers jutted forth adamantly, deformed the horrible purple jacket. In addition to the jacket, she was wearing a very short black miniskirt, black stockings, black high heels. Her legs were long, slender, perfect.

"Hi," I said, trying to exude a certain amount of warmth.

The young hooker offered no reply. She stood on the wood-plank veranda, hands in her jacket, shivering.

"I'm Peter," I said. I let her in the room.

She stepped, hesitantly, onto the matted carpeting.

"How're you doing?" I said.

She moved toward the bed, her head angled down.

"Your name is…?"

"Melissa…."

"How you doing, Melissa?"

"Okay...."

She started to unzip her jacket, but then stopped, and, with a serrated edge in her voice, asked, "Ya got the money?"

"Yeah, sure, of course," I said.

I gave her the $125 that the escort service charged. Plus a $35 tip. A total of $160.

She counted the bills.

"Thanks," she said, blankly, jamming the money into her handbag.

She took off her jacket. She was wearing a black top, a clingy jersey that revealed, rather explicitly, her contours. Her tits were extremely big, bigger than I'd suspected. They were mammoth.

She draped the skijacket over the television. A crooked purple arm fell across the dark screen.

"Hey," I said. "I thought we could watch some TV."

"Do ya want to?" she said.

"No," I said. "I was just kidding...." I put my arms around her, ran my fingers along the waistline of her miniskirt, pressed my fingertips against the cheap fabric. "With you around," I said, "why would I want to watch TV...." I kissed her neck, tasted her particular mixture of flesh, perspiration, inexpensive perfume. I kissed her ear. I kissed her jaw. Then I tried to kiss her mouth, but she pulled back, quickly, reflexively, the way every hooker pulls back when you try to put your mouth on theirs. She was young and probably didn't have much experience as a prostitute, but she reacted, in this instance, like a seasoned pro.

"Ya gonna take your clothes off?" she asked. She had a severe Long Island accent. Her voice was shaved, warped.

"I guess I should...," I said, sliding my hands under her skirt.

She stared past my shoulder, toward the motel room wall.

"I should get undressed, shouldn't I...." I held her ass through her underwear.

"If ya want to," she said.

"I do," I said.

I removed my sweatshirt.

"Is Melissa your real name?" I asked her.

"No."

"I like the name," I said, unhooking my jeans.

"Whenever I hear the name Melissa," I said, pushing down my jeans, "I think of the Allman Brothers song 'Sweet Melissa.'"

"Of course," I said, "you probably don't even know who the Allman Brothers are."

"Right?"

"Right, Melissa?"

"What?" She sat against the bed, pulled off her stockings.

"The Allman Brothers. Ever hear of them?"

"I don't think so."

"They were a great American rock and roll band of my youth."

I discarded my underpants.

"If you didn't get your name from the Allman Brothers song, how'd you get it?"

My cock stuck out, stiffly, like a length of garden hose.

"How'd you get the name Melissa?"

"It was the name of a girl in a movie I saw."

She pulled her shirt over her head. Her hair splayed, disarranged, against her bare shoulders.

"What movie?"

"What movie?" I asked her.

"It was some movie I saw on TV," she said.

She took off her bra.

"Can you tell me your real name?" I stared at her breasts. They were extraordinarily large. And they were extraordinarily firm, they seemed to defy gravity, they seemed to float on the air, like those giant balloons at the Macy's Thanksgiving Day Parade.

"What's your real name?" I asked her.

"I never tell," she said, using a slightly belligerent tone.

"I won't let anybody know," I said.

"I can keep a secret," I said.

"I never tell anybody," she said.

"Not even me?"

"No."

"Cmon."

"Sorry."

"Cmon. I'm not going to tell anybody."

"Sorry."

"Cmon."

She grimaced.

"It's Ellen," she said.

"That's a good name," I said.

"It's alright," she said.

"So can I call you Ellen?" I asked.

"No. Ya better not." She felt strongly about this. She felt that it was important to obey certain protocols. "Ya better call me Melissa."

"Okay, fair enough," I said, "I'll call you Melissa...."

She opened the condom package, tearing the foil with her bittendown red fingernails. She pushed the condom, down, over my long stiff cock. She executed the task slowly, carefully, like an exemplary high school student performing an important science experiment.

Then she lowered her head and wrapped her mouth around my shaft and moved her mouth deliberately up and down and up and down.

❦   ❦   ❦

I got on top of her, guided my sheathed prick inside her. And I fucked her. I plunged my cock, deep, into her.

She pressed the side of her face against the motel room pillow. She kept her eyes shut. She didn't move. She didn't twitch.

She pulled off the condom, and, holding it gingerly between her thumb and forefinger, carried it into the bathroom.

She sat on the mattress, and, using a hot damp washcloth, cleaned my prick. She tamped the crown, enveloped the flaccid shaft, squeezed gently. I watched her. I examined her face, her smooth young visage. She looked alot like Gwen Purkey, a girl I'd known when I was in high school. She looked just like Gwen Purkey, I thought. She was, I thought, a dead ringer for Gwen.

I'd had a prodigious crush on Gwen Purkey, a crush that'd blossomed when we had sat at adjacent desks in English in the eleventh grade. This crush, of course, never had a chance of developing into anything more than a crush. Gwen had a steady boyfriend, Neil Kornhoeffer, a tall, goodlooking, not unintelligent guy who starred on the football team as a rangy defensive end with a penchant for sacking quarterbacks. But if Gwen hadn't been involved with Kornhoeffer, I still wouldn't have been able to start up any kind of romantic, or semi-romantic, relationship with her. The fact of the matter was, I was incapable of interacting with girls in anything but the most superficial manner when I was a teenager. When it came to relating to the opposite sex, I was impossibly fearful. I suffered an unerring paralysis. Going out on a date, having a girlfriend, these were activities, seemingly part of a normal highschooler's life, that I wasn't able to participate in.

They were beyond my scope. I could no more orchestrate a boy-girl linkage, it seemed, than I could speak Russian. Or dunk a basketball. Or fly.

I didn't go out on a single date during high school. I never took a girl to the movies or a local ice cream parlor or the diner or the beach. I never walked through a park holding hands with a pretty sixteen year old girl. I never kissed a girl, never pressed my teen-aged lips against a girl's warm soft lips while I held her and felt her tits against my bony chest and slid my hand through her hair.

I never did any of that.

Never.

This absence of any sort of connection with any sort of girl during that part of my life was something I'd always regretted. And I still regretted it. I still felt an ache, a pang, when I thought about it.

And, I guessed, I'd probably always regret it.

Melissa sat on the edge of the bed, pulled on her stockings.

"So what are you doing now?" I asked her. I lay across the bed, my naked corpse depressing the shitbrown bedspread. My pecker hung, shrunken, like a cocktail frank, against my leg.

"Do you have someplace else to go?" I asked her.

"I don't know," she said.

"Do you?"

"Maybe."

"Why don't you spend the night with me…," I said. I ran my fingers across her thigh.

"I can't," she said.

"Cmon," I said. "Spend the night with me…."

"I can't."

"Cmon."

"I can't."

She slid off the bed.

"I could give you more money," I said.

"How much?"

"I've got about a hundred dollars."

"You're gonna need alot more than that if ya want me ta stay all night," she said with a veteran hooker's timeworn arrogance.

She grabbed her bra.

"I'd give you more," I said, "but that's all I've got left...."

She fitted the bra over her tits.

"I'd really like you to stay...," I said.

"I can't," she said, with a sharp edge. "I got somebody waitin outside in a car for me. I gotta get outta here."

"I'm sure you could just go out there and tell'em you're gonna stay...."

"That's what you think," she said, picking up her skirt.

"I think you should think about it...," I said. "I think you should give it some consideration...I know it's not something you'd ordinarily do...but I think you should think about making an exception...."

She put on the black miniskirt.

"Stay the night with me...," I said.

She looked at me, her lipstick-smeared mouth scrunched, indicating a building exasperation.

"Stay with me...."

"I can't."

"Stay with me, Melissa...."

"I can't."

"Cmon...."

"I can't."

"I'm sure you can if you want to...," I said.

"I can't."

"I'm sure you can...," I said.

"I can't," she said.

"Stay with me…," I said.

"Stop it!" she said, nearly screaming. She glared at me. She was beginning to despise me.

"I'm sorry…," I said. "I'd just like to spend more time with you…I just thought it'd be nice…."

7

I spent Sunday morning in bed, bent, splintered, like a tree branch that'd been knocked to the street during a violent storm.

I got up sometime after 1pm.

I left the motel room.

I drove down Sunrise Highway.

It was a cold grey day.

I found a delicatessen, bought some things that I hoped would mollify my ravaged digestive tract, that I hoped would soothe my hungover condition. A buttered bagel. Two containers of vanilla yogurt. A big bottle of ginger ale.

I went back to the motel. Climbed onto the bed with my provisions. Propped myself against the plywood headboard. Flicked on the Jets-Dolphins game. I figured I'd watch the game, and then I'd watch the game that came on next, and after that I'd watch something else, and then something else. I figured I wasn't going to be able to do much more than this. I wasn't going to be able to attend to the tasks I had to attend to. I wasn't going to be able to look for a place to live. And I wasn't going to be able to call Willy Smithberger.

I put my focus on the screen, the spiralling passes, the players colliding, the big helmeted athletes tromping up and down the artificial turf. On the motel room TV the artificial surface gave off a glossy green tint, like a tacky neon sign on a suburban bar and grill.

I watched the game with a good amount of interest for about three quarters. But toward the end of the third quarter, Marino, the Dolphins quarterback, threw two quick touchdown passes, and all of a sudden the Jets, who, of course, were my team, were behind by a wide margin. At that point I began to pay less attention to the goings-on on the TV, and I began to pay more attention, alot more attention, to the sounds, the lusty yawps, coming through the motel room walls.

Since I'd checked into the South Shore Motel, I had been treated to a non-stop symphony of erotic cries and fervid dialogs, a continuous demonstration of the different forms of communication, articulate and inarticulate, that men and women utilize when in the throes of sexual intercourse, oral sex, bondage and discipline, you name it. Not a minute, not a moment, had passed when I hadn't been able to hear something. More often than not, I could hear some sort of lewd noise coming from both of the adjoining rooms. And I never, at any time, had to make an effort to hear these sounds, they trespassed the cheap plaster with extraordinary facility, as though they were being piped into the room, the way muzak is piped into a dentist's office.

The couples who visited the South Shore Motel were a vociferous lot. They were constantly voicing their passions, bleating, yelping, exhorting, exulting, groaning, in an uninhibited, often aggressive manner. I was developing a theory. It was my growing belief that the men and women who rented the South Shore's rooms were probably moved to express themselves in such dramatic fashion by the simple fact of their surroundings. They were probably more inclined to scream and gasp in these faceless rooms than they would've been if closeted in some tiny bedroom, in some boxshaped house, in some suburban grid. They were probably prodded by a sudden experience of boundarylessness. They were probably inspired by a newfound sense of freedom.

At some point, about five minutes into the fourth quarter, I all but stopped watching the game. I pressed the mute button, silenced the TV. And I concentrated on the sounds coming through the feeble walls. I concentrated mainly on the sounds coming through the wall to my left, the sounds being emitted by a woman who was, obviously, in the midst of a furious encounter. This woman and her all-but-silent partner were, obviously, fucking. And she was making all kinds of noises. She was spewing all sorts of things, indecipherable phrases, untranslatable fragments. But her primary means of expressing herself was an unusually shrill, dissonant chirping sound. It was the sort of sound, I thought, that a certain type of bird might make, a frail low-flying bird perhaps, the kind of bird that might inhabit the marshy areas near the Great South Bay. She made this chirping sound frequently, but at irregular intervals. All of a sudden she'd start, and she'd chirp wildly, and sometimes she'd go on for long stretches, thirty seconds or longer, and she'd chirp louder, and louder, and louder, with the tenacity of a car alarm, as though she wanted to stop, but couldn't, or didn't know how.

After listening to this woman for a few minutes, I unsnapped my jeans, pushed them down, and I pushed down my underpants, and I clutched my prick, held it firmly, tugged it, pulled it.

I stroked my rod. And I pictured her. I pictured a birdlike creature. A woman, maybe thirty-five, with shortcropped brown hair, small brown eyes. In my mind, she had a skinny body, small pointy tits. And, of course, she was sexy, she was decidedly sexy, in a hungry, pecking-in-the-dirt-for-food way.

I stroked my cock effortfully, moved my hand rapidly, up and down, over my hard elongated shaft.

I envisioned her, straddling her partner, bouncing on his prick, flapping her arms. I saw her arching her back, her mouth twisting, her lips vibrating, that chirping sound rising unavoidably from her quivering throat. I visualized her cunt, shuddering, moist. And her ass, glistening in the grey-yellow room light.

I yanked my cock.

I moved my hand up and down, faster and faster.

She chirped and chirped.

I grabbed my balls.

I stroked fiercely.

Then I loosened my grip.

I slipped off the bed. Pulled up my pants. Put on my leather-jacket. Left the room.

I figured I would get another prostitute.

I drove to the Citibank just past the intersection of Sunrise and Route 140. I withdrew $160 from the ATM.

Taking the money from the ATM, I felt a twinge of despair, of self-loathing. I realized that, from a moral standpoint, I shouldn't be doing what I was doing. And I realized, more importantly, that I shouldn't be spending my money, my all-too-precious resources, in this manner. But as I walked across the parking lot to the Toyota, I pushed away these difficult feelings. I was doing what I had to do, I told myself. I was tending to an innate human desire. I was living, I told myself, the way I had to live. I was, simply, trying to live fully, passionately, on the edge, on the extremest verge, to use Whitman's phrase. I was acquiring the sort of experiences that a writer, an artist, had to have, I told myself.

I got back in the car, drove down Sunrise, stopped at a deli, picked up a couple of six-packs and a big bag of potato chips.

Then I headed back to the motel. I drove down Sunrise, I sped down the car-ridden road, eager to get back, to fuck, to ram my cock into a goodlooking hooker's practiced cunt.

I streaked down the concrete.

Then I got an idea.

I would get two hookers.

I was thoroughly inspired. I had never had sex with two women at the same time, but, like most redblooded American males, I had always wanted to. I'd harbored a desire to partake in such a triad for quite awhile, for years. I'd often fantasized about it. And now, it seemed, I had an opportunity to do it. I was standing at a half-open window, a window I could easily crawl through. It was, it seemed, the time to do it.

I steered the Toyota into the left-turn lane, made a U-turn, drove back to the bank.

I withdrew another $160.

And then, again, I headed for the motel. I drove fast. 55, 60 mph. I flashed down Sunrise, changing lanes, passing car after car, shooting past all the suburban vehicles trekking numbly through the grey Sunday afternoon. I realized that I was speeding, that I was driving recklessly. But I couldn't do anything about it.

I stabbed the accelerator, thinking about the menage a trois.

I flew down the road.

Back in my motel room, I called an escort service. Superb Escorts.

"I'd like two girls," I told the woman who answered the phone.

"Two?"

"Yeah. Two girls."

"Two girls," she repeated, emotionlessly, as though she was taking an order for a couple of pizzas.

"Okay?"

"No problem," she said.

❧   ❧   ❧

About an hour later, there was a hard rap on the motel room door.

I opened the door.

The two hookers, the representatives from Superb Escorts, stood on the veranda, bundled in their coats, hunched against the cold.

They were a miserable looking pair. They looked like a couple of forlorn hitchhikers, they looked like a couple of vagabonds, directionless misfits who'd stumbled on the motel and were knocking on random doors looking for handouts.

Needless to say, I was profoundly disappointed.

"You call Superb Escorts?" asked the prostitute standing closest to the door.

"Yeah," I said.

"I'm Billie," she said.

"How you doing, Billie?" I said.

"Not bad," she said, stepping past me, spearing me with an inadvertently extended elbow. She walked into the room, slapping her decrepit sneakers against the carpeting. She had a brazen quality, like the leader of a pack of wild dogs.

"Fuck it's cold," she said, blowing on her hands. "I hope to fuck they got heat in this fucking place."

"They do," I said.

"Thank fucking god for that." She was wearing an old peacoat, buttoned tight over her scrawny form. She had a hard pocked face, small grey eyes like pieces of gravel. Her hair, which was brownish and rather short, looked like it'd been shorn with a pair of rusty hedgeclippers.

"Say hi to Janey," she said, glancing over her shoulder.

Locking the door, I acknowledged the second hooker, half-smiled, said, "How you doing?"

She said nothing. She was a tall girl. Outfitted in a working girl's basic footwear, black stiletto heels, she was a good three or four inches taller than me. Standing near the door, full of uncertainty, she looked like she might topple over. She was wearing a ripped orange down coat, big dirty lavender mittens. Her hair was long and dyed red, the color of dead rose petals. Her face was pale, cadaverous, seemingly incapable of moving.

"Let's take care of first things first," Billie said. She had a harsh, bruised voice. She'd probably destroyed her vocal cords, smoking millions of cigarettes, drinking, cursing, swallowing gallons of male ejaculate.

"You got the money?" she asked.

"Sure," I said. I knew that I was going to have to pay up. I was quite familiar with the rules that governed these transactions. I knew that I wasn't going to be able to send the two hookers back, the way you send back an omelette when you discover a dead cockroach nestled amongst the broccoli and cheddar cheese, I knew that I wasn't going to be able to tell them that I didn't want to have sex with them and that therefore I wasn't going to compensate them. I knew that even if I rejected the opportunity to utilize Billie's and Janey's services I was still going to have to give them the money, the $250 that I'd told the woman from Superb Escorts I'd give them. As far as the money went, I was well beyond the point of no return.

And besides, the truth was, I still wanted to have sex with them. Despite everything, despite their horrendous appearance, and their dearth of charm, I still wanted to roll around with the two of them, for my allotted hour, on the sagging kingsized bed.

I took out the wad of bills, the money I'd just withdrawn from my savings account, and I counted off $250.

I put the $250 in Billie's scaly red hand.

"Here's two hundred fifty," I said.

And then I peeled off another $50, and I gave it to her, explaining, "This is a little something extra for the two of you."

Billie counted the bills, dampening her finger with her cracked red tongue.

She shoved the money in her back pocket.

Then she gave me a stern look.

"I wanna get one thing straight right up front," she said.

"Uh huh."

"I ain't eatin her pussy," she said.

"Uh huh."

She looked toward Janey. The tall prostitute was still standing near the door. She was still wearing her orange coat and lavender mittens.

"And she ain't lickin me," Billie said.

I nodded.

"You got that?"

"Yeah, sure."

"I don't want you to get the wrong impression."

"I wouldn't want to get the wrong impression," I said, applying a little gentle sarcasm.

"I know what you guys like," she said. "You like to watch girls eatin pussy."

"I guess you can't blame us for liking what we like," I said.

"You like to watch a coupla girls stickin their faces in each other's cunts."

"I guess there's probably some truth to that."

"Well, it ain't gonna happen."

"I've got to admit, I'm sorry to hear that," I said. "I wouldn't have minded watching the two of you go down on each other."

"I'm sure you wouldn't've."

"I would've enjoyed it."

"Well, it ain't on the agenda."

"That's too bad."

"That's the way it goes," she said.

"I guess we'll just have to find something else to do," I said.

"That won't be a problem," she said.

"I'm glad to hear that."

"We'll make a nice sandwich for you," she said.

"That sounds good."

She looked at her companion.

"We'll make him a nice sandwich, won't we? Right, Janey?"

"Sure," the tall girl replied.

Billie crawled across the bed, on a mission, headed for my crotch. Her naked body was a disturbing sight. Her skin had a yellow tint and didn't seem to fit properly over her skeleton. Her bones jutted out at odd angles. Her chest was utterly flat, her nipples worndown like old pencil erasers. Her ass was shaped like a deflated soccer ball and covered with red spots.

She grabbed my cock, yanked it, coaxed it to a partially stiff status. She encased my not-exactly-steel-hard cock in a lime green condom. Then she dropped her head and engulfed it. She took most of its tenuous length in her mouth. And she began cranking up and down, mechanically, like a machine on an assembly line in some Detroit factory.

At the same time, Janey sat on the bed, her bleach-white legs hanging over the side. Her nakedness was as off-putting as Billie's. Her breasts were thin, oblong, like Polish kielbasa. Her shoulders were narrow and her ribs were clearly visible, but beneath her ribs she was thick, doughy. A terrific patch of mangy black growth descended from her snatch and reached down between her big thighs like a religious fanatic's untended-for beard. She sat on the edge, the precipice, of the bed, trailed her hand in slow motion across my abdomen.

Billie moved her head up and down. Her lips pinched my long, hard, if not quite crowbar-like prick.

She moved up and down at a fairly rapid pace.

Then she retracted her mouth.

She eyeballed me.

"Ready to fuck?"

"I guess so," I breathed.

She slapped my tottering cock.

"I think you're ready," she said.

Janey lay dead-still on her back on top of the bedspread. And I got on top of her and forced my cock inside her. And I fucked her.

Billie kneeled behind me. She clasped my ass. She dug her fingers into my flesh, deep in, and she squeezed, viciously. Her fingers were strong, like talons.

"Is it good?" she asked diabolically.

"Yeah," I breathed.

"You like fucking her?"

"Yeah."

"You like it?"

"Yeah."

"I bet you like it," she said. And then she spanked me. She spanked me hard. The resultant sound, a definitive phlack, was quite loud, easily discernible, no doubt, in the adjoining rooms.

"Fuck her," she said.

Then she spanked me again.

"Fuck her good," she said.

"I will...," I said.

"Fuck her good," she said, spanking me again.

"I will...I will...," I said.

8

I remembered how the light slanted through the bare trees, onto the roofs of the boxshaped houses.

I was riding my bicycle down Jefferson Street.

It was a March evening.

I was ten years old.

I pedalled onto the driveway, pushed up the garage door, leaned my bike against the wall inside the garage.

I knew that I was getting home late, I knew that there was a chance I was going to be in trouble.

I went into the house. My brother, Eddie, who was eight, was sprawled on the living room floor, watching TV. My sister, Denise, who was two, was sitting in the playpen. This was a bad sign. It probably meant that my brother and sister had already had dinner, it probably meant that I had missed dinner, it probably meant that I was quite late.

I stood on the carpeting in the middle of the living room. I didn't know what to do.

Then I heard my father's angry, jagged-edged voice.

"Pete! Get the hell in here!"

I walked into the kitchen.

My father was standing next to the kitchen table, dragging on a cigarette, holding the butt to his twisted, turned-down mouth.

My mother was sitting, bent over the table. Her long brown hair dropped in messy clumps. She looked like a backyard weed struggling to survive after having been sprayed with some sort of chemical.

The green formica table was littered with the remains of the evening's meal, burnt frankfurters, dried-up french fries lying at the bottom of a Tupperware bowl.

"Where the hell have you been?!" my father screamed.

He dragged on his cigarette, then threw it, backwards, into the sink. The butt bounced against the porcelain, landed, hissing, in a waterfilled pot.

He shifted toward me. He moved toward me. He moved across the kitchen floor. His big body pushed against the dimensions of the space, the small wallpapered kitchen. He had that ability, particularly when he was angry, like now, to completely disrupt the structure of whatever room he was in.

He scowled, his face distorted, like the picture on the TV when a tube burned out. His dark brown hair was skewed. His big bushy eyebrows were mangled, like a couple of overused brillo pads. He was wearing his usual salesman's garb, the navy blue blazer, white shirt, tie, polyester slacks, black shoes. This probably meant that he'd spent the day, or part of the day, looking for employment. He'd recently lost his job. He was an insurance salesman, he'd been working for a large insurance company in the city. He hadn't, however, had that job for very long. And, in fact, he hadn't been able to hold any of the sales positions he'd had with different insurance companies during the past few years, he'd been fired, or laid off, or he'd quit—I didn't know the details—after he'd had these jobs for just a short time, a few months, six or seven months at the most.

Since his most recent descent into unemployment, there hadn't been many, if any, moments, at least when I'd seen him, when he hadn't been consumed with fastburning anger. And right now he was enraged. It seemed, to me, like he'd moved beyond an edge. It seemed like he'd turned, like a character in a science fiction movie, into a kind of monster. His body, already enormous, seemed to have expanded. His arms bulged into his jacket, threatening to rip the seams. The flaps of his shirt hung over his belt. His shirt was open at the collar, several buttons had been unbuttoned, or perhaps they'd flown off, his tie had been loosened, and his chest hair sprouted out, madly, like rampant chaotic foliage in a deserted empty lot.

"What the hell were you doing?!" he roared. "Where were you?!"

"I was playing baseball," I said weakly. I had spent the afternoon playing baseball in front of Kenny Pelligrini's house. It had been a beautiful March day, the first warm day that spring, and when school had let out my friends and I had grabbed our bats and gloves and had headed to Kenny's. We had played until the sun had all but disappeared. And although it was true that we had played longer than we should have, it was only because we had waited for a day like this for so long, for the course of the winter. But I couldn't tell my father this. I couldn't even begin to tell him.

"Do you know what time it is?!"

I said nothing.

"You were supposed to be home an hour ago!"

I remained silent.

"What is this crap?!"

"I'm sorry," I said. And I started to cry. My thin body heaved, forcing up tears. The tears rolled off my face, onto my blue jacket with the insignias of the twenty major league teams.

My father screamed.

"I've had it with your bullshit, Pete! I've fucking had it!"

"David…," my mother broke in, imploring him in a strained, almost inaudible voice, "that's enough…."

My father screamed at her.

"Shut up! Shut the fuck up!"

He returned to me.

"I'm sick and tired of your bullshit! Who do you think you are?! Who the hell do you think you are?!"

He stepped toward me.

"You goddam little prick!"

He raised his big arm. He held his arm behind his head. Then he swung. He swung. He slammed the base of his hand against my shoulder.

I crashed to the floor.

I lay against the linoleum.

"Get up!" he said.

I struggled to my knees.

He stood over me.

"You goddam piece of shit!" he growled. Then he hit me again. He smashed his massive paw against the side of my head.

I fell backwards. I landed against the refrigerator, the back of my skull banged the white thinmetal door.

I lay, crumpled, against the refrigerator door.

"Cmon you piece of shit!" my father screamed. "Get up!"

"David…stop it…," my mother exhaled. She looked down, at the table, as animated as the flowers in the wallpaper design. "You're going to hurt him…."

My father turned to her.

"He's got to learn a lesson! He thinks he can do whatever he wants! He thinks he can come and go as he goddam pleases! I've had it with his bullshit! I've had it, Maryanne! I've had it!"

While I had the chance, while my father was screaming at my mother, I crawled to the kitchen door. I grabbed the door knob. I opened the door. Normally I wouldn't have tried something like this. Normally I wouldn't have tried to get away from him, because I knew full well that any attempt I might make to escape, to avoid his fury, would only further infuriate him. But this situation, I sensed, was different. It was, I sensed, a more dangerous situation than other situations I'd been in.

In trying to get away from my father, I was responding, I suppose, to an inherent desire to survive.

I stumbled, half-crawling, half-running, through the door.

I moved down the steps that led to the backyard.

But I slipped. And fell.

I landed against the concrete path in front of the steps. And as I hit the ground I became aware of my father, his palpitating bulk, charging down the steps.

"What the hell do you think you're doing!" He hovered over me, a mass of rage set against the evening's dark. "What kind of crap are you trying to pull! What the hell is going on!"

I lay, curled up, my face pressed to the cold concrete.

"Get up!" he screamed. "Get up, goddammit!"

I didn't follow his instructions.

"Get up, Pete!"

I didn't make any attempt to get up. Instead, I pulled my legs to my chest and wrapped my arms around my knees and tried to make myself into a ball, like a small animal trying to protect itself from a much larger, superior predator.

"Get up, Pete! Get up!"

My father's voice reverberated against the placid suburban night, the dormant yards, the flat expanse of Jefferson Street.

"I've fucking had it with you!" he screamed.

Then he kicked me. He kicked me violently. He kicked me with an unglued ferocity. He drove his big black shoe into my arm, my right arm. His shoe, the hard toe, smashed into my arm near the elbow.

"You lousy piece of shit!" he screamed. "You goddam lousy piece of shit!"

Then he kicked me again. He drove his shoe, once again, into my arm. The hard leather shoe struck my arm in just about the same place where it'd struck before.

"You little cocksucker!" he growled.

Then he went up the steps.

"Go to your room," he said, opening the kitchen door. "No dinner for you tonight."

When I got to school the next morning, I went straight to the nurse's office. I told the nurse that I had fallen off my bicycle on my way to school and that I'd hurt my arm. From then on this was what I told people, this was how I explained how I had broken my arm. In the days and months and years to follow this was the story I gave.

The nurse drove me to Mid Island Hospital, where my arm was put in a cast that extended from the knuckles of my right hand to my elbow, where it made a right angle, then continued almost to my shoulder.

Before I left the hospital one of the doctors gave me an X-ray of the arm, figuring that I'd like to keep it as a souvenir of my travails. But when I walked into the waiting room and saw my mother, I quickly folded the X-ray and shoved it in my pants. She was sitting on a vinyl couch. She was wearing a crummy blue raincoat. Her hair was tied in a greasy ponytail. Her eyes were half-closed, black.

She was obviously struggling with her despair.

She was thirty-two years old, but her life was beyond the point where she could do anything about it. Her life was shit. Every impenetrable moment was shit. And getting worse every day. And this was another of those moments that magnified, clarified the other moments. Another in a series, a life, of disasters.

I forced the X-ray into my pants. And after I got home I walked around the house to the garbage cans and I stuffed it into one of the dented metal cans, deep inside, with the rotting food and miscellaneous refuse.

Needless to say, I wasn't able to play Little League baseball that spring. I drudged around until the third week in May, lugging the monstrous cast like some unfortunate mythological character forced by a spiteful god to carry a heavy white log for the remainder of his earthbound days, and then, when I went back to the hospital to have the cast removed, I was told that my arm hadn't healed completely and that I was going to have to wear another, less elaborate, cast for another six weeks.

The day after the second cast was taken off, I tried to throw a baseball.

I stood on Jefferson Street with Chris Adelkravitich. We had our baseball gloves and a hardball. The ball was scuffed, the stitches loose, coming undone.

It was a cloudy morning. Large white clouds moved, like busses, across the July sky.

The street was wet, it'd rained the night before, everything, the street, the lawns, the trees, smelled like the rain.

"You're making a comeback," Chris said, grinning, holding up his mitt.

I gripped the baseball apprehensively.

I threw it.

The ball angled downwards, ricochetted off the street, a good ten feet in front of Adelkravitich.

Chris stuck out his glove, speared the ball.

"Can't expect the first throw to be good," he said cheerfully.

"It feels weird," I said.

"That's not surprising," he said.

I tried again. And, again, I threw wildly. This time the ball sailed over Chris's head.

Chris ran after the baseball, grabbed it just before it rolled into the sewer.

"Don't try too hard," he said, walking back to me, his sneakers scraping the rain discolored street. "Just throw nice and easy."

"I think something's wrong," I said.

"You're just out of practice," Chris said. He flipped me the ball.

"I never throw like this," I said. "I think something's wrong with my arm."

I made a few more throws. I made nine, ten throws. I didn't try to fire the ball. I tried to throw nice and easy, as Chris'd suggested. But I didn't make one accurate toss. I winged the ball over Chris's head. I bounced the ball off the pavement. I threw wide left, wide right.

"Something's wrong," I said.

"It's just gonna take some time," Chris said. He was out-of-breath. He'd expended an undue amount of energy, running down the street, crawling under cars, searching in bushes, tracking down my errant throws.

"It doesn't feel good," I said. "It feels like there's something wrong with it."

"Maybe you should take a break," Chris said.

"Let me try a few more," I said.

I attempted five or six more throws. But I had no success. Each throw was disastrously off-line.

"That's enough," I said finally.

I took off my glove, tucked it under my arm.

"You're just out of shape," Chris said consolingly.

"I can't throw," I said.

I was profoundly discouraged. The expectations, the hope, that I'd felt when Chris and I had stepped onto the street had been crushed, like an aluminum can beneath the wheels of a garbage truck.

"Don't worry," Chris said.

"There's something wrong with my arm," I said.

"It'll get better."

"Something's wrong with it."

"You just got the cast off," Chris said.

"It shouldn't feel like this," I said.

"It's gonna take awhile before you can throw right," Chris said.

"I should be able to throw better than this," I said.

"Don't worry," Chris said. "Pretty soon you'll be throwing like Tony Kubek."

"I hope you're right," I said, "but I think something's wrong with it."

July moved into August, the summer sun parched the rectangular lawns, baked the long straight streets. But I still wasn't able to throw. I wasn't able to throw with any sort of accuracy. I had no idea when I let go of the baseball where it was going to go, and it almost never went where I wanted it to go.

Although I still played baseball on the street with my friends, I didn't play nearly as much as I used to. I frequently avoided Chris and Willy and Kevin and Louie when they were starting up a game. There were many times that summer when they knocked on my door and asked if I wanted to play when I rejected them, when I told them that I had something else that I wanted to do, when I told them that I didn't feel well, when I told them, quite simply, that I didn't "feel like it."

When I played, I played first base. In the past I'd always played shortstop, but now, of course, I couldn't play short, I couldn't throw well enough. Now the only position that I could play with any skill and facility was first base. It was the only position at which I didn't have to throw, the only position at which I didn't run the risk of hampering the smooth flow of the game with my wayward tosses. It was the only place my friends could put me without compromising the quality and integrity of the game.

Of course, the truth was, before I broke my arm we almost never deployed a first baseman when we played baseball on the street. We never had enough players to field an entire team. And, besides, there wasn't enough room on the narrow street for a full complement, for nine players, somebody at every position. Whenever we played on the street we improvised. If we played in front of my house or Chris's house we made a big tree first base, and if we played in front of Kenny Pelligrini's it was a mailbox. When an infielder picked up a grounder he simply threw the ball at the tree or the mailbox and if he hit his target the batter was out. We had always gotten along nicely without putting a live body at first.

In letting me play first base, my friends were carving out a space for me, in much the same way that space in a parking lot is apportioned for handicapped drivers.

I was, of course, afraid to talk to my father about the trouble I was having. But if I hadn't been afraid, I don't know that I would've been able to talk to him, I don't know that I would've been able to find the opportunity to talk to him. The fact was, I hardly ever saw my father during the months that followed that March evening when he kicked me and ruined my arm. For two or three weeks immediately following the incident, I didn't see him at all. He disappeared. And then, after he reappeared, I saw him infrequently, and when I saw him I saw him only briefly, I glimpsed him, sitting at the kitchen table digging a big spoon into a sloppy half-gallon of vanilla fudge ice cream, standing at the workbench in the garage angrily jamming a screwdriver inside the guts of a brokendown toaster. At some point he got a job as a salesman for a small insurance company in Flushing, Queens, and after that I almost never saw him during the week. He rarely came directly home to Jefferson Street after finishing a day of work. He rarely sat at the dinner table with my mother and my brother and my sister and me. He hardly ever planted himself on the easychair in the living room and watched the evening TV programs. He usually didn't come home, when, and if, he did come home, until long after I went to bed.

Sometimes I heard him coming home, sometimes I was wakened by the abrupt sound, my father barging through the front door, finding his way, with difficulty, across the living room. Sometimes I lay in bed, three, four, in the morning, kept awake, tensely awake, by the sound of my father and my mother fighting, my father screaming, spewing derogatory comments, cursing her, calling her a bitch, whore, cunt, cocksucker, my mother countering desperately, shrieking, hurling her pain and contempt like somebody who'd been shoved into a hole flinging bits of mud at her attacker.

Where did my father go after work? How did he pass his evenings, those hours before he clattered through the front door, before he lashed out at my mother? I never knew exactly. But based on pieces of information I gathered, mostly by listening to my parents' verbal wars, it's likely that he spent much of that time drinking, sitting on barstools in grim gin mills in Flushing and along Hempstead Turnpike and Jerusalem Avenue. And if he wasn't perched at some bar, he was probably gambling, playing poker, or putting down bets on the trotters at Roosevelt and Yonkers.

The bottom line was, he was never around. I hardly ever saw him anymore.

For awhile I thought I'd try to tell my mother that I was having a problem, that I couldn't throw. But when push came to shove, I was afraid to talk to her, too.

I'd approach her, thinking that I was going to talk to her, thinking that I was going to tell her everything I had to tell her, but when I got close to her, when I noticed her black eyes, when I smelled her despair, I couldn't do it, I backed down, any inclination I had, any resolve, was quickly negated, the way light in a room is negated by the flick of a switch.

In September my mother took Eddie and me to see Dr. Untermeyer, the pediatrician that we went to every fall for our beginning-the-school-year checkup, and when Untermeyer was finished examining me I asked him if he would look at my arm.

"I think something's wrong with it," I explained.

"Does it hurt?" he asked, writing on his clipboard.

"Not really," I said. "But ever since I got the cast off I can't move it the way I want to. I can't move it the way I used to. I can't throw a baseball anymore. I can't throw straight...."

Untermeyer was tall, thin, with black hair, black glasses. He held my arm, pressed his long hairy fingers into my flesh.

"Do you feel any pain?"

"No," I said. "It doesn't really hurt...but I can't throw...."

"Not at all?"

"I can throw...," I said, "but not like I used to...I can't control where the ball is going...I can't control it at all...."

Untermeyer manipulated my arm, turned it side to side, bended it, like he was adjusting the rabbit ears on a television.

"How does it feel?"

"It feels like something inside it is doing something it isn't supposed to be doing...," I said. "It doesn't feel the same way it used to feel before I broke it...."

"It bothers you mostly when you throw a baseball?"

"Yeah."

"Make a throwing motion for me," Untermeyer suggested. "Pretend you're throwing a ball."

Sitting on the examining table in my underpants, my legs dangling, I pantomimed throwing a baseball.

"Does that hurt?"

"No, not really...."

"How does it feel?"

"It feels like it's stiff, like it's crooked...," I said. "It doesn't feel right...."

Untermeyer plucked a cotton ball from a large glass jar.

"Try throwing this," he said.

I held the cotton ball in my fingers. Threw it. The small fluffy piece of cotton floated jerkily, dropped to the floor.

"How did that feel?"

"The same...," I said. "I can't move it the way I used to be able to move it...it feels weird...it feels awkward...it doesn't feel right...."

Untermeyer scribbled something on his clipboard.

"When I throw a baseball I can't throw it the way I want to...," I said. "The ball goes everywhere except where I want it to go...."

My mother came into the room, and Dr. Untermeyer told her that he was going to give her the name of a doctor who could look at my arm. An orthopedist.

My mother nodded, respectfully, concernedly. Her hair fell, a tangle of greasy knots. Beneath her eyes were dark raccoon circles. She was wearing a wrinkled dress cinched at her waist, which was very thin, with a frayed rope belt.

Untermeyer jotted the doctor's name and number on a small pad, tore off the paper, handed it to her.

My mother dropped the slip of paper into her handbag.

"The problem could be psychological," Untermeyer told her, speaking in a near whisper as he uttered the key word "psychological." He tapped his pencil, twice, against his temple.

My mother nodded.

On the way home, as my mother drove the station wagon down Sunrise Highway, I leaned toward the front seat—I was sitting in the back with Eddie, Denise was strapped into a car seat in front. I put my hands on the top of the seat, and I said, "Mom, are you going to call the specialist?"

"Yes," she said.

"When?"

"I'll call tomorrow," she said.

But I think I knew that she would never make the call.

And, of course, she didn't.

The next spring, despite the fact that my arm hadn't improved, despite the fact that I still couldn't throw, I registered for Little League baseball.

I was placed on the Braves, a team in the Bayview Central League minor leagues. The coach of the Braves was Al Stoudafere, the father of Wayne Stoudafere, a kid I knew from Furley Elementary School. Stoudafere fancied himself a brilliant field general, a Little League Casey Stengel or Leo Durocher. He wanted, more than anything else, to win. That was his priority. That was his mission. He declared, in fact, at our first practice, that, "Our job is winning baseball games. That's what we're here for. To bring home a trophy." Stoudafere quickly decided, probably after the first time he saw me throw, that I wasn't the kind of ballplayer who was going to help him capture a championship. He immediately appointed me to an obscure role, he made me a backup outfielder, and he indicated, clearly, mostly by the way he ignored me, that I wasn't going to be an integral part of his pennant-bound squad. I tried to let him know that I was best suited to play first base. But he wouldn't listen. He had somebody to play first. A kid named Tommy Baumgartner. Baumgartner, apparently, was one of the team's stars, one of the young athletes who was going to lead Stoudafere's troops to the promised land. There was no way that I was going to interfere with Tommy Baumgartner's skilled dominion over the balding turf around first base.

Once the schedule of games began, Stoudafere gave me very little opportunity to play, just enough to comply with the league's stipulations that every boy had to play a minimum number of innings during the fifteen game season. For the bulk of each game, and sometimes for the whole game, I sat on the bench along with a cast of dubious ballplayers, kids like pintsized Billy Ferguson and frighteningly skinny Toby Wick, a boy who lived on Van Buren Street who once before a game hit himself in the face with his bat, knocking off his glasses and giving himself a bloody nose.

I didn't say anything to my father about my participation, or lack of participation, with the Braves.

And he didn't say anything to me about it.

In the past my father had taken a keen, often feverish, interest in my baseball playing. In his own youth he had apparently been a pretty good player, a standout performer on his high school team, a third baseman with a marked ability to hit the long ball. After high school he'd played for a well-known semi-pro team, the

Woodhaven Lancers. He'd been scouted, he'd once told me, by the Brooklyn Dodgers. There was one time, he'd told me, when a Dodgers scout had come to one of his games and had seen my father hit two gargantuan home runs. The scout had talked to my father after the game and had told him that the Dodgers were interested in signing him. But nothing had ever happened, he never heard from the Dodgers, no contract was ever offered.

When I was four years old my father bought me a plastic mitt and a small wooden bat, and he spent a number of summer evenings and weekend afternoons when I was four, five, six, playing with me in the backyard, playing catch, throwing me grounders and pop flies, pitching tennis balls to me, giving instruction, explaining the fundamentals of the game, espousing his hardass philosophies concerning sports. When I got older he would take me to 52 Acres field and he'd work with me, he'd put me through a series of gruelling drills. First he'd hit grounders to me. I'd stand on the rockhard infield, amidst the swirling dirt, and he'd hit me hundreds of grounders, he'd hit hard shots, wicked shots, he'd hit balls that I couldn't possibly catch, balls that would bounce off my shins and my chest, balls that I would have to dive after, fling my body after, and he'd exhort me, "Get in front of the goddam ball!" And then he'd pitch to me. He'd stand on the mound, he'd go into a herky-jerky windup, kick his leg, twist his massive body, and he'd fire the ball, he'd throw vicious fastballs and sharpbreaking curves and changeups, sometimes he'd even throw knuckleballs. "Step into the ball!" he'd yell. "Snap your wrists! Be aggressive!"

But since he'd broken my arm my father hadn't say anything to me about baseball. Of course, he hadn't been around much, but during those rare moments when we'd had contact he hadn't suggested that we go to 52 Acres, or that we have a catch on the street, or play wiffleball in the backyard. He hadn't mentioned baseball at all. He hadn't even said anything about the Yankees or the Mets.

He hadn't said anything that had anything to do with baseball, he'd avoided the subject, he'd discarded it, the way somebody might discard a dilapidated car by sliding it into a ditch along a remote section of highway.

I assumed that he wouldn't attend any of the games that I played with the Braves. And as far as I was concerned, that was okay. I didn't want him to come to any of the games.

When he didn't make an appearance at the first eight or nine games, I figured that I didn't have anything to worry about, I figured that there was no way that he was going to come to any of the games.

And then one evening he showed up.

We were playing at Richard Place Field.

It was a weekday evening.

A grey evening.

The game was just about to start.

And I saw him.

I saw him walking across the street, walking toward the field. He was wearing a ratty brown sportsjacket. The jacket and his tie were flapping in the breeze and his stomach was protruding into his white shirt. He was smoking a cigarette. He clodded toward the field, holding the cigarette to his curved-down mouth. Eschewing the small set of bleachers where the other parents were sitting, he lodged himself behind home plate, behind the chain-link backstop. He stood there, by himself, his shoes stuck in the dried mud. He stared maliciously at the leaden sky. Pulled on his cigarette.

My teammates took the field, jogged to their positions. And I settled onto my familiar spot on the splintered wooden bench. I glanced, several times, at my father. I was hoping he'd take off when he realized that I wasn't in the starting lineup. But he didn't budge.

The game began. We were playing the Pirates. They were the best team in the league. And despite Stoudafere's impassioned efforts to mold us into a winner, we were undoubtedly the worst. Up to that point we had tasted victory just once, and in most of our games we'd gotten our asses kicked rather thoroughly. We didn't stand a chance against the Pirates.

From the beginning the game was a blow-out. The Pirates scored seven runs in the top half of the first inning, and in the bottom half of the inning our first three batters struck out. After the second inning the Pirates were leading 11–0, and after the third inning the score was 14–1.

I kept checking my father. I was hoping that he'd tire of the painful spectacle, that he'd decide he'd seen enough, that he'd leave, that he'd get in his car and drive off. But he didn't move. He remained behind the cage. He stared at the field, his eyebrows bunched, his face smeared with a growing disgust, the ubiquitous cigarette glued between his bentdown lips.

At the end of the fourth inning the score was 16–2, and before the start of the fifth a demoralized Stoudafere walked to the end of the bench, to the section of the timber where the second stringers, including myself, were sitting, and, undoubtedly concluding that there was no possible way that we could win and that this was a good time to give the scrubs a chance to play, to accumulate some innings, he grabbed my shoulder and said, "Okay Pete. Go to left field. Show'em what you got. Play some baseball."

I didn't want to have to go in the game. But I had no choice but to obey Stoudafere's orders.

I trotted out to left field. I took my position, hands on my knees, in the expanse of crabgrass, dandelions and bumpy dirt. Needless to say, I was terrified. I didn't want to have to do anything, didn't want to have to make any kind of play. I didn't want to have to make a catch. I certainly didn't want to have to throw. I hoped, I prayed, that the ball wouldn't be hit to me.

I looked across the diamond, toward home plate. I tried to focus on the Pirates first batter, Brian Finbow. But I couldn't prevent my gaze from slipping, shifting to my father, standing behind the backstop, dragging on his cigarette.

The inning began.

Brian Finbow, to my not insubstantial relief, hit a weak roller to the first baseman, Tommy Baumgartner.

The next Pirate batter walked.

The next batter was a chubby blondeheaded kid named Stephen Louden.

Louden let a couple of pitches go by. Then he took a hard swing. And he smacked the ball. He hit a line drive, a rocket, over the shortstop's head.

The ball shot through the grey air, into left field, toward me.

I started forward.

The baseball hit the ground sharply.

I moved toward the ball. But I felt like I didn't have control of my basic motor functions. I couldn't feel my body moving. I felt like I'd lost contact with my arms and legs, the way you lose contact with an out-of-town radio station.

The ball bounced furiously against the hard turf. It bore down on me, like an angry rodent, teeth bared, hellbent on taking a bite out of my leg.

I leaned toward the ball. I tried to make the play. I tried to bend down, tried to put my glove down, to touch the leather fingers to the ground, the way my father had shown me, again and again. I tried, but I couldn't move my glove the way I wanted to.

The ball hit my knee, deflected away, behind me.

I went after it.

I stumbled.

Fell.

Got up.

I finally reached the ball. It was resting against a clump of weeds. I picked it up. Dropped it. Picked it up again.

Turning to the infield, I saw Stephen Louden running, lumbering, toward third base. I reared back. And I threw the baseball. I threw the ball so hard, so forcefully, that I fell down, I collapsed to the bonehard ground.

The ball took off. It soared. It soared like a berserk seagull. It soared over the head of the third baseman, Paul Cooper, it cleared Cooper's head by at least ten feet, and it flew into the bleachers, and it hit Tommy Baumgartner's grandmother smackdab on her ankle.

Lying on the ground in the wasteland of left field, I watched everything, the whole ugly scene. Stephen Louden chugging home, shooting his arms triumphantly above his head. Tommy Baumgartner's grandmother clutching her ankle. Baumgartner's parents attending to the stricken grandmother. And behind the backstop, my father, looking at the sky, his face clenched, as though rigged with an awkward system of wires that were being pulled to their limit and then some.

After the game my father put my bike in the station wagon and drove me back to Jefferson Street. He guided the car through the neighborhood streets, dragged on a cigarette, said nothing. I sat beside him, peered through the window.

We reached the house, the small boxshaped house with the green shingles and chipped white trim. My father pulled the station wagon into the driveway. He stifled the engine.

He scrutinized me.

"You wanna tell me what that was all about?" he said.

He pulled on his cigarette.

"What the hell was that all about, Pete?"

"It was a bad game," I said. And I started to cry.

"It was pathetic," my father said.

"I'm sorry," I said, the tears trickling down my face in myriad paths.

"I've never been so humiliated in my whole goddam life," he said. "Do you have any idea how much I was humiliated? Watching you sit on the bench. With those other kids. With those spastics. Do you know how humiliating that was? And then when you got in the game. That was the worst. That was the worst thing I've ever seen. The worst thing. Kicking that ball. Throwing it in the stands. Hitting that old cunt. Jesus Christ, Pete."

I sat there, throbbing, the tears dripping onto my dark green Braves shirt.

"Do you realize how much you're embarrassing yourself?"

"It's just a game," I said, fitting the words through a narrow passageway.

"You've gotta have some pride in yourself," he said. "You're letting that cocksucker Stoudafere make a jackass out of you. You can't do that. You can't let that happen. Do you know what I'm talking about, Pete? You don't want to look like those other kids. Like Toby Wick. Is that what you want? Do you want people to laugh at you? Because that's what's going on out there. They're laughing at you."

My father glared at me. His face looked like it might split open, like a piece of rotten fruit.

"I think you should quit the team," he said.

"I don't want to," I said.

"I think you should."

"I don't want to."

He glared at me. But he said nothing. He knew, I think, that he could only go so far, given what he'd done. He'd lost the right to go any further.

He looked through the windshield, toward the garage. Behind the garage, the sky was almost completely dark, only the edges were tinged with the remnants of the day's grey colors.

"I don't know what to tell you...," he said, finally. "I guess if you wanna make an ass out of yourself, that's your business...."

I didn't take my father's advice. I didn't quit. I stayed on the team until the last game was completed, the last inning played, the last put-out recorded.

But that was the last season of Little League baseball I played.

I was never again able to throw.

I never recovered.

For awhile I still played baseball on the street. I didn't play often, but I played. But then, toward the end of the summer of my twelfth year, I decided that I'd had it. I stashed my mitt in the recesses of the bedroom closet. And I vowed that I would never play baseball again.

When my friends asked me to play, I rebuffed them. And after awhile they no longer importuned me, they no longer sought to include me.

The way I saw it, I was through. That part of my life, the part when I played baseball, was done with. It was over.

He tried, I think, to talk to me about what'd happened.

He tried. At least that's what I'd like to think. That he tried. But that he just couldn't pull it off.

I was thirteen years old.

I was in the living room, sitting on the couch, watching *The Tonight Show*. The house was quiet. Eddie and Denise had gone to bed. My mother had disappeared into her bedroom.

I heard his car, the decrepit Chevy Malibu, turning into the driveway, clanking, coughing.

Normally if I'd heard my father's car I would've slipped off the couch and jogged upstairs, to my room. But I didn't move.

My father came through the door. He stepped, taking short unbalanced steps, across the living room. He was categorically drunk. Gone. He noticed me. He squinted, as though he recognized me but wasn't quite sure who I was.

He fell against the easychair opposite the couch. Lying there, he stared, incoherently, thick-eyed, into the room's blank spaces. He was, at forty-two, the picture of somebody who'd conceded the fight. His face sagged, its angularity gone, his once well-defined jawline obscured by loose flesh. His visage was marred by stubble, which wasn't unusual, but the stubble had taken a different form, had turned, it seemed, into a kind of rot. He was wearing a stained tan raincoat. Underneath, the usual salesman's garb, the sports-jacket, tie, grey slacks, black shoes. He was working at Gorman and Fusco, an appliance store on Hempstead Turnpike. It'd been some time since he'd worked as an insurance salesman, which for many years, of course, had been his bailiwick. In the past few years he'd toiled as a salesman for a number of different unrelated concerns. He'd sold wine and liquor, advertising space, Buicks, Hondas, used cars, cardboard boxes, potato chips, and probably some other things that I didn't know about. Now he passed his days shuffling up and down the brightly-lit aisles in Gorman and Fusco, selling dishwashers, refrigerators, air conditioners, and washing machines to suburban couples looking to outfit their houses with dependable, technologically advanced appliances that they might purchase at a reasonable cost.

For a minute or so, he just sat there, slumped, against the easy-chair.

Then suddenly he pivoted his head, looked directly at me.

"Hey Pete," he said.

"Hi Dad," I said.

"What's going on?"

"Nothing."

"How're you doing?" he asked. There was a warmth, an affection, in his voice. It was something I hadn't heard in a long time. It was as though he'd suddenly found it, this cache of affection, it was as though he'd been looking for something in the attic and had come across it, hidden behind old tools and broken lamps and sundry forms of junk.

"Everything okay?" he asked.

I didn't respond.

"Talk to me," he said.

I looked at the TV. Johnny Carson bantering with Ed McMahon.

"We never talk…," he said.

This was certainly true. In the past several years we'd had just a few, remarkably insignificant conversations.

"It's not right…," he said. "A father and his son should talk every once in awhile…."

I looked, sideways, at him.

"I guess you don't have much use for me…," he said. "You must think I really screwed you…."

"No…," I said.

"You must think I really messed you up…."

"No, I don't…," I said. And I started to cry.

"I know what you must think…," he said. "You must think I really fucked you up…you must think I fucked you up good…."

"No…," I said.

"You're probably mad at me...you're probably mad...you probably hate my guts...don't you...don't you, Pete...?"

"No...," I said.

"I don't blame you if you do...," he said. "I fucked up...I fucked up alot...."

He reached into his raincoat, produced a pack of Kents, a plastic lighter.

He fitted a cigarette between his lips, flicked the lighter, lit the butt, the flame leaping, nearly scorching his face.

He took a long drag.

"I did the best I could," he said. Now, suddenly, he was angry. "What can I tell you?"

He puffed on his cigarette.

"I don't know what to tell you," he said. The affection was completely gone from his voice.

"I know you haven't had it so easy...," he said. He couldn't help it. He couldn't allay his venom. Every word dripped. "I know it's been tough...it's been tough for everyone...it's been tough for your mother...it's been tough for Eddie and Denise...that's just the way it is sometimes...that's life, Pete...that's life...things don't always go your way...you gotta take some hard knocks sometimes...you gotta take some hard knocks...."

He scowled at me.

"Are you crying? What the hell are you crying for?"

He dragged, effortfully, on his cigarette.

"You gotta learn to accept things, Pete...you take everything too hard...you take everything too goddam hard...it's no good, Pete...you're gonna be a miserable sonofabitch your whole goddam life...."

He stubbed out his cigarette.

"You're never gonna be anything but a goddam miserable sonofabitch...," he said.

Then he fell back against the chair.

And he passed out.

He died not long after that, on a cold March night.

My mother didn't provide my brother and my sister and me with the specific details surrounding his death, but I was able to acquire some of the details by eavesdropping on conversations that my mother, zonked on tranquilizers, had with a neighbor, Joan Galvin, during the days following his demise.

Apparently my father left Gorman and Fusco that night just after the store closed, shortly after 9pm.

He probably went straight to Crowley's, the nondescript gin mill that he went to almost every night after he left work.

He stayed at Crowley's for a few hours. He sat at the bar, drank a number of glasses of vodka.

He left Crowley's at approximately 1am.

He got in his car, the clunky Malibu.

He drove down Hempstead Turnpike, then got on the Wantagh Parkway.

He headed south, down the parkway. This was the route he normally took when coming home from Crowley's. He normally travelled on the Wantagh for a couple of miles, got off at the Sunrise Highway exit, then drove to Bayview. But on this particular March night my father didn't take the Sunrise Highway exit. Why? Perhaps, in his inebriated state, he simply missed the exit. Or perhaps he knew what he was doing. Perhaps he had no intention of getting off at Sunrise, of returning to Jefferson Street.

He continued down the Wantagh. He passed the Merrick Road exit, another exit that he could've taken.

He headed down the parkway toward Jones Beach. He drove past tall winterstripped trees. The road was dark. There were probably just a few cars. This segment of the Wantagh was used primarily by Long Islanders headed for the south shore beaches, and it was therefore likely, given the time of year, and the time of night, that my father's Chevy was one of just a handful of cars driving along the dark asphalt. It was likely, in fact, that at different points my father didn't see any other vehicles, coming or going.

He kept driving south.

He rattled past pockets of water, parts of the Great South Bay.

He was probably moving at a good clip, 65, 70, maybe 75 mph. He was probably driving the beatup Chevy alot faster than he usually drove it. And he was undoubtedly driving in his trademark style, one hand clutching the wheel, the other holding a cigarette.

He came to a bridge, one of several small concrete bridges that spanned pieces of the bay. The bridge was under construction. A succession of signs instructed oncoming motorists to slow down, to reduce their speed to 15 mph, a few more signs indicated to drivers that they had to veer to the right, and a series of orange pylons funnelled the traffic into a single narrow lane.

The detour was poorly lit.

And the road conditions were not good. It was a bitterly cold night, one of those March nights that refused to let go of winter's vagaries. The temperature was in the low thirties. And the air, this near the water, was filled with moisture. As a result, the surface of the bridge was covered with a thin glaze of ice.

My father came upon the construction site.

It's possible that he never saw the signs. Or that by the time he saw them it was too late.

The Chevy skidded. It skidded wildly. It knocked over a couple of signs and some pylons. And crashed through a makeshift fence. And flew off the bridge into the Great South Bay.

They didn't pull the car out of the water until the next afternoon.

❦   ❦   ❦

A couple of months after my father died, my mother decided that she would have to sell the house.

When I was younger, my mother hadn't worked, she'd been a housewife, like all my friend's mothers, like the majority of the women of her generation. She'd never had any career, she'd never developed any skills that she could translate into making money.

In high school she'd been an excellent student, at the top of her class at Jamaica High. She had gone to CCNY. But she had quit after two years, and a year or so after she'd quit she had married my father, and a year or so after that she had given birth to me. She had been just twenty-two when I was born.

In recent years she had taken various part-time jobs in order to help defray the debts that'd mounted as the result of my father's wayward habits, his drinking and gambling, and his general inability to meet his responsibilities. At the time of my father's passing, she was working in the office of a carpet cleaning company on Jerusalem Avenue, performing simple administrative duties, filing stuff, typing, etc. But she was working just twelve to fifteen hours a week and wasn't making much money. She was going to have to find some kind of full-time employment, she realized. She was going to have to figure out a way to support herself and my brother and my sister and me. In the meantime, she wasn't going to be able to afford to keep the house, she didn't think.

During the summer she put the house on the market. The real estate company planted a large red and white FOR SALE sign on the front lawn. Strange people came and looked at the house, peered into the rooms, young couples vying for their share of the American Dream.

And in September my mother found a buyer. She sold the house.

And in October, during the beginning of my freshman year at Bayview High School, my mother and Eddie and Denise and I moved into my mother's parents' house in Bellerose, Queens.

I wrote a number of short stories during my senior year at Benjamin Cardozo High School, and at the urging of my English teacher, Mrs. Raffin, I submitted the most accomplished story to a small, utterly inconspicuous literary journal, *The Flip Side*. The story was rejected, but, in a moment of youthful brashness, I submitted it to another publication, a significantly more well-known publication, *The Paris Review*. And it was accepted.

The story, to some extent, was about my father. The title, "The Dancing Gorilla," derived from the memory I had of a time that my parents took Eddie and me to the Bronx Zoo.

I was five, maybe six.

My father and I were looking at the gorillas. They were sitting on big pink rocks, just sitting there, scratching their asses. Then, suddenly, one of the apes jumped to his feet and started dancing, started wiggling in a frenetic, jerky fashion. Like he was doing the Twist.

And my father started laughing. He laughed uncontrollably. He dropped to his knees, held his stomach, and laughed, guffawed. It was as though something inside him that'd been stuck had suddenly become unstuck.

It was a memory that had always seemed to rise when I thought about him.

Until I sold "The Dancing Gorilla" to *The Paris Review*, I'd never considered having a career as a writer. It'd never occurred to me that somebody like myself, the product of a middleclass suburb, the son of a deceased salesman, might pursue that sort of artistic path. Certainly "writer" didn't fall into the category of logical middleclass occupations, the sort of occupations I'd been indoctrinated to consider by my mother, my grandparents, my school, the general situation comedy mentality, the treadmill culture that I'd been brought up in. When I had met with my guidance counselor at the beginning of my senior year, I had told him that I thought I might want to be a lawyer. But after I learned that I'd sold my story I began to think that perhaps I wasn't meant to be an attorney, I began to think that perhaps I was destined to fulfill the role of an author, an author of astonishing, revelatory fictions.

I was quite certain that I could do it, that I could be a writer.

I was sure.

As my senior year came to a close I pieced together a dream. I would write a novel while I was in college. A blindingly beautiful novel. A groundbreaking novel. It would be published before I graduated, by the time I graduated I would be an established writer, and after I graduated I would move smoothly into the writer's life. I would be a full time, self-sufficient writer. And I would never have to subject myself to the hellish routines of a nine-to-five life. I wouldn't have to live the way my father had lived, the way the men who lived in the suburbs and places like Bellerose lived. I'd watched these men all my life, getting off the railroad, trudging through the doors of their dismal houses. I would never have to follow that deadly course.

But I didn't write the novel, I didn't write anything during college.

And after I graduated I got a job, I got a job with L.G. Buchanan School Supplies, a job as a sales rep, a job selling educational materials, scotch tape, rulers, protractors, calculators, colored paper, paper clips, file cabinets, chalk, pencils, to schools in the

Bronx, Brooklyn, Manhattan, Queens and Staten Island. I figured I'd keep this job for awhile, for a year or so, I figured I'd put a minimum amount of effort into it, I'd execute my salesman's duties to the extent that I had to, in order to maintain my standing with the company, in order to pay my bills and support myself, but I would direct my most heartfelt energies into my writing, into writing a book, into writing the book, the novel, the exhilaratingly wrought, joltingly gorgeous novel that I had vowed, when I was in high school, that I would write.

But for six years I didn't write, I didn't write anything.

Then, finally, when I was twenty-eight, I started, I started to write, I started to write a novel, *the* novel, the novel that I'd promised myself I would write, the novel that I hoped would change the course of my life, that would establish me as a writer, an artist, a painter of startling, and startlingly poetic, landscapes.

I worked on this novel for more than ten years. I still, of course, worked for L.G. Buchanan, but when I wasn't plying my salesman's trade, when I wasn't making a sales pitch to some tired assistant principal, or manning the booth at some ridiculous materials exhibit, when I wasn't working, I wrote. Whenever I could, I wrote. On a typical day I worked for Buchanan until about 3pm, until the schools let out, and then I came home, back to my apartment in Forest Hills, and I wrote for the remainder of the afternoon and into the evening. I often wrote well into the night, until 10, 11pm. I sat at my desk, a wooden table positioned against the living room wall, and I wrote, I wrote doggedly. I usually set aside an hour or so, and I cooked something, spaghetti, hamburgers, or I ordered Chinese food or a pizza, and I ate, and then I sat down again at my desk and I wrote. For those ten plus years I didn't do much else except work for Buchanan and hammer away on my novel. I wrote almost every day. I wrote on the weekends. I wrote on the school vacations. And I wrote during my own personal vacation time, I didn't go anywhere, I stayed in Forest Hills and wrote.

I accumulated thousands, tens of thousands, of pages of manuscript. I piled up countless legal pads, dozens of spiral notebooks, mountains of typewritten pages, and then, when I got a computer, even larger mountains of computer paper. I stored these pages, burdened with the paragraphs and chapters, the various drafts of my novel, in cardboard boxes, boxes that I kept, because I had no other place to put them, in my bedroom. I lined the boxes against the wall opposite my bed, and for a couple of years they made a neat row against the wall and I put my jeans and sweatshirts and tee shirts on them, and then after a few years I began to stack the boxes, I stacked them three, four high, and then I began to add additional rows, and eventually the boxes jutted into the room, and as the years went on they began to resemble some sort of cardboard architecture, an odd version of the forts and cities that I'd constructed with blocks when I was a kindergartner at Furley Elementary School.

Then I trashed the manuscript.

I worked on the book for the last time on a Wednesday night in mid-July. I worked through the afternoon, into the hot, oppressively humid summer night. I sat at my table, in my air-conditioning-bereft apartment, and I slogged away until about 10pm. For the last couple of hours I worked on a section that comprised roughly one-fourth of a page. I rewrote this remarkably uncomplicated section at least twenty times. Then finally I gave up. I couldn't get the sentences right, and it didn't seem like I ever would. I left the apartment. I got in my car, drove down Queens Blvd, to a local Forest Hills tavern, the Background Lounge. I sat at the bar, glugged five or six beers. Then I got back in my car and headed down Queens Blvd, over the Queensboro Bridge, into Manhattan. I drove up and down 57th and 58th Streets for about an hour, looking for a hooker, looking for the right hooker. There were plenty of girls to choose from, but I didn't spot anyone who intrigued me, who provoked me. Eventually I picked up my car phone and I called a whorehouse, a place on Second Avenue that I visited on a fairly regular basis.

At the whorehouse I was pleased to find sitting in the "waiting room" a girl by the name of Ingrid, an attractive young blonde with whom I'd had sex a number of times in the recent past. I spent an hour with her in a small room with abscessed pink walls. I fucked her. I fondled her tits, her ass. Talked to her. Then I went back to Forest Hills, to my apartment.

I woke up the next morning at about 11am. I went into the kitchen, prepared myself a bowl of cereal, Raisin Bran with lowfat milk. I sat on the couch in the living room, slurped the cereal. Then I just sat there. I sat there for two hours, three hours. I sat there, doing nothing, I stared out the window, I studied the sun slanting off the apartment building across the street from my apartment building.

Finally I got off the couch. I grabbed my handtruck, a contrivance I normally used for hauling L.G. Buchanan materials. I went into the bedroom, started loading the cardboard boxes, the boxes that held my manuscript, the pages of my book, the many drafts of my long-gestating novel. I put five or six boxes on the handtruck, carted them downstairs, around the building, to the large steel receptacle into which you were supposed to deposit recyclable paper products. I tossed the boxes into the big silver container. Then I went back upstairs, re-loaded the handtruck. It took several trips, but eventually I dumped every last box, every last page, every last sentence, every last word.

The next afternoon I drove to New Jersey, to the L.G. Buchanan office, and I told Dave Finchen, the regional sales manager, that I was quitting. And the next day I called Nadine, the woman who worked in the management office for the building I lived in, and I told her that I was moving out of my apartment.

Over the next couple of weeks I cleaned out my apartment. I got rid of the bulk of my possessions, I kept just a few things, some clothes, some kitchen supplies, my old manual typewriter, some books, *Leaves of Grass*, *Walden*, a collection of Emerson's essays. I turned in everything I had that belonged to L.G. Buchanan, my computer, my fax machine, my telephone answering machine. I returned my company car, and bought the Toyota.

I left Queens on the last day of July with all of my belongings, the few things I'd held onto, packed into the Toyota's minuscule trunk. I headed north, up the Thruway, then west on Route 17. In the small upstate New York town of Liberty I found a place to live. A rundown shack, appointed with some cruddy furniture and a woodburning stove, situated in the middle of nowhere, in the midst of alot of tall unperturbed trees. It was, I thought, the perfect place for me to do what I had to do, to write, to pound out a book, a novel, a goddam masterwork.

I started writing. I started, in fact, on the day I moved into the shack. I started writing another novel.

I worked on this novel for three months.

I wrote every day, usually for about ten hours, usually from about 10am to 8pm. I took breaks now and then, primarily to attend to necessary bodily functions, eating, pissing, shitting, masturbating, but for the most part I worked, I wrote, I sat at a wobbly card table, banged away on my portable typewriter, the ancient Olivetti that I'd received for Christmas from my mother, when I was in high school. I hardly ever left the typewriter, I sat there, all day, just kept hitting the plastic keys. I just kept my fingers moving. I wasn't propelled by any kind of inspiration, I wasn't possessed by any great creative urge, I moved ahead through sheer determination, I grinded forward, like a truck grinding cross-country, grinding day after day along a long string of monotonous interstates.

I completed a first draft during the first week of November. It totalled 1,352 typewritten pages.

I finished the draft on a Friday morning. I knocked out the last ten, twelve pages, then pushed away from the card table, away from the embattled Olivetti, away from my beleaguered manuscript, the lopsided heap of typed-on sheets of cheaply manufactured paper. I stood. I went outside. I stood in front of the shack, on the dirt road, and stared at the trees. The leaves, this far north, were already brown and crisp. They were already falling.

After a few minutes I went back inside. And I began to shove the manuscript, my bloated first draft, into the woodburning stove. I fed the smudged paper into the stove methodically, eighty, a hundred pages at a time, until every last page was destroyed, reduced to ash. Then I left the shack.

I headed down Route 17, then down the Thruway, toward the city.

At first I didn't know where I was going to go.

Then I had an insight. And I knew.

I drove to Bayview.

I got a room at the South Shore Motel.

And I had another insight. I realized that I had to call Willy Smithberger. If I was able to make contact with Willy I might learn something, I might get answers. I had to call him, I was dead certain of this, I didn't know when I'd been this certain of anything.

9

I sat on the motel room bed the day after my encounter with Billie and Janey and I unfolded the page I'd torn from *Newsday*, the page that included the listings for apartments and rooms. I re-examined the listings, grabbed a pen, circled a half dozen ads. I was in terrible shape. I was blatantly hungover. Physically sick. Emotionally and spiritually depleted. But I felt like I had to do something, I felt a sense of urgency, I felt desperate, I felt like I had to take action, I had to move forward. I selected one of the ads, an ad for a studio apartment located in Bayview, and I called the number. I was greeted, however, by an answering machine. I didn't leave a message. I figured I shouldn't. I figured I shouldn't leave the motel phone number. I figured I'd lose any chance I'd have of renting the place if the person I was hoping to rent from ascertained that I was staying at the South Shore Motel.

I chose another ad, an ad for another studio apartment. I called. And got another answering machine.

I picked another ad. I tried the number. A woman answered. A woman named Victoria. She lived, she said, on Dogwood Street, on the other side of Bayview from the neighborhood where I'd grown up. She had a basement apartment that she was looking to rent. I told her I'd like to look at the place, that if possible I'd like to look at it that afternoon. She said okay. And I told her I'd come by in an hour or so.

Hanging up, I felt encouraged. The apartment seemed to fit the profile for the sort of living quarters I was looking for. The rent was low. Victoria didn't require that her tenant sign a lease. The place was furnished. And it was ready to be moved into. It seemed ideal. I figured that if I found it acceptable, or close to acceptable, I'd take it. I wouldn't procrastinate. I'd put down a deposit, perhaps even write a check for the first month's rent. And I'd move in right away.

All in all, I felt inspired. I figured that there was a good chance that by the end of the day I'd have a place to live.

I changed into a relatively clean shirt, a black turtleneck, and I put on my most presentable pair of jeans. I grabbed my checkbook. And left the motel room.

I drove down Jerusalem Avenue, with the shimmy of cars, through the grey November afternoon.

I stopped at a liquor store. Bought a pint of Johnny Walker Red.

I drove to Cotter Park. I sat in the car, held the pint bottle, wrapped in a brown paper bag, to my mouth, sipped the scotch. I studied the park. I remembered my mother taking me to this park when I was two, three years old. I remembered walking on the gravel paths, my mother beside me, her hair rumpling, pushing a carriage inside which my brother, Eddie, lay, wrapped in wooly clothes. I remembered standing at the edge of the tiny pond, feeding pieces of stale bread to the ducks.

I drove to Dogwood Street. I found Victoria's house, a split level with a brick exterior set in a long row of identical brickfaced split levels. I parked at the curb. Checked my visage in the rearview mirror. Fixed my hair. Picked some crust off my nostrils. I opened the pint, took a slug. Then I got out of the car.

I walked to the door. Rang the bell.

Victoria let me in the house.

"How're you doing," I said. I tried to present myself in an upbeat, incontestably likeable manner. "I'm Peter."

She nodded perfunctorily. Unquestionably attractive, she had an intimidating guise, long dark hair, dark eyes, a large mouth curved downward into a tough haughty expression. Probably in her late thirties, she exuded a definitive female power. She was tall, about 5'10", big-boned, strong-looking. The thing she was wearing, a skintight black bodysuit, highlighted her amazonish form, her muscular shoulders, cannonball breasts, long thick legs.

"I'll show you the apartment," she said. She had a hard, cold voice.

She escorted me down a hallway, then down a short drop of stairs. Then she opened a door and led me down a longer flight of creaky wooden stairs.

"There isn't a separate entrance," she said warningly.

"Uh huh."

"That's a problem for some people."

"I don't think it would be a problem for me," I said.

I followed her down the stairs. I inhaled her musty female scent. I ogled her big ass. And I couldn't help but fantasize, couldn't help but think about the steamy landlord-tenant scenarios that we might engage in. I couldn't help but imagine it. Victoria descending the stairs on pale winter afternoons, finding me at my desk, laboring away on my novel. Saying, "Time for your break, baby." Discarding her pants. Sitting, right in front of me, on the desk. Spreading her legs, giving me an up-close view of her cunt. Grasping my head with her long plier-like fingers, jamming, forcing, my mouth against her snatch. Then turning around, sticking her ass in the air, displaying the meaty lips of her vagina, telling me to put my cock in, tell me in no uncertain terms to fuck her…and me, unsnapping my jeans, taking out my stalwart rod, driving it in….

"This is it," she said, blankly. She stepped into the basement, flicked a lightswitch.

Gauzy fluorescent light illuminated, to some degree, the cramped low-ceilinged apartment.

I shuffled onto the center of the floor. Looked around. The room that Victoria and I had descended into, the living room, for lack of a better definition, was a slapdash affair, in need of much repair and refurbishing. The walls were adorned with brown panelling, rather substandard panelling, that in some places had come loose from its moorings and needed to be rehammered. The floor was covered with a piece of warped linoleum. The ceiling, which was disturbingly low, so low that if I'd been just a few inches taller than my six feet my head would've brushed against it, was made of cork tiles, some of which were hanging down, ready to fall, others of which had already fallen, revealing networks of pipes and electrical cables. The room had only one window, a small rectangular aperture that lay flush to the ceiling. The window, however, was caked with scum, making it impossible for whatever light was left on this grey afternoon to eke through. The furnishings included a shabby couch, an old wooden coffee table, two rather suspect wooden chairs, a couple of beatup lamps. As was the case in every basement apartment I'd ever been in, a dank odor clung to the air, as though pasted to the molecules.

"It looks great," I said.

The place, of course, was dismal. But, the truth was, it was exactly the sort of place I was hoping to find.

"The bedroom is this way," Victoria said. She led me down a short dark sheetrock lined hallway.

She showed me the bedroom, equipped with a narrow single bed, the bathroom, the kitchenette. The entire tour took less than two minutes.

We stepped back into the room with panelled walls.

The apartment, as far as I was concerned, was fine. It was suitable enough.

I was ready to tell Victoria that I'd take it.

I didn't see any reason why I should hesitate.

"I think this place would be great for me," I said.

Victoria said nothing.

"I'm definitely interested," I said.

She didn't respond.

"I like it," I said. I looked at Victoria. Tried to smile. But my mouth caught, awkwardly, against my teeth.

"I'll take it," I said, trying to apply the appropriate amount of resolve.

Victoria considered me. She gazed at me, skeptically, her eyes narrowed, her mouth pursed, as though sewn shut with nylon fishing line.

"I should tell you what the situation is," she said. Her tone was uncompromising, cold, icy, as icy as a chunk of ice hanging from the eaves of somebody's house the day after a winter storm. "I live here with my kids. I've got two boys. They're not home right now, but when they're home they make alot of noise. They make a hell of alot of noise. They're kids. That's what they do. They make alot of noise. That's the way it is. Whoever lives down here has got to put up with it. You can hear everything that goes on upstairs. It gets noisy. There's nothing you can do about it."

I nodded.

"They make a hell of a racket," she said.

"That's alright," I said.

"You'd be surprised how noisy it gets."

"Uh huh."

"Alot of people don't like having kids around."

"I don't think it would matter to me," I said.

"I just think you should know what it's like," she said. It was obvious that she was trying to discourage me. It was obvious that she had serious doubts as to whether I was somebody she wanted living in her basement, beneath her and her cacophonous offspring. Why was she so wary of having me as a tenant? It was my guess that she was put off by my appearance. My hair was sort of long, sort of disheveled. My leatherjacket—an item I'd purchased on Orchard Street fifteen years earlier for just $100—was badly defaced, riddled with small tears. My jeans were grimy. My black lowcut basketball sneakers were awfully worn, beginning to decompose. It was my guess that she was inclined to believe that I was a shiftless sort, a purposeless transient, a bum.

"Do you know what the rent is?" she asked.

"Six hundred."

"I ask for two months rent up front," she said.

"Okay."

"Plus one month security deposit."

"Okay."

She smirked.

"What do you do?" she asked.

"What do you mean?"

"What do you do? What kind of work do you do?"

"What do I do for a living?"

"Yes."

"I'm a writer," I said.

"A writer?" The skepticism congealed on her lips like day-old gravy.

"Yeah…I'm a writer…."

"What kind of writer?"

"I'm working on a book right now," I said.

"A book?"

"Yeah."

"What kind of book?"

"A novel."

"Is that how you make your living? By writing novels?" Clearly, she found the notion ludicrous.

"I'm not supporting myself at the moment with my writing...," I said. "But I hope to be able to in the near future...."

"So how do you support yourself?"

"I was in sales, I was a sales rep for a number of years...," I explained. "I was able to save up quite a bit of money...and I took a leave of absence...a sabbatical...so I could write...so I could work on this book I'm writing...."

"What you're telling me," Victoria said, "is that you don't have a job."

"Not in the conventional sense."

"You're unemployed."

"I've got quite alot of money in the bank," I said. "I wouldn't have any problem paying the rent."

"You're unemployed," she said bluntly.

"I would definitely be able to handle the rent," I said.

"I've got to have somebody living here who's got a job," she said. She was annoyed. She was angry. I had wasted her time. I had wasted her valuable time. I had wasted her fucking valuable time. I was an asshole. A bum.

"I could give you a few months rent in advance...," I said.

"It's not going to work," she said.

"I could give you three, four months rent...."

"You've got to have a job," she said.

"I could make whatever arrangement with you that would work for you...," I said.

"If you haven't got a job, I can't have you living here," she said.

We went back up the stairs.

I followed her, directly behind her, my face inches from, nearly touching, the shifting clefts of her formidable ass.

"Is it worth giving you a call in a day or two?" I asked.

"No," she said.

I drove down Victoria's street, past the brickfronted houses, the yellow lawns.

And as I drove through the wan afternoon light I perceived what seemed an indisputable truth:

I wasn't going to be able to find a place to live.

If I continued to look for an apartment, or a room, or whatever, I was only going to have experiences similar to the demoralizing, debilitating experience I'd just had. I was going to face roadblocks, wherever I went. I was going to be rejected, wherever I went.

I drove out of Victoria's neighborhood, onto Sunrise Highway. I drove down Sunrise.

I would abandon my plans to find an apartment, I decided.

I would shuck the whole thing, I decided. The whole scheme I'd concocted just a few days before. The whole ridiculous scheme.

I'd been a fool, I concluded. I'd devised a fool's scheme. Returning to Bayview. Setting up camp in this inglorious suburb. Exploring the landscape, digging in the psychic soil for clues to the meaning of my goddam life, for answers. Seeking out Willy Smithberger. The whole thing was crazy. It was an absurd idea. It was the sort of idea that you might have, that anybody might have, in a weak moment, but it was the sort of idea that should remain just that, an idea, it was the sort of idea that you should never try to follow through on.

I headed down Sunrise, with the endless thread of cars, trucks.

I would leave Bayview, I decided. I would check out of the motel, and leave, within the next twenty-four hours.

I would go.

I squeezed the wheel, pressed my sneaker against the gas pedal. And as I pushed the Toyota forward I had an insight.

I had returned, I had come back to Bayview, I now perceived, because I'd had to find out that I had to leave.

1 0

But I didn't leave. I didn't make any sort of move, in any direction.

I stayed put, like carpeting, nailed to the floor.

After my excursion to Victoria's house, I didn't make any more attempts to find an apartment, to find a more suitable, more affordable place to live. I didn't make any more calls. I didn't check the classified ads. I didn't think about trying to find different lodgings. I gave up completely on the idea. I resigned myself to living at the motel. I surrendered to the fact that I was going to be there for awhile, at least for awhile.

I spent the rest of November doing nothing. I did nothing. I did nothing that amounted to anything. I drove the Toyota up and down the long straight streets, up and down the cluttered thoroughfares. I traversed the same streets, the same highways, again and again. And then again. And again. I habituated the various taverns that dotted the roadsides in Bayview and the neighboring towns, I sat at the various bars, studied the human bodies, listened to the outdated jukebox music, and I drank beer, usually from the bottle, Michelob, Budweiser, and I downed shots, usually only if the bartender was setting them up for free, shots of tequila, sambuca, 151. And of course I spent alot of time, a tremendous amount of time, in my motel room, I lounged on the kingsized bed, and I watched the tube, I spent hours watching the tube, flicking the remote, going through the channels, again and again. And again. And typically when I watched TV I drank, I drank beer, I drank scotch. And I spent a significant portion of the time, the long hours inside the motel room, I spent a big piece of time with my hand wrapped around my cock, jerking off. I jerked off every day, and there were many days when I jerked off two or three or four times. I refrained, for the most part, from calling escort services. I couldn't afford to pay for hookers. I didn't have that kind of money. So instead of placating my lust by having sex with suburban call girls, I satisfied my seemingly everpresent desire, my need for sexual gratification, at least to some extent, by listening to the couples fornicating in the adjoining rooms and whacking off. I whittled away several hours just about every day listening to the men and women with whom I shared the thin plaster walls, listening to their homespun pornographies, absorbing the rhythms of their lurid interactions, my hand steadfastly stroking, up and down, up and down, my fingers grinding my bonehard flesh.

I didn't write. I didn't write at all. I didn't start working on another novel. I didn't make any attempt to get started. No. I didn't fish out any of my chewed-up ballpoint pens from the bowels of my suitcase. I didn't take out a spiral notebook. I didn't remove my typewriter from the trunk of my car. I didn't ponder the course of action I might take in order to procure the other supplies I'd need, legal pads, more spiral notebooks, more pens, typing paper, correct-a-type, white-out. I didn't make any of these necessary preliminary moves. Nor did I think about the novel. I didn't think about it at all. I didn't think about what it might be like, how I might construct it. I didn't think about the story I might want to tell, the plotlines, the characters, the settings, the time frames. I didn't think about any of this. It wasn't that I didn't want to think about it. I wanted to. I knew that I needed to. I just wasn't able to.

The thing of it was, I was stuck. I was stuck like a Ford stuck in deep thick ruts of mud. I couldn't move, I couldn't do much of anything, I couldn't pry myself loose, couldn't pull myself from the muck, the pervasive glop. I was stuck and I couldn't get unstuck.

And as the month wore on, as the days grew shorter and colder, I came to believe that the only way I was going to get unstuck was going to be by calling Willy Smithberger. I came to believe, with everything inside me that enabled me to believe, that the only way I was going to be able to extricate myself from the South Shore Motel, the only way I was going to be able to write, the only way I was going to be able to move forward, to move into something akin to a new life, the only way I was going to be able to do it was going to be by taking the action I had vowed to take on the day I came to Bayview: I had to call Willy Smithberger. If I was going to make any progress, if I was going to get anywhere, I was going to have to call Smithberger and I was going to have to meet with him.

Smithberger was the key. Smithberger was the linchpin.

If I could contact Smithberger, I might have a chance, I might acquire the answers I needed to acquire. I might see something, I might learn something, on a subterranean, cellular level, I might undergo a certain shift, a certain displacement. I might, in sum, gain inspiration. And, fueled by this inspiration, I might be able to yank myself out of the rut I was in, and I might be able to take positive steps forward.

Smithberger was a way-out.

Having read the likes of Sartre and Camus when I was in college, I knew that there came a time in a man's life when he needed a way-out. I was stuck, embedded in something, something that I didn't quite understand, something that was sucking me in, and under, a little further, every day, and I needed a way-out. And, it seemed, Willy Smithberger was my way-out.

He was, it seemed, my only way-out. Or let's put it this way, he was the only way-out that I could discern.

The bottom line was, I had to call him.

I had to call him.

I had to call Willy Smithberger.

It'd dwindled down to this. My days and nights in Bayview, the arc of my life, the currents of my mind, the pings and throbs of my heart, it'd come down to this, everything led to this, pointed clearly to this, to this one thing, this one simple action, this one act: calling Smithberger.

I had to do it. It was the thing I had to do. It was the thing. It was it.

The problem was, I wasn't able to do it. I wasn't able to perform this simple task. Pick up the phone. Punch out the numbers. Speak into the receiver. Say hello.

I wasn't able to do it, and I didn't know when I'd be able to do it, or, for that matter, if I'd be able to do it…I just knew, I knew, that I had to do it….

I spent Thanksgiving by myself. I stopped by the Jerusalem Avenue Deli and picked up a Thanksgiving Dinner package, a complete Thanksgiving meal that cost just $12.99, and included white and dark meat turkey, stuffing, mashed potatoes, yams, string beans, cranberry sauce, and a couple of rolls. I took the meal, which came packed in a white cardboard box, back to my motel room, and I sat on the bed, the styrofoam plates loaded with just-barely-warm partly-quashed food positioned tenuously on the bedspread, and, using the plastic utensils that the deli had provided, I ate, I had my Thanksgiving dinner.

I devoured my holiday repast. I watched the Lions-Chargers game. And I drank a bit of scotch. I actually drank quite a bit of scotch. I drained more than half of a bottle of Johnny Walker Red.

After the sun went down, I thought about calling an escort service. It was a holiday, I reasoned. It was a time to celebrate, to enjoy, to taste not just turkey and cranberry sauce, but life's other pleasures as well. In the end, however, I didn't commission a hooker. I didn't want to spend the money, didn't want to relinquish such a big chunk of my diminishing savings. Instead, I jerked off. I stretched out on the bed, the drapes pulled, the room coated with yellow light, as though smeared with margarine, and I listened to the men and women in the adjacent rooms, and I jerked off. Although it was Thanksgiving, there wasn't any shortage of erotic sounds to listen to; the fact that it was a holiday didn't prevent the South Shore's faithful customers from venturing to the motel and carrying on in their usual fashion, their lustful exclamations penetrated the walls all day and all night long, without cease.

I jerked off for several hours. I paced myself. I stroked my prick, hardened it, stroked aggressively, then relaxed my grip, slowed my tempo, let my prick soften, and then once again brought it to stiffness, and stroked, and stroked, and then I let it go limp. And so on. And so on.

I came twice.

I probably would've come a third, and perhaps a fourth time. But my cock grew sore. After awhile I was barely able to touch it. I held it gingerly, stroked slowly, very, very slowly. And then it began to bleed. And, reluctantly, I stopped.

The way I saw it, I didn't have any choice but to spend Thanksgiving alone.

I normally spent Thanksgiving with my family. I had gone to my brother's house on Long Island on the previous Thanksgiving,

I'd had Thanksgiving dinner with Eddie and his wife, Susan, and their son, Aaron, and my mother, and my sister, Denise, and her boyfriend. But I didn't want to have to do anything like that. The fact was, I found the occasions when I got together with my family members to be highly anxiety-producing. The fact was, I had a difficult relationship with everybody in my family. My relationship with my mother was excruciatingly difficult. My relationship with my brother wasn't much better. And while I got along more compatibly with my sister, I still didn't have a smooth, easy relationship with her.

It was a given that when I got together with my family members that I was going to struggle. And I figured that I'd find being with them on this particular Thanksgiving more of a struggle than usual. I certainly didn't want to have to try to explain my situation to them, my unemployed state, my residence at the South Shore Motel, my desire to write a novel despite the fact that I'd been trying to write one for more than ten years and hadn't made any progress at all. I didn't want to have to explain anything to them, describe any part of my life to them. I didn't want to have to talk to them, to have to try to relate to them in any way. I was sure that being with my mother, brother and sister, or any configuration that included any of them, would be gutwrenchingly, mind-frazzlingly awful, I was quite sure that it'd be painfully difficult.

If I'd had a friend, or a group of friends, that I'd thought I might've wanted to have Thanksgiving dinner with, I might've made some calls, tried to arrange something. But the truth, of course, was that I didn't have any friends. That was the plain unembellished fact of the matter. I had no friends. I had nobody in my life that I could call a friend. I didn't even have any casual friends. I had nobody. *Nobody.*

I had, of course, lost touch with the friends I'd had when I was a kid growing up in Bayview.

And I'd lost touch with the friends, the few friends, I'd had when I was in high school, at Benjamin Cardozo.

I'd had several reasonably close friends when I was in college—Wayne Podkorny, Keith Furtusk, Andy Steinberg—but none of those friendships had lasted. After college they'd withered and died pretty quickly.

And in the years following college I hadn't developed any new friendships. I hadn't tried to make new friends. I simply hadn't tried. I'd lost sight of the importance of friendship, the profound value of friendship. As the years had faded, I'd been like a person with a worsening visual impairment. I'd gradually gone blind. I'd been unable to see any reason why I should have friends, why I should try to cultivate a friendship with anybody. There'd been a few guys who worked for L.G. Buchanan—Bob Rondell, Glen Paxton, Burt Forest—who I'd had a rapport with, who I might've forged a viable relationship, something like a friendship, with. But I had never made the effort. If anything, I'd scoffed at the idea. These guys, I'd told myself, weren't the kinds of individuals that I wanted to associate with beyond the constructs of the work environment. They were salesmen, after all. They were prototypical salesmen, destined to be nothing but salesmen. They were disastrously limited, intellectually, personality wise. They were losers.

And I guess some of the reason why I hadn't put any effort into maintaining and establishing friendships was that I'd assumed during my twenties and thirties that I would derive the benefits of companionship through my interactions with women, in other words the women I had romantic liaisons with, girlfriends, etc. But, of course, things hadn't worked out the way I'd envisioned. During the course of my quote-unquote adult life, I'd shared a close, or moderately close, bond with just a few women. Beth Kroge. Sandy Mizner. And Karen. And the fact, the hard-to-digest fact, was that none of those relationships had endured for very long. My relationship with Karen was the longest I'd had. And it'd lasted just nine months. And, of course, Karen was the last woman I'd had any sort of involvement with. And it'd been three and a half years since we'd split apart, it'd been three and a half years. And since we'd broken up, since she'd left, since she'd walked out of my apartment, smirking and tearstained, I'd had almost no contact with anybody I might've deemed a prospective mate. For the longest time the only substantial interactions I'd had with women had been the interactions, the strictly business collaborations, I'd had with prostitutes.

I called my sister about a week after Thanksgiving.

I called her partly because I wanted to know whether I'd received any important, or semi-important, mail. I had arranged when I'd left Forest Hills to have my mail forwarded to Denise's Brooklyn address, and I wanted to know if she'd received anything for me that I needed to know about, that I needed to do something about.

I was pretty sure that I was in good stead with the institutions to which I had a regular financial responsibility. Since I'd left Queens I'd made sure to continue to pay the bills that I knew I had to pay, namely the bills for my car insurance and health insurance. A couple of days before I had moved out of the shack I had mailed a quarterly payment to the company that provided my car insurance. And I had remitted a payment for my health insurance every month since I'd left Forest Hills, I had inserted a check and a payment coupon in a pre-addressed envelope, and I'd mailed the envelope in a timely fashion to the insurance company. When I had quit my job, I had enrolled in a COBRA plan, in order to be able to continue to receive health benefits, and the insurance company had sent me a booklet filled with coupons, one for each month, that showed how much my premium was and when I had to pay it. As a matter of fact, Denise had received the coupon booklet sometime in August, after I'd moved into the shack, and I had spoken to her on the phone and had asked her to send it to my landlord's house in Liberty since I didn't have a bona fide mailing address. That conversation we'd had toward the tail end of August had, in fact, been the last conversation we'd had, that'd been the last time I'd spoken to her.

I was confident that I was keeping up with the payments for my car insurance and health insurance. I wasn't worried about that. But I was worried that I might not be taking care of some other things that I needed to take care of. I was worried that Denise might've received some other bills, for what I didn't know, that I needed to pay. Or that she might've received other pieces of mail that I needed to respond to.

But the main reason why I called my sister was that I felt like I *should* call her. I felt like it was something I had to do. I felt like it was the right thing to do.

I felt like I should make contact with somebody from my family. I felt like I should try to communicate with somebody, in light of the fact that I hadn't had any communication with anybody, with Denise, or Eddie, or my mother, in an inordinately long time. I hadn't spoken to Denise since August. And I hadn't talked to my mother in about six months. And I hadn't talked to Eddie in almost a year.

I figured I should let my sister know where I was. I figured I should let her know that I was no longer living in Liberty, and that I was currently domiciled on Long Island, in Bayview. I figured that I didn't have to give her too many specifics. I definitely didn't want to have to tell her that I was living at the South Shore Motel. I figured I'd tell her I was staying with a friend. I'd leave it at that. The important thing was that I connect with her, and give her at least a general idea of my whereabouts, let her know that I, indeed, had whereabouts.

I called her on a weekday night during the first week of December.

I put down four or five glasses of scotch before I picked up the phone. I was apprehensive about speaking to her. I was afraid that Denise might be angry with me. I was afraid that she might be upset with me, considering that I hadn't made an effort to get together with her and the rest of my family for Thanksgiving, considering that I'd been out of contact with her and everyone else for such a long time. My recent behavior, I feared, was the sort of behavior that might stir up angry feelings in just about anybody, even somebody like Denise who was typically sweet and compassionate.

Shoving, sort of elbowing my way through my apprehension, I finally dialed her number.

Denise answered.

"Hi Denise," I said.

"Peter?"

"How you doing?"

"I can't believe it's you." She didn't seem angry. But she did seem disconcerted.

"I know it's been awhile...."

"I can't believe you're calling...."

"I'm sorry...," I said. "I know I've been out of touch...."

"We've been trying to find you," she said.

"I'm sorry...," I said. "I've had alot going on...."

"You wouldn't believe what we've been going through, trying to find you...."

"Is something wrong?"

It was obvious there was.

"Mom died," she said.

"You've got to be kidding…."

"We tried to find you…."

"I'm so sorry, Denise…."

"We went upstate, to Liberty…we went to the place where you were living…."

"Yeah, I moved out of there…."

"We didn't know where to find you…," she said. She was crying.

"When did she die?" I asked.

"About a month ago."

"Jesus."

"At the beginning of November…November eighth…."

"What happened?"

"She had an accident…a car accident…."

"Oh Jesus."

"It happened right in front of where she lived…," Denise said.

"Oh god."

"I'm really sorry, Peter…."

She cried, she sobbed, her sobs like something moving over something bumpy, like car tires moving over a bumpy street.

For a few moments I didn't say anything, I listened to my sister cry, then finally I said, "I don't know what to say, Denise…."

11

I waited a couple of days before I called my brother. Then I did what I had to do.

I called him.

I reached Eddie at home, at his house in Suffolk County, and we had a brief conversation at the end of which we agreed that we'd go together, on the ensuing Saturday, to visit my mother's grave.

We met on Saturday afternoon at the Dunkin' Donuts on Sunrise Highway across from the Bayview train station. I was sitting next to the plate glass window, eating a jelly donut, when my brother pulled into the parking lot. He was driving a black BMW. The car gleamed, glistened, glittered, threw diamonds of light, despite the fact that the afternoon had turned grey. And although I wanted to maintain a level of calmness, of forbearance, for this meeting with my brother, I couldn't help but feel revulsed, watching the BMW glide across the craggy pavement. As far as I was concerned, the car was the symbol of everything that was wrong, the desperate urge to achieve the American Dream, the lurching attempt to climb the middleclass ladder, the neverending groping after material success. As far as I was concerned, it was a loathsome object.

Eddie emerged from the BMW, bedecked in a huge burgundy parka. A pair of wire rimmed spectacles bridged his pale white nose. It was the first time I'd seen him wearing glasses.

He looked at the Dunkin' Donuts building. Grimaced.

He came through the glass doors.

He stepped across the tile floor.

I felt a wave of aversion, surging, inside me.

I called to him.

"Eddie!"

He approached.

"How you doing, Pete." He exhibited a grim look, his mouth pinched, as though he was trying to hold a watermelon seed between his lips.

"I'm alright," I said. "How you doing?"

"I'm okay," he said.

"Wanna cup of coffee or something?"

"Nah," he said. "Let's get out of here."

We went out to the parking lot.

"I'll drive if you want," I said.

"Where's your car?" my brother asked.

I pointed to the Toyota.

"I'll drive," he said, disdainfully, probably thinking that the last thing he wanted to do was place his misshapen late thirties ass on the worn vinyl inside my miserable shitbox.

We got into the BMW.

Eddie drove out of the lot. Staring rigidly through the windshield, he headed the BMW down Sunrise.

I studied him. My brother was two years younger than me, but, I thought, he looked older than me. His face was bone pale. His hair, blondish and slicked back, had thinned, and toward the back of his skull there was a goodsized bald patch, an area devoid of hair that resembled a section of forest that'd been destroyed by fire. Beneath his glasses, his eyes bespoke a certain weariness, an irreconcilableness, a surrender. They were the eyes, I thought, of someone who'd sold out, who'd sold his soul.

My brother had achieved a degree of success, according to society's standard measurements. He had a high-paying job as a sales manager for a computer software company. He had a big house in the suburbs. He had a shiny European sedan. He had an attractive wife. He had a kid. He even had a dog, a big blubbering pooch named Viceroy that roamed the spacious backyard of his stately Suffolk County manse. He had the things that you supposedly had to have if you wanted to be happy. But, as far as I could tell, he wasn't happy. It seemed, to me, like he'd drifted a good distance from the possibility of happiness. He'd faded into the joyless ether of suburban life. He'd faded badly.

I felt vindicated, looking at him. I'd taken the better path, I told myself. I'd done the better thing, in quitting my job, in directing my efforts toward having a different kind of life, a life dedicated to the exposition of a deeper truth, to giving birth to some kind of poetry.

I certainly didn't want to live the way he lived, I told myself.

"How's Willy Smithberger doing?" Eddie asked.

"He's good," I said. I had told Eddie when we'd talked on the phone that I was living temporarily in Bayview, and that I was staying at Willy Smithberger's house, in the small apartment that Willy had above his garage.

"I didn't realize you kept in touch with him," Eddie said, in a distant, detached voice.

"Yeah," I said. "We've kept in touch...."

"I didn't realize that...." He forced the BMW down Sunrise. He drove fast, aggressively, he kept a vicious pace.

"I've always felt like I wanted to maintain a connection with someone from Bayview," I explained, "so I've made it a point to keep in touch with him...."

"You in touch with anyone else from Bayview?"

"No, not really...."

"Just Willy."

"Yeah."

"I think I remember him," Eddie said. "He was a skinny kid, wasn't he?"

"Yeah, he was...," I said, and, in an effort to paint a credible picture of a modern-day Willy, I added, "he's not as skinny as he used to be...he's put on a few pounds...."

"I know what that's all about," Eddie said morosely. I couldn't tell how much weight my brother had put on—his oversized parka obscured his contours—but I didn't find it hard to believe that he'd acquired a middleaged paunch, the sort of girth that results from a steady diet of thick meats and dense starches and rich desserts and an array of snacks procured from overstuffed refrigerator and pantry shelves, chocolate chip cookies, cupcakes, pretzels, potato chips, designer ice creams.

"Willy's married?" Eddie asked.

"Yeah," I said.

"He marry someone from Bayview?"

"No...she's not from Bayview...she's from the north shore, I think...."

"Nice chick?"

"Yeah, sure...."

"Goodlooking?"

"Yeah, she's not bad...."

"He's got kids?"

"Yeah."

"How many?"

"Two."

"What's he got?"

"Boy and a girl."

"How old?"

"His son is six…," I said, "and his daughter is three…."

Eddie changed lanes, scorched past a laggard Mazda.

"What does Smithberger do?" he asked. It was clear that he wasn't asking these questions because he was genuinely interested in finding out more about Willy Smithberger, or because he had a compelling desire to converse with me. It was something he figured he was obliged to do.

"He works for some company that makes fax machines, office equipment…," I said. This seemed a likely form of employment for the adult Willy Smithberger.

"What company?"

"I don't know, I'm not sure…," I said.

"A big company?"

"I don't know, I don't remember…," I said. "He told me, but I don't remember…."

"You don't remember?" Eddie was appalled.

"I'm not great at remembering that kind of stuff," I said.

"What does he do there?" he asked.

"To be honest, I'm not sure…."

"Jesus Christ."

"He's got some kind of desk job…."

"Doing what?"

"I don't know…," I said, and, in a decidedly acid tone, I said, "I guess my mind just goes blank when it comes to that sort of thing…."

"He works in the city?"

"Yeah."

"And he's got a house in Bayview?"

"North Bayview."

"Up by the Southern State?"

"Yeah."

Ahead, the traffic light turned yellow, and Eddie, in an attempt to beat the light, drove his foot against the gas pedal.

But the car in front of us slowed. And Eddie had to hit the brake.

The BMW lurched, stopped.

My brother bashed his hand against the steering wheel.

"Cocksucker!" he growled.

We headed down the Southern State Parkway toward the Nassau-Queens border.

Eddie propelled the BMW down the car-infested parkway. He drove 75, 80 mph. He stayed for the most part in the middle lane, but when he came upon a slower vehicle he moved quickly into the left lane and passed the vehicle, hurtling the BMW forward maliciously, with the intent fervor of somebody throwing a punch.

For awhile we didn't say anything.

Eddie stared through the windshield, his jaw locked, his facial muscles clenched.

I leaned against the plush black leather upholstery, looked at the passing roadside, the trees, naked but for a few crinkled brown leaves, and beyond the trees, the dull outlines of boxshaped houses.

There were certainly things that we could have talked about. We were brothers, after all. We had passed a good part of our lives in close proximity. We had, in fact, shared the same bedroom, we had slept just a few feet apart for many years. There had been a time when we'd been tight, there'd been a time when we'd enjoyed a truly harmonious bond, when I had played rather adroitly the part of the older brother and Eddie had played just as adroitly the part of the younger brother. Although our relationship might not have been as picture perfect as those depicted on the TV shows we watched so religiously, it probably wasn't too much of a stretch to say that I had played Wally to Eddie's Beaver in a way not unlike the way that that character had interacted with his little brother in the beloved situation comedy. There had been a time, when we were boys, when I had served as a role model to my brother. I had guided him. I had tutored him. I had shown him how to catch a baseball, how to swing a bat. I had taught him how to ride a two wheeler. I had answered his countless dumbfounded questions. I had supported him during those moments when he had failed, or had thought he'd failed. I had attempted to buoy his young boy's spirit. I had urged him on.

Eddie and I had gone through alot together. We had shared the vicissitudes of life in that house on Jefferson Street, that life lived under the dubious influence of my father and mother. We'd shared the difficulties, the terrible disappointments. We had stuck together. I remembered, for instance, when Eddie's bicycle was stolen during the summer when I was twelve and he was ten. My father refused to buy him a new bike, he said he couldn't afford to. So I rode Eddie around on my bike. I had a Stingray, with V-shaped handlebars, and I pedalled all over Bayview, all summer, with Eddie sitting on the handlebars.

Eventually I tried to get Eddie to participate in a meaningful conversation. I asked him about his son.

"Aaron is how old? Two?"

"Two and a half," Eddie said brusquely.

"How's he doing?"

"Okay."

"It's been awhile since I've seen him," I said.

I hadn't seen my nephew since the previous Christmas. And I'd seen him just twice since he'd been born.

"He must be getting big," I said.

"Uh huh," Eddie said.

"I guess he's walking pretty good by now," I said.

"He's been walking for more than a year," Eddie said, not bothering to hide his irritation.

"He's all over the place, I bet."

"Uh huh."

"Is he going to preschool or anything like that?"

"No," Eddie said. "He's just two."

"I guess he's still a little young."

"Yeah."

"I figured you'd have him enrolled in some college-preparatory preschool program…," I said, trying to inject some humor.

"Right."

"I imagine you've got him reading…," I said. "He's probably already gotten through the abridged children's versions of *Moby Dick* and *The Brothers Karamazov*…."

"Right."

"I wouldn't expect anything less from your progeny, Eddie."

My brother turned his head, displayed a wry smile that degenerated almost instantly into a frown.

"Are there alot of kids in the neighborhood for him to play with?"

"There's a few."

"We always had alot of kids in our neighborhood when we were growing up," I said.

My brother said nothing.

"There was always somebody to play with."

Eddie stared ahead, silent.

"You remember how it was?"

"Uh huh." He swerved the BMW into the left lane, shot past a green Dodge minivan.

"Well," I said. "I hope I get a chance to see Aaron one of these days...."

"Come out to the house," he said, coldly.

"I'd like to," I said. I knew, however, that my brother wasn't going to extend any formal invitation any day soon, he wasn't going to ask me to come to his place for Sunday dinner or anything like that. And, by the same token, I knew that I wasn't going to try to orchestrate any kind of get-together with Eddie and his perky blonde wife and young son, I knew that, although I did want to see my nephew, I wasn't going to take any initiative that might lead to a visit to my brother's tastefully appointed suburban hacienda.

We continued down the Southern State Parkway.

We passed the exits for south shore towns. Freeport. Baldwin. Rockville Centre. Lynbrook.

We said hardly anything.

Then suddenly Eddie lashed out at me.

"I've gotta ask you something," he said. He put his eyes on me. Tiny beads of perspiration dotted his upper lip. I could smell him, his deodorant, his aftershave, the stuff he put in his hair.

"I wanna know something," he said.

"What?"

"Have you been drinking?" The words bursted out like water from a damaged pipe under the kitchen sink.

"What?"

"Have you been drinking?"

"What are you talking about?"

"Are you drunk?"

"Why are you asking me that?" I made it clear that I was offended by his line of questioning.

"I smell alcohol on you," he said.

"You do?"

"Yeah. I do. It's pretty fucking obvious, Pete."

"I don't know what to tell you," I said.

"Just tell me," he said. He stared through the windshield. "Have you been drinking?"

"Hardly."

"Cmon Pete."

"I definitely wouldn't say that I've been drinking."

"Just give me a straight answer," he said. "Are you drunk?"

"No," I said. "I'm not."

"I find that hard to believe," he said.

"I had one drink," I said. "Just before I met you…I had one drink…."

I was lying, of course. I had spent the first part of the afternoon secluded in my motel room, drinking scotch. I had slugged down eight or nine glasses of Johnny Walker Red, glasses filled to the brim with nothing but scotch. And, the truth was, I was quite intoxicated.

"Don't bullshit me," Eddie said.

"I'm not bullshitting you," I said.

"You fucking reek," he said. Approaching a bend in the parkway, he pressed the gas, whipped the BMW through the curve.

"You stink," he said, glancing at me.

"Give me a break, Eddie."

"You're drunk," he said.

"I'm not drunk," I said. I was angry. I was fucking angry. I wanted to grab my brother by his throat and dig my fingers into his pale flesh and strangle him. Fucking strangle him.

"I know when someone's drunk," he said.

"I had one drink," I said. "One goddam drink."

"You're drunk, Pete." He glanced at me. "You're fucked up."

"You're fucking crazy," I said. My words ricochetted off the sleek black seats.

"Don't get pissed," he said.

"I'm not pissed," I said. "You're pissed."

"Maybe I am."

"I don't know what your fucking problem is," I said.

"It just doesn't seem right," he said.

"What doesn't seem right?"

"We're going to Mom's grave...you weren't there when she died...."

"I'm sorry about that...."

"You weren't there for the funeral...."

"There's nothing I can do about that now, Eddie...."

"It just doesn't seem like you should be fucked up."

"I'm *not* fucked up, Eddie."

"You stink," he said. "It smells like you poured a bottle of whiskey over your head."

"I'm not fucked up," I said. "But even if I was, so what? So fucking what? It's none of your business, Eddie. I'm a grown man. I'm thirty-nine fucking years old. I can do whatever I goddam please."

"It would just be nice if you weren't drunk," he said.

"I'm not," I said.

We turned into the cemetery. We drove through an iron gate, down a corridor of tall scruffy hedges.

I could see hundreds of grey headstones.

We went down several thin roads, ribbons of corrugated pavement barely wide enough to allow a single vehicle to pass through.

Eddie pulled the BMW to the side of the road. He parked, two wheels on the road, two wheels on the dirt next to the road. He killed the engine.

"Let's forget about it," he said weakly.

"Okay," I said.

We got out of the car.

We walked through the sea of markers. It was cold. A cold wind cut across the flat grey landscape. The few random trees, grey, crooked, devoid of leaves, swayed, rattled.

I followed my brother, my hands stuffed into the pockets of my leatherjacket.

"How come Mom wasn't buried in the same cemetery that Dad is buried in?" I asked him. It was something I'd been wondering about.

"I don't know," Eddie said, trudging forward, stubbing the hard turf with his undoubtedly state-of-the-art hiking boots.

"You don't know?"

"This is where Aunt Carol wanted her buried."

"Aunt Carol?"

"Yeah."

"It was her decision?"

"She wanted her buried here," Eddie said. "She wanted some things. Denise and I made most of the arrangements. We made most of the decisions. We took care of almost everything. But Aunt Carol wanted some things. I didn't see any reason to argue with her."

"It just seems strange," I said.

"It was okay with me," Eddie said.

"I always thought it was customary for a person to be buried in the same place as the person they were married to."

"Maybe it is," he snapped.

"It just seems like it would be the appropriate thing to do."

"Maybe it is."

We walked through the stones. Eddie squinted behind his glasses, the wind slapping his forehead and lenses, pushing strands of hair across his pasty scalp.

"I guess part of the reason why it was decided to bury her here," he said, "was because the place where Dad is buried isn't that great."

"What do you mean?"

"The way I understand it, the way I heard it, is that Mom didn't have a hell of alot of money to pay for Dad's funeral, so she had to have him buried in what I'd guess you'd call a pauper's grave."

"What are you talking about?" I said. I made sure to exhibit a good measure of outrage.

"That's the way I understand it," Eddie said.

"That's bullshit, Eddie."

"All I know is what I got from what I heard…."

"Dad isn't buried in a pauper's grave," I said. "That's fucking nonsense."

"What I was told was that it's a pauper's grave," Eddie said. "Or at least the equivalent of a pauper's grave."

"That's crazy."

"That's the story I got."

"When was the last time you were there?" I asked, acrimoniously.

"I couldn't tell you."

"Maybe you should go sometime," I said. "Check it out."

"Maybe I should."

We walked about ten yards in silence.

I knew that I should drop the subject. But I couldn't.

"It's not a pauper's grave," I said.

"Maybe it isn't," Eddie said. He spit out the words, as though they were pieces of mangled rotten-tasting food. "Maybe it fucking isn't."

We walked a little further.

Then Eddie stopped.

"This is it," he muttered.

We stood in front of a rectangular patch of light brown dirt. A small wooden stake was stuck in the ground at the top of the plot. A strip of yellow tape, fluttering in the wind, was attached to the stake, and my mother's name was written on it in black magic marker.

Eddie jammed his gloved hands into his parka, looked toward the grave.

I bent my head, scrutinized the ground, the brown rectangle. The dirt, recently turned over, would, of course, remain like this, grass-less, until the spring. I stared at the dirt. I tried to concentrate. The wind blew my hair, filtered past my collar, into my shirt. Above my head, a jet rumbled through the grey air, descending, bound for Kennedy.

I stared at the dirt. I tried to feel something.

"I'm going back to the car," Eddie said, after we'd been standing there for a minute or two.

"I'm gonna stay a little longer," I said.

"Take your time," he said tersely.

He turned.

He walked from the grave.

For a moment I watched him. The colorless head. The glasses. The massive parka. Plodding through the scape of graves.

Then I returned my attention to my mother's plot.

I was hoping I'd be able to focus more effectively, concentrate more intensely, now that Eddie had departed.

I stared.

I stared at the dirt.

I stared at the grey background, the vista of markers, the choked sky, the dissolving afternoon.

I was hoping I might feel something. I was hoping I might experience some sort of release. I was hoping I might cry.

I stared at the grave for five, ten minutes.

But I felt nothing.

And finally I turned from the brown rectangle, and I walked back, slowly, through the cemetery, to my brother's car.

I roll over on the bed, scraping my white skin against the coarse motelroom sheets.

These sheets aren't meant for sleeping.

In fact, it'd be my guess that most of the men and women who come to the South Shore Motel, like the couple presently fornicating, boisterously, in the room past my left shoulder, never make contact with the sheets. They probably never bother to turn down the bedspread and blanket, they probably get right to business, they probably strip quickly and dive on top of the un-turned-down bed.

My fate, however, rests with these sheets, these rough white sheets, these abrasive sheets, these sandpaper sheets.

I press my face against the pillow, try to avert the morning sunlight, creeping, weak, grey, through the breaks in the drapes. I try to block out the couple in the next room, they're yelping, like participants in a crude tribal ritual, the sort of thing you might see on a *National Geographic* special.

I try to sleep.

I try to sleep, in hopes that sleep might heal my scourged body. If I had any scotch, a cupful, a thimbleful, I'd sock it down. I wouldn't think twice about it. But I've got nothing left. The bottle standing on the bedside table is empty, bone dry. And so, for now, I don't know what else I can do except to try to sleep, to sleep, perchance to sleep.

I didn't sleep much, hardly at all, during the night. I lay on the bed, between the grating sheets, sharply awake, forced to listen to the sounds coming through the paperthin walls, the barbaric exclamations, the lusty grunts, the sounds of couples perpetrating an assortment of sexual maneuvers. These sounds never let up, never softened. They haven't abated, not for a minute, not slightly, since I checked into the motel.

And I should make this clear: I no longer find these sounds arousing. I no longer find them even mildly amusing.

I don't want to hear this stuff. But I can't escape it.

This, apparently, is my sentence. Or at least part of it. To have to listen, through the night, and through the day, to the sounds of men and women copulating.

It's a painful, wicked sentence.

During the night just passed, I was subjected to a series of highly unsettling lewd declarations.

At one point I hear a woman screaming like the female lead in a badly-made horror flick.

And shortly after that I hear a couple articulating their every move, in a rather precise, specific manner, like they're chefs on a television cooking program.

And then a couple roaring and snorting like a pair of wildebeests.

And then, at about 5am, a couple that prefers the kinky forms. I hear the female barking commands, I hear her ordering her male counterpart to get on his hands and knees, and then I hear her spanking him, presumably on his bare ass, again and again, and after each resounding smack I hear the male swooning, "Thank you...thank you...."

Then I hear her telling him to give her oral sex, I hear her telling him to lick her "delicious pussy," and I'm pretty sure I hear the male executing the said task, I'm pretty sure I hear him slobbering, sloshing his tongue up and down, back and forth, against her snatch.

And as I listen to this couple I'm reminded of a liaison I had with a woman named Audrey, a woman who weighed more than two hundred pounds, who liked to wear skimpy brassieres, crotchless black leather panties, garters, and spiked heels, who liked to tie me up with clothesline twine and spank me for long stretches with a large steel spoon, the sort of utensil you might use to serve a casserole.

And then I remember getting spanked in a different context, not by a woman, but by my father, my goddam old man...I remember lying across his knees, my pants pulled down to my ankles, and I remember him telling me that I was a "goddam cocksucker," and I remember him slamming his hand against my small naked bottom, again and again....

And then I remember being very young, a baby...I'm somehow granted access to a deep part of my subconscious, and I remember lying in a crib, crying...and I have this sense that what I'm remembering is the day I was born, the very godforsaken day....

I must have cried profusely that day, I must've wailed....

It was a sorry day, I know that....

The truth.

The truth is that I am a miserable human being.

The truth is that I am a deplorable example of the human form.

I've been living at the South Shore Motel since the beginning of November, and now it's January, it's late January, it's almost February. I've been living in this dump, in this forlorn room situated at the end of mankind's last deadend street, I've been here three months, three months, three goddam months. And in three months I haven't done anything, I haven't done a damn thing, except drive up and down the mundane suburban streets, except loaf in my motel room, on the motelroom bed, and watch TV, and jerk off, and drink. And I can't stop drinking. For weeks I've been drinking every day, throughout the day. And I can't stop.

I had come to Bayview with such vaunted expectations. I was going to make a heroic return to the site of my childhood. I was going to dig up answers. I was going to find a long discarded sense of joy. But the truth, the truth is, I haven't done anything, I haven't found anything. The truth is, I haven't taken any of the actions that I had said I'd take when I arrived in Bayview. Most critically, I still haven't called Willy Smithberger. I still believe that if I call Smithberger and then meet with him that I might acquire some sort of life-altering insight. I might get answers.

I still consider Smithberger a way-out. My only way-out.

But I'm not able to call him. I'm not able to perform this highly uncomplicated task. I think about it alot. I think about it every day. I think about it throughout the day. I think about it wherever I am, whatever I'm doing. It's the thing I think about more than anything else.

It's the thing, the one thing, that I know I have to do.

I have to call Willy Smithberger.

But I'm not able to do it.

The truth is, I'm pathetically inept.

I'm a loser.

My autobiography should be called *The Autobiography of a Loser*.

I've deluded myself, I've deluded myself into thinking that I'm headed toward some extraordinary destination, some sort of joyful life, but the truth is I'm headed toward nothing, I'm headed toward utter desolation, I'm headed down, like a plane that's lost its engines, nosediving into a black valley.

The truth is, I've become exactly what I've always been afraid I'd become. A bum. An insubstantial piece of meat.

I roll side to side, the sheets rubbing my hypersensitive flesh. What I am, the truth, screams in my mind, like a chorus of ambulance and policecar sirens demolishing the morning air:

Bum.
Loser.
Failure.
Rotten.
No good.
Pathetic.
Reprehensible.
Repulsive.
Deviant.
Degenerate.
Dog.
Worthless mutt.
Cur.
Lowlife.
Scumbag.
Stupid fuck.
Stupid asshole.
Shithead.
Bastard.
Cocksucker.
Stupid cocksucker.
Motherfucker.
Motherfucking asshole.
Stupid motherfucking asshole.
Sonofabitch.
Prick.
Prick bastard.
Piece of shit.

Goddam piece of shit.
Goddam repugnant piece of shit.

I leave the motel room, as quietly, as inconspicuously, as a veteran cat burglar. I slide, I slither, through the door. I go down the wooden stairs, shuffle across the parking lot.

I get in the Toyota, position my ass on the bitterly cold vinyl.

I fit the key, turn it.

The engine coughs.

Won't start.

I wait. Turn the key again.

But the engine just coughs.

I walk across the lot. I don't have any choice, I'm going to have to go into the registration office, I'm going to have to ask Howard, the obnoxious desk clerk, to give me a jump.

I don't want to have to go into the office. I try to go in there as infrequently as possible. I try, as a rule, to avoid the people who work at the motel. I find the interactions I have with them, even the most inconsequential interactions, to be terrifically humiliating. After all, as far as I'm concerned, I'm in a rather humiliating spot, having been living in this scurrilous sex ranch for such a long time. I can't help but think that the men and women employed by the South Shore, the desk clerks, the maids, the porters, must view me with a negative eye. I can't help but think that they must think I'm a derelict, a sleazy desperado, a bum.

I can't help but think, for instance, that Gladys, the maid who most frequently cleans my room, must think that I'm a despicable character.

Gladys is a diminutive black woman, perhaps in her forties, or fifties. I can't provide a detailed description of her because when-

143

ever I encounter her I try to cut short the encounter, and I always bow my head, I never look directly at her. It's my guess, however, that my existence rankles her. It's my guess that when she has to confront the fact that she has to clean my room, that she has to, in effect, serve me, that she fills with anger, centuries-old anger. She probably abhors me. She probably considers me her oppressor.

I try not to upset her. I try to keep my room clean. I try to maintain a certain orderliness. If I create any sort of mess I make sure to tidy things up. If I drop crumbs on the carpeting I pick them up carefully with my fingers. If I've left the newspaper on the bathroom floor I place it neatly on the dresser. If I take a crap and leave a brown smudge inside the bowl I grab a wad of toilet paper, stick my hand in the bowl, underwater if necessary, wipe it off.

And, of course, I make sure to remove the most incriminating evidences of my plight. I scrub clean the sheets if I squirt jism on them when I'm masturbating. I stash my porno magazines in the dresser, under my sweaters. And, of course, I dispose of all my empty scotch bottles and beer cans. In fact, I don't even put the bottles and cans in the wastebasket; I stuff them in a plastic bag, carry them outside, toss them in the big dumpster on the side of the building.

Of course I don't always succeed in making an impeccable presentation.

I recently had a rather unfortunate experience that involved Gladys. It was a weekday afternoon. I was lying in bed, jerking off. In one of the adjacent rooms, the inhabitants were yelling ferociously, both the man and the woman, it was as if they were dueling, trying to see who could yell the loudest. The couple in the other adjacent room was also making a considerable racket, the woman was howling like a backyard dog, and the man was producing an awful guttural vibration, it sounded as if he had a ball of tinfoil caught in his throat. Compounding this cacophony, there was a garbage truck in the parking lot, grinding clamorously. And because of all this noise, I didn't hear Gladys knocking on the door.

And when I didn't respond to her knocks, she opened the door. Sometimes I latched the door with the metal chain, but I'd neglected to before I'd gone to sleep the night before, and, as a result, Gladys was able to step unimpeded into the room.

As she entered, I was jerking off rather furiously. I was lying beneath the sheets and blankets. My legs were propped. My left middle finger was inserted in my ass. And I was stroking, stroking rapidly, moving my hand up and down my hardened shaft.

The door swung open. A plane of greyish light fell across the room, across the bed. And Gladys's bony figure materialized in the door frame.

I saw the door move, and I saw her, and I quickly removed my finger from my ass and my hand from my cock, and turned onto my side, away from her. "Please come back later...," I said, as nicely as I could. "I'm sleeping...."

"Oh, sorry...," she grumbled, pulling the door shut.

I go into the registration office.

I find Howard sitting behind the counter, watching TV. He's watching a soap opera.

He's a short, painfully scrawny guy. About forty. He's bald, his eggshaped pate is bare, but for a few crinkled hairs. His face is pitted. It's an insect's face. His eyes bulge behind thick blackframed glasses. His mouth is a wound, festering, pus-filled.

He's a decidedly unpleasant sort. In all the times I've gone into the office, to pay for my accommodations, or to do whatever else, he's never attempted to speak to me in a friendly, or even vaguely friendly manner. He typically says very little to me. Typically, he just sneers.

I certainly don't want to have to ask him to help me get my car started. Particularly since this isn't the first time I've had to ask him for this kind of assistance. During the past few weeks I've had to ask him for a jump on two other occasions.

I step to the counter. Trying to effect a cheerful tone, I say, "How you doing, Howard?"

He glances at me. Then returns his gaze to the pintsized TV.

"Cold out there, huh? Must be about twenty degrees. Maybe colder."

He stares at the set.

"I'm sorry to bother you," I say, "but I wanted to ask you if you could give me a hand...."

He keeps his vision on the soap opera.

"I'm having a hard time getting my car started...I guess it must be the cold...if you could give me a jump I'd really appreciate it...."

He stays glued to the vapid drama, the inane interplay, an exceedingly goodlooking man talking to a knockout prefabricated blonde.

"You'd be doing me a big favor...."

He remains focussed on the screen.

"I hate to disturb you...," I say, "but I could really use a jump...."

He finally speaks. He doesn't look at me, doesn't turn his head at all, not a fraction. Riveted to the TV, he moves his mouth just slightly, he just barely wriggles his thin infected lips.

"You're gonna have to give me a few minutes," he says.

Howard parks his battered Ford Escort next to the Toyota. Working quickly in the cold, we connect the jumper cables.

I get in the Toyota. Turn the key. The engine starts, no problem.

Howard unclamps the cables, grabbing the plastic-coated handles with his scabby red hands. He frowns. The whole thing has taken maybe five minutes, maybe less, but from his look, his supremely irritated look, you'd think I'd asked him to overhaul the goddam carburetor.

He put the cables in his trunk.

I get out of the Toyota. Close the hood.

I nod towards Howard.

"Thanks alot, man," I say.

He steps to the car door, gagging on the cold January air. The wind lifts the few kinked hairs off his scalp, they're like pubic hairs, dancing on his grey dome. He looks toward me, but not quite right at me. He scowls. His mouth twists grotesquely.

"You need a new battery," he says, the syllables oozing from his lips like hazardous waste.

He gets in the Escort.

I drive down Route 140, steer the Toyota into the parking lot in front of a strip mall, a collection of unremarkable businesses, a bakery, a beauty parlor, a video store, a Carvel, a liquor store. The liquor store, Bertram's Wines and Liquors, is an establishment I've patronized before, numerous times, during the past months.

I get out of the car—I leave the engine running, I want to let the battery recharge—and I go into the liquor store and buy a quart of Johnny Walker Red.

I sit in the car in the lot, the cars and trucks clambering down 140, I open the bottle, hold the spout to my mouth, glug the scotch.

I take in a measured amount of scotch. Just enough. Just enough to quell the worst ache. Just enough to erode the sharpest edges of pain. I'm careful not to pour too much down my throat.

I put the bottle under the seat. I figure I'll wait another half hour or so before I take another hit.

During the past weeks I've developed a system, a strategy for imbibing, that I call my Spaced Maintenance program. It's a simple program. I buy one quart bottle of Johnny Walker every day, and I drink from this bottle throughout the day. I make the bottle last the whole day. Each time I open the bottle I swallow a moderate amount of scotch. And I space out these dosages, I take a slug every thirty or forty minutes. I don't worry about trying to adhere to a strict, synchronized schedule, I just try to space my drinks far enough apart so that the bottle will last, so that, ideally, I'll gulp down the last half inch or so of scotch just before I go to sleep, just before I shut my eyes.

The key to the program is that I drink one bottle, *just one bottle*, during a twenty-four hour period. That's what I'm aiming for.

The way I look at it, if I can regulate my consumption, if I can limit my daily intake to just one quart of scotch, then I'm not doing so badly, I'm not doing as badly as I could be doing.

Of course, I know the truth. I know that drinking a quart of scotch a day is not a recommended habit, not a healthy practice. But to my way of thinking, at least I'm staying somewhat in control of things, I'm not letting things get too far away from me.

I'm holding on, I'm hanging in, to some extent.

I drive to Phil's Pizza.

I park in front, I leave the engine running, and I go in and I get a slice.

I drive to Furley School.

I pull to the curb. I figure I'll remain here, parked in front of the school, for awhile, and let the motor run. I figure I should probably give the battery more time to recharge.

I light a cigarette.

I study the school.

The Bayview School District had built a number of schools, including Furley, during the 1950s and early 1960s, in order to accommodate the burgeoning school-age population, the so-called Baby Boom generation, but as the members of this generation, my generation, had grown up and graduated from these schools the amount of kids in the school system had decreased precipitously. During the 80s there hadn't been nearly enough students to fill the buildings. And because of this dearth of young suburban boys and girls, the school district had decided to close down some schools, including Furley.

During the days when I had inhabited its classrooms, when I had sat at its wooden desks and stared at its chalkboards, Furley School had been a radiant place, an emblem of possibility. But now, after having been shut down for a length of time, it's in dismal condition. The school building has been battered, beaten down by the long groaning years and blatant neglect. The brick exterior, once a resilient red hue, is now a dingy brown. Many of the windows are boarded up, covered with sheets of warped grey plywood. The trim between the roof and the brick is peeling. Small trees grow in the raingutters. The schoolyard, the vast playground where my friends and I once romped and laughed and dreamed, is enclosed by a tall chainlink fence. The yard is now little more than a field of scraggly half-alive weeds. It's plagued with litter, all kinds, pieces of newspaper, fastfood wrappers, plastic soda bottles, squashed cigarette packs.

From my vantage point I can see the windows of the room that I was situated in when I was in third grade, in Miss Thompson's class. A couple of big pieces of plywood have been nailed over the windows, and somebody, in a burst of creativity, has spraypainted on the corroded wood, in fuzzy orange letters, the trenchant slogan, "FUCK YOU."

I drag on my cigarette.

I pull out the bottle of scotch. Take a slug. A measured slug.

The engine grunts. A weak stream of warm air wafts from the ducts near my feet.

I think about Willy Smithberger.

I still believe that if I contact Smithberger I might get the answers I'm looking for.

But I also realize that I might not.

I've got good reason, I figure, to think that when, or if, I get together with Smithberger that I won't be able to get through to him, or to the sense of things I'm hoping to get through to.

The fact is, at the time I left Bayview, at fourteen, I no longer had a strong connection with Willy Smithberger.

Willy and I had been good friends. We'd had a close friendship. We'd had a joyful friendship. But the friendship that Willy and I had known had flourished when we were young boys. It had been a friendship created by the facts of our boyhood, and when our boyhood dissolved, when we no longer played on the streets, when we no longer participated in those seminal boyhood activities, riding bikes, playing baseball, at that point the bond between Willy and me had begun to fade.

As we'd entered adolescence, Willy Smithberger and I had drifted apart, we had scattered in the hazy near-void of our early teenaged years, like sheets of looseleaf paper blowing in different directions, pushed by the sharp irregular breezes cutting across the walkways outside Bayview Junior High School. After we started junior high, we didn't spend alot of time together. We walked to school almost every morning, usually with Chris Adelkravitich and Kevin Anderson and Louie Plunkett, but this excursion along the neighborhood sidewalks was for the most part the only endeavor that we shared. After school, Willy and I went our separate ways.

There was nothing unusual about our splitting apart. There wasn't any difficulty between us, any disagreement. The rift wasn't caused by resentment or even misunderstanding. We had simply evolved into different individuals.

Willy and I discovered our differences rather quickly as we moved into adolescence.

The discrepancy between us was perhaps most evident in the way in which we performed academically. I was an excellent student. I received mostly As, a few B plusses. Willy, on the other hand, was a mediocre pupil. A C student at the very best. Not particularly bright, if not stupid, he demonstrated little interest in school. Whereas I was dead serious, driven by a clear sense of the importance, the crucialness, of classroom success, Willy possessed a lackadaisical attitude.

Beyond the hallways of Bayview Junior High School, our inclinations were also quite divergent. I was intrigued by the critical newsworthy matters of the time. I was interested in developing an awareness and a viewpoint concerning the manic shifts and changes that were shaking America. This, of course, was the 60s. There was alot going on. Viet Nam. Columbia. Nixon. I was mesmerized by these monumental current events, this wash of history pouring out each day. Willy, conversely, didn't have much interest in this stuff. He probably couldn't have told you what SDS stood for, or who Eugene McCarthy was. He probably still couldn't.

We were aligned differently. Even as a kid I was prone to examine the existential questions. I was moved by the poetry in things. I longed to hear the music embedded in life. Willy, however, wasn't one to delve. He was interested, almost exclusively, with what happened inside the constricted circle of adolescent social life. He was interested in girls. He was interested in clothes, he called them "threads." More than anything else, he was enthusiastic about "hanging out." He put his most diligent efforts into hanging out. Hanging out on strategic streetcorners. Hanging out at the Ripley Park handball courts. Hanging out at the junior high dances and the Battle of the Bands. Hanging out at the McDonald's on Jerusalem Avenue.

In junior high Willy and I gravitated to different sets of friends. I maintained my friendships with Chris Adelkravitich and Kevin Anderson and, to some extent, Louie Plunkett, and I developed new friendships with some other kids, Bob Filch, Steve Longeran, Rich Zoolman. And Willy forged bonds with an altogether different lot of kids. In the eighth grade he became involved with a group of other eighth-grade boys and girls, a clique comprised of similarly disposed kids. The members of this clique fit a rather definitive profile, they were poor students, they shirked the traditional aspects of junior high life, athletics, clubs, etc. They were, essentially, unimpressive, minor characters, but they had a flair for late-60s style, and they had a decided social facility that most noticeably manifested in boyfriend-girlfriend linkages and forays into the uncharted territories of their sexuality.

I couldn't relate at all to Willy's new gaggle of friends. From my perspective, they were alien creatures. They might as well have been wearing horns and covered with fur.

I suppose that part of the reason why I felt such a lack of affinity for this unspectacular collection of eighth graders had to do with the fact that the clique included girls. I was, of course, afraid of girls. I was incapable of intermingling with girls, the way that other boys my age were beginning to intermingle with them. I wasn't able to talk to girls, I wasn't able to engage a girl, any girl, in any sort of conversation, except perhaps the most innocuous conversation, about a math assignment or something. The sort of boy-girl pairing up prevalent in Willy's clique was something that I yearned for but was thousands of miles from being able to achieve. It was way beyond my range, it was inconceivably far-off, like some distant land, Antarctica, or something.

Willy's enmeshment in this clique represented a major point of departure. It signified, to me, that our friendship had suffered an irremediable break.

After Willy became a full-fledged member of this clique, he spent the bulk of his time hanging out with his newfound cohorts. I hardly ever saw him. When I did interact with him, usually during the times when we trekked the long neighborhood streets on the way to school, I felt like I could no longer communicate with him. I felt like I couldn't identify with him. He'd metamorphosized into an odd, unknowable sort. He didn't look the same. His hair flared down his neck. He wore strange clothes, turtlenecks, bellbottom pants, boots with enormous plastic heels. He spoke with a queer accent. He had a new vocabulary, everything suddenly was "boss" and "far out" and "uptight" and "cool."

Then he garnered a girlfriend. And that, to my way of seeing it, was the ultimate breaking off point. The point of no return. The end.

I knew in my young fourteen year old heart that my friendship with Willy Smithberger would never be the same.

Her name was Doreen Higeboth. Like most of the girls in Willy's social circle, she was disturbingly attractive. Like the others, she was crashlanding in the middle of puberty, trying hard to articulate her femaleness, her substantial power. She was learning to provoke. And learning well. She fixed her hair in offbeat, sometimes daring styles, daubed her face with pastel makeup, wore revealing tops in an effort to announce her emerging bosom. To me, she was terrifyingly appealing. And she was, simply, terrifying. I couldn't get anywhere near her without being thrown back conclusively by her female energy, her innate sexual electricity.

Willy's romance with Doreen Higeboth commenced in March, and from then on I had very little contact with him. He spent his time, all of his time, it seemed, with Doreen. Most mornings he didn't walk to school with Chris, Kevin, Louie and me. Instead he journeyed to Doreen's house—she lived a good mile away, on the other side of Sunrise Highway—and he walked to school with her. Sometimes my friends and I would see the two of them, scuffing down the sidewalk, past the dewcovered lawns, the fuzzy houses. And Willy'd be holding Doreen's books and clutching her hand, and he'd be wearing a dazed look, as though he had the flu or something. I know that I must have seen them when they weren't with each other, but it seemed like I never did, it seemed like they were always together, it seemed, to me, to my cynical way of seeing it, as though they'd become utterly dependent on each other, it seemed as if their bloodstreams had been attached with a plastic tube, it seemed like it would be impossible to pull them apart without annihilating both of them.

Of course, I didn't try to pull them apart. I didn't try to connect with Willy. I made no attempt during that spring and the ensuing summer to resuscitate my friendship with him. To the contrary, I avoided him.

In the weeks before I left Bayview, the first weeks of my freshman year at Bayview High School, I didn't exchange more than a handful of sentences with Willy Smithberger. But I realized, during the last days that I lived on Jefferson Street, that I wanted to talk to Willy before I left. I wanted to say goodbye to him. I wanted to effect an appropriate parting. I wanted to let Willy know that I was cognizant of the important role that he had played in my life. I wanted to let him know that I regarded him with affection.

The day before we moved, I went to Willy's house.

It was a grey October day.

I went to Willy's front door. Rang the bell.

Nobody came to the door.

I opened the screen door, pushed open the wooden door, stuck my head inside the house, and called, "Willy!" It was something I had been doing since I was four years old.

"Willy!" I tried again when there was no response.

There was still no answer.

I stepped into the house. Peered into the Smithberger's living room.

And I saw: Willy and Doreen Higeboth. They were sprawled on the couch. Willy was lying across Doreen's legs. His hair was hanging in his eyes. He was looking toward me, confusedly. Doreen was stretched out on her back. She was barechested. Flustered, she was trying to hold something, a shirt or something, in front of her. But she wasn't covering herself very effectively. And I could see one of her breasts. It stood out, determinedly, burnished, like an apple. Her bra lay crumpled on the coffee table, beside an assortment of magazines. *Time. Newsweek. Ladies' Home Journal.*

"Sorry…," I breathed. I backtracked quickly. I went back through the door. Leaped down the cement stoop. Ran across the Smithberger's lawn.

Willy, to his credit, came to my house the next afternoon.

We stood on the bare wood floor in my bedroom. The room was suddenly barren, everything had been removed, my Knicks and Yankees posters, the beds, the dresser. Willy and I said good bye. We didn't say anything about what'd happened the day before.

We stood facing each other, amid shanks of dust, between the blank walls. My transistor radio, sitting on the windowsill, played popular AM tunes. 77 WABC. Outside the window, the movers were hauling the last few pieces of bedraggled furniture across the lawn.

Willy and I shook hands.

We said we'd stay in touch.

But, of course, we didn't.

That was the last time I saw him, or spoke with him, or had any contact with him.

I sit in the car in front of Furley School.

I turn off the engine.

I take another glug of scotch.

I light another cigarette.

I've been smoking for about three weeks. I had never smoked before this. And I'd always thought I never would. I'd always loathed smoking, partly because my father had been such a prolific smoker. I had always thought, watching my father, who was never without a cigarette sutured to his mouth, that smoking was reprehensible habit. I had always despised the act, every facet, the ceaseless puffing, the smoke, the reek, the smushed butts, the overflowing ashtrays. And, of course, I'd been appalled by the smoker's willingness to risk his health, his life.

I had been at first shocked and then horrified when I discovered, when I was in junior high, that some of my friends had decided to experiment with the filthy habit.

Louie Plunkett was the first of my friends to try smoking. I remember when I found him out. I was riding my bike along Main Street when I espied Louie and Jack Mockley standing in the alley between Brunnerkamp's Meats and Martin's Hardware Store. Louie was leaning against the hardware store's concrete wall, holding a cigarette to his mouth. He was striking, or trying to strike, a blasé pose. He was trying to exhibit a certain cool. Caressing the cigarette with his thin lips, he took a long, long drag, his head cocked, his chest expanded, and then he exhaled, slowly, blowing a long meandering trail of smoke into the grey suburban air. Jack Mockley, a kid who lived on Adams Street who

157

had a huge penchant for getting into trouble, was shuffling, kicking the pavement, lecturing Louie, waving his cigarette, like an orchestra conductor waving his baton.

I bicycled quickly past.

A few days later I was biking down Jefferson Street when I caught sight of Louie standing on the corner of Delaware Avenue. Again, he was smoking.

I stopped my bike against the curb.

Louie nodded, grumbled, "Pete."

"Smoking?" I said, with what I deemed the proper degree of incredulity.

"Sure," he slurred.

"Since when?"

"I've been known to take a drag every once in awhile," he said.

"Who're you kidding?"

"I ain't kiddin nobody," he said.

"Cmon Louie." I made clear my outrage.

"I enjoy a Marlboro as much as the next man," he said.

"Give me a break," I said.

He sucked on his cigarette, pinching the butt with his dirty pink fingers.

"What's your problem?" I said.

"I ain't got no problem," he said, bands of smoke floating past his mouth.

I shook my head disparagingly. And pedalled away.

I had always condemned kids like Louie Plunkett when I'd found out that they'd taken up smoking. Certainly I had condemned them in my mind, if not directly.

When it came to smoking, I had always assumed a righteous stance. I'd been staunchly opposed to the unseemly behavior.

And I'd vowed that I would never smoke.

But for the last several weeks, I've smoked at least a pack of Marlboros every day.

I drive down Sunrise, eastward, into Suffolk County.

I keep driving eastward.

I drive past a sign indicating that I've entered West Breakwater, the town where my mother had lived, and died.

I think about visiting the scene of her demise.

I've been thinking about doing this for some time, ever since my sister told me that my mother had died, and how, and where, she'd died.

According to Denise, my mother was driving home, in her ten year old Chevy Nova.

She was driving down Bridley Avenue. She lived in a small one-bedroom apartment in a garden apartment complex on the corner of Bridley and Route 116. She was driving down Bridley, she was approaching Route 116. She had to cross 116, then turn right into the lot where she parked her car.

It was a cold November night. It'd been raining, but the temperature had dropped, and for a half hour or so the precipitation had consisted of a slanting freezing rain.

The road was covered with a thin glaze of ice.

As she approached 116 my mother lost control of the Nova. The car skidded. It skidded through the intersection. And crashed head-on into a telephone pole.

My mother, who wasn't wearing her seatbelt, flew through the windshield and landed on the hood of the car.

Although Denise hadn't wanted to describe the final result in the most explicit detail, from what I gathered my mother had been decapitated, or at least partially decapitated.

I continue driving, eastward, down Sunrise.

I could try to find a florist shop, I think. I could pick up a bouquet of flowers, nothing too fancy, but something nice, carnations, some roses, and I could drive to the spot where she met her end, the corner of Bridley and Route 116, and I could place the bouquet at the base of the telephone pole...I could do something like that...and maybe I could offer some kind of prayer...I could implore God, if in fact there is such a thing as God, I could ask God to facilitate my mother's transition into wherever it is she's going...and maybe I could try to connect, somehow, in some way, with my mother's disembodied spirit, and maybe I could let her know that I hoped she was okay, that I hoped she'd found some sort of peace...and maybe I could tell her I was sorry, that I was sorry about the less-than-warmhearted way I'd oftentimes behaved, the unpleasantness I'd often exhibited, the anger I'd frequently displayed...maybe I could tell her I was sorry that we hadn't gotten along better....

I pass a sign for Route 116.

If I turn right onto 116, and drive about a half mile, I'll come to Bridley Avenue, to the intersection where she bought it.

But I don't make the required adjustments.

No.

I don't turn right.

No.

Instead, I slide into the lefthand lane.

And I make a U-turn.

And I head back down Sunrise, back toward Bayview.

I called my sister a couple of weeks after that December night when she told me that my mother had died. I called her primarily because I wanted to tell her that I was no longer staying with Willy Smithberger. I had told Denise that I was staying at Smithberger's house, and I was afraid that she might try to reach me there, perhaps in an attempt to organize some kind of Christmas Day get-together. I hadn't, needless to say, given her Smithberger's phone number, but I was afraid she might look it up and that she might try to contact me at Smithberger's North Bayview domicile.

"I'm not staying at Willy Smithberger's anymore," I told her almost as soon as I got on the phone with her.

"Where are you staying?"

"I've got my own place."

"Where?"

"In Bayview." I didn't have any choice, I didn't think, except to present her with an outright fabrication. "There're these condominiums on Route 140." There are, in fact. "I'm subletting an apartment there…."

"How long are you going to be there?"

"I'm not sure."

"Can I get your phone number?" Denise asked.

"Actually, at the moment I don't have a phone number…," I said. "The guy I'm subletting from had his phone turned off…and I've been trying to get it turned back on, but I've been having trouble getting it straightened out with the phone company…."

"So there's no way I can get in touch with you?" She was disappointed, distressed. "There's no way I can call you?"

"Not at the moment."

"Well...," she said, "please let me know when you get a number...."

"I will," I said. "As soon as I get it worked out, I'll let you know...."

"Please...," she said.

"I will...," I said.

I didn't want to have to say too much, I didn't want to have to say anything, about myself, so I asked my sister about herself. I asked her how she was doing.

She didn't have alot to say. She talked briefly about her job. But it was obviously a subject that depressed her. She worked as an administrative assistant for a Madison Avenue advertising agency. Prior to this job she'd tried to piece together a career as an artist, a painter, although she'd supported herself mostly by waiting tables. Based on the little I knew, the tiny bit of her work I'd seen, she had a fair amount of talent. But, from what I could tell, she'd abandoned her dream. From what I could tell, she didn't paint anymore.

Was she happy? It was hard to say, I didn't know her well enough to say. I didn't think, however, that she was.

It seemed like she'd resigned herself to living a less than full, less than joyful life. It seemed like she'd resigned herself to living half a life. As though that was all that was available to her.

She asked about my plans for the upcoming holiday.

"What are you going to do for Christmas?"

"I don't know...," I said.

"Are you going to go to Eddie's?" she asked.

"Is that what you're going to do?"

"Yeah. Are you going to?"

"I don't think so…," I said.

"No?"

"I don't think so…."

"Do you have other plans?"

"No. Not really."

"Then you should go to Eddie's," she said.

"I don't think I'm going to…," I said.

"You should." She was urging me gently.

"I just don't think I'm up to it," I said.

"Don't you think it would be good for you to go?"

"I don't know…I don't think so…."

"Don't you think that you're going to want to be with everyone, with Eddie, and Susan, and Aaron…?"

"I don't know…."

"Since Mom just died…."

"I don't know, Denise…." I sighed, clarifying my anguish. "I just think, right now, at this point, it wouldn't be the best thing for me…I think I need to be by myself…I feel bad about not going and being there with everybody, but I think that's just the way it's going to have to be…."

"I wish you'd go."

"I don't think I'm going to."

"What'll you do?"

"I don't know."

There was a silence.

"I have present for you," Denise said, finally.

I didn't respond.

"I'd like to give it to you," she said. And she started to cry.

"I'm sure you'll be able to give it to me," I said.

"I guess I could put it in the mail to you…." She was crying softly. "Do you want me to mail it to you…?"

"I don't think that's gonna work…," I said.

"Why?"

"Unfortunately, I don't think you're gonna be able to mail it to me...," I said. I manufactured an explanation. "The guy I'm subletting the apartment from didn't give me the key to the mailbox, so I haven't been able to get any mail...and he's in Europe...I don't know when he's gonna be able to get the key to me...."

"What am I going to do?" she said.

"Maybe we can get together...," I said.

"When?"

"Let me call you."

"I can't call you...you don't have a phone...." She was still crying. She pushed her words through her sobs. "You're going to have to call me...."

"I'll call you," I said.

"When?" she asked.

"Soon...," I said.

But I still haven't called her.

It's been a month, it's been more than a month, and I still haven't called her.

After talking to Peter I wonder if Ill ever have anything resembling a truly close relationship with him. Ive got my doubts about it. I would like to have a relationship with him but I dont know if its possible if Ill ever be able to get close to him or if hell ever be able to get close to me to be fair about it.

I know that there are things going on with him. I have a dark feeling about it. Its obvious that hes in a dark place. I can hear it can feel it. Its not hard to tell.

I think hes probably in alot of pain not your ordinary stub your toe toothache pain but really heavy duty pain. I think hes anguished that's how Id describe it what I hear.

Whats going on with him scares me. Im afraid hes on a self destructive path that hes headed towards a disaster something horrible maybe even death. Maybe this is an irrational fear but its how I feel like he might die.

Maybe I feel like this because I compare my brother with my father. Maybe I perceive that theyre alike. Maybe I see things in Peter that remind me of my father although I barely knew my father and I barely know Peter for that matter. But I wonder if hes emulating my father not consciously of course but I wonder if its the pattern for the men in my family to move into these dark places to die before their time.

It makes me wonder about the men I choose. Do I choose men like the men in my family? Do I choose men who are out and out incapable of having a relationship? Who are completely unavailable to me the way my father was unavailable to me the way my brother is unavailable to me? Is this the truth? Do I choose guys who are on some kind of self destructive path? Is this my pattern to choose guys who are anguished who cant get past their unhappiness?

If I force myself to be honest I have to say that Im really unhappy. I really dont think I want to be in this relationship with Darren if you can call it a relationship. I think I want out. All my instincts tell me I should get out that its the only sensible thing to do and I think I would do it if I was able to but right now I dont feel like Im able to. Why is this? Is it that I have to be so miserable that I cant stand it anymore before I break up with somebody? Is it that somebody has to beat me up or slap me around or commit some other abusive act before I can break up with him?

I havent been happy for a long time since the first few months of the relationship to be honest about it. Im not getting what I want or what I need. I dont want to look at the truth but the truth is that Darren has been withholding himself from me for months he pulls back a little more every time I see him he doesnt open up to me anymore not that he ever did very much. He hardly talks to me. Hes angry most of the time. He grumbles. He snaps thats his main form of communication. He snaps hes like a turtle he stays inside his shell 90% of the time and sticks his head out once in awhile and snaps at something usually me. Its not like were having great sex anymore. For a long time the sex kept me going for a long time that was the thing that kept me attracted that made me want him. I guess Id be lying if I said I still didnt crave him sometimes if I said I still didnt feel a physical pull but Im not getting anything from the sex. I want him to fuck me but when he fucks me I feel terrible I feel awful about myself.

I have to tell him I want out. I just wish I could do it.

Sometimes I feel like I need to make a clean break. Get out of this relationship quit my job leave the city ideally Id like to go someplace that Ive never been before someplace where I can start my life over on a clean slate.

Ive never given up on that vision I had when I was a little girl that vision from the *Mary Tyler Moore Show* that vision of Mary moving to Minneapolis starting a new life from scratch everything summed up in that theme song about love being all around and you can have it and you can make it. I still hold on to that vision still dream about someday doing something like that moving to my own Minneapolis a new job new friends a new life.

I drive to the Big Burger. I get the same thing I always get, the same thing I've been getting since I was a kid, three burgers, two bags of fries, medium coke.

I drive to Biltmore Beach, park in the mutilated lot, facing the Great South Bay.

I devour my evening's meal, study the beach.

When I was a boy, my mother used to take Eddie and Denise and me to this beach. A narrow band of sand fronting a very small segment of the bay, it'd never been much of a beach. Mostly it'd been a place for young kids, a place where they could burrow in the sand, splash in the shallow water, maybe try their first swimming stokes. It'd been a good place, I suppose, for young suburban mothers to take their kids on hot July and August days. It's been a number of years, however, since any mothers have sat on the sand in their one-piece bathing suits and sunglasses, sipping iced tea from paper cups, since any kids have doused themselves in the unruffled green water. The beach, unfortunately, has been closed for seven or eight years. It's been closed, of course, because the water is polluted. According to articles I've read in the newspaper, the level of contamination in the water far exceeds the acceptable limit and the odds are that the denizens of Bayview will never again be able to use the beach for recreational purposes.

The beach certainly looks like it's been out of use for some time. A shoddy cyclone fence stands between the parking lot and the sand. Attached to the fence are several signs warning, NO BATHING. POLLUTED WATER. Past the fence the sand is grey, hardened, like a wad of chewing gum that's been stuck under a fourth grader's desk for the better part of the school year. The sand is littered with driftwood, tires, hunks of cardboard, styrofoam, aluminum cans. A lifeguard chair lays on its side, the planks dislodged, splintered. On a jutting slat, a quickwitted trespasser has scrawled in black magic marker the pungent epithet, "FUCK YOU."

I polish off my humble repast, the hamburgers, thin slices of grey meat garnished with pickle and ketchup encased in a damp bun, the rubbery salt-encrusted french fries. I sip the coke.

I watch the afternoon descend, die. Beyond the crummy sand, the bay churns slowly, the water, a dark dull green, turns, shifts, folds, in the dying January light. An occasional whitecap forms, a bit of foam, like an abrasion, on the greenish surface.

I watch the daylight fade.

The water's brackish smell seeps into the car.

The sun drops. The sun drops quickly behind the thick, the eternal sweep, the impossible grey, the grey and greyblack smear, the long blanket of clouds. The sun nears the horizon. The sky is grey, like a burned-out lightbulb. Then the sun touches the horizon, and the sky turns darker, and darker, grey. There's no pretty sunset, no suggestion of color, no hint of red or orange or purple. And then the sun goes down. And the sky gets darker. And darker. And even darker. And then the sky is black.

I drive down Sunrise Highway, bring the Toyota to a halt in front of a Citibank.

I withdraw $200 from my savings account. Taking the money from the ATM machine, I check the screen, note my balance. I've got a little more than $2,200 left in my account. This, of course, is the full extent of my financial resources. This is it.

When this money, this $2,200, is gone, I won't have anything left, I won't have any means by which I might support myself, sustain myself.

If I had a credit card I could use it to bail myself out, I could use it, when my savings disappear, to pay for my motel room, to buy food. But I no longer have any credit cards. I'd had two, an American Express and a Visa, but I got rid of both cards about two weeks ago.

I got rid of the cards after I used the Visa twice, on consecutive nights, to pay for a hooker.

The first night I called an escort service, Extraordinary Escorts, and I asked them to send a hooker to my room, and I had them charge the $125 fee to my credit card. I even had them add an extra $25 for a tip.

They delivered to my room a lanky bleachblonde, a girl named Heather.

The next evening I called another escort service, Sweet Thing Escorts. And, again, I paid the $125 fee, and the $25 tip, with my Visa.

This place, Sweet Thing, sent over a girl by the name of Frances. She was frail, marginally attractive, with unevenly cut brown hair, big slow eyes. She sucked my cock. Rather expertly, I must admit. And I rammed her. I slammed my prick inside her.

But after she left, I felt intensely depressed. And I decided that I wasn't going to squander any more of my funds on prostitutes. And, in turn, I decided that I was going to cancel my credit cards. I realized that if I didn't cancel my cards I'd almost certainly use them again to purchase the services of a hooker. If I felt the desire, if the urge struck, I wouldn't be able to defer it, I'd call an escort service. And so the next day I did what I had to do. I called American Express and Visa, found out my balances, and then I wrote each company a check and a note indicating that I was terminating my account. And then I destroyed my cards. I broke them apart and dropped the jagged pieces in the motelroom wastebasket.

I drive down Sunrise.

I pull into the parking lot next to the Liquor Bazaar, a large supermarket-style liquor store.

I pick up a quart of Johnny Walker Red.

I'm not thinking about deviating from my Spaced Maintenance program. I'm not planning on opening this bottle tonight. I've still got a fair amount of booze left in the bottle I bought earlier, and I figure I'll go back to the motel, watch TV, and gradually deplete that bottle. And, if things go right, I'll empty the bottle just before I go to sleep.

I'm buying this bottle of Johnny Walker Red simply because I don't want to wake up tomorrow morning without a supply of scotch within arm's reach. I don't want to wake up, sick as a scrabbly mutt, fighting the shakes, without some booze to gulp down immediately, even before I roll off the bed, if that's necessary. I'm planning ahead, that's all. I'm preparing for every eventuality. It's something you've got to do.

I leave the liquor store, toting the bottle of scotch in an orange plastic bag.

I scuttle down the sidewalk, along Sunrise. Streetlamps illuminate the road. Cars and trucks whoosh past, headlights gleaming. Exhaust fumes singe my nostrils. The wind and blasts from the traffic blow my hair in various directions, pound my leather-jacket, my jeans.

I come to a strip mall, step across the parking lot. The strip mall features a pizza place, a laundromat, an OTB parlor, a deli, a drugstore, a shoe repair shop. I go into the deli. Buy a pack of Marlboros. There are ten or eleven cigarettes in the pack in my leatherjacket pocket. But, again, I'm planning ahead. Making sure I've got enough supplies. Stockpiling the required provisions. When the sirens go off, and the bombs start falling, and there's no place to go, I want to be ready.

Holed up for the night, I assume my regular position on the motelroom bed. My head rests on the two pillows propped against the plywood headboard. My ass dents the mattress. My legs stretch across the tragic bedspread.

My bottle of scotch and my cigarettes sit, close by, on the night table.

The television, my lone fellow rider on this night's journey, my last sidekick, my enduring night nurse, is pivoted toward the bed. The screen burns faithfully, if slightly blurrily, the color imprecise, the picture marred by gently vibrating snow.

My right hand clutches the remote control. My thumb touches the buttons with a sure ease, an earned dexterity.

Flicking repeatedly, I change channels, try to find something, a show, a part of a show, a sequence, a redeeming snippet, an unglued moment, a view, a pretty face, anything....

A woman, she's got an outrageous blonde
    coiffure
Kathy
46DD
I think, she says, one of the hardest
    things is
is you don't know if a fellow
is interested in you because
of who you are
or because you have big breasts
well, let's ask your boyfriend

175

says the blonde female host
would you feel the same way about
Kathy
if she didn't have big breasts?
I really don't think that's a fair question
he says
sincerely
he's gawky, bespectacled
wears a brown corduroy jacket
I mean, if you think about it
he says
she wouldn't be
Kathy
if she didn't have big breasts.

You might think
Reed Burroughs says
tall, chiselled
he walks across a grassy square
in front of a large rectilinear school building
you might think
that if a high school principal was
        going to have an affair with
        a student
that he'd choose the class
        valedictorian, or the senior class
        president
or even perhaps the prettiest girl from
        the cheerleading squad
but that wasn't the case with
Bill Murbridge, the principal of Pottsville High
no, Bill Murbridge decided to

have an affair
with Charisse Ulbeck
a C minus student with a
history of getting into
        trouble.
Charisse Ulbeck sits
on the concrete, in front of Pottsville High
legs crossed, smoking a cigarette
shortcropped purple hair
rings in
        ears, nose, lips, eyebrows
wears ripped gunsnroses tee shirt
        torn jeans
        boots
holds her cigarette, probably a Marlboro
        to her smudged red mouth
        takes a drag
when you're in love with someone
she says
she blows smoke into the
        suburban air
when you're in love
you do all kinds of stupid crap.

The President gnaws
on a slice of pizza
strings
of cheese
stick
to his cuff.

The Playmate of the Year

gets out
of a limousine
breasts shaking
laughing.

The just barely post-pubescent rockstar bashes away
    at his electric guitar
a tall
supermodel
long blonde hair
lingerie
dryhumps
the guitar
her exquisite rump
grazes
the fiberglass.

Brick Towne
square-jawed, square-shouldered, wearing
an expensive suit
claps
like a robot
says, welcome to *Guys and Dolls*
    and now
    let's meet
    our first guest
    Jennifer
a tall blonde
    piece-of-ass
Jennifer grips Brick's hand
    smiles
    perfect teeth

years of orthodontry
hi.

Eddie drives into the parking lot of the South Shore Motel.

He gets out of the BMW along with Joanne Glidden, a girl who works in his office, answering phones, making copies, typing letters, refilling the coffee machine.

"Looks like we gotta go up these stairs," he says, staring disgustedly at the motel building.

He takes the steps, two steps at a time, his $250 black Italian dress shoes clipping the rotted wood.

They go into the motel room.

"I'm gonna go in the bathroom and do you-know-what," Joanne says.

"Go ahead," Eddie mutters.

He lays his trenchcoat on the easychair. He takes off his suitjacket, lays it on top of the trenchcoat. He picks up the remote. Flicks on the TV. *Guys and Dolls* materializes. The show's broadshouldered host, Brick Towne, is sitting on a lavender couch, chatting with a terrifically goodlooking blonde.

"I got this spermicide stuff," Joanne says through the half-open bathroom door.

"Uh huh," Eddie grunts.

"I'm gonna use some of it," she says.

"Good idea," he says, sardonically. He's revulsed by her. He finds her incredibly stupid.

"It tastes like strawberry," she says. "Supposedly."

"Great," he says.

❦   ❦   ❦

Joanne walks across the matted-down carpeting. She's untied her hair and her brown tresses fall wildly, cascade flamboyantly past her shoulders. She's wearing a lacy black bra that can't possibly contain her enormous breasts and a pair of black underpants that are being stretched well beyond their limit by her abundant hips and big cornucopia of an ass.

Eddie is stricken by the sight of her.

And, at least for now, he remembers what he likes about her.

He remembers.

He ogles her, he ogles her big voluptuous body, he ogles her breasts, he studies the way they project into the room, the way they bob, like a couple of buoys on the Great South Bay. His cock juts into his pants.

He moves toward her, clamps her, pulls her breasts to his plain white perspiration-sticky shirt. He presses his underdeveloped pectoral muscles against her, craving the lewd friction. He kisses her, jabs his elongated tongue into the recesses of her mouth.

He guides her onto the kingsized bed, climbs on top of her.

"Ya want Joanne?" she asks.

"Yeah," Eddie says.

He paws her tits. He grinds his crotch against her. His cock, stiff as a crowbar, sticks into his trousers, threatens to punch a hole in the pricey fabric.

He pushes down her bra.

"Ya like Joanne's breasts?" she asks.

He buries his head between her tits, irked, annoyed by the way she refers to herself using the third person. He wishes she wouldn't say anything. He wishes she'd keep her fucking mouth shut.

He crawls backwards, down the bed. Yanks off her underpants. Fits his head between her thighs, mashes his face against her cunt, jams his mouth, his chafed lips, into her wet crease, pokes his tongue, up, into, inside her corrugated folds, as far as he can get it, and then a bit further.

"Oh yeah...," she says. "That's what Joanne likes...."

He grabs her fleshy indent with his lips and teeth, pulls and thrashes, like a hyena tearing the flesh from a just-found carcass.

He growls hyperbolically.

"Oh yeah...," she moans. "Eat Joanne's pussy...."

Eddie flails away, viciously.

Then suddenly he retracts his head. He jerks back and away from her slit, as though he's cut himself on a wickedly sharp edge.

"Fuck!" he cries.

He sits on his knees on the mattress.

"What's wrong?" she asks.

"Motherfucker!" he curses. He fingers his necktie. The tie is wet. It's not completely drenched, but in a few spots it's wet, it's soaked through with Joanne's rank fluid.

"What's wrong?" Joanne cranes her neck. Her long masses of curly brown hair fall against her knockers.

"I can't believe this!" he bleats. "This is fucked up!"

"What is it?"

"My fucking tie!"

"What's wrong?"

"It's fucking ruined!"

"Is it that bad?"

"Look at this!" He holds up the blue paisley tie, shows her the wet rhomboid-shaped blotches. What makes the situation especially disturbing is that this is the tie that Susan, his wife, gave to him this past Christmas. "Look at this!"

"Can't you take it to the dry cleaners?" Joanne says.

"Whattam I gonna tell my wife?!"

Eddie slides off the bed. Stands on the carpeting. He unfastens the tie.

"What the fuck am I gonna do!"

"Maybe you could wash it in the sink."

"It's a fucking silk tie!"

He lays the tie over the back of the easychair.

He looks away from the bed, away from her. He's afraid that if he looks at her, he'll explode. He stares at the wall. Studies the shadows created by the motelroom furniture.

"Are you okay?" she asks.

"I'm great...," he mutters. "I'm fucking great...."

He steps toward the TV. Inspects the screen. *Guys and Dolls* is still on. A black woman is sitting on the couch, talking to Brick Towne. She's very attractive, lightskinned, with an almost shaved head, a triangular face, shiny front teeth.

"Ya like her?" Joanne asks playfully, trying to reel him back in.

Eddie stares at the fuzzy screen, grimaces.

"Wouldya go out with a black girl?" she asks.

"I don't think my wife would appreciate it," he says, snapping his reply.

"Whattaya think she'd say about ya goin out with me?"

"Not much."

Eddie glares at the set. The black woman jabbering.

"I can't watch this shit when the contestants are black," he says venomously.

"Yeah, I know what ya mean," she says.

"Fucking coons. It's fucking bullshit."

"I know, I can't get into it, either," she says. She shows agreement only because she doesn't want to show disagreement. She realizes that his view is faulty, morally incorrect. But she doesn't want to dispute him, doesn't want to prod his anger, doesn't want to say anything that might move him further away from her than he's already moved. She wants, if possible, to placate him, please him, she wants to regain his favor. Bottom line, she wants him, she wants his big thick cock inside her.

It's always like this when they get together. At some point he acts like a jerk, he's nasty, he gets angry. But she wants him anyway. She wants what she wants. She can't help it.

She says, "I usually change the channel when they're black."

"Seems like every time I turn it on they got blacks on," he says. "I guess they've got some kind of fucking quota. Gotta have a certain number of coons. Everything is fucked up like that. All this Affirmative Action bullshit. It's just reverse racism. I mean, we got guys like Alvin Fisher working for us. I mean, what the fuck is that all about. The guy can't sell. He can't sell shit. The only reason he's got the job is because he's black. That's the only goddam reason. If he wasn't a fucking coon they never would've hired him. They wouldn't've hired him to clean the fucking toilets."

"I didn't realize he was that bad," she says.

"He's a fucking piece of shit. If it was up to me, he'd be out on his coon ass. But there's no way they'll ever fire him. He'd have to punch out Venturi, and even then they probably wouldn't fire him. They'd say it wasn't his fault, he did it because of his poor oppressed ghetto upbringing."

"I always thought he was a nice guy," she says lightly, careful not to antagonize him.

"He's no salesman, that's for goddam sure." Eddie picks up the remote, flicks off the TV.

He steps to the window. Separates the drapes.

"I'll say one thing for Bayview," he says. "At least they got no coons living here."

"They don't?"

"No way."

"They don't have any?"

"Nope."

"None?"

"Nope. They won't let'em in. They don't want the place to fall apart."

He looks out, at Sunrise, the cars, the lights.

"You gotta give'em credit for that," he says.

He fucks her. From behind. He kneels on the sagging mattress, holds on to her ass, stabilizing himself. He shoves his cock in, pulls it out, shoves it in, pulls it out, shoves it in.

He fucks her violently. And, as he fucks her, he roars. A loud roughedged noise rides up his throat, exits his body through his bent, deformed mouth. An animal roar, the sort of pained lament, desperate cry, made by a furry, fangtoothed denizen of the deep forest.

He roars dramatically. His anguished exclamations blast the motelroom air, pierce the thin plaster walls.

He roars.

America is disintegrating.

America is disintegrating, crumbling into indistinguishable fragments, breaking apart into hopeless pieces.

The Typical Middleclass American will admit, perhaps, that parts of America are disintegrating, that, specifically, certain sections of certain cities are disintegrating. He's observed this disintegration, he'll say, he's seen the pictures, on TV, in newspapers, in magazines, or maybe he's glanced this disintegration firsthand, from a distance, of course, maybe he's viewed scenes of this disintegration through the window, the rolled up window, of his car, maybe he's driven down, say, the Cross Bronx Expressway, in his shiny middleclass vehicle, and he's seen the burned-out buildings and desolate lots, the smashed brick, the striking ruin.

But the truth, the truth that the Typical Middleclass American is incapable of perceiving, is that the most profound, most devastating disintegration taking place in America isn't taking place in the cities, in those poverty-stricken enclaves, the worst disintegration, the most severe disintegration, is taking place in the suburbs, in the middle of the middleclass neighborhoods, in places like Bayview. This is where the most catastrophic decay is taking place. This is where the corrosion is most telling, most significant. In the suburbs. Inside the boxshaped houses. On the dull concrete streets. On the commuter trains. In the fucking malls.

The Typical Middleclass American will, of course, refute what I'm saying, but that's only because the Typical Middleclass American can't see what's happening, can't see, or won't see, what's transpiring in his own backyard. Because, let's face it, the Typical Middleclass American is something of an asshole.

But if he would take a good look, if he would open his eyes, if he would take an honest, penetrating look, the Typical Middleclass American would see the disintegration I'm talking about, if he would look past the suburban cosmetics, the aluminum siding, the trimmed shrubs, if he would look inside his fellow suburbanites, or, better yet, if he would look inside himself (I realize that this is too much to ask, but I've got to suggest it), if he would look inside himself, past the namebrand clothes, the accurate haircut, the gymnasium-altered muscle groups, and if he would look past the layers of what-he-thinks-he-knows, the opinions, the muck of views, if he would look into his mind, and heart, if he would *really* look, he would find horrible disintegration, he would find a diseased cavity, a putrefying hole. Because the truth, the truth is, the truth is the Typical Middleclass American is a loathsome specimen, he's fearful, hateful, violence-inclined, racist, greedy, lustful, narrowminded, visionless, spiritless, godless (I'm not referring to the sort of god that most people refer to when they talk about god, the sort of god I'm referring to when I use the term godless is most definitely not the sort of god that's worshipped on Sunday mornings in the churches I drive past on my way to wherever I'm going, it's not the same god that the Typical Middleclass American prays to. This god I'm referring to is something else entirely, I'm not exactly sure how I might define this god, the whole notion of god isn't one that I've bothered much to consider, I've always thought myself an agnostic, perhaps an atheist, certainly an existentialist, but I am beginning, just beginning, to sense that perhaps, maybe, although I may be wrong, that there might be some sort of god, a god distinctly different from that other sort of god....)....

I lay across the motelroom bed.

1am.

I drag on a cigarette.

I flick the remote.

The bottle of Johnny Walker Red, the bottle I drank from throughout the day, stands on the night table, empty, scotchless.

The bottle I bought just before I came back to the motel stands on the dresser, unopened, it stands there, proudly, like a trophy, a statuette, an Academy Award, or an Emmy, or something. I have a tremendous desire to open this bottle. I'm aching to open it. I'm dying to open it. I don't want to forsake my Spaced Maintenance program. I don't want to violate the rules I've set. I don't want to surrender to my inability to control my intake. I don't want to relinquish my grasp of choice. But I'm still wide awake. I'm severely, sharply awake. And it seems like I'm going to be awake for a while longer. And I just don't think that I'm going to be able to get through the next hour or two, or three, without pouring more scotch into my system, without pouring a few more cans of oil into the crankcase, without shovelling more coal into the furnace.

I glance intermittently at the dresser. I glance every now and then, I glance at intervals, at the untouched bottle.

Finally I roll off the bed. Limp across the room. Grab the bottle. I sit on the bed, unscrew the cap, with a quick twist, break the seal. I pour some scotch in my glass: I pour the scotch until the glass is two-thirds full: I pour a significant amount of scotch: I

188

pour it, slowly, mindfully, until there's enough, the right amount, in the glass.

I hold the glass to my mouth. I hold the glass to my mouth, take a long, much-needed sip. I take a long sip, let the scotch stream down, into my blood.

I flick the remote, press my thumb against the upward-pointing rubber triangle, the button that advances the channels. I press the button, again and again.

Then I stop. I rest my thumb against the rubber triangle, settle on the image of a young man, a guy maybe in his early thirties, sitting at a big round table talking about the book that he's apparently just written. This guy's got thick dipsydoodling dark hair. He speaks with an upperclass drawl and there's an unmistakable arrogance ironed on to his pasty visage. He's wearing a blazer, a black turtleneck, the same sort of garb he's been wearing, undoubtedly, since his fucking prep school days.

He's apparently written a work of fiction, a novel.

He looks familiar. But I really have no idea who he is.

Then a graphic appears at the bottom of the screen, revealing that he's Josh Fairchild. According to the graphic, Fairchild's just published novel is called *Devil Dog*.

I don't know alot about Josh Fairchild, but I probably know more than I need to know. I know that he's considered, by the people who do such considering, to be something of a phenom, a rising star. His first book, *Love Fiend*, which he wrote when he was a student in some graduate school program, received tons of notoriety, turned him into a veritable literary celebrity. Since then he's written two more novels, both of which have garnered a heap of critical acclaim and public notice.

I haven't read any of Fairchild's books. But I know enough about them, having read some reviews in the *New York Times Book Review*, and having skimmed some pages from one or two of his novels that I've pulled from shelves in bookstores, I know enough to know that I have no affinity for the sort of stuff he writes. I know enough to know that he writes precisely the sort of stuff that I don't want to write. I know enough to know that his stuff is crap. It's pathetic, insipid garbage, written for an overinflated clique of trendmongers and psuedo-academics. It's worthless, self-absorbed blather, the sort of meaningless folderol that offers nothing to the society, to the people, that contains none of the attributes of poetry that Whitman talked about.

I've got no desire to watch Fairchild expound on his so-called literary process. I've got no interest in listening to him pontificate on his goddam personal vision and his opinion of contemporary American fiction and anything else he might choose to babble about.

I flick the remote.

I lay on the bed, propped against the plywood headboard, covered by the scabrous bedclothes. I'm wearing, under the covers, a grungy sweatshirt, underpants, a pair of white socks. The room is dark, the lights are off, the only illumination is provided by the TV, glowing steadfastly, bouncing dull rays off the bedspread.

I can't sleep.

It's past 4am, it's encroaching on 5am, but I can't sleep, I'm wide awake, jaggedly awake.

I want desperately to sleep, to drop, to descend from the conscious world. But I don't seem to have access to the way down. I can't seem to find the way.

I pour more scotch into my glass. I sip the lukewarm scotch. Put the glass on the night table. Then pick it up. Take another sip.

I flick the remote.

The images flash.

A man with bushy sideburns standing next to an old dusty Chevy.

A young woman wearing an orange shirt and bellbottoms.

A grainy black and white image, a man and a woman slow-dancing.

I flick.

I light a cigarette.

I listen, half-listen, to the man and woman in the adjacent room. They're panting, vociferously, like a couple of dogs that've just run the length of a football field on a stifling July afternoon.

I drag on my cigarette. Tap ashes into the ashtray. The ashtray is an unsightly mess, loaded with squushed butts.

I slide off the bed. Slide into the bathroom. Toss my cigarette in the toilet. Piss.

I crawl back into bed.

I flick the remote. I keep flicking, keep moving, from channel to channel to channel to channel, don't remain for more than a few seconds on any image.

Then, to my delight, I stumble on a *Leave it to Beaver* rerun.

The program is just starting.

The familiar theme music pipes, the familiar characters emerge, step, one by one, through the front door of Beaver's house, Beaver's mother, June, played by Barbara Billingsley, Beaver's dad, Ward, played by Hugh Beaumont, Wally, played by Tony Dow, and then, grinning that ageless, enduring grin, the Beaver himself, the announcer intoning, "And Jerry Mathers as the Beaver."

I lay the remote on the bedspread.

The episode begins.

I watch raptly. I concentrate on the black and white picture. I try to absorb everything, every piece of action, every line of dialog.

And at some point I remember a summer evening when I was seven, eight years old, when I watched *Leave it to Beaver* with my friends, Chris Adelkravitich and Willy Smithberger. I remember lying on the floor, in the den in Chris's house, lying beside my two friends. It was the end of the summer, and the sun slanted across the room, the day's last slants, they slanted across the room at that low angle that the sun makes during summer's final weeks. And my friends and I lay there, the sun slanting across our slim bodies, and we watched *Leave it to Beaver*.

And now, beneath the squalid covers, in my endarkened room, in the South Shore Motel, I remember that feeling, that feeling that that summer had driven into me, that feeling that'd infiltrated my young bones as I'd sprawled on the floor with Chris and Willy. I remember that joy I'd felt, that I'd known, back then, when I was with them.

And, to some extent, I can feel that joy right now, thirty years later, I can actually *feel* it, inside me, in my body, in my throat, at the bottom of my throat. It lodges itself there, a small warm mass, about the size of a golf ball.

The show ends. Theme music plays. Credits appear, along with that indestructible closing sequence, the image of Wally and the Beaver walking down the sidewalk, past the meticulous houses, the meticulous yards of their suburban neighborhood.

I flick off the TV. Lay my cheek against the rough industrial pillowcase. I can still feel that joy, a bit of it. It lingers, faintly, like the taste left by something you ate awhile ago.

And holding on to this smidgen of joy, this vague taste, holding on dearly, I make the slow muddled descent, I find sleep.

It's Saturday, I think. It's the first thing I think when I wake.

I've always figured that Saturday would be the best day to call Willy Smithberger. I've always figured that if I contacted Willy on a Saturday I'd have a better chance of apprehending him when he was in a relaxed mood, an amiable mood, a mood in which he'd be able, more able, to deal with a strange unexpected phone call, a mood in which he'd be able to handle without too much strain a conversation with somebody he hadn't spoken to in twenty-five years. I've always figured that Smithberger would be more approachable on a Saturday, that he'd be more receptive to a call from me. He'd be, hopefully, somewhat removed from his job, his scraping worklife, he'd be free, at least to some degree, from the workweek stress, the Monday-Friday anxiety and despair. I've always figured that Saturday would be the day on which I'd have the best opportunity to engage him in a spirited dialog, Saturday afternoon, perhaps later, after he'd performed his rote weekend tasks, his husbandly and fatherly tasks, his prototypically suburban tasks, taking the kids to gymnastics lessons, repairing the molding in the dining room, putting shit in the attic.

I've always figured that Saturday would be the day I'd call him.

I roll off the bed.

I wobble into the bathroom.

I sit on the toilet. I don't have to take a dump, but I know, I know from experience, that with the way my hands are shaking, with the way my legs are shaking, that if I try to urinate while I'm standing I'll almost certainly misfire, I'll probably miss the bowl entirely, I'll probably splurt streams of piss against the wall and floor.

I finish pissing. Stand. Stuff my cock back into my underpants.

I walk back across the motel room, I walk slowly, my socks skidding against the carpeting, every inch of motion cut with pain.

I sit on the bed, grab the bottle of Johnny Walker. I hold the bottle to my lips, take a long, long slug.

I pull on a hooded sweatshirt. I pull on my leatherjacket. I need to get to a liquor store.

I step outside. I peer around, like I'm leaving the scene of a crime. And perhaps I am.

I get in the freezing Toyota.

I fit the key in the ignition.

I mutter a short prayer. I ask God to please let the car start.

Usually, of course, I don't beseech God with these sorts of prayers, primarily because I doubt whether a God exists who listens to such prayers, who ponders such prayers, who answers such prayers. I don't think that God is a He, or She, with a human form, with ears, that He, or She, listens to the trivial prayers uttered by unemployed salesmen sitting in motel parking lots, that He, or She, receives these utterances, these requests, while seated at a giant control panel, or computer, that He, or She, makes a decision, then hits a switch and makes the unemployed salesman's car start, or not start. But in this instance, I pray as though this kind of God does exist.

I turn the key slowly.

The engine grunts. I pump the gas, hold the key in the turned position.

And the damn thing starts.

I drive down Sunrise Highway.
   I turn onto Jerusalem Avenue.
   Drive down Jerusalem.
   I park against the curb in front of Dingham's Liquors.
   I pick up a bottle of Johnny Walker Red.

I lay on the motelroom bed.

I pour some scotch into the cruddy bathroom glass. About a shot's worth. I bring the glass to my mouth, knock down the booze, in a quick, slightly desperate gulp.

I put down the glass.

I wait. I wait to feel something.

But I feel nothing. Absolutely nothing.

Nothing.

And I'm concerned.

It's been about an hour since I returned from the liquor store, and in this hour I've glugged down quite alot of scotch, I've picked up the bottle nine or ten or eleven times and I've poured an amount of scotch, roughly a shot's worth, into the glass, and I've just about inhaled the scotch. And I don't feel anything. I don't feel anything at all.

I look toward the TV, there's a college basketball game on, St. John's vs. Providence.

I try to watch the game. A St. John's player, a skinny black kid, stands at the foul line, bouncing the ball, flexing his knees.

The kid shoots.

I pick up the bottle, pour more scotch in my glass. I pour several inches of scotch into the glass, and I take a prodigious slug, I completely ignore, defy the guidelines I've constructed, the principles of Spaced Maintenance, and I drain the glass.

But I feel nothing.

I don't feel at all intoxicated.

It's crazy, unexplainable.

I'm sober.
I'm completely sober.
Cold sober.
Dead sober.
I feel more sober, in fact, than I've felt in weeks, in months.
I don't know when I've felt this sober.

I fill the glass more than halfway. And I take a long, very long, slug. And then I take another long slug.

I'm still hopeful. I'm still hopeful that I might cross the threshold, that I might finally gain a certain drunkenness, that I might at last attain a stuporous, semi-paralyzed state.

I wait.

But I don't feel anything.

No.

I don't feel even mildly inebriated.

If anything, I feel more sober.

I feel more intensely sober.

I lay on the bed.

The TV flashes.

In one of the adjacent rooms, a man and a woman are yelling frantically. As though it's the last time they'll ever fuck. And maybe it is. Maybe it is.

I tilt the bottle, refill my glass.

I take a protracted slug.

I hold the glass between my thighs. I lean my head back against the plywood headboard.

I feel remarkably sober.

To put it another way, I feel closer.

I feel like I'm getting closer, I feel like I'm getting closer to the moment, to the present moment, to the moment in which I exist....

I lay on the bed. Stuck. Embedded. Right here. In this blisteringly real place. In this moment.

I lay, on my spine, on the grimy bedspread.

I feel an insane, ratcheting anxiety.

I feel like I'm going to destruct. I feel like I'm going to break down, like a dilapidated machine, clattering, collapsing, gears clashing, bolts dropping, screws rolling away.

I feel like I'm going to break into a million unidentifiable fragments.

And then, suddenly, I feel calm. I feel imperturbably calm.

Everything is still.

Everything, for a moment, stops.

And I can see things in a way that I wasn't previously able to see them. I can see much more clearly. I can see with much greater comprehension. I can see my life, my basic existence, as though it's standing outside me, as though it's a separate object, as though it's a big rock sitting on the motelroom carpeting, as though it's a boulder, the kind you might find on the side of the road, in the Adirondacks, or something.

And then this perception yields to another swiftly arising perception. And I can make out a passageway. An unobstructed, decently-lit passageway. It's right there, in the place where I've been looking for it, for months. It's right in front of me.

And I know that I've got to act, I've got to act *right now*, before I lose sight of it.

I lean to the bedside table.

I pick up the telephone.

I stand there, in front of Willy Smithberger's small boxshaped house. I stand there, the light above the door glossing my leather-jacketed form. I stand there, breathing the cold evening air. I stand there, hesitating.

Finally I ring the bell.

And the door opens.

And Willy Smithberger appears.

He stands in front of me, grinning.

And I know. I know that I'm not going to get what I came for, I'm not going to get answers, I'm not going to get a goddam thing.

I know, before he says anything.

I know, just by looking at him.

I know.

This man is nothing like the Willy Smithberger I had known, the Willy Smithberger I had grown up with. This man is a depressing substitute, a disappointing replacement for Willy Smithberger.

He looks nothing like Willy Smithberger.

He's bald. His big pink head is barren but for scruffs of growth, scrubby vegetation, near his ears. His face is big, round, pinkish, overrun by an enormous mustache, a profusion of brown hair that hangs from his nostrils like a dead rodent. He's a big man, with a massive chest and a giant stomach that protrudes into his shirt like an in-season watermelon.

He's a bear.

Nothing about him reminds me of Willy Smithberger. There isn't a hint of Willy anywhere. It's as if this man, this alleged Willy

Smithberger, this bear, has devoured my boyhood friend, it's as if he's swallowed him whole.

He pushes open the glass storm door.

"Pete!" he grins, showing a set of yellow teeth. "It's great to see you!"

He extends his big paw.

"Hi Willy," I say, clasping his hand.

"This is great!" he says, grinning.

I stand there, dumbly, shaking his swollen hand.

"Come on in," he says.

"Thanks," I say.

I retract my hand.

But I don't move. I feel like I don't want to move. I feel like I don't want to go any further, like I don't want to go in the house...I feel like I want to turn and run....

Finally, though, I lift my sneaker, and move it slowly, and I move my body, slowly, through the door....

I follow Smithberger into the heart of his decidedly suburban living room. The room is small, bland. The carpeting, a beige tone, is lackluster, worn. The furniture is unimpressive, inexpensive-looking, most of the items were probably purchased, it's my guess, at the discount warehouses on Route 140.

Smithberger introduces his wife. Rosalind.

She's sitting on the couch, holding a copy of *People* magazine. She puts the magazine on the coffee table. Smiles.

"Hi Peter," she says.

She's extremely goodlooking. Blonde hair. Slender body. Streamlined legs, crossed, highlighted by sleek jeans.

She's a genuine piece-of-ass.

"Hi," I say, clumsily.

"Give me your coat," Smithberger says.

I take off my leatherjacket.

"Can I getcha something to drink?" he asks.

"Sure."

"Beer?"

"You have any scotch?"

"Sure, I have scotch," he says. "How do you like it?"

"On the rocks is fine."

"No soda or anything?"

"Nah, that's not necessary."

"I've got club soda," he says.

"That's okay," I say. "On the rocks is good."

Smithberger nods, as though impressed.

"Make yourself at home," he says.

"Thanks," I say.

"I'll get your drink," he says.

"Thanks," I say.

I sit on an easychair, across from Rosalind. Scrumptious Rosalind. She's exceptionally goodlooking. She's the sort of girl you'd expect to find leaning against a Corvette at the Nassau Coliseum Auto Show. Or, better yet, she's the sort of girl you'd expect to see on TV, reporting on some story for the Channel 9 evening news. Or, even better yet, she's the sort of girl you'd expect to see playing a sexy young thing in a commercial for some shampoo or toothpaste or something. The last place you'd expect to find her is right here, sitting on the couch in Willy Smithberger's living room, playing the role of Willy Smithberger's wife.

And as I recline, stiffly, against the easychair, I can't help but ask myself:

How did Willy Smithberger land a girl like this?

How does this sort of thing happen?

How is it that a fat bald ignoramus like Smithberger is able to hook up with somebody like this when I can't seem to establish any connection with any kind of woman?

Why does it always turn out like this?

Why?

"You live in Queens?" Rosalind says.

"Yeah. In Forest Hills," I say.

I had told Willy, when I'd spoken to him on the phone, that I lived in Forest Hills.

"Do you like it?"

"It's okay." It's nervewracking, talking to her. It's always nervewracking, when I'm trying to make conversation with a good-looking woman.

"I'm not that familiar with Queens," she says.

"If there's not any reason to be familiar with it," I say, "then it's unlikely that you'd be familiar with it."

She nods.

"Where are your kids?" I ask, in an attempt to facilitate the dialog.

"They're upstairs," she says. "They're watching a video…they'll come down in a little while, when we have dinner…."

"Great."

"They're looking forward to meeting you."

"I'm looking forward to meeting them," I say. "You've got a boy and a girl?"

"Yeah," she smiles. "Ben and Lisa Anne."

"And they're how old?"

"Ben is seven. And Lisa Anne is four."

"That's great…."

Willy hands me a tall glass filled halfway with scotch and ice cubes. He gives Rosalind a glass filled with white wine, and he sits next to her on the couch, clutching his beverage of choice, a bottle of Heineken.

I bring my glass to my mouth, gulp down a good amount of the cold biting scotch. I'm already inebriated, of course. I had passed the afternoon, in my motel room, drinking. I had, in fact, polished off a quart of Johnny Walker Red before I'd left for Smithberger's. But right now I feel an urgent need to take in more alcohol. I feel like I need replenishment. I feel, in fact, like I'm going to need constant replenishment while I'm here, while I'm in the presence of this bearish Willy Smithberger, this imposterish Smithberger, I feel like I'm going to need to drink non-stop, I'm going to need continuous liquid sustenance, like a tropical plant that needs to absorb some form of moisture twenty-four hours a day if it's going to survive.

"This is great," Smithberger grins, putting his bottle of beer to his mouth.

"Yeah," I say flatly.

"It's great to see you, Pete."

"It's good to see you, Willy...."

"I figured I'd never see you again."

"Yeah, I know...."

"It's like I told you on the phone," Smithberger says. "I haven't heard from anybody from the old neighborhood in years."

"I guess everybody's moved on...."

"I haven't heard from anybody, nobody, in ten years...I get a Christmas card every year from Louie Plunkett...that's about it...." Smithberger turns to his wife, asks her, "Did we get a Christmas card from Louie Plunkett this year?"

"I'm not sure, I think so...," Rosalind says.

"I was really surprised when you called," Smithberger says.

"I can imagine...," I say.

"For a minute I didn't know who you were."

"That's understandable."

"For a second I thought you were some joker tryin to sell me something."

"Sorry I threw you off."

"Then I figured it out."

I nod.

I sip my scotch.

Smithberger pulls on his beer.

"So what are you doing these days?" he asks.

"What do you mean?"

"What do you do?"

"For work?"

"Yeah."

I sip my scotch, delay my response. I can't help but think that if I tell Smithberger about my efforts to write that he won't be able to relate. I can't help but think that he'll think that I'm some kind of flake, some kind of nut.

"Well…," I say eventually, "I'm sort of in a period of transition…I'm sort of in the middle of what I guess you could call a career change…I was working for a company that sells educational materials…I actually worked for that company for a number of years…I was a sales rep…but I left that job fairly recently…just a few months ago…right now I'm doing some writing…."

"Writing?"

"Yeah."

"You're a writer?"

"Yeah…."

"That's great!" Willy says.

"Yeah…," I say. "Right now I'm working on a book…."

"A book!" he exudes. "That's great!"

"That's terrific," Rosalind chimes.

"Yeah…." I lift my glass to my mouth.

"I can't believe you're writing a book!" Willy says.

"That's exciting," Rosalind says.

"Yeah," I say, sipping my scotch.

"What kind of book is it?" she asks.

"A novel."

"Wow," she says.

"You mean, it's fiction?" Willy says.

"Right," I say.

"Like a story?"

"Right."

"Have you written any books before?" he asks.

"No…," I say. "It's what I've wanted to do, for a long time…it's what I'd planned to do when I was in college, it's what I wanted to do when I got out of college…but I had this job…it was a demanding job, it took up alot of my time, most of my time, most of my life…I wanted to write, but I didn't have the time to write…that's why I left…so I could write…now that I've left, now that I'm not working forty, fifty hours a week, I can put the time into my writing…which is what you've got to do if you want to write a book, you've got to put the time into it, you've got to put a full effort into it…."

Smithberger nods, slugs his beer. The green bottleneck disappears beneath his humongous mustache.

"What's the title of the book?" he asks.

"I never reveal that," I say. "I never tell anyone. It's sort of a writer's superstition."

"Can you tell us what it's about?" he asks.

"Yeah, what's it about?" Rosalind choruses.

"In twenty-five words or less?"

"Whatever," Willy laughs.

"Can you tell us?" Rosalind begs.

"Tell us," Willy urges.

I sip my scotch. I take a long sip.

"Cmon Peter," Rosalind says. "Tell us something about it."

"I guess I could…I guess I could tell you a little bit about it…," I say. "It's hard…it's hard to explain it…I'm afraid I'm not very good at explaining it…I think it's actually hard for alot of writers to talk about what they're working on, when they're working on it…."

"Just give us a general idea what it's about," Rosalind says.

"I'll try…," I say. I sip my drink. I look into my glass. I've already downed most of the scotch. "I guess you could say it's autobiographical…."

"It's about your experiences," Willy says.

He's an astute bastard.

"It's primarily autobiographical…I write about what I know…," I say. "I guess I've always been prone to go along with what Thoreau said, what he said about his writing…he said that he wrote about his own experiences because it's what he knew the most about, if he knew about anything else as well then he would have written about that…but he didn't, of course, so he wrote about his own life…."

I'm sure that Smithberger doesn't have the slightest idea who Thoreau is. For all big dumb Willy knows, he might be a columnist for *Newsday*.

"It's autobiographical to an extent…," I say. "I take my experiences, things that've happened to me, and I draw on them…I take them up to a certain point, and then I guess you could say I leap off, I let my imagination take over…I extrapolate…."

"Great," Willy says.

I have no doubt that he doesn't know what "extrapolate" means.

"I actually write alot about the suburbs," I say.

"Yeah?" Smithberger laughs.

"Yeah, I write alot about places like Bayview, what it was like growing up in a place like this, stuff like that...."

"That's wild," Smithberger says.

"I figure it's fertile ground...I figure there's alot to write about...."

I take another sip of scotch.

"It's always been my belief," I go on, "that where we grew up, Long Island, the suburbs, in the sixties, it's where the tide of things turned, it's where the America we know took shape...if you want to find out about America, if you go back to that place, that time, you can really find out alot about what it's all about...."

"I never really thought about it like that," Smithberger says. "But you're probably right."

"That was an extraordinary time, when we were growing up...."

Smithberger nods.

His wife nods.

"I think it makes for really pertinent, really viable subject matter...the suburbs are the ideal place, I think, in which to make a study of American life...."

I take a long sip of scotch, slowly dribble the booze over my gums, my tongue, down my throat. I consider Smithberger. He's sitting there, grinning, his beer tilted to his mouth. He's showing interest in my creative proclivities, the nuances of my writer's craft, my personal vision. But I can't help but think that he thinks that I'm a fool. I can't help but think that he thinks that I'm deluded. I can't help but think that he thinks that I'm a lost soul, a dreamer, trying to be a writer, trying to write a novel, a novel about the suburbs, of all things. I can't help but think that he's analyzed me, my less-than-elegant appearance, my long hair, my sweater with the hole in the shoulder, my beatup jeans, my decomposing basketball sneakers, and that he's concluded that I'm some sort of crazed vagabond, a lunatic, a bum.

I look at him. I look at this late twentieth century Willy Smithberger. I gaze at his bald head, his mustache, the Heineken bottle soldered to his mouth like a length of pipe.

This is what I should expect him to think, I realize.

This is *exactly* what I should expect him to think.

Because, the thing is, this Willy Smithberger is a categorical bonehead. He's a prototypical suburban bonehead. He's the sort of person who's incapable, who always will be incapable, of appreciating the artist's posture. The guy, I tell myself, lacks any kind of depth. He's about as deep, I tell myself, as the puddles that form on the bathroom tiles when he takes his morning shower.

I keep my glass pressed to my lips, let the scotch trickle, slowly, down. I empty the glass.

Smithberger glugs his beer. He rests the green bottle on the coffee table.

He grins amusedly, his mustache spottled with beer foam.

"I gotta tell you," he says. "You got me worried."

"Why's that?"

"I'm just thinking," he says, "that if you're writin a book about Bayview, about when we were kids and stuff like that, I'm just thinking that I might be in there somewhere. I might be one of your characters."

"There's a chance of that," I allow.

"That's what I was afraid of." He laughs. His mustache rumbles. "Just promise me," he says, "that you'll go easy on me."

"I will," I say. "You don't have anything to worry about...."

"I'm a cop," Smithberger tells me.

"Oh yeah?"

"Yeah, I've been on the job fifteen years."

"Great."

"I made detective a coupla years ago."

"That's great," I say.

"Yeah, I work right here in Nassau County."

"Great."

I'm feigning an affirmative reaction. I'm pretending that I'm enthused by what he's telling me. The truth, of course, is that I'm horrified.

Smithberger is a cop!

A cop!

I feel like I've been dealt a crushing blow.

Willy Smithberger is a cop!

I've been getting hit with all kinds of painful, damaging blows since I mounted the steps to Willy Smithberger's house. But this, it would seem, is the culminating blow. This is the blow, it would seem, that's going to finish me off.

Smithberger is a fucking cop!

I have always, of course, had a terrifically negative opinion of cops. Growing up in the sixties, I had learned to despise cops. I had watched cops every night on TV committing all sorts of atrocious acts. I had watched cops attacking the very people who, as far as I was concerned, were trying to do something about the disease that'd infected America's bones. I had watched cops cracking young men and women with nightsticks, throwing these young people, these kids, against the concrete, dragging them by their long hair, bombarding them with tear gas, shooting them, *fucking shooting them.*

And perhaps I'm biased (I know I'm biased), but I still consider cops brutalizers, bullies, purveyors of ignorance and anger and hatred and violence. To me, cops will always be what we called them way-back-when: pigs.

The fact that Willy Smithberger is a cop, a pig, is, to my way of seeing things, conclusively damning. It seals the case. Now I know, *I know*, I know that there's no way that I'm going to be able to connect with this oversized Willy Smithberger, I know that there's no way that I'm going to be able to establish any sort of meaningful connection with him.

Now I know that there's no way, *no way*, that I'm going to find answers here, in this place. If I was still clinging to some faint hope that this encounter with Willy Smithberger might yield answers, and perhaps I was, now I know that I have no reason to have even the slightest shred of hope, now I know, now I know that I've got a better chance of finding gold in Smithberger's raingutters than finding answers through an interaction with this man.

"I did run into somebody a coupla years ago," Willy Smithberger says. "Not somebody we used to hang out with...but somebody we used to know...."

"Yeah?"

"Yeah," Smithberger says. "Jack Mockley."

"Oh yeah?"

"Yeah," Smithberger laughs. "I busted him."

"Really?"

"Yeah, it's a pretty comical story." He quaffs his beer. "I was working on this case...marijuana dealers...these guys who were operating out of the marina, they had this big old wooden cabin cruiser...one night we go down to this boat, this piece-of-shit tub...and there's four or five guys sitting there, putting the dope in plastic bags...there's pounds of the shit on the table...and these guys, they're all stoned, they're fucked up...the cabin is all smoky, you can barely see there's so much goddam smoke...and we come in, and none of these guys does much of anything, they just sit there, out of their fucking gourds, and they look at us, all glassy-eyed...and one of 'em is Jack Mockley...he's a two-bit player it turns out, a middleman at best, deals one or two pounds at a time, strictly local...anyway, he looks at me, and recognizes me, and starts talking to me, he starts trying to convince me that I should let him go, for old times sake...'Cmon Willy,' he says. 'You know me. You know me from Adams Street. I'm alright. I'm cool'...he's completely burned out...he's talking to me, making his case...and then he tries to get away...." Smithberger laughs. Pulls on his Heineken. "He knocks over some stuff and he climbs through this hatch...and he jumps off the goddam boat...of course the stupid bastard can't swim...."

I listen to Smithberger, but, as I listen, as I focus on his big pink head, I think to myself that I've got to terminate this reunion, that I've got to cut short this visit, this ill advised get-together with Willy Smithberger.

I've got to get out of here, I think.

I've got to remove myself from the premises.

Take off.

Split.

I don't want to have to stay for dinner, I think.

I can't think of anything that I might find more trying, more excruciating, than having to sit at the dinner table, for an hour, or maybe longer, with this transmogrified Willy Smithberger, this big clod, this cop. I know, I know that it would be an ordeal, a torturous exercise. I don't know, in fact, that I'd be able to endure it, that I'd make it through. I'm afraid, I'm afraid I wouldn't last, I'm afraid I might not be able to stand it, that I might fall apart, that after awhile I might be reduced to indistinguishable matter, that when all was said and done there might not be anything left of me, except a pile of grey ashes, dental fillings, the zipper from my Levi's, and a few sneaker eyelets.

As I listen to Detective Smithberger, I try to figure out how I might orchestrate a quick and relatively graceful exit from his suburban lair. I try to figure out how I might be able to excuse myself from having dinner with Smithberger and his wife and kids.

I try to form a strategy. I try to decide what I might tell Smithberger in an effort to explain why I won't be able to stay, why I won't be able to have dinner with him and Rosalind and his as-yet-unseen son and daughter.

I could tell him, I think, that I'm not feeling well...I could tell him that I'm just getting over the flu, and that I don't feel well enough to stay for dinner...or I could tell him that I think I'm coming down with something, the flu or something, and that I think I should go....

Or, I think, I could announce that I have plans to meet somebody, my brother perhaps, for dinner...I could tell Smithberger that I didn't realize I'd been invited for dinner, that I'd thought I was coming over simply to have a few drinks....

Smithberger goes on.

"I go up on the deck," he says, laughing, "and there's Mockley, splashing around, practically drowning...."

"What happened?" I ask.

"We had a coupla boats in the water, next to the fucking cabin cruiser...somebody pulled Mockley outta the soup...probably saved his goddam life...." Smithberger laughs. A lawman's rugged, satisfied laugh. The just rewards for a task neatly completed.

"What happened to Mockley?" I ask. "Did he go to jail?"

"Sure did," Smithberger says. "He got a nice chunk of time...eight, ten years, something like that...it wasn't the first time he'd been convicted, the fucker had a pretty long rap sheet...last I heard he was upstate somewhere...Dannemora, I think...he's probably still up there...."

❧   ❧   ❧

"Lemme put some more scotch in your glass," Smithberger says, grabbing my empty glass from the coffee table.

He goes into the kitchen, comes back, holding the tall glass with the yellow horizontal stripes. He hands me the glass, refilled with scotch and cubes. Then he sits on the couch beside Rosalind. He repositions his burly, bearlike body, depresses the abraded green and yellow cushions.

I sip the scotch.

I sit there, on the easychair, and I hold my glass, lift it, sip from it. I don't say much. I let Willy talk. I make a few truncated remarks, but for the most part I keep silent, I sip the scotch, and I nod toward Smithberger as he banters on.

Willy, perhaps recognizing my reluctance to speak, perhaps surmising that I've got some sort of social handicap, is more than willing to shoulder the bulk of the conversational load.

He tells the story of how he met Rosalind. He gives a thorough account of the genesis of his relationship with his now-wife, describing in adjective-laden detail the series of chance occurrences that linked him to her.

Willy's path intersected with Rosalind's for the first time in Macy's in the Sunrise Mall.

Willy was riding the escalator, going up.

And as he headed upwards, he farted. He cut a loud rippling fart.

He probably wouldn't've farted if he'd realized that an attractive blonde woman was riding the escalator, that this blonde woman was in fact just behind him, just two or three steps behind him.

The blonde woman, of course, was Rosalind.

Rosalind, needless to say, was appalled by the rude act perpetrated by the broadshouldered, windbreaker-clad man in front of her. She was also sickened, physically sickened, by the noxious fumes wafting directly at her. Gagging, she jogged swiftly up the moving steps, past Willy.

And as she hurried up the steps, she turned, and she looked back. And she saw Willy. And Willy saw her.

Rosalind disappeared into the Women's Clothing department.

But Willy knew. He knew, right then, that she was somebody he could fall in love with.

Six months later, Willy and a couple of his buddies went to an Islanders game.

The first period had begun when Willy, to his astonishment, espied Rosalind coming up the aisle, accompanied by a male personage.

Rosalind and her date sat down in the row in front of Willy and his cohorts. And as she sat down, Rosalind noticed Smithberger. And recognized him. And smiled.

At several points during the game Willy and Rosalind glanced at each other.

Between the second and third periods, Rosalind's boyfriend went to the concession stand, and while he was gone Willy caught Rosalind's gaze, and said, "How you doin?" and Rosalind said, "Okay."

Those were the only words they spoke.

And when Rosalind took off, toward the end of the third period, Willy was painfully disappointed, crestfallen. He figured he'd never see her again.

Then, a year later, Police Officer Willy Smithberger and his partner, Rudy, were chasing a burglary suspect across a succession of suburban backyards when Willy, attempting to scale a chain-link fence, was speared by an exposed metal prong.

The prong pierced Smithberger's upper thigh, went fairly deep into the flesh.

Willy was taken to the Nassau County Medical Center, where he had his leg stitched up and was given a tetanus shot.

And Rosalind was one of the nurses who attended to him. In fact, she gave him the tetanus shot.

And, in fact, while she was giving him the shot Willy asked her if she wanted to have dinner with him.

And, in fact, they had dinner a few nights later, at a restaurant on Main Street, a place called The Flying Bridge.

The Flying Bridge was noted for its superb seafood, but Willy, who ordered the swordfish, and Rosalind, who had the scallops, barely touched their food.

According to Willy, he realized at some point, while they were sitting at their cozy corner table, that he would marry her, that he would live with her for the rest of his goddam life.

After dinner they went to a bar, the Lion's Den, they sat in a dark booth, drank a number of cocktails, and talked and talked and talked, until the place closed.

It was 4am, but neither of them wanted to go home.

They drove, instead, to Biltmore Beach.

They sat in Willy's Chevy, watched the sun come up. All orange and shit.

And then they climbed into the backseat, and fucked, in ecstatic fashion.

They were engaged a few months later.

And they were married the following June.

"It happened fast," Willy says, concluding the romantic tale. "But I was sure. I was never so sure about anything in my life. It was the easiest decision I ever had to make."

"It was meant to be," Rosalind says.

"There's no doubt about that," Willy says, squeezing her knee, his stout policeman's fingers pressing her smooth perfect-fitting jeans.

"That's a great story," I say, but what I'm thinking, of course, is that it's one of the most banal, most idiotic stories I've ever heard. What I'm thinking is that they're extraordinarily shallow, limited people, this Willy and Rosalind. They haven't got any idea about what love is. They've got a mundane, suburban, television-generated understanding of what love is.

They're people, I think, who have never had, and never will have, the ability to grasp the poetry in things.

I hold my glass against my mouth, siphon off the last drops of booze. I haven't been at Willy Smithberger's that long, but I've already sucked down four, or five, scotches.

Pressing the glass to my mouth, I let an ice cube slide onto my tongue.

I rest the depleted glass against my leg, suck on the ice, crunch the cube with my sensitive silver-filled molars.

"Lemme get you another scotch," Willy Smithberger says, removing his onerous corpus from the couch.

I should say something, I think.

I should say something right now, I think.

I should tell Smithberger that I don't want another drink, that I'm going to take off in a few minutes, that I'm not going to be able to stay for dinner....

Or, at the very least, I should tell him that I'm going to have just one more drink, and that then I'm going to go....

I should tell him what I've got to tell him, I think, I should do it now...I should do it right now....

But I don't say anything....

I give him my glass....

❦   ❦   ❦

Smithberger returns from the kitchen, holding in one hand my glass, once again refilled with scotch and ice cubes, and in the other hand a bottle of Chivas Regal.

"This is your lucky day," he says. "I ran out of scotch. But I found this bottle of Chivas. Somebody gave it to me for Christmas a coupla years ago. I never opened it. Never drink the stuff. Never graduated from beer."

He puts the bottle on the coffee table.

"I hope you like Chivas," he says.

"I love it," I say.

"I kinda figured that might be the case," he says.

I nod. And I grin. But I feel angry. I can't help but think that Smithberger is merely patronizing me, I can't help but think that he's responding like this, in this benevolent fashion, because he thinks I'm sick, because he thinks I'm a drunk, a derelict, I can't help but think that in proffering this bottle of scotch he's merely attempting to attend to my dereliction. It seems, to me, like he's decided to assume the role of my caretaker. The way he's suddenly found this bottle. The way he's placed it so carefully on the table, so close to me. He's treating me, it seems, as though I'm a hapless sot.

The fat fuck!

I feel a wave of aversion, a black wave, passing through me, as I watch him, as I watch him set the bottle on the coffee table, as I watch him sit down next to Rosalind on the couch.

I've got to get the hell out of here, I think....

I definitely don't want to have to stay for dinner, I think....

"I'm going to put the lasagna in the oven," Rosalind says. She focusses on me. Her blue eyes are saturated, drenched through with compassion. She, too, obviously, believes that I'm a sick individual, an unfortunate spectacle.

"I made a lasagna," she says. "I hope that's okay, Peter."

I nod, almost imperceptibly.

If I'm going to try to get out of staying for dinner, I've got to say something *now*, I've got to say something *right now*....

This is the time to do it, I realize.

This probably will be my last reasonable opportunity, I realize.

If I don't say something now, I'm probably going to have to stay, I'm probably going to have to sit down at the dinner table with Willy Smithberger and his suburban clan....

I know, pretty much, what I want to say....

I don't need to go into any long explanations...I just need to make a simple excuse....

I'm sorry, but I don't think I'm going to stay for dinner...I'm not feeling that well...I really don't think I'm up to eating anything...I think I should probably go....

But I can't do it....

I can't mouth the simple, straightforward words...I can't propel the words from the back of my throat into the air....

I can't pull the trigger....

I can't do it, I can't even get close to doing it....

I can't do it....

"I love lasagna," I say.

"I'm glad," Rosalind says, smiling.

"You're not married?" Smithberger says.

Rosalind has gone into the kitchen, and Willy apparently figures that this is the appropriate time to have a man-to-man discussion. It's the right time to discuss what else, women, girls, chicks, broads, cunts.

"No," I report.

"Divorced?"

"No."

"You've never been married?"

"No."

"That boggles my mind," he says, laughing.

"Does it?"

"I guess I just can't conceive of what it must be like not to be married," he says. "I guess maybe because I've been married for so long."

"Yeah," I say. "I just haven't gotten around to it."

I lift my glass, take a long slug of scotch.

Smithberger tilts his beer.

"I was close a couple of times," I say, "but I never went through with it....." This, of course is a lie, a complete prevarication. I've never been close, I've never been within miles of getting married. I've given Smithberger this piece of false information primarily because I don't want him to think that I'm a homosexual.

"Got a girlfriend?" he asks.

"Uh, yeah...," I say.

"She live in Queens?"

"Uh, no...." I sip from my glass, try to decide on a suitable place of residence for a fictitious girlfriend, somebody I'd dig, thoroughly, if she existed. Finally I say, "She lives in Manhattan."

Smithberger nods, draws on his beer.

"What does she do?" he asks.

I bit the rim of my glass. If figure I could use Karen as the model for my supposed girlfriend. I'm not inspired, however, by this potential tack. I mean, there wouldn't be alot of noteworthy facts that I could present. I mean, what could tell him? That my girlfriend is a frustrated cellist who hasn't touched a bow in five years? That the object of my affection works as a receptionist in a podiatrist's office? That she spends the better part of her paltry take-home pay on therapy and antidepressants?

No, if I'm going to provide Smithberger with a portrait of a bogus girlfriend, I might as well create a completely different girlfriend, an interesting-sounding girlfriend, an exemplary girlfriend. I might as well try to impress him.

"She's an actress," I say.

"No shit," Smithberger responds.

"Yeah, she's an actress...."

"She must be a knockout," he says.

"She's alright," I say.

"She must be incredible."

"Yeah, she's okay...."

Smithberger guzzles his Heineken.

"She performs and stuff?"

"Yeah, sure."

"That's great."

"Don't get me wrong," I say. "She spends her fair share of time waiting tables...but she gets a decent amount of work as an actress...she gets a good number of acting jobs...."

"She ever on television?" Smithberger asks.

"Yeah, sure...." I'm not sure how far I want to go. I'm afraid that if I go too far, if I paint the picture of a truly exceptional woman, that Smithberger will begin to question my story, he'll start to think that I must be bullshitting, he'll start to think that it couldn't possibly be true, that a scurrilous character, a lowly dog such as myself, couldn't possibly be having a relationship with such a woman. Nevertheless, I tell him, "She does some TV...she's been on a few shows...she does commercials...she does different things...she's been in a couple of movies...."

"That's wild," Smithberger says.

"She's talented," I say matter of factly.

"She been in anything you think I mighta seen?"

"Maybe."

"Like what?"

"She was in Clint Eastwood's last movie...."

"Shit."

"I can't remember the name of it...."

"Yeah, I didn't see it...."

I bring my glass to my mouth, hold it, for awhile, against my teeth, let a good amount of scotch stream down, down my throat.

"She's been on some TV shows?" Smithberger asks.

"Yeah."

"Anything I'd know?"

"Maybe."

"Yeah? Like what?"

"She was in an episode of *Cheers*...."

"You're kidding." Smithberger laughs. "Roz and I watch *Cheers* all the time. I betcha we saw the episode she was in."

"Maybe you did."

"What episode was it?"

"I really don't remember...," I say. "I don't remember that much about it...it was on a year or two before we started going out...."

Willy nods, his big bald head reflecting the room's incandescent light, glinting.

"She played Sam's girlfriend...," I say. "She was actually on the screen for only about ten seconds...she walked into the bar and then walked out...."

"I bet I saw that episode," Smithberger says.

"You probably did."

"I'll have to look for it on the reruns," he says.

I nod, sip my scotch.

"What's her name?"

"What's my girlfriend's name?"

"Yeah. What's her name?"

"It's Vicki…," I say. "Vicki Sheridan…."

Vicki Sheridan was a girl, a pretty blondehaired girl, I'd had a crush on when I was in high school.

"Vicki Sheridan," Smithberger repeats the name.

"Yeah."

"I'll have to remember that."

He swigs his beer.

"Vicki Sheridan."

"Right."

"How long you been goin out with her?"

"About six months," I say.

"You think it's getting serious?"

"I don't know," I say. "I don't know if I want it to get too serious…."

"Why not? She sounds like a great chick."

"She is," I say. "She's cool…but, the thing is, I've just got too much going on right now…I'm trying to write this book…it's a big job…it requires alot of my energy, most of my energy…it's hard for me, at this juncture, to think about getting into anything too serious with anyone…."

"Yeah?"

"Yeah."

I drain the last half inch of scotch from my glass.

I grab the Chivas Regal bottle.

"How old is she?" Smithberger asks.

"My girlfriend?"

"Yeah."

"She's twenty-six," I say.

"Twenty-six! Jesus Christ!"

"Too young?" I pour some scotch in my glass, over a smattering of shrunken pea-sized ice cubes.

"It's not too young as far as I'm concerned." Smithberger laughs. "I just can't believe you're goin out with a twenty-six year old chick. That's unreal. More power to you, man."

"She's only thirteen years younger than me," I note, conspiratorially.

The portly detective laughs. His mustache flaps, like laundry hanging on a clothesline flapping in the breeze.

"Twenty-six!"

"It does have a nice ring to it," I say, "doesn't it?"

"It sure as hell does," he laughs.

Rosalind re-enters the living room.

She re-sits her exquisite ass on the couch.

"About fifteen minutes and we'll eat," she says. "I made a salad. And I'm heating up some Italian bread, to go with the lasagna. I hope that's okay, Peter. It's nothing too fancy."

"It sounds great," I say.

"Roz makes a fantastic lasagna," Willy says.

I nod, I move my head up and down, stiffly, not quite sure how to respond to Willy's prideful claim.

Then I tell Willy and Rosalind that, "I'm going to smoke a cigarette...."

I need a cigarette. I haven't smoked a single butt since I stepped inside Willy Smithberger's house. I need one badly. And, just as importantly, I feel like I need to get away, away from Smithberger, at least for a few minutes. If I'm going to have dinner with the rotund policeman and his family, and it looks like I am, then, the way I figure it, I'm going to need some time by myself, to calm myself, resuscitate myself, rebuild my strength, before I sit down at the table. To this end, I tell Willy and Rosalind that, "I'll go out-side…I don't want to bother you with the smoke and every-thing…."

"You don't have to go outside," Willy says.

"I don't mind," I say.

"It's not necessary," he says.

"I really don't mind," I say. "I'd actually kind of like to get some fresh air…."

"It's cold, Pete," he says. "It's thirty degrees. It's not even thirty…."

"I don't mind the cold," I say.

"Smoke your cigarette right here," he says. He looks at Rosal-ind. "You wanna get Pete an ashtray?"

Rosalind says nothing. Doesn't move.

"I don't have a problem going outside," I say. "I know that most people prefer it if you don't smoke in the house…."

"It doesn't bother me," Smithberger says. "My old man comes over here all the time and smokes like a goddam chimney. It's no big deal, Pete."

I check Rosalind. I'm guessing, judging by her reticence, that she isn't thrilled with the idea of somebody lighting up a Marl-boro, puffing away, blowing smoke into the relatively unpolluted living room air.

"I'll just go outside," I say, and, pinpointing my vision on Rosalind, I say, "That would be better, wouldn't it?"

"I really would appreciate it if you wouldn't smoke in the house," she confesses.

"Whatta you talkin about?" Willy spits. He scowls at her.

"I'm gonna go outside," I say. I edge off the easychair, place my glass on the coffee table.

"You don't have to," Willy insists.

"It's okay," I say.

"I don't want you to have to go out in the cold," Rosalind says. "It is cold. Maybe you could go in the garage."

"Jesus Christ," Willy groans.

"I'll go outside," I say. "Like I said, I wouldn't mind getting a little fresh air...."

"Are you sure, Peter?" Rosalind says.

"Yeah, definitely."

"This is nonsense, Roz." Willy glares at his wife. His mustache twitches like a rat undergoing electroshock.

Rosalind eyes her roly-poly spouse. She's not going to give in. Sometimes she does, sometimes she plays the subservient nurse to his macho detective. Sometimes she slips automatically into that role. But in certain carefully chosen situations she won't give up her ground. She won't permit him to move her, not an inch, not a fraction of an inch. And this is one of those situations.

She addresses Willy with a calm, contained force.

"Peter says he doesn't have any problem going outside."

Willy frowns.

"He's being very agreeable," she says. "And it would be nice if you'd be agreeable, too."

"Alright, alright," Willy sighs.

Rosalind looks at me.

"Thanks for being understanding, Peter."

"No problem."

I stand.

"I'll get you your coat," she says, getting off the couch.

"If you're gonna go outside," Willy says, "you should go in the backyard...it's nicer back there...."

"Okay," I say. I nod toward Smithberger, as though thanking him for the helpful suggestion. But I'm irked. I can't help but think that Smithberger has recommended that I go in the back-yard not because he wants me to enjoy a more pleasant setting, but because he's afraid that if I smoke in front of the house that one, or more, of his neighbors might notice me, might notice a dubious figure, standing on the front steps, slouching, inhaling a cancerstick, striking a classic malingerer's pose. I can't help but think that he's afraid that his reputation as an upstanding member of the community might be jeopardized.

I stand on the narrow cement patio adjacent to the kitchen door.

The cement is barren, the plastic outdoor furniture, barbecue grill, and children's toys having been removed for winter's frozen length.

I drag on my cigarette, exhale a thin line of smoke. The smoke, caught briefly in the diffuse light from the lamp above the door, filters into the backyard. It's a typical backyard, from what I can see, small, rectangular, lined with scrawny bushes, bordered by a wooden fence, graced with a solitary winterstripped tree. The scant green-brown grass, like the patio, is devoid of the usual signs of suburban life, simplified by winter's desolate turn.

I drag slowly on my Marlboro. I feel better. I feel significantly better. The outside air is very nearly rejuvenating. The air is cold, crisp. It's fresh, it's appreciably fresher, I notice, than the air that surrounds the South Shore Motel, which of course is permanently fouled, besmirched with exhaust fumes.

I flick ashes onto the patio, reasonably confident that the winter breeze'll scatter them, that my sordid tracks will be sufficiently erased. I study the yard. Try, for a moment, to find something, something meaningful, in the small endarkened plot. Something perhaps beneath the surface. Some clue. Some answer.

Still trying.

I laugh, scornfully, at myself.

You fool.

You jerk.

There's nothing here, I tell myself, I remind myself.

Nothing.

Nothing.

I take a final drag, bend down, stub the cigarette's burning end against the patio. I toss the extinguished butt behind a shrub. Then I kick the smudge, the blackish mark I've made on the cement. Don't want to leave any traces. Don't want to leave any evidence.

I kick the smudge several times.

Then, suddenly, I realize that, if I want, I can escape. I can take off. Nothing is stopping me. I can walk around the house, find the gate that leads to the street, and jog to my car, get in, and go…and if I can't find the gate I can climb the fence—I had climbed similar fences many times when I was a youth—I can scale the fence, and then I can run, like a Marine paratrooper, across Smithberger's lawn, to my car….

I can, I think. I can flee….

I step off the patio.

I don't know if I'm going to try to escape, but I want to investigate the possibility, I want to see what it feels like to begin to move in the direction of my freedom….

I walk on the decimated grass…I walk toward the side of the house…I walk slowly, practically in slow motion….

Then I hear the kitchen door opening. I hear the door clacking, screeking. And I stop. I freeze.

I look backwards.

Willy Smithberger, massive Willy Smithberger, the bear, the cop, is coming through the door.

"Hey Pete!" he says, walking across the patio, toward me.

I turn toward him.

"We're gonna eat in a coupla minutes," he says.

He shuffles across the patio. He isn't wearing a coat, but he doesn't seem cold, doesn't seem uncomfortable. Apparently his flannel shirt, and his tough cop's hide, and his not insignificant flesh, keep him warm, the way a bear's fur keeps him warm.

He walks across the grass.

He approaches me.

He stops, beside me, his workboots thlokking the hard ground.

"I was just looking at the backyard," I say.

"Yeah, it's not much of a yard," he says.

We both stare into the yard, at the patchy darkness.

"I wish we had a little more property," he says.

"It's not a bad yard," I say sympathetically. "It kind of reminds me of the yard we had when I lived on Jefferson Street."

"Yeah, it's like the yard we had, too." Willy laughs. "All these houses have the same layout."

"I guess so."

"I think I'm gonna get the kids some swings," he says offhandedly. "Swings, a slide, maybe monkey bars…they love that stuff…they've got these real nice swing sets nowadays, they're wooden, they're real sturdy…they're a helluva lot better than those metal deals we had when we were kids…they got all rusted up, fell apart in a coupla years…."

"I remember the swings we had," I say. "They were broken for years, you couldn't use them anymore, they were shot, but my old man never bothered to get rid of them…the damn metal frame was standing there, in the backyard, for years, for years, just the metal frame, with no swings attached to it…it was like some kind of goddam sculpture…."

Willy laughs.

And I find myself laughing. I find myself sharing a moment, a warmhearted moment, with this fat chrome-domed Willy Smithberger.

"I think about those days sometimes," Willy says.

"Yeah, I do, too," I say.

"That was a good time, wasn't it? When we were kids. In the old neighborhood."

"It was."

"You, and me, and Chris Adelkravitich, and Bobby Merton."

"Kevin Anderson, Louie Plunkett, Kenny Pelligrini, Mark Carroway."

"Yeah," Smithberger muses. "It wasn't such a bad place to grow up."

"I think about it alot," I say, with an increased solemnity. "Growing up around here. The stuff we used to do. Those days. I think about it alot."

"Yeah?"

"Yeah, I think about it alot." I decide to take a risk, to expose myself, to open up, a bit, to this bearish Willy Smithberger. "I guess," I say, "that I've always had this feeling that so much of who I am can be traced back to those days."

"Yeah, I think I know what you're talkin about," Smithberger says.

"I mean," I say, I venture forth, "I mean, for all intents and purposes, my life, my essential being, my elemental spirit, the core of who I am, the deep truth of what my life is about, was formed during those days…living on Jefferson Street…hanging out with everybody, with all the friends we had…riding bikes…playing baseball…playing baseball on the street…all those baseball games we played…those amazing games…."

"We played alot of baseball, didn't we?"

"We used to play all the time…we used to play every day…we used to play for hours…during the summer we'd play for hours and hours, we'd play all day long…."

"Yeah," Willy says.

"We used to play until it got too dark to see the damn ball...."

"Yeah."

I stare into the dark silent backyard.

"I think," I say, "that those were probably the best times I've ever had."

"Yeah," Willy says. "I think they probably were for me, too."

"Yeah."

"I remember when you broke your arm," he says.

"Yeah."

"That was something."

"You know, it was my father who broke it," I say.

I've never told anyone what I've just told Smithberger. For the past twenty-nine years I've stuck to the story I gave the school nurse. I've always said that I fell off my bike, that I crashed badly, and that, in the process, I wrecked my arm.

This is the first time I've revealed what actually happened.

"He beat the shit out of me," I say.

"Are you kidding?" Smithberger says.

"I mean," I say, "that was a fairly regular occurrence. He beat the shit out of me on a regular basis. But this time he really lost control, he got really fucking wild, really crazed. He kicked me. He fucking kicked me, and he broke my arm."

"Shit. You're serious?"

"Yeah," I say. "I was down on the ground, in the backyard, and he kicked me, he kicked me in the arm, boom, boom, boom, he kicked me a bunch of fucking times, he kicked me really hard, really viciously, like he was trying to kick a fucking football through a brick wall. He broke my arm in three places."

"Jesus Christ," Willy Smithberger says.

"Yeah," I say. "That was how it happened."

Willy and I go into the house.

We go into the dining room, an exceedingly narrow room squeezed between the kitchen and living room. The room barely holds a table and five chairs. A chintzy chandelier hangs down, over the table, disseminating harsh yellow light. The wallpaper, a mishmash of pink, blue and yellow flowers intertwined in an uncoordinated fashion, is blemished, peeling.

Rosalind has arranged the table in a pleasant, if not elaborate, manner. She's probably paid a little more attention to form and detail than she usually does, on an ordinary Saturday night. Dishes with yellow and gold crisscrossing lines and geometric shapes rest on a dark yellow tablecloth. A big pan, overflowing with Rosalind's prize lasagna, sits at the middle of the table, along with a ceramic bowl filled with greens and tomato, and a wood board adorned with a loaf of Italian bread.

Smithberger's children, Ben and Lisa Anne, are sitting at the table. They're beautiful kids. Ben is a pale, skinny boy with short brown hair. Lisa Anne is positively adorable. She's inherited a number of her mother's attributes, the blonde hair, the blue eyes. She's a budding angel.

Willy stands behind his daughter, tugs playfully on her blonde ponytail.

"Lisa Anne," he says. "This is my friend. His name is Pete."

The little girl looks toward me, sheepishly.

"Hi Lisa Anne," I say.

"Hi," she says.

"Ben," Willy says. "This is Pete."

Ben pivots his head, but keeps his gaze trained downwards, at the table.

"Hi Ben," I say.

"Hello," he says softly.

"Jesus Christ!" Willy growls. He rails at the kid. "Is that how you say hello to an adult! Look him in the eye when you say hello!

And speak up, for chrissakes! How many times do I have to tell you that!"

Standing next to Smithberger, I'm staggered, I'm shattered, by his sudden malice, his violence. If I'd been feeling a flicker of affection for Smithberger when I'd re-entered the house, I no longer feel anything like it. Standing there, watching the corpulent detective attack his son, I feel a rage. I feel a powerful rage. I feel a rage that transcends all of the other forms of rage that I typically experience. There is, of course, nothing, *nothing*, that infuriates me more than when a father abuses his kid. It scorches me. It inflames me.

"You wanna give it another try?!" Willy says.

Ben looks toward me hesitantly, fixes his small brown eyes on my standing form.

"Hello," he says, somewhat louder.

"Hi Ben. It's good to meet you," I say. I try to speak with an unmistakable kindness.

I offer the kid my hand. I want to extend myself to him. I want to let him know that I respect him, even if his father doesn't. I want to let him know that I support him. I want him to know that I'm his ally.

Ben grips my hand, wraps his thin fingers around my knuckles. We shake.

Willy Smithberger plants himself in the time-honored position at the head of the table. I sit next to him, across from the kids. I'm shaking, in the aftermath of Smithberger's attack on young Ben. I'm perspiring, the tee shirt under my sweater is sticking to my back, droplets of sweat slide down my armpits, down my flanks. I pick up my glass, which Rosalind, bless her heart, has refilled and placed next to my plate. I take a long swallow of scotch.

Rosalind enters the room, carrying a couple of bottles of salad dressing and a small container of apple juice. She puts the bottles on the table, rests the juice beside Lisa Anne's plate. She sits opposite Willy.

Everybody covers their plates with the gooey lasagna.

And then everybody starts eating.

Willy shovels huge clumps of lasagna into his mouth. He eats like bear gorging himself after passing the winter in a cave, hibernating. His jowls expand, his mouth curves, twists, his mustache wriggles. He says hardly anything, he makes a few inconsequential comments, his mouth stuffed with food, his words garbled, but for five, ten minutes he says almost nothing.

But then he turns, glares at Ben, and, in a hard admonishing voice, says, "I want to see you finish everything."

Ben acknowledges his father, then lowers his head, his brown hair shining in the excessive dining room light. He stabs the lasagna. He moves his fork tentatively inside the conglomeration of noodles, cheese, ground beef and tomato sauce.

"You hear me?" Willy says.

The boy glances apprehensively at Smithberger.

"You hear me, Ben?"

"Yes," Ben says.

"Leave him alone," Rosalind says. "He's doing fine."

Willy turns to me.

"The kid just picks at his food," he explains.

I nod grimly.

"He eats like a bird," Smithberger says.

I squeeze my fork.

"Like a sparrow."

Smithberger imitates a bird.

"Tweet. Tweet."

I drive my fork into the lasagna, the amorphous heap lying on my plate.

I'm enraged.

I find Smithberger's behavior inexcusable, the way he's lashing out at the kid, berating him, belittling him.

I thrust my fork, through the lasagna. The points hit sharply, scrape the plate.

I want to destroy Willy Smithberger. I want to crush him. I want to smash his bald head. I want to pummel his big gut.

Once again Smithberger imitates a small pathetic bird.

"Tweet. Tweet."

I put down my fork.

I stand up.

I've got to get away from the table, I've got to get away from Smithberger. I'm afraid that if I remain at the table, I'll lose it. I'll blow apart.

"Excuse me," I say.

I'm wobbling.

"I'm going to get myself a drink," I say.

"Want me to get it for you?" Smithberger asks.

"No, I can get it," I say, clutching my glass.

"You sure?"

"Yeah."

"I put the bottle in the kitchen," Rosalind says. "It's on the counter."

"Thanks," I say.

I scuffle into the kitchen. Find the bottle. Pour some scotch into my glass. My hands are quivering, the booze splashes against the sides of the glass, forms waves, spills. I bring the glass to my mouth, hold it, firmly, against my lips, take a slug.

Then, realizing that if Willy Smithberger turns his head he'll be able to see me, I move, I move out of Smithberger's line of sight, I slither along the counter, into a sort of alcove, a small dark area that houses a washing machine and a clothes dryer. I lean against the dryer. Sip the scotch.

I try to steady myself. I stare at the opposite wall, at a shelf that holds several boxes and bottles of laundry detergent, a big bottle of Clorox, a few other articles of the homemaker's trade. I try to focus my attention on a large orange box of Tide. Like a meditator attempting to put his full attention on his breath, I try to put my full attention on the box, just the box. And I try to let go of my virulent emotions, my rage.

I lean against the dryer and I scrutinize the orange box for a few minutes.

Then, finally, I hear Willy Smithberger's sharp policeman's snarl.

"Hey Pete! What's going on?!"

I walk back into the dining room.

"I'm sorry...," I say, and then I try to explain my lengthy absence, I provide my hosts, the Smithbergers, with what seems like a plausible excuse, in other words I lie, I tell them, "I don't feel well...I've got a bad headache, a bad sinus headache...I get these headaches every once in awhile, and it usually helps if I stand for awhile...."

"Can I get you something for it?" Rosalind asks, full of concern.

"No, thanks...," I say. I re-take my seat. "I took something before I left my place...I could feel it coming on, so I took something...unfortunately it doesn't seem to be working that well...."

"Oh, that's too bad," Rosalind says.

"Yeah," I say. "These headaches can be really painful sometimes...."

"Well," she says, "just let me know if you want something."

"Thanks," I say.

"We've got Tylenol, Ibuprofen, aspirin…."

"Thanks."

"Just let me know," she says.

"I will," I say.

I sit there, at the table, with Willy, Rosalind, Ben, Lisa Anne. I don't feel like I have any room, any space where I can put the food, the lasagna, the salad, the piece of bread, lying on my plate. I feel glutted, filled with alcohol, and filled with rage, but I figure I should try to assume the posture of the correct guest, I figure I should try to eat something, I figure I should try to put a dent in this bland, though not unpleasant, meal that Rosalind has prepared.

I lop off a fragment of lasagna. Put it in my mouth. Chew slowly.

Chewing, I look toward Rosalind as she turns her slim curved body, considers her son and daughter, says,

"Ben. Lisa Anne. Did you know that Daddy and Peter grew up together? They were friends when they were little boys."

"I've known Pete since I was Lisa Anne's age," Willy says. "Since I was four years old." He crams a tremendous hunk of lasagna into his mouth. A bulge forms in his cheek. "We lived around the corner from each other."

"I thought you lived on the same street," Rosalind says.

"No," Willy says, irritated. "I lived on Adams Street. Pete lived on Jefferson."

"I didn't realize that."

"I told you that."

"I guess I forgot."

"I guess."

Willy looks toward the children.

"Pete and me played together all the time when we were kids. Right, Pete?"

"That's right." I rest my vision on Ben and Lisa Anne. "Your dad and I played together just about every day when we were your age."

I try to smile, try to bend my mouth, try to form an upward curve.

"I guess it's probably hard for you guys to believe that your dad and I could've once been kids."

I keep my vision on them, expecting them to say something, expecting them to respond in that sweet, ingenuous, delightfully insightful way that children are so capable of responding.

But they don't say anything.

Ben leans over his plate, contemplates the mangled lasagna.

Lisa Anne glances furtively in my direction, as thought she'd like to speak, but isn't sure if it's permissible, if it's acceptable behavior.

"It's probably hard for you to believe that your dad and I were once your age," I say.

I smile, warmly, as warmly as I can, in these difficult circumstances.

"Can you believe that?" I say.

They don't respond.

"What do you think about that?" I say.

But, still, they don't respond. They don't respond in any way, they don't even respond in any sort of nonverbal fashion, they don't offer indicative facial expressions, they don't smile, they don't nod bashfully.

They're afraid, I realize, studying them. They're afraid to speak. They're afraid to present themselves to me. They've been battered, physically, I'd guess, and emotionally, I know for a fact, by their father, the malevolent cop, Willy Smithberger, and they're afraid to say anything, to do anything, because they know that if they say, or do, the wrong thing, or anything that might be perceived to be wrong, that they might very well incur Smithberger's potent wrath.

I pick up my glass, and I study them, I study them carefully, their pale faces, their little eyes, their small tense bodies. I study them with a heightened earnestness, with more earnestness than I've studied anything since I returned to Bayview.

And my heart breaks.

My heart disintegrates.

Because I know. I know what they're going through. I know what their suffering is like.

I know.

"When me and Pete were kids," Willy Smithberger tells his son and daughter, "we played alot of baseball."

He looks at me.

"Right, Pete?"

"Yeah," I say.

"We played all the time."

"Yeah."

"You shoulda seen this guy," Willy says. "He played with a bum arm, but he still played. It didn't stop him. He couldn't throw, but he still played. Played first base. Played it pretty good, if I recall."

"It was the only position they could put me at," I explain.

"It took alot of guts, man. Tryin to play with that arm."

"It took alot of foolhardiness."

"You never see kids nowadays playin baseball on the street the way we used to," Willy says disparagingly. "You never see'em playin ball. You never see it. I bought Ben a glove, I don't think he's ever used it." Smithberger eyes his son, asks him, "You ever use that baseball glove I got you?"

The boys looks up from his messy plate.

"Sometimes," he says.

"I've never seen you using it."

"I do sometimes."

"It's the middle of the winter," Rosalind intercedes. "You wouldn't see him using it this time of year."

"I didn't see him using it all last summer," Smithberger growls.

"I used it," Ben says.

"I remember you playing baseball," Rosalind says, turning toward the boy. "With Clifford Lewis. And some of your other friends."

"He's no ballplayer," Smithberger says disdainfully.

"For godssakes, Willy." Rosalind can't restrain her anger. "He's only seven years old."

"When me and Pete were seven we played baseball every day," Willy says. "We played every damn day. We played in the rain. We played in the snow."

Willy holds up his Heineken bottle, and, with a decided arrogance, pours a long stream of beer down his gullet.

"I don't know what the kid is doin," he says, "but he ain't playin baseball."

He takes another glug of beer.

"Maybe he's playin tiddlywinks," he says.

He laughs.

"Maybe he's playin with Lisa Anne's Barbie."

I stand.

I'm thoroughly enraged.

I grip the back of my chair.

I'm shaking, I'm shaking violently, I'm shaking like the last leaf, the last crinkled, desiccated leaf, the last leaf remaining on a tree in somebody's backyard in the middle of January, shaking in the uninterruptible winter wind.

"Excuse me," I say. I can barely talk.

"I've got to go to the bathroom," I say.

I go into the bathroom. Unzip my jeans. Piss.

The bathroom, in all likelihood, has been tidied up for the purpose of my visit. It's fairly immaculate. The toilet bowl, a light blue color, is devoid of stains and grime and random pubic hairs. The sink, also light blue, is equally spotless. The blue floor shines. The blue towels, hanging opposite the sink, are fluffy, fresh-looking, probably've just been laundered. A sharp ammonia smell, the sort of smell left by a household cleaner, tinges the air.

Finished pissing, I zip my pants. I put down the plastic toilet lid. And I sit on the lid.

I sit on the lid, elbows on my thighs, my hair hanging in my face, and I stare at the wall, I stare at the wallpaper, the peculiar design, light blue windmills, pink bicycles, butterflies, anvils, dachshunds. I try to concentrate on the wallpaper. I try to calm down.

I figure I'll stay in the bathroom for as long as I have to. I figure I won't go back into the dining room until my rage diminishes, at least some.

I sit on the toilet lid.

I stare at the wallpaper, try to locate a zone of peace, somewhere within.

After awhile, however, I begin to worry, I begin to worry about what Willy and Rosalind might be thinking, I begin to worry that they might wondering what I'm doing, that they might be wondering if I'm doing something I shouldn't be doing. They might, I think, be speculating that I'm taking drugs, that I'm snorting coke, or smoking crack, or something. Or perhaps, I think, they're hypothesizing that I'm performing a sexual act, that I'm jerking off, squirting jizz into the well-scrubbed sink....

But, finally, I decide that I probably don't have anything to worry about, that they're probably assuming that there's a logical explanation for my lengthy stay in the head. They're probably assuming, I decide, that I'm merely taking a dump, that I'm taking an ordinary, if protracted, crap....

I leave the bathroom.

I step into the dining room, intending to once again sit at the table, to once again attempt to eat some of Rosalind's lasagna....

But as I get near the table, as I get near Willy Smithberger, as I put my vision on him, as I get a whiff of his rank middleaged meat, I feel my rage flaring, escalating....

I'm not going to be able to sit down, I realize.

I walk past the table, past the fork-wielding Smithbergers.

Willy turns his head, looks toward me, suspiciously.

Rosalind shifts her pretty head, toward me.

Ben and Lisa Anne glimpse me.

"I'm going to make myself a drink," I say, picking up my glass.

I go into the kitchen.

I pour some scotch in my glass.

I slide into the little room that contains the Smithbergers' valued appliances. Lean my butt against the dryer. Drink the scotch.

I empty the glass.

I still don't feel ready, however. I still don't feel ready to go into the dining room, to sit at the table, next to Willy Smithberger, within his arm's reach, his hairy animal arm's reach.

I'll smoke a cigarette, I figure. I'll go outside, into the backyard, smoke a cigarette.

The only problem, as I see it, is that I'm going to have to walk back through the dining room, past the lasagna-chomping Smithbergers, in order to get my leatherjacket, which is in the living room, draped over the couch. I need the jacket, not just because it's the middle of the goddam winter, but because my Marlboros are in the front pocket.

I certainly don't want to have to walk through the dining room, past Willy and Rosalind and Ben and Lisa Anne, but I don't have any choice, I'm going to have to, I'm going to have to make the difficult journey.

I step into the dining room.

I shuffle past the table.

"I'm going to smoke a cigarette," I indicate.

I get my jacket. I pull it on. Then, once again, I walk through the dining room, past the Smithbergers. I stay close to the wall, I brush the wallpaper with my shoulder, and I keep my head down, I look down, at the carpeting.

I go into the kitchen, and as I move to the door that opens to the backyard, I hear Lisa Anne say, "Is he going out?"

"Yes," Rosalind says. "Just for a minute."

"It's cold, isn't it?" the little girl says.

"Yes," Rosalind says. "That's why he got his coat."

I stand on the patio, drag slowly on my cigarette.

I finish the cigarette. But I don't go back into the house. I stand on the blank cement, my hands in my pockets, and I stare into the backyard, into the darkness. I stand there for awhile, for ten, fifteen minutes.

Finally Rosalind opens the kitchen door, pokes her blonde head into the chilly night air.

"Peter...," she calls.

I turn, slightly, toward her.

"Peter…come on in…," she says, calling me the way she might call the family dog, the way she might call a benign, but sometimes recalcitrant mutt.

"Come on…," she says.

I go back into the house.

I go back into the dining room.

I sit down.

I stare at my plate, still burdened with most of the lasagna I initially put there, most of the salad, the better part of the piece of Italian bread. I stick my fork into the lasagna. Slice off a small chunk. Put it in my mouth.

The lasagna, to be truthful, isn't bad. It's not the best lasagna I've ever had, it's not as good, for instance, as the lasagna you get at Divini's on Queens Blvd, but it's not the worst I've ever had. It's good serviceable suburban lasagna.

I just don't feel like I can eat much.

"Finish up," Willy Smithberger says. Willy's plate is empty, like a strip mall parking lot at 5am. He's finally surrendered his all-out assault on his wife's lasagna. Rosalind and the kids also seem to have expended their desire to eat any more lasagna. At this point nobody's paying alot of attention to what's left on their plate.

"I'm afraid I don't have much appetite…," I tell Smithberger. "I just don't feel well…."

"That's too bad," he says, without an ounce of compassion.

For the next several minutes I jab halfheartedly at my plate. I swallow a few ragged shards of lasagna, a few torn bits of lettuce. I gnaw lethargically on the bread.

Then I give up.

I lay down my fork.

I sit there, silent. I look down, study the yellow tablecloth.

Finally Rosalind turns, smiles, asks me, "Do you think you're going to want to eat more?"

"I don't think so…," I say.

"I'll take your plate then," she says.

She stands, her blonde strands realigning, falling against her shoulders, her breasts.

I hand her my plate, say, "I'm sorry I didn't have more of an appetite…."

"Don't worry about it, Peter," she says.

"The lasagna was great," I say.

"Thanks," she says.

She picks up Ben's and Lisa Anne's plates, asks, "Do you think you're going to want dessert, Peter?"

"I don't think so…," I say.

"Maybe you'll have something later," she says. "I've got a cherry pie. And plenty of ice cream."

She looks toward the children.

"You guys want some dessert?"

"Yeah," Ben responds.

"I want ice cream," Lisa Anne says.

Willy turns his big bald head, focusses his redveined eyes on me.

"I should probably pass on dessert myself," he says.

I nod.

"Let's go in the den," he says. "The Knick game is on."

"Oh yeah?"

"They're playin the Celtics."

"Can I watch?" Ben blurts out.

"You can watch upstairs," Willy says, in a hard abrupt voice.

Ben nods, knocked down, rejected.

"Cmon Pete," Smithberger says. He pushes away from the table. "Bring your bottle if you want."

"Actually," I say, "I was thinking that I would get going...."

"Whatta you talkin about," Smithberger says. "You just got here."

"This headache is pretty bad," I say. "I should go...."

"Cmon," he says. "Watch the game with me."

"I'd like to...," I say, "but this headache is really killing me...I really should go home...."

"Cmon," he says. "Stay awhile."

"I wish I felt like I was up to it...," I say. "I just feel lousy...."

"Cmon," he says. "Who knows when we're gonna see each other again."

"That's true."

"Cmon Pete." Smithberger grins. "You got the Knick game on the tube. You got a bottle of Chivas Regal. What more could you ask for?"

"You've got a point."

"Stick around," he says.

"I should probably go, I should probably go home and go to bed...," I say.

"Cmon." He clamps my shoulder with his strong cop's paw. "Watch the game with me."

I study Smithberger's pink face, his eyes, his big drooping walrus mustache.

"Whatta ya say?" he says, grinning, squeezing my shoulder through my worn sweater.

"Alright...," I breathe.

"Good man," he says.

"I'll watch a little of the game...," I say, "then I'm gonna go...."

Smithberger's den is prototypical middleclass suburban fare, a constricted room, an afterthought of a room, appointed with cheap furniture, lined with cheap panelling, decorated with cheap five-and-dime paintings. Smithberger sits on a big green recliner that's bandaged with strips of duct tape. I rest my drunken carcass on the beat-to-shit couch. In front of us, an enormous TV flashes the Knicks-Celtics game.

"You like the Knicks?" Smithberger asks.

"Yeah, sure," I reply, weakly. The fact is, I'm an ardent Knicks fan. But I don't want to give Smithberger the satisfaction of knowing this.

"I watch, but sometimes it's hard to get into it," Smithberger says. He checks the screen. The Celtics spindly point guard dribbles to the top of the key, throws up an errant jump shot. Ewing, the Knicks center, grabs the rebound.

"It's hard to identify with these guys," he says. "They make so much fucking money."

"They do," I say.

"Maybe I wouldn't have such a hard time if they had a few more white guys on the team," he says. "I think they got one. And he sucks." Smithberger laughs, rubs his mustache with the end of his beer bottle. "He never plays. And that's it. They got just the one guy. Everyone else is a coon."

I nod, pressing my lips together unsympathetically.

"It's not the same game," he says. "It's changed."

"Everything changes," I remark, acerbically.

"I guess so."

"Except Bayview, right?"

"Bayview's changed," Smithberger says.

"I suppose it has."

"It's definitely changed."

"Everything changes," I say. "Everything remains the same."

Smithberger eyes me, curiously. Pulls on his beer.

"Still aren't any blacks living around here," I say. "No minorities at all. It's still lily white."

"That's not exactly true," Smithberger says.

"No?"

"We've got a few black families living in this neighborhood," he informs me.

"I didn't think they let blacks into Bayview."

"You gotta remember, this ain't Bayview. It's North Bayview."

"I guess it's completely different."

"It is. It's a whole different ball game. You might find a black family or two living in Bayview, but you'd have to search like hell to find'em. But North Bayview is a different story. We've had Orientals and some Hispanics living in this neighborhood since we bought the house. And now some coons are movin in. Not a whole lot. It's not an influx or anything. But in the last coupla years there've been some black families that've moved in around here."

I wedge my glass against my mouth and teeth, take an extended slug of scotch. The bottle of Chivas Regal stands beside me on a scratched wooden end table. The bottle, by now, is filled with more air than scotch. There isn't much booze left.

"I guess," I say, "that it's a little upsetting, having blacks moving in…."

"I really don't care that much," Smithberger says.

"No? You don't?" I participate in the dialog in an agreeable manner, as though I have an affinity for Smithberger's way of seeing things. Of course, I don't. As far as I'm concerned, he's a pointblank racist. I pretend to empathize with his fucked-up view because I want Smithberger to expose himself. I want to infiltrate the storehouse of his hateful racist attitudes. In effect, I'm going undercover, I'm gathering evidence, evidence that will prove Smithberger's guilt. In effect, I'm playing detective, I'm turning the tables on Detective Smithberger.

"I don't care if some coons move in," he says. "Not as long as they're middleclass, middleclass coons. You know, business types, white-collar coons. College-educated coons. I've got no problem with that. That's okay. As long as they don't turn the place into a fucking slum, I really don't give a damn."

"So from what you can tell," I say, "you think that the blacks who are moving in are middleclass? You think they're business people? Professionals?"

"I figure they gotta be," Smithberger says. "This black family that just moved into this place around the corner, on Belmont Street, they moved into this real nice split, with a big fucking extension off the side of the house, a fucking finished basement, a built-in fucking pool. Place musta went for two hundred grand. Maybe more. I mean, you can't afford to buy a place like that if you ain't makin pretty good dough. You can't afford a place like that if you're workin some bullshit job, if you're a porter in some goddam office building."

"Makes sense," I say.

"Rosalind says she saw the wife at the Grand Union. Says she seemed like a real upwardly mobile type. Like that broad on *The Cosby Show*. You know?"

"Uh huh."

"The kids are in Ben's school. Ben says they're okay. Although I don't think he really knows'em."

"That must be tough," I say. "Being a black kid in a predominantly white school."

"I guess." Smithberger slugs his beer. "It would be a helluva lot tougher for a white kid in an all-black school."

"Why do you say that?" I ask.

"A white kid in a black school would get his head kicked in every day of the week," Smithberger says. "Nothing really bad happens to the black kids in Ben's school. Hell, they're practically fucking celebrities. But a white kid, if he was in a black school, he'd get the shit beat out of him on a daily basis. It'd be part of the fucking curriculum."

"You think?"

"I know. A kid like Ben, he wouldn't last a week in a black school. They'd eat him up alive. There wouldn't be anything left of him when they were done with him."

"You think it would be that bad?"

"I have no doubt about it."

I sip my scotch, glimpse the television. Ewing taking his trademark fallaway jumper.

"Do you think more black families will move in around here?" I ask, with a measured nonchalance. "Do you think it's a significant trend?"

"I don't know," Smithberger says. "I don't know if there's a pattern developing. I kind of think that so far most of the cases where blacks have moved in have been isolated incidents."

"How would you feel if it was a developing pattern?" I ask. "How would you feel if this became a fully integrated neighborhood?"

"I don't know...," Smithberger says. "I guess it wouldn't bother me...I got nothing, basically, against the coons...."

I nod.

"I would just hope that what I've seen happen in some other places doesn't happen here...."

"What do you mean?"

"Sometimes, when blacks start movin into a neighborhood, sometimes the white people, the people who've been living there all along, for years, sometimes they get scared...they get scared, and they start movin out...and more and more blacks start movin in...and pretty soon all the whites are sellin their houses because they're afraid that the neighborhood is gonna turn into a black neighborhood...and then, because everybody is sellin, then everybody fucking panics, they start getting desperate, and they start sellin for next to nothing, they're practically givin their houses away...and then, because the houses are sellin for almost nothing, then you start getting lower class blacks movin in, they start movin in from the Bronx, from Harlem...and before you know it the neighborhood has turned into a goddam ghetto...that's what happened in Davis Park...the whites all got scared and moved out and the place turned black...now they got all kinds of problems, all kinds of crime, drugs, crack, they're sellin it everywhere, they got prostitutes on Whitworth Avenue walkin up and down the street wearin silver miniskirts...it's a fucking zoo...."

"I didn't realize that," I say.

"I would just hope that that wouldn't happen here," Smithberger says.

"You think it could?"

"I don't know, I don't think so...." Smithberger brings his beer to his mouth. Since I've arrived, he's knocked down six, maybe seven, maybe eight Heinekens. He's obviously soused. He slugs the beer. Studies the TV. Then looks toward me, a glint of seriousness in his bloody eyes. "I'd really hate to see this place change too much," he says. "I've always liked it here."

"You must."

"I do, Pete."

"You must. You've lived here your whole life."

"I've never had any urge to leave," he says.

"I guess you and me are different," I say, cynically. "I've never had any urge, any urge whatsoever, to live in the suburbs."

Willy laughs.

"I don't think I could live in the city," he says. "I know I couldn't. I can't stand the place, to be honest with you. Roz and I take the kids in once or twice a year, to the circus and the Radio City Christmas Show, and that's it. That's more than enough for me."

"Yeah, we think in exactly the opposite way," I tell Smithberger. "I can't stand the suburbs."

I sip my scotch.

"I hate the fucking suburbs," I say.

I take another sip.

"I'd never want to live around here," I say. "*Never.*"

"You don't think the day might come when you might wanna live around here? In Bayview? Or somewhere around here?" Smithberger doesn't seem rankled, doesn't seem upset by my less-than-positive stance regarding his beloved suburbs. He stares at the TV. The Celtics center, Robert Parish, executing an uncannily serene dunk shot. "You don't think you might wanna come back some day? This is where you're from. It's where you grew up. Like you said before, this place has always been important to you."

"I would *never* move back here," I say. I can't defer my anger. "That would *never* happen."

"What if you decide to settle down? What if you decide to marry this chick you've been seein, this actress?"

"I'm a long way from doing that," I say.

"Let's just say," Willy continues. "Let's just say you marry her, and you have a couple of kids. You don't think you'd wanna get out of the city? You don't think that Bayview would be a good place to live?"

"No," I say. "I don't."

"No? You'd bring up your kids in the city? You think that's such a good idea?"

"I don't know that it's necessarily such a bad idea," I retort. My anger, my rage, is rising quickly. Like fire. I'm warm. I'm trembling. And, speaking with an increased intensity, I go on, saying,

"I know that I could *never* live around here. *Never.* I could *never* do it. If I know anything, it's that there's *nothing* here for me. There's *nothing* here for me, Willy. *Nothing.*" I sip my scotch. I look at Willy Smithberger, and I say, "I've been coming around here every now and then lately, sort of doing research for this book I'm writing, and one of the most powerful, one of the most profound things I've come to understand is that this place is dead for me…it's dead…it's as dead as the corpse in my father's grave…it's as dead as the corpse in my mother's grave…as far as I'm concerned, it's dead, it's fucking dead…."

Ben Smithberger, clad in his pajamas, walks shyly into the den. He steps toward his father.

"Good night," he says.

"Good night kid," Willy says. He hooks his arm around his son's small knobby shoulders, yanks the boy to his chest, kisses him on top of his brown hair.

"Good night Ben," I say. "It was really good to meet you."

Ben glances at me.

"Good night," he says dutifully.

And then he goes. He pads across the tile floor, his bare feet nudging the worn linoleum.

And he leaves the room.

I pour more scotch into my glass. I lift the glass to my mouth, take a long slow drink, let the booze flow slowly down my ravaged throat.

I put the glass on the end table.

I look at Willy Smithberger. I look directly at Willy Smith-berger. I study Willy Smithberger, fat, bald Willy Smithberger, this malignant Willy Smithberger, this gruesome incarnation of my boyhood friend.

I move forward. I perch my ass on the edge of the couch, and I scrutinize Willy Smithberger.

I lean forward, look right at him.

I feel like I might as well say anything I want to say. I feel like I've got nothing to lose.

"I gotta tell you," I say, "I thought it would be different, coming here."

Smithberger, staring at the TV, says, "Yeah?"

"Maybe I was crazy, but I was kind of expecting it to be a powerful experience."

Smithberger laughs. "It hasn't been, huh?"

"Unfortunately, no, it hasn't. It hasn't been nearly as powerful as I thought it would be."

I pick up my glass, take a quick sip.

"There was a time," I say, "when I thought that coming here, seeing you, making contact with you after all these years, would be inspiring...I thought I'd find something, I thought I'd find answers, to something, to something I've been trying to figure out for a long time, a fucking long time...I thought I'd find some kind of release, or redemption, or affirmation, or validation, or insight, or enlightenment...."

"Oh yeah?"

"I thought I'd be able to make some kind of connection...to something...I thought, I guess, in a strange way, that I'd find the kid I grew up with...."

"Oh yeah?"

"I thought I'd find the kid I played with, the kid I played baseball with...I thought I'd find the Willy Smithberger I played with on the street, on those perfect summer afternoons, the pavement glistening, the sun slanting down...that's the Willy Smithberger I was thinking I'd find...."

"Instead you found a fat old fuck. A fat old fuck who's lost his hair." Smithberger laughs, a chopped-off, ironic laugh. "Is that the way you look at it?"

"Precisely."

"I guess it couldn't be avoided."

"I guess not."

"If I had my way," Smithberger says, "I wouldn't've lost my hair. I wouldn't've gotten old."

I take a quick sip of scotch.

Then I go on.

"I'm not delusional...," I say. "Although it may appear that I am...." My words make big gashes in the dull TV-lit atmosphere. "I knew I wouldn't find an exact replica of the Willy Smithberger I knew...I knew I wouldn't find a four foot, seven inch Willy Smithberger...but I thought I'd find a reasonable facsimile of the kid I used to know...but you don't even faintly resemble the Willy Smithberger I used to know...."

Smithberger snorts. His mustache bends. He's been trying, like a good cop, to maintain a certain equanimity, but now he can't help but show his annoyance, his disgust.

"You've really changed," I say. "You've changed, Willy. You've changed *alot.*"

"That's what happens," he says brusquely. He checks the TV. Robert Parish throwing a long outlet pass.

"I mean, it's incredible how much you've changed. I mean, physically you're not recognizable, that goes without saying...I didn't recognize you at all when you came to the door.... If I had run into you somewhere, I never would've recognized you. If I'd been in the deli, or something, and you were right in front of me, standing at the counter, ordering a ham and cheese sandwich, or something, I wouldn't've recognized you. I wouldn't've recognized you if you'd knocked into me. I wouldn't've recognized you if you'd kicked me in the nuts…. But it's more than just a physical thing. You've undergone more than just a physical transformation. It's more than that. It's alot more than that."

"Oh yeah?"

"It's an intangible thing."

"Is that right?" He glares at the TV.

I bob against the edge of the couch, the bones in my ass pressing the wooden skeleton, the couch groaning, creaking. I slide my hands through my hair. And then I continue forth, forward, unrestrainedly, I say,

"I don't know quite how to put it, Willy…I guess the only way to put it is that you've turned into a real *adult. A genuine adult.*"

"What'd you expect, Pete?"

"I don't know, I guess I didn't expect to find such an adult figure, such an irrefutable example of the adult form…. It's just kind of sad…."

"I guess it is," Willy says. He gives me a skeptical look. He thinks, quite obviously, that I'm some kind of madman.

He puts his vision on the TV. A Celtics player is standing at the foul line. Willy examines the screen. The Celtics player makes a couple of free throws. The Knicks and Celtics run up and down the court several times.

Finally Smithberger turns to me.

"You finish that?" he asks, angling his big cranium toward the Chivas Regal bottle.

"Not quite," I respond.

He returns his attention to the TV.

For a few minutes the room is quiet. The only sound is provided by the Knicks' announcer, Marv Albert, droning in his familiar nasal tone, and the radiator, belching and ticking.

Then Smithberger speaks.

"The Knicks should beat these fuckers," he says, keeping his gaze on the TV.

"Yeah," I say.

"They always have problems with the Celtics when they play'em in Boston," he says.

I'm not oblivious. I'm not blind to what's going on. I realize that Smithberger has no desire to continue to discuss the subject I've introduced, the subject of his transformation and my accompanying disillusionment. I know that he wants to avoid the discussion, to shove it as far out of sight as he can get it. But I'm determined to keep the discussion going.

"I really thought I'd feel inspired," I say.

"So how *do* you feel?" Smithberger asks wearily.

"I feel empty," I say. "I feel a profound emptiness."

"That's too bad."

"Yeah. It is."

Smithberger contemplates the television. He says nothing.

I sip my scotch. And for awhile I, too, remain silent.

The third quarter ends, Oakley scoring on a tap-in just before the buzzer.

Commercials flash, brash colors, loud voices, loud clangy music. Smithberger studies the screen, intently.

Graphics delineating the third quarter statistics are thrown up, and Willy inspects them with a keen eye.

Finally I break in.

"Can I ask you something, Willy?"

"Yeah, sure."

"It's just that I've been here for a couple of hours. I've been observing how you live.... I've been coming out here alot, like I said, doing my research, making my observations of suburban life, and I was wondering, I was wondering: *Do you ever feel a sense of responsibility?*"

"What?"

"*Do you ever feel a sense of responsibility?* Do you ever feel a sense of responsibility for what's going on in the world? For what's going on in this country? I wonder about that alot when it comes to people like yourself who've entrenched themselves in the suburbs. It seems to be a particular characteristic of suburbanites not to want to have anything to do with anything that's going on beyond the boundaries of their own neighborhoods, or, more accurately, beyond the boundaries of their own houses, their own fenced-in yards."

Smithberger eyeballs me, his big round pink face blotched with contempt.

"So what I was wondering is, do you ever feel a sense of responsibility?" I speak rapidly, recklessly. I know I'm losing hold. But I don't care. I want to lose hold. I want to lose it, totally lose it. I want to let go of everything. Fling everything. "Do you ever feel that the problems we have in this country, problems like poverty, like violence, like racism, all the different forms of oppression, the rampant materialism, the incessant struggle to acquire possessions, the desire to achieve financial gain at the expense of everything else, the general state of suffering that most people live in, the despair, the misery, the anguish, the anger, the hatred, the greed, the great unending unhappiness, the deep embedded depression, do you ever feel that it's your responsibility, as a citizen in the democratic society, as an American, as a human being, to do something about what's going on, to make some sort of contribution to the betterment of the society, to help to alleviate all the suffering? Do you ever feel that you have a responsibility to help improve the way things are? Do you *ever* think about that?"

"I think that as a police officer I do my part," Smithberger says.

"As a police officer you enforce the laws. You arrest people who've done something wrong, who've already fucked up. What you do is a reaction, perhaps, to wrongdoing, but it doesn't help to alleviate wrongdoing."

"I don't know what the hell you're talking about," he says disgustedly.

"I think you do."

"I don't, Pete. I honestly don't."

"I think you know precisely what I'm talking about," I say, "even if you don't know what I'm talking about."

"Jesus Christ."

"I think you do."

"It's a bullshit conversation."

"No it isn't."

"Yes it is."

"I just want to know," I say, "if you ever think about doing anything to help to change the world."

"Jesus." Smithberger laughs, deprecatingly.

"It's always been my belief," I say, "that every man, every person in the democratic society, is responsible for the condition that the society, the nation, finds itself in. *Every man* is accountable. *Nobody* is exempt. *Everyone* is responsible, Willy. But the problem is, *people don't want to accept their responsibility.* What I've come to see, as I've made my little survey of suburban life, is that a tremendously large, tremendously significant, portion of the population has retreated to the suburbs. *Retreated.* Retreated is the key word here. They've *retreated.* They've barricaded themselves inside their houses, they've boarded up the windows, and they've closed themselves off from what's going on, they've separated themselves from the filth, the viciousness, the plain horror, the omnipresent despair, the interminable suffering, the truth. They've separated themselves from the truth. *They've separated themselves from the truth.* From the fact that this country is disintegrating. *Fucking disintegrating.* They don't care. As long as they've got food in the refrigerator, and enough resiliency in the couch cushions, and good reception on the TV, they don't care. They don't know how to care. That's what I'm starting to see, Willy. *They don't know how to care.* They're too fucking numb. All across this country we've got these immense sprawling suburbs, inhabited by millions upon millions of people, we've got all these fucking people living in these suburbs, and every one of them is numb. They've all shot themselves full of psychic novocaine, with all the television they watch, all the videos they rent, with their goddam relentless forays to the mall, with all the shit they buy, the endless accumulation of things, countless things. They've numbed themselves. They've become zombies. Fucking zombies. And the last thing they want is to accept their responsibility for what's happening to the world. That's absolutely the last thing they want. And yet, and I believe this with all my heart, all my soul, the only way things are ever going to change is if these very people, these very people who've sequestered themselves inside their suburban fortresses, the only way things are ever going to change is if they do something. The only way things are ever going to change is if these very people decide to take responsibility. The government isn't going to change things. That's what everybody who lives in a place like Bayview is hoping, counting on. But the fucking government is never going to change anything. The only way things are ever going to change is if the people take responsibility. The people. *The people who live in the suburbs.* The Average Suburban Americans. The Blind Suburbans. They're going to have to be the ones to change things. They're going to have to be the ones. Because, when you come right down to it, Willy, they're the *only ones* who can change things. Because, *who else* is going to change things? *Who else?* They're the only ones, ironically enough, who can change the world."

Smithberger regards me, disdainfully.

"I think that's alot of sixties crap," he says. "Changing the world. Fuck. I've got my hands full, trying to do my job, support my family, take care of my kids, make sure my wife is satisfied. There's enough for me to do right here. More than enough. I can't even think about changing the world. That's so far outta my realm I can't even think about it."

"I see." I nod my head incrementally.

I grab the Chivas bottle. Pour a little more scotch into my glass. It's not an easy task, the way my hand is shaking, the way my arm is shaking, the way my whole body is shaking.

I slug the scotch. There's no ice in the glass, the scotch is lukewarm, it burns, scorches my throat, going down.

"I'm gonna change the subject," I say. "I want to ask you something else, in the spirit of this research I've been doing."

"What?" Smithberger groans.

"I was wondering if you ever experience real joy, Willy. You know the kind of joy I'm talking about. The kind of joy we experienced when we were kids. Pure joy. Ecstatic joy. That limitless joy. That kind of joy that comes from just being alive. *Just being alive.* Do you ever experience that kind of joy?"

"I don't know." Smithberger would rather discuss almost anything else. He'd rather discuss Rosalind's lasagna recipe. "It's not something I think about."

"I'm not asking if you think about it," I say, increasing the force I put behind each word, each syllable. "I just wanna know if you ever *feel* it. If you ever *feel* that kind of joy. If you ever *feel* any kind of joy."

"I'm a happy guy, for the most part," he says, begrudgingly.

"Yeah, that's cool," I say. "But I'm not asking if you're happy. This is an entirely different thing. I'm asking you if you ever feel *joy*! Unfettered, transcendent *joy*!"

"Who knows?"

"That's what I want!" I tell him. I'm practically screaming. My ass bounces against the couch. My body jerks. "I want joy! I want a joyful life! I don't want to live a mundane bullshit life! I did that for years! Fucking years! Working as a salesman! A goddam motherfucking salesman! Just like my old man! Killing myself! Dying! I don't want to live like that anymore, Willy! I want to get beyond the dull tragedy of everyday life! I want joy!"

I stand. I stand on the besmirched suburban linoleum. I stand, wobblylegged, and I shake my fist at the panelled walls. "I want to experience the joy of life! I want to sing! I want to dance! I want to fuck! I want to play, Willy! I want to play!"

I stand there, on the dismal linoleum, vibrating.

I glance at the TV. The Knicks, the Celtics, moving, a mishmash of colors.

Out of the corner of my eye, I discern Smithberger. Holding his beer to his mouth. Scowling. His mustache squirming like a rabid hamster. He'd probably like to dispose of me, quickly and efficiently, the way he disposes of petty criminals during his daily rounds as a suburban lawman. Probably wishes he could cuff me, throw me in the back of a squad car, and, if I try to say something, smack me a few times with a billyclub.

I turn, partways, toward him.

I tell him, "I've gotta take a leak...."

I go into the bathroom.

I feel incoherent.

Sick.

Everything is moving, shifting, sliding, out of sync. The walls slide, as though rolling on greased runners.

I kneel in front of the toilet. Puke.

I stay there, kneeling, my knees pressing the blue tile, my head suspended above the bowl. Then, with a struggle, I stand. I splash cold water on my face. I collect a hunk of toilet paper, clean the toilet, wipe off the brownish streaks, the tiny bits of regurgitated food sticking to the previously immaculate rim.

I sit on the bowl, piss.

I stand, zip my pants.

I still feel incoherent, fuzzy. But I know what I'm going to do. I'm going to go. I'm going to go into the den and tell Willy Smithberger that I'm going to go, and then I'm going to go, I'm going to take off.

I exit the bathroom, shuffle, stumble, down the hall, toward the kitchen. Still aspiring to be the proper guest, I want to say goodbye to Rosalind, I want to thank her for her sincerely hospitable efforts.

I step into the kitchen.

Rosalind is standing at the sink, holding a large plastic serving spoon under the running faucet. I watch her. I watch her place the spoon in the dishwasher. I watch her bend to the machine. I watch her ass, protruding, stretching the threads of her jeans. I watch her blonde hair, nestling against her shoulders with an exhilarating haphazardness. I wouldn't mind taking her right now, I think. No, I think, I wouldn't mind it at all. Taking her from behind. Unsnapping her jeans. Draping her over the dishwasher. Kneading her ass. Sticking my prick up into her undoubtedly delectable snatch. Again and again.

"I'm going to get going," I say.

She turns.

"I just wanted to thank you," I say.

"Oh, you're welcome, Peter." She wipes her fingers on the front of her jeans. "It was nice to meet you."

"It was nice to meet you."

"I'm sorry you weren't feeling better."

"Yeah, I wish I was, too…."
"I hope we see you again."
"I hope so."
She smiles.
"Well, take it easy…," I say.
"Bye Peter," she says.
"Bye," I say.

I go, I go down, I lurch down, the hallway.

I go into the den. I take a few steps into the room. Then stop.
I pivot toward Willy Smithberger.
"I'm gonna take off," I say.
Smithberger, welded to the recliner, gives me a terrifically skeptical look.
"You're driving?"
"Yeah."
"You think that's such a good idea?"
"Yeah, sure."
"You've had a helluva lot to drink," he says.
"I'm fine," I say.
"Why don't you stay here tonight," he says. "You can sleep in here. The couch pulls out. It's not bad, it's pretty comfortable."
"That's okay," I say. "I'm gonna go home."
"You're gonna drive to Queens?"
"Yeah."
"That's gotta be a forty-five minute drive."
"More like thirty-five."
Smithberger scratches his neck, digs his fingers into his thick putty flesh.

"I'm not real comfortable with the idea of you driving back to Queens," he says, with a clearly placed gravity. "To be honest, I'm not real comfortable with the idea of you driving anywhere."

"There's really no reason why I can't drive," I say.

Smithberger laughs.

"You've had too much to drink."

"I'm fine."

"I'm not sure how fine you are."

"I'd really like to get going," I say. "I need to get back. I've got alot of stuff I gotta do in the morning...."

"Stay the night," Smithberger says easily. "Get a good night's sleep. And you can get an early start in the morning. That is, if you can get your tail up after all the booze you've put away...."

"I really should get going," I say.

"I know for a fact that you'll sleep good on the couch," he says, with a touch of humor. "I sleep on it all the time, whenever Roz and I fight."

"I really feel like I can drive without any problem," I say. I try to speak in a clear, confident manner, like a conscientious high school student engaged in a conversation with the school principal. "I feel okay, Willy. I really do."

"You've drunk a quart of scotch, Pete. More than a quart."

"Have I?"

"You sure as hell have."

"I didn't realize I drank that much."

Smithberger laughs.

"I really feel pretty good."

"Cmon Pete," he says. "Don't shit me. You're fucked up."

"I'm not," I say.

"Believe me," he says. "You are."

"I'm going to go," I say.

"Jesus Christ." Smithberger laughs. "I don't remember you being such a stubborn sonofabitch."

"I'm going to split," I say.

"You're not going anywhere," he says decisively. He looks at the TV. The game has tightened up. The Knicks had been losing by 16, but they've made a furious run and now they're down by just 4 points. The score is Celtics 85, Knicks 81.

"You're forgetting," Willy says. "I'm a cop. If you get in your car I could have you locked up."

"Oh yeah?"

"There's no fucking way you'd pass a breathalyzer."

"You wouldn't bust an old chum, would you?"

"I might."

"Yeah?"

"I don't want you to drive, Pete."

This is his final word. This is his official intractable policeman's position.

I don't bother to argue.

I'm going to have to try another strategy, I realize. Smithberger isn't going to relent. He isn't going to let me get in my car.

I put my eyes on the TV. A Celtics player taking a baseline jumper. The ball swishing through the net.

I'll pretend to give in, I decide.

I'll pretend to acquiesce to Detective Smithberger's wish, or should I say his demand, that I stay the night…I'll tell him that I'll stay, that I'll sleep on the pitiful pull-out couch…then I'll sit down, and watch, or pretend to watch, the basketball game, and then, after I've watched for awhile, I'll manufacture some reason to leave the room, I'll tell Smithberger that I have to go to the bathroom, or something, and I'll leave the room, and I'll go straight to the front door, and straight through the door…I'll flee, while Smithberger is sitting on his big ass, watching the tube….

"You really don't think I should drive?" I say, as though I've gained a willingness to concede.

"You shouldn't get anywhere near a car," Smithberger says.

"I really didn't think I was that fucked up...."

"You are."

"I guess maybe I'm more fucked up than I thought I was...."

"I guess."

"I guess it would be okay if I stayed the night," I say.

"I think it's your only alternative," he says.

"Alright...," I say. "I'll stay...."

"Good," he says.

He points his beer bottle at the couch.

"Sit down," he says.

I step, haltingly, across the dirty linoleum floor.

I drop onto the couch.

I sit there, on the couch, sunk against the cushions. I lean my skull against the soiled upholstery, sniff the couch's stale odor. I watch the game. The screen seems far away. The picture blurs, the Knicks and Celtics players streaming up and down.

"I don't think the Knicks are gonna pull it out," I say.

"It doesn't look good, does it?" Smithberger says.

"No, it doesn't."

Smithberger and I stare at the set. For a couple of minutes we don't say anything.

The Knicks call time out. There's a minute and twenty-five seconds left in the game. The Knicks are down by 8.

A commercial comes on. A gorgeous blonde, clad in a minuscule bikini, driving a jeep along a mountain road.

"Looks like the Knicks have had it," I say.

"I think you're right," Smithberger says.

"I think I'm gonna smoke a cigarette," I tell him.

"Go ahead."

"I'll go in the backyard," I say.

"You sure?"

"Yeah."

"Roz is funny about the smoke," he says apologetically.

"It's not a problem," I say.

I look at the TV.

Then I glance at Smithberger.

"I guess my coat is in the closet?"

"Yeah," he says, his big head trained on the color screen. "I think so."

I wait another couple of seconds.

Then I start to move....

I start to move, I start to raise myself, to hoist my inebriated corpse from the deep oversoft cushions....

But I can't lift my body up. Not because I'm physically incapable. No, I'm held back by something other than a physical inability, I'm held back by some heavy force, some thickened gravity....

I can't move....

The game resumes. A Celtics player misses a foul shot. Oakley grabs the rebound. The Knicks call time out.

A commercial runs. A man sitting in a canoe, next to a tub stocked with bottles of a popular domestic beer. Two blondes, wielding oars, powering the boat down a churning river.

Smithberger watches, examines the screen, like an art history student perusing a painting by Cezanne, or somebody.

I try again. I try to make my move, my getaway move...I try to get off the couch....

I try to thrust myself forward....

But, again, I can't eject myself from the cushions....

I can't move....

The game continues. There are 50, 45 seconds left.

There are 35 seconds left.

Smithberger eyes me.

"Can I ask you something, Pete?"

"What?"

"I don't mean to butt in where I shouldn't," he says, almost gently, almost kindly, "but I was wondering if you thought you might have a drinking problem."

"What?"

"Do you think you have a drinking problem?"

"What're you talking about?"

"Have you ever thought about it?"

"No," I say.

"I just get the impression," he says, "from watching you, watching how much you've drunk tonight, and how you've drunk it, I just get the impression that maybe you have a drinking problem."

"Tonight's an aberration," I tell Smithberger. "I usually don't drink this much."

"I deal with alot of people who got a problem with drinking," he explains. "I kind of know the signs. The way you've been socking down that scotch makes me wonder if you don't got a problem."

"I don't," I say.

"I wouldn't say anything if I didn't think that there was a possibility that you did."

"I don't."

"I was just thinking that if you thought you did, that maybe I could help you out," he says. "I could get you in touch with someplace where you could go, where you could get some help."

"I don't have a problem," I say.

"There's a couple of rehabs," he says. "They're right out here, on Long Island. They're supposed to be pretty good. Supposedly they can help you get yourself straightened out."

I nod perfunctorily, watch the lamplight gloss off Smithberger's denuded pate.

"I could probably hook you up with one of these places, if you want."

"Thanks," I say. "But it's not necessary."

"I just want you to know that if you want you can give me a call."

I nod.

"You can call me anytime," Smithberger says.

"Thanks," I say flatly.

"You got it," he says.

He grins.

"I'm gonna smoke my cigarette," I say.

"Okay," he says.

I walk into the living room. I walk across the room, across the flattened-down carpeting. I go to the closet. Open it. My hearts beats fiercely, like a broken lawnmower blade beating the ground. My leatherjacket is hanging on a wire hanger, pressed between coats and jackets belonging to various Smithberger family members. I remove the jacket. Put it on.

I step to the front door.

I put my hand on the brass-colored doorknob. Turn it. Very slowly. Very carefully.

I pull open the wooden door.

I push open the glass stormdoor. Step onto the concrete stoop. Into the cold night. I pull the wooden door close to the jamb. I don't close the door, I don't want Willy Smithberger to hear the door shutting. I'm afraid he'll hear the clunk, the phlank, and that he'll bound from the recliner, charge across the living room, throw his big arm around my neck. I pull the door, until it almost touches the jamb. Then I close the stormdoor. I close the stormdoor with extraordinary care, I very slowly retract my thumb from the metal button, release the mechanism, allow the door to gradually latch.

I descend the stoop.

I run.

The Toyota sits at the curb, the beaten blue finish reflecting streetlamp light, glinting.

I run across Willy Smithberger's lawn. I run as fast as I can. My sneakers jab the turf, the horribly worn soles lift, move swiftly through the cold air. I fly.

I reach the car, open the door. Slide in.

I don't shut the door. I don't want Smithberger to hear the resultant thwank.

I fit the key in the ignition. Turn it.

The engine coughs.

I try again.

The engine coughs pathetically, like a ninety year old emphysema patient.

I can't keep trying, I realize. I can't keep cranking the engine. Sooner or later Smithberger will hear me, he'll hear me trying to get the goddam thing to start.

There's only one thing I can do, I figure.

I shift into neutral.

I get out of the car.

And I push the Toyota, I push the Toyota away from the curb.

I push the car down the street, down the middle of Willy Smithberger's suburban street, past the houses, the lit windows.

I push the Toyota 50, maybe 100, maybe 150 yards.

Finally I let the car come to a halt, near the curb, in front of somebody's boxshaped house.

I get in. I close the door, as gently as I can.

I sit against the cold vinyl.

Catch my breath.

Close my eyes, for a minute, just a minute.

Then I try the engine.

It coughs weakly.

I wait. Then try again.

And it starts.

I hold my sneaker against the gas pedal, let the engine warm.

And then I drive down the street, through the fractured darkness, the irredeemable suburban night.

I lay on the motelroom bed. End of February.

Still waiting.

Still waiting for answers.

I've got to believe, however, that I haven't got much longer to wait, another day, another couple of days at the very most....

I've got to believe, you see, that the answers will come when everything has been stripped away, when all the encumbrances and shackles and attachments have been eliminated, when all the things that've tied me to my life have been discarded. I've got to believe that the doors will swing open, and I'll see what I'm supposed to see, when I've lost everything. Everything.

And I'm almost there. I've already lost just about everything I had that I could've lost. I've got almost nothing left. I've let go of my job. I've relinquished my apartment, most of my belongings. And now I'm almost completely broke. I've got just a small amount of money left. I've got ninety-eight dollars in my bank account. Fifty-seven dollars in my wallet. About a dollar's worth of change in the pocket of my leatherjacket. And that's it. That's the extent of my financial resources. One hundred fifty-six dollars.

And, needless to say, this one hundred fifty-six dollars isn't going to last very long.

I lay on the bed, propped against the plywood headboard.

I stare through the motelroom window. I've pulled apart the drapes, as far as they'll go, giving myself a wide view of things, and I stare intensely at the February afternoon.

277

The afternoon is deteriorating, dissolving into fuzzy, futile greyness. The light is frail. The sky is blanketed with grey clouds, layers of dark grey clouds.

I light a cigarette.

I exhale smoke into the thin motelroom air.

I stare at the diminishing afternoon.

Changes, it seems, are already starting to occur. The old laws are starting to break down, lose their hard form. I feel differently. I feel like I can see further into things. This scene beyond the window has never seemed quite so beautiful. The grey sky, blending with the grey landscape, the cars moving on Sunrise, forcing their way into the grey folds, into the crevices of dying light. I've always been able to grasp the poetry in this view of suburban life, but never have I grasped it, understood it, felt it, the way I now seem to be able to....

I sip my scotch.

I stare through the window.

The sky darkens, the grey turns darker grey.

I'm moved viciously, close to tears.

In the farflung distance, past the railroad tracks, naked black tree branches make thin wistful cracks against the darkening sky. And I can see, beneath the branches, the roofs of houses, and I can sense, so clearly, the life thrumming beneath these roofs, all the wonderment, happiness, pain, loss, disappointment, grief, the irrepressible sadness.

Past Sunrise, the railroad tracks reach into the growing darkness, disappear into the night's holy throat. And on Sunrise, the rush hour traffic grinds forward, the ceaseless procession of cars, lights burning, edging through the grey, homeward.

O Sunrise! Heartbreakingly beautiful Sunrise, with your countless automobiles piercing the falling dark, every one of them lost, looking for warmth, for temporary redemption. You long broad road, road of my childhood, making your sighing trail through the heart of the suburbs, the heart of America, through all the middleclassness, the white sorrow. O Sunrise! Always leading sadly forward, through the years, into all that terrible nothingness, sweet concrete river, eternal passageway, the way home. O Sunrise! You long enduring highway!

O Sunrise!

I lay on the bed.

The room is dark. The TV's off, the only light is provided by the dull generalized glow from streetlights and headlights coming through the window.

I light a cigarette.

I hold the cigarette between my thumb and forefinger. My hand is twitching, and I sort of wave the butt at the window, at the night sky. The reason, of course, why my hand is twitching, why I'm waving the lit cigarette, is that I've put too much alcohol in my body, during the course of the day, during the course of the past several weeks, the past months, the past twenty years. But it almost seems as if there's another reason why I'm waving the cigarette, it almost seems as if I'm sending a flare, as if I'm sending a signal, to some unseen force, like God, or something.

I hold the cigarette against my lips, take a slow drag. I stare at the sky. I can feel, I'm pretty sure I can feel, the presence of God, or something like God, lurking, not all that far from where I lay, somewhere out there, just beyond the window, in the night, in the suburban darkness....

I lay on the bed, in the dark room.

I listen, can't help but listen, to the couple in the next room. I can hear this couple very clearly, extremely clearly, more clearly, it seems, than I've been able to hear any other couple in the four months I've resided at the motel. It's as if they're fucking in my room, on the carpeting, next to my bed. The man grunts. The woman wails soulfully. I hear them climaxing, simultaneously.

And then I hear their becalmed, post-intercourse voices. I hear them putting on their clothes, I hear them tugging their zippers, pulling on their coats. And then I hear them leaving the room, their hushed in-transit elocutions. I hear the motelroom door shutting, thwacking.

And then I see them.

They walk past my window. The man, tall, bedecked in a trenchcoat, walks past. The woman follows.

The man disappears.

But, to my surprise, the woman stops. She stops right in front of the window. She stops, and she stares right through the window, directly at me.

She's tall. She's very tall. She's wearing a long dark coat. She's got long straight dark hair, a madonna's cascade of dark hair, hair that plummets down her back, past her waist, resolutely, like water falling, like dark light.

She's got a moonshaped face. I can't, however, see much of her face. I can't make a detailed assessment of her features. It's too dark. And I'm probably too drunk. But from what I can see, she's looking quite purposefully at me, she's focussing intently on my reclined form.

And I can't help but think that maybe, just maybe, she's standing there, staring into my room, for a very specific reason.

Maybe she's letting me know something.

Maybe she's giving some kind of indication.

Maybe she's some sort of messenger. Maybe she's God's pointwoman, sent ahead, to give word.

She looks through the scuzzy window. She just stands there, as still as can be, and stares in.

And perhaps I'm wrong, perhaps she's just another suburban bimbo, who, in that disoriented interval following frenetic sex, has simply stopped to check her visage in the big pane of glass.

But I'm not convinced I'm wrong, I'm not convinced that she's not an authentic messenger, that she's not giving me some sort of sign.

She stares through the glass, steadfastly.

Then, finally, she vanishes. Like every vision. She turns. And she goes. And she's gone.

The next afternoon.

I extricate myself from the rough bedclothes, cast off the sheets and blankets, slowly, like a snake shedding his skin. I sit on the edge of the bed, wearing an ancient Mets tee shirt and nothing else, and I pour what's left in the bottle of Johnny Walker, an inch or so of scotch, into my glass, and I down this meager bit of scotch, quickly, in one wrenching gulp.

I walk to the bathroom. My body juts. Each step, each movement, each contact with the motelroom air, brings inconceivable ranting pain.

I sit on the toilet. Piss.

I walk back across the room. The carpeting feels hard, damp, like clay, against my bare feet. I open the closet. Two pillowcases stuffed with dirty laundry lean against the closet wall. They're both bulging, overflowing with caked, balled-up clothes. I pull out one of the pillowcases, root around inside, dig my hand into the densely packed clothes, try to find a pair of underpants and a pair of socks. I look for articles that aren't overly offensive, that have a modicum of battlescars, that don't smell too badly. Eventually I remove a pair of dark blue briefs and a couple of black socks that might, or might not, match.

I pull the underpants over my grotty pecker and balls. I yank on the limp socks. I put on jeans. I pull a black sweatshirt over my Mets tee shirt, then pull on a bedraggled burgundy sweater, something my mother gave to me for Christmas about fifteen years ago.

I put on my leatherjacket. Pull on my old scuffed brown leather gloves. Leave the room.

I drive to Price Right Liquors. I buy a bottle of Johnny Walker Red. Sit in the car, open the bottle, take several hefty slugs, drinking, of course, directly from the bottle, my head thrown back, my lips squeezing the glass spout.

I drive to the Citibank on Main Street. Using the ATM, I ascertain what's left, the exact balance, in my savings account. I've got $98.24. I make out a withdrawal slip for the entire amount. Then I get on line, behind two old ladies, a truckdriver type, a woman carrying a baby strapped to her chest. I reach one of the tellers. A darkhaired girl. Perhaps mid-twenties. Bespectacled. Kind of cute. I slide her my withdrawal slip and my bank card. Try not to look at her, try not to let her see my face, try not to let her get a good view of my forlorn countenance. She gives me my money. My $98.24. I fit the bills in my wallet. Drop the coins in my leatherjacket. Leave the bank.

I drive down Main Street. Pull the Toyota to the curb in front of a strip mall, a lineup of dirtspecked establishments that includes an ice cream shop, a real estate office, a delicatessen, a plumbing supply store, a bagel store. I go into the deli. Buy a pack of Marlboros and a big box of pretzels.

I go back to the motel. Park alongside the registration office. Slink, head down, into the office. Howard, surprisingly, isn't sitting behind the counter. Instead, there's a woman sitting there, somebody I haven't seen before. She's not half-bad-looking. Thirty-fiveish. Brunette. I tell her I'm going to pay for another night's lodgings. Just one night's lodgings.

I've got enough cash to pay for two more nights at the South Shore, but I don't think I should pay for two nights. I don't quite yet know how I want to spend my last monies. I know that, besides shelter, that there are some things I'm probably going to want to purchase. I'm probably going to want to procure certain basics, like food, like scotch. But I'm not sure how much I want to spend on these items. Or if I might want to spend my last few dollars on something else, something entirely different.

I give the brunette two twenties and a ten.

"There you go," she says, handing me my change.

"Thanks," I say, glancing, shyly, at her.

She smiles, flatly, her lips stapled together.

She's definitely got something going for her.

She's definitely fuckable.

No doubt about that.

"Take care," I say.

"Bye," she says.

I pass the afternoon in my room, lying on the kingsized bed, watching TV, drinking, smoking, eating pretzels. I eat all of the pretzels. I scarf down everything in the goodsized box, every pretzel, every broken-off piece, every fragment, every stub. And for awhile the pretzels sustain me. They keep me going. But as the afternoon darkens and turns into evening, I begin to feel hungry, I begin to feel like I need to put something else, something more substantial, in my stomach.

I think about getting dinner.

I go over my options.

I could go to a deli, get a sandwich, maybe a chicken cutlet on a roll.

Or I could go to Wing Fat, the Chinese take-out place on Jerusalem Avenue, and I could pick up something, wonton soup, fried rice.

Or I could go to Phil's Pizza, get a couple of slices.

Or I could go to the Big Burger.

I consider each of these possibilities. I examine the pros and cons of each.

Then I get an idea. It's a brilliant idea, as far as I'm concerned. It's an idea that's got genius in it, that's got poetry in it.

I jump off the bed. I pull off my sweater, and I put on the most presentable sweater I've got, a dark green number, the same sweater, as a matter of fact, that I wore to Willy Smithberger's house. I go to the closet. I grab my navy blue blazer. I haven't worn the blazer in months, since I left my job. There'd been a time, of course, when I'd worn it alot. It'd been a garment that I'd worn almost exhaustively during my tenure as a sales rep for L.G. Buchanan. I'd trudged through many a school building, wended my way down many a derelict city street wearing this jacket. It'd been a key part of my salesman's wardrobe, it'd seen a hell of alot of action, it'd been through numerous wars, as evident by its shiny lapels, misshapen shoulders, frayed cuffs.

I don the blazer, tug it over the thickish sweater.

I go into the bathroom. Stand in front of the mirror. Try to fix my hair. My brown mop is in an incorrigibly disheveled state. I haven't had a haircut in eight or nine months. I did attempt to trim my bangs, about a month ago, using a pair of dull grade-school scissors, a pair of scissors, in fact, that I once carried in my L.G. Buchanan sample case. That attempt, however, didn't yield an especially successful result. Now there isn't alot I can accomplish. The situation is pretty much beyond my control. But I try. I wet my hands under the sink faucet, run them through my hair, try to push the more recalcitrant and wayward strands off my forehead, behind my ears, try to tamp, to pat, to pull my long unruly locks into some sort of pleasant-looking shape.

I contemplate shaving. I haven't put a blade to my face in several days. I look rather scruffy. I sort of resemble an Alaskan sea otter. I gaze at the mirror, analyze my unsmooth puss. I decide, finally, however, that I'm not going to shave. I'm going to go with the stubbled, unkempt look. This, fortunately, is a look that's somewhat in vogue. If somebody happens to notice my grizzled visage, there's a fair chance, I figure, that they'll think that I'm merely keeping up with the latest trends.

I go to the night table, grab my bottle of scotch, take a long slug. Then I put on my leatherjacket. It's about 25 degrees outside, and windy. The blazer isn't going to guard me adequately from the cold. I'm going to need all the protection I can get from the wintry elements.

I grip the bottle, take another long slug.

I pull on my gloves.

I take another slug.

Then, sticking the bottle inside my jacket, I leave the room.

I drive to Musicello's. To my way to seeing things, Musicello's is something of a landmark in this suburb that, almost by definition, denies the existence of landmarks. The restaurant has been standing on the same piece of land, on Main Street, since I was a kid. This fact alone should be enough to give it landmark status. But Musicello's is more than just a building that's been standing for forty years. It's more than a hunk of concrete and wood that's somehow survived the wrecking ball. It's an establishment that, at least when I was a youth, had owned a prominent position on the Bayview landscape. Noted for its simple, equitably priced, but altogether tasty Italian fare, Musicello's had been a highly popular spot, perhaps the most popular eatery in the area. It'd been a place that young suburban families had flocked to, in droves, like seagulls descending on a bulkhead strewn with fish parts. When I was a boy, many of my friends went to Musicello's with their families on a regular basis, on those nights when their mothers were given a reprieve from putting dinner, the usual meat and potatoes, on the kitchen table. Chris Adelkravitich, for instance, went to Musicello's with his parents and his three sisters every Saturday night.

Musicello's was also a place where teenaged boys and girls went on dates on Friday and Saturday nights, it was a place where they sat opposite each other at little tables, clumsily forked spaghetti, and uttered halting halfsentences, in those days before their innocence was shot to hell. I remember hearing Willy Smithberger's sister, Louise, telling a friend that the guy she'd had a date with on the previous Saturday night had taken her to Musicello's. And, ironically, I remember Willy telling me, one afternoon when I ran into him at Tony's Candystore, that he'd taken Doreen Higeboth to the much-loved trattoria.

All in all, Musicello's seems like the ideal place to have what, to my way of seeing it, is going to be the equivalent of my Last Supper.

I roll into the parking lot behind the smudged white stucco building. The lot, I'm surprised to find, is nearly deserted. Just two cars, a Chevy and a rusted Lincoln, are sitting on the crater-ridden asphalt.

I park.

I take a few swigs from my bottle, drain the bottle.

I get out of the car.

I walk around the building, go into the restaurant.

I'm met, as I come through the door, by a short squatty unsmiling man wearing a wrinkled white shirt and black pants. For lack of a better way of describing him, I'll call him the maitre d'. He leads me to a small table pressed against the wall toward the back of the dining floor.

I pull off my leatherjacket, hang it over my chair, sit down, facing the front of the restaurant.

Strangely enough, I haven't been to Musicello's before. Whenever my parents took my siblings and me someplace to eat they took us to less refined venues like the Big Burger and McDonald's. On special occasions they might've taken us to Howard Johnson or the Bayview Diner. But they never took us to Musicello's. As a result, I'm quite interested to see what the place is like.

I scan the restaurant, inspect the premises with a scrupulous eye.

Unfortunately, I'm not impressed. This latter-day Musicello's is a weary-looking establishment. It's enveloped in a lethargic murkiness. The lighting is poor, so poor, so anemic, that you get the feeling that a minimal amount of electricity is being pumped into the building. It's as though the proprietors have decided to cut back the power in an effort to adhere to some kind of austerity budget. The walls are covered with dark red wallpaper that reminds you of ancient Christmas wrapping, stuff that's been lying in the attic for a couple of decades. The floors are covered with dark purplish carpeting. The carpeting, quite possibly the same carpeting that Chris Adelkravitich and Willy Smithberger trodded upon when they were youngsters, is beatendown and discolored, it's obviously been significantly altered by tens of thousands of trampling feet, innumerable spilled wine glasses, and a variety of misdirected food particles, as well as the unavoidable ignominies that the passage of time confers, the crusts, grimes, random erosions.

The place, basically, is empty. There are about twenty tables, each covered with a red-and-white checkered tablecloth, decorated with a small glass vase that holds a wilting red carnation. Just one table, however, other than mine, is occupied. This table is being held down, in a manner of speaking, by an elderly man and woman. They're a feeble-looking, whitehaired duo. They sit there, precariously, on their rickety wooden chairs, poke their utensils in painful slow motion at their tomato-sauce splotched food.

Besides myself and the senior citizen couple, the only other paying customers in Musicello's on this winter's night are the men sitting at the small padded bar near the front entrance. There are two of them. A business type attired in a grey suit. And a guy wearing a Yankee cap, a red flannel shirt, shitty jeans, and work-boots.

And that's it.

The place is dead.

And I get the feeling that this is what a typical night at Musicello's is like, at this point, as the century moves toward its conclusion. I'm willing to consider some possible logical reasons as to why the place is this lifeless. It's a weekday night. It's a work night. It's a school night. It's still early, just past seven. I might've chosen to visit the restaurant on an unusually slow night. But my gut feeling is that Musicello's is an establishment that has seen its best days come and go. My gut feeling is that the place is heading down, quickly, on a path toward its extinction.

A group of waiters stands near the bar. There are three or four, they're all male, they all look the same, dressed in white shirts and black pants. They stand there, aimlessly, hands in pockets, shifting their weight, eyeballing the ceiling.

Eventually one of the waiters breaks free from the pack, shuffles across the purple carpeting, approaches my table. He's medium height, medium weight, very Italian looking. Thick wire-brush hair. Olive skin. A square jaw permeated with dark stubble.

"How ya doin," he says. He's got a strong Brooklyn accent. In fact, I'm inclined to believe that he must commute to Musicello's from that very borough, from Brooklyn itself. He's too Italian to be from Long Island. Italians who reside on Long Island tend to be watered down. The suburbs dilute their Italian-ness. But this waiter is an undiluted character. He's the real deal.

"Ahm Victor," he says. "Ahm ya waita this evenin."

"How ya doin," I say.

"Can I getcha a drink?" he asks.

I tell him I'll have a Johnny Walker Red, on the rocks.

"You got it," he says.

"Thanks alot," I say, attempting to show sincerity, warmth. I want to let him know that I'm truly grateful for his efforts. I want to extend myself to Victor. I want to make a positive heartfelt connection with him. I'm quite cognizant, you see, of the critical role that he's going to play. He's going to chaperone my transition. He's going to facilitate my passage. For tonight, for my purposes, he's going to be more than just a waiter, he's going to take the part of a spiritual guide, an angel. He's going to accompany me on my journey, from my old life to a new life, from darkness to light.

He brings my drink.

"Ya ready ta orda?" he asks.

"No...sorry...," I say.

I still haven't figured out exactly what I should order, what items I should select so that, firstly, I'll be able to enjoy a delicious and celebratory repast, and, secondly, and most importantly, so that the numbers will compute, so that the cost of the meal will add up to what it's got to add up to.

"Can you give me a minute?" I say.

"No problem," Victor says.

"Thanks," I say.

I study the menu. I make some calculations. They aren't complicated calculations, but my mathematical ability, thanks to my prolific alcohol consumption, has been severely impaired. In other words, it's hard to add.

Victor returns.

"Ready ta orda?"

"Sure."

I check the menu.

"I'll have the soup, the minestrone," I say.

"Minestrone," he says, writing on a small pad with a stub of a pencil.

"And for an appetizer, I'll have the cold antipasto."

"Uh huh."

"And also give me the oysters."

Victor nods.

"And I'm going to have the veal chop."

"How da ya want dat?"

"Medium."

"Ya want spaghetti? Ziti? Vegetable?"

"I'll have spaghetti," I say.

"Anything else?"

"What's the vegetable?"

"Broccoli."

"I tell you what," I say. "Give me the spaghetti and the broccoli."

"Ya want both?"

"Yeah."

"No problem."

"And give me another Johnny Walker."

"You got it," Victor says.

He goes.

I've put the wheels into motion rather effectively, I think.

I've moved myself into the final stages.

Everything, it seems, is in place.

I'll have a sumptuous meal, the most sumptuous meal that you can have in a place like Musicello's. And when I'm finished with this meal, when I've paid the check, and have left a nice tip for my waiter, the taciturn Victor, then, if my math is correct, I'll have reached point zero. I'll have extinguished the last of my monetary reserves. I'll be bankrupt. Dead broke. Empty.

And I'll be able to see whatever it is I'm supposed to see. And I'll be ready to move on, to wherever it is I'm meant to move on to.

Victor brings the minestrone.

"Thanks," I say.

I gaze upon the soup, reflectively. I try to absorb, fully sense, what I'm doing, the meaning of what's going on.

I pick up my soup spoon.

I dip the spoon into the bowl, lift it to my mouth. Some of the soup slides off the implement, my hand quaking, the alcohol shakes impossible to control, no point in even trying to control them. I put the spoon in my mouth. Let the soup loiter against my tongue.

The minestrone, unfortunately, isn't very good. No. It's lousy. Tasteless.

But I should eat it, I figure, I should try to eat as much of it as I can, in an effort to maintain the spirit of the occasion, in an effort to preserve the celebratory nature of the moment....

I devour the soup.

And I devour the appetizers. I slurp the gooey, acrid-tasting oysters. And I eat most of the antipasto, the raggedy pieces of ham, pepperoni, cheese, the dilapidated artichoke hearts, the olives.

Unfortunately, by the time I've decided that I've eaten enough of the antipasto, I don't feel so well. I feel sick. I don't know if it's the food, which isn't exactly mouthwateringly delicious, which is in fact rather unpalatable, or if it's all the alcohol I've slugged down, probably it's a combination of both, but whatever the cause is, I feel crummy.

I feel queasy.

I feel like I might throw up.

Victor brings the veal chop, the spaghetti, the broccoli.

I stick my knife into the chop. Cut a small piece. Put it in my mouth.

I chew, effortfully, grinding my molars against the tough sinewy meat.

The chop, like everything else, is alarmingly unappetizing. It tastes like cardboard. Actually, if you took a hunk of cardboard, sautéed it in a little olive oil, with a little garlic, a little salt and pepper, it might very well taste better than this veal chop.

I don't want to have to eat the chop. It's detestable. And, besides that, I don't feel well. I don't feel well enough, well enough to eat it.

I feel pretty damn sick.

But I feel like I should eat at least a reasonable, representative portion of the chop. I feel like I should eat at least half of it....

The thing is, I'm afraid that if I leave the chop untouched, or relatively untouched, I'll compromise the integrity of the occasion...I'm afraid that if I don't make a considerable dent in the chop, and if I don't eat at least some of the spaghetti and the broccoli, I'm afraid it won't be much of a Last Supper...I'm afraid that, as far as Last Suppers go, it'll be a failure....

I put down my knife and fork. I've eaten about a third of the chop. And I've demolished most of the saucesplattered pasta. And I've consumed one of the rubbery pale-green stalks of broccoli. And I'm almost sure that if I try to eat anything else, I'll puke, I'll vomit torrentially.

The fact of the matter is, I feel really sick.

I feel really sick.

I plunge a couple of fingers into my water glass, press my cold wet fingers against the bridge of my nose.

I feel like there's a chance, a very good chance, that I'm going to throw up, no matter what, even if I don't ingest another scrap, another morsel of food.

I look away, away from the tablecloth, away from the plates covered with clumps, leavings of pallid food. I stare across the restaurant. Two men come through the door. They're both wearing trenchcoats. One of the men is elderly. The other is appreciably younger. They might, I think, be father and son. They move, escorted by the maitre d', into the dining room, through the geometric of tables. I watch them. They distort, like images in a funhouse mirror. Their bodies elongate, shimmy, shimmer.

I look toward the ceiling.

I feel really fucking sick. Nauseous. The front of my head pulses, morphs.

I look across the restaurant, toward the front, the bar, the guys sitting on tall stools, tilting drinks. My head pulses.

I feel really sick.

I feel really sick. As sick as a dog. As sick as the sickest, mangiest, scraggliest, ungainliest dog that ever limped through an ice-cold fast-beating rain, down a dirty litter infested alley, behind a decrepit suburban strip mall.

I look out on the landscape of tables.

My eyes throb, arrhythmically, against the bones of their sockets.

The restaurant revolves, kaleidoscopically, a fractured, fragmented collision of dark crimson surfaces, and human beings, just a few of them, shifting, gesticulating.

I'm going to puke, I realize.

I stand.

I move, I stutterstep, toward the restroom. I move down a darkred corridor. I lunge at the men's room door. Push open the door with my forearm and hip.

I throw myself halfblindly at one of the stalls. Smack my elbow against the metal door. Fall to my knees. Grab the pisscoated toilet. Stick my head in the bowl.

I return to my table.

I feel better. I feel better physically, but more importantly, I feel better psychologically, spiritually. I feel like I've let go of something, something besides the vomit I've expelled, I feel like I've let go of at least some of the burden I've been carrying around, like a knapsack filled with bricks, for the better part of my thirty-nine years.

Victor steps across the purple carpeting.

"Ya finished?"

"Yeah, I am," I say.

"Ya wan me ta wrap up any a dis for ya?" he asks, snatching the plate on which the partially eaten veal chop lays, like a piece of driftwood.

"Nah, don't bother," I say.

"Can I getcha some dessert?"

"Nah, I don't think so." I realize that if I don't get dessert I'm probably not going to run up a high enough bill, a bill that, when paid, will force me to empty my wallet. When I had worked out what I would order so that I might deplete my finances, I had figured I would order a somewhat expensive dessert. Now, of course, after having barfed, I don't want to have to try to stomach any kind of dessert, not even the most subtle dessert. I could, of course, order a dessert and then simply ignore it, let it sit, unmolested, on its plate. I don't think, however, that this would be the right thing to do. I'm afraid I'd be making a mockery of things. If

I took this kind of action, I'm afraid, I'd be undermining the importance, the meaningfulness of the occasion.

"We got a nice chocolate mousse cake," Victor says.

"Thanks," I say, "but I think I'm gonna pass."

"What about coffee?"

"No thanks."

"Cappuccino? Espresso?"

"Nah, I think that'll do it for me," I say.

"Alright," Victor says.

He departs.

And I watch him, I study him, I study him walking across the purple rug, my still cluttered plates balanced against his arm, I study him walking to the kitchen, strutting, his shoulders jamming the dull air, his trousers shining in the dim light, his black shoes scraping the hellish rug....

And I study the people sitting at the tables covered with red-and-white tablecloths. The old enfeebled man and woman. The two men, probably father and son, sitting across from each other. And I study the men perched at the bar. And I study the bartender. And the dilatory waiters, the maitre d'....

I study them, each of these apparently unexceptional beings who, for whatever reason, has found his or her way to Musicello's on this cold February night....

They're angels, I realize. They're angels. They're all angels. They've brought me through. They've shepherded me. They've ensured my safe transport.

And, as I study them, as I put my focus directly, steadfastly, on them, I see something I hadn't seen before, at least I think I see something I hadn't seen before, I see a light emanating from them, from each of them, I see a light emanating from their ordinary, unassuming bodies, not a blinding light or anything like that, but a light, a pinkish light, a hazy pinkish light....

And as I continue to study them, I see them rise, the old couple, the father and son, the guys at the bar, the waiters, they rise, they leave the ground, and they hang, four, five feet above the floor, above the slanderous carpeting, they hang there, in mid-air, legs dangling, forks and glasses raised, they hang there, glowing softly, giving off that pinkish light....

Victor places the check on the table.

"Thanks," I say.

"You got it," he says.

He heads toward the kitchen.

I examine the check. As I'd expected, I haven't reached my goal, I haven't hit my mark. Since I didn't order dessert, and didn't order as many drinks as I'd thought I would've, I haven't run up the bill as high as I'd wanted to.

The total charge comes to $52.50.

And I've got about $79.

I think:

I could give Victor a $15 tip, a very generous gratuity by anybody's standards.

If I give Victor $15 that would mean I'd be leaving $68 on the table.

I'd still be $11 short.

I'd still have $11.

I try to decide if there's another course I might pursue.

I could give Victor a bigger tip, I think. I could give him all of the cash that's left after I pay the bill. That would amount to roughly a $26 tip.

If I give him the $26 I'd be through with it. I'd be consummately broke. My funds would be gone.

But I don't think I should do it.

I don't think I should give Victor such a big tip. I don't want to taint the moment by giving him an incongruous tip, a ridiculously enormous tip. I'm afraid that if I give him this sort of tip I'd be turning this Last Supper into a veritable farce.

I don't want to let go of my last dollars in such an absurd, irregular way.

I want to proceed in a symbolically correct manner.

I'm going to give him a $15 tip, I decide.

I take out my wallet. I count out enough money to cover the bill and Victor's quite ample gratuity. $68.

I lay the cash, in a neat pile, on the tablecloth.

Then I get up.

I pull on my leatherjacket. Remove two quarters from the jacket pocket. Place the quarters on top of the little pile of cash.

Then I go.

I get in the Toyota.

I try to start the engine.

It sputters.

Gags.

I try again.

The engine coughs.

And coughs.

And then starts.

I hold my sneaker against the accelerator.

I don't know what I should do about the car. I don't know whether or not I should get rid of it. If I'm going to discard all my encumbrances, divest myself of all my attachments, then, I think, I should probably divest myself of the car, I should probably let it go, the way I'm letting go of everything else....

Then again, I think, there might be some good reasons why I should hold on to the Toyota. From a purely philosophical standpoint, there might be some valid reasons. Isn't, after all, a man's car, an American man's car, an integral component of his spiritual life, isn't it one of the most important instruments he's got with which to explore the most poetic, most transcendent aspects of American life, those aspects explicated by Whitman in his ruminations on the open road, and gloried, of course, by the likes of Kerouac....

I'm not sure what I should do. I should probably get rid of the car, I think, but I'm not yet convinced that I should....

I'll decide soon enough, I figure....

I pull out of Musicello's parking lot, drive down Main Street, past the now familiar architectures, office buildings, strip malls, supermarkets, gas stations. The radio, tuned to the oldies station, WCBS, plays a song I remember, with not a small amount of fondness, from the summer of 1968, the Rascals' "People Got to Be Free."

I drive slowly, try to figure out how I should spend the money I've got left, my last eleven-plus dollars. I try to determine the best way, the most appropriate, most fitting way to empty my coffers.

I drive, very slowly, down Main. A Beatles song, from 1965, "Eight Days a Week," scratches, broken-up, from the dashboard speakers.

I cross Park Blvd, drive through the intersection, under the traffic light, and I glimpse the 7-Eleven, just ahead, on the left-hand side of the road. And I realize, in an instant, that this is the place. *It's the place.* It's the right place, the symbolically correct place. It's the perfect place to dissipate my monetary assets.

I don't know what I'm going to buy in this 7-Eleven, but I know that this is the place where I should let go, empty, release, my last few crinkly dollars, my last few coins.

I turn, sharply, into the glass-strewn lot.

I park the Toyota.

I check my wallet. I've got two five-dollar bills, a single. I remove the change from my jacket pocket. I've got two nickels, a dime.

I get out of the car.

I go into the 7-Eleven.

The store, like all 7-Elevens, is indifferent, grungy. It's brightly lit, but the bright, eye pummelling light only clarifies the store's grunginess. Everything about the place seems forgotten, decayed. There are just a few customers. They drag across the tile floor, laggardly, unenthusiastically. Like tired apparitions. A middleaged woman wearing a bulbous down coat paces an incremental length in front of a magazine rack. A man attired in a beige trenchcoat walks toward the cash register, toting a half gallon of milk and an Entenmann's box.

Behind the register, an adolescent male sits on a stool. Long-haired, besieged with red pimples, wearing a Motley Crue tee shirt, he slouches emphatically, projects a cosmic lethargy.

I walk slowly past shelves crammed with boxes, cans, jars. I try to decide what I should buy.

I stride, short strides, on the soiled tile. I stride toward the back of the store. Catch sight of the long refrigerated case loaded with bottles and cans of various beverages. And then I know. I know what I should buy. Beer.

I go, quickly, to the section of the refrigerated case where the beer is stored. Slide the glass door. Remove a six-pack of Budweiser. Cans.

I can't think of a more symbolically correct purchase.

Because what could be more symbolic of an American life, like mine, like yours, than a six-pack of Budweiser?

What better way could I wait for the end of what's coming to an end than by drinking some beer? It just seems right that I should prepare for the apocalypse with a six-pack at my side, a cold Bud pressed to my mouth.

And, on a more pragmatic level, I know that I'm going to want, to need, to put some alcohol in my body. I don't have any scotch left. The beer, hopefully, will placate the craving, the sharp craving, the vehement craving, that's surely going to strike, that, in fact, I'm already beginning to feel....

I move through the store, clutching the six-pack. I do some quick math. I've got 11 dollars, 20 cents. The six-pack costs $5.99. There's tax. If I'm going to completely drain my financial reservoirs I'm going to have to buy something else, I'm going to have to find something to buy that costs roughly 4 dollars.

I walk slowly, I barely walk, my sneakers, the thin, almost non-existent soles, chafe the dingy floor.

I walk, at an ever-slowing pace, in the general direction of the cash register.

And then I realize what I should buy.

Cigarettes.

Cigarettes are the perfect thing to spend my final dollars on. The cigarette, traditionally, is the last attachment, the last thing left after everything else has been taken away. Consider the classic loser, the bum, puffing away on a butt. He's got nothing, but somehow he's always got that cigarette glued between his grubby fingers. Or consider the prisoner, remanded to a dark jail cell, deprived of every pleasure that life offers, except for the cigarette. Or better yet, consider the condemned man, bound for his execution, given that final cigarette before he walks, down a long corridor, through a steel door, to the electric chair.

Certainly it seems right, it seems fitting, that I should have a cigarette fixed between my own embattled lips as I wait for the end of this life, this excuse for a life, this set of sorry gyrations I've been involved with for the last several decades.

And besides, I'm going to need cigarettes.

I step to the cash register. I rest the six-pack on the counter, eye the slouching clerk.

"Give me a pack of Marlboros…the hard pack…," I say.

The kid nods languidly, strands of hair falling over his eyes, leaving a greasemark on his cheek.

He puts the cigarettes on the counter.

"That should do it," I say.

The kid manipulates the cash register.

I stare at the digital read-out. The green numbers flicker, show the total: $11.08.

"Shit," I mutter.

I'm still short.

"Eleven oh-eight," the clerk says.

"Hold on a second," I say. I've got to figure a way to spend another 12 cents. "I'm gonna get something else."

The kid doesn't react, just stares, ambiguously, into the bright chemical air.

I scan the selection of candy, gum, lifesavers, etc., displayed on the rack next to the register.

I reach for a Milky Way, a candy bar that I favored, and frequently devoured, when I was a boy.

Then I notice a small box filled with baseball cards. And I know. I know that this is what I should buy. Baseball cards. Collecting baseball cards was, of course, one of those inexpressibly joyful activities that I had participated in when I was growing up. Some of the most memorable, most sublime moments of my life had taken place sitting on the chaste sidewalks of my suburban neighborhood, along with Chris Adelkravitich, Willy Smithberger, Kevin Anderson, Louie Plunkett, opening packs of baseball cards, going through the cards, scrutinizing, exulting, laughing. In the final analysis, I don't know if there's a more suitable, more symbolically correct purchase that I could make. Buying baseball cards is, I think, an exquisite way to part with my last few cents.

I grab a pack of cards. I don't pick up the pack on top, but the pack underneath the pack on top. This was a practice, a ritual, if you will, that I'd always observed. I lay the cards on the counter, next to the beer and the cigarettes.

"I'll take these," I tell the pimply clerk.

The kid hits the register.

The green digits transmute. Read $11.18.

Still two cents short.

Damn.

"You got any Bazooka?" I ask the clerk. I'm a bit frantic.

"What's that?"

"It's gum. You know, it's a small piece of gum." I hold my thumb and index finger an inch or so apart. "It's that hard pink gum. It comes with a little comic. It used to cost a penny. Do you have any?"

"I don't know." The kid stares over my head. He doesn't know. He doesn't care.

"You got anything that costs two cents? Or less? A penny?"

"I don't think so."

"You sure?"

"Yeah."

"Yeah?"

He shrugs, sort of.

"Alright," I sigh. I open my wallet. I take out the eleven dollars, the two fives, the single. I give the kid the bills.

I reach into my pocket, find the two nickels, the dime. I give him the coins.

The kid takes my money. He inserts the bills into their respective slots in the cash register drawer. He drops the coins in the drawer.

He puts my change, two pennies, in my palm.

"Thanks," I say.

I grasp the plastic bag containing my purchases. Turn from the counter. Head for the exit.

I move, slowly, across the grimy dirtcrusted floor.

I move toward the glass doors.

Then, suddenly, she appears.

She pulls open the door.

She steps into the store.

She's the girl.

She's the girl. She's the girl I've been looking for. She's the girl I've been looking for, for my entire goddam life. She's the girl I've been looking for since I was a kid, sitting in the classrooms at Furley Elementary School, bicycling the Bayview streets...she's the girl I've been looking for, all along, through the aching span of years, my lonely teenaged years, my twenties, my thirties...she's the girl, she's the girl I've dreamed about, I've had a recurring dream about her since I was six, seven years old, a dream after which I wake up soaked with a warm, uplifted feeling...she's the girl, I've glimpsed her before, on different occasions, maybe I've been driving, cruising down the highway, and I've moved alongside another car, and I've looked over, and I've seen her, or maybe I've been riding the subway, and the train has stopped at a certain station, and then it's started to pull out of the station, and I've looked through the window, and I've seen her walking along the platform....

She's the girl.

She is, of course, categorically pretty. She's got blonde hair, straight blonde hair that reaches almost, but not quite, to her shoulders. She's got blue eyes. She's got smooth unmarked skin.

But, the truth is, there's no way that I can accurately describe her. I don't have the skill, the verbal agility. I don't have the goods, not like some of those other hotshot writers (maybe if I'd had a different upbringing, maybe if I'd gone to a better college, an Ivy League college, or maybe if I'd enrolled in some goddam graduate school writing program, maybe if I'd attended the fucking University of Iowa Writers' Workshop....). All I can say right now is that she opens up something in me, she opens some sort of long-shut, long-stuck trapdoor in my heart....

I stand there, on the blotched 7-Eleven floor, my sneakers nailed to the tile.

She moves toward me. She looks toward me. And, for a moment, a speck of a moment, she connects her gaze to my stupefied gaze. She erects a cable, albeit a thin cable, between her eyes and my eyes. Then she looks beyond me, snaps the cable. And she walks past me.

I shift toward her.

She stands in front of the cash register, bedecked in her long blue cloth coat, her blonde hair just above her shoulders, hovering. She investigates the rack filled with candy, gum, other sugar-laden items.

She picks up a roll of mints. Examines it.

She puts the mints on the counter.

I stand near the door and I watch her. I stand there, dead still, like a statue, missing an arm, birdcrap spattered, standing in a people-less park in the middle of winter.

She takes money from her bag.

Then everything collapses. The moment, the delicate structure, falls apart.

The glass doors fly open. And a tall brownhaired girl wearing a big coat barges through the door, calls to the blonde,

"Hey Lawrie! I'm gonna get a cup a cawfee!"

The tall girl clambers past me, her coat heaving, her arms swinging. She almost knocks into me.

She goes to the cash register, tells the clerk that she wants a cup of cawfee, light and sweet.

"What the hell," she laughs.

"I don't know," the blonde says.

"I'm impossible," the tall brownhaired girl says.

"You are."

"I know."

I turn. I turn toward the glass doors. I don't want to leave the store. I don't want to leave the blonde. I'd like to remain near her. Of course, what I'd like to be able to do, more than anything else, is to approach her…but I know that I'm not going to be able to approach her, not with her friend standing there…to be honest, I don't know that I'd be able to approach her anyway, even if the tall brownhaired girl wasn't standing right there…I'd like to think I'd be able to…but I know, for sure, that there's no way that I'm going to be able to walk over to her, to start a conversation with her, with the brownhaired girl standing there, asserting her brash reality, monopolizing the air…I don't even feel comfortable loitering on the tile, watching the blonde, now that the other girl has entered the store….

I push open the door, slide into the cold breezestruck night.

I step to the Toyota.

I start to open the car door, but realize, as I reach for the handle, that I've still got my hand enclosed around the two pennies, the remnants of my once dynamic financial portfolio. I whip the pennies across the parking lot, toward Main, the cars moving to and fro, headlights beaming, daubing the night. I hear the coins, clinking, rolling.

I get in the car. Start the engine. Peer through the windshield, peer through the 7-Eleven's lightsplashed plate glass. I watch the blonde. Laurie. She stands at the cash register, next to her friend. She moves her mouth, says something to the tall brownhaired girl. She pulls on her black leather gloves.

I watch her, closely.

She leaves the cruddy convenience store. She comes through the glass doors. She is undeniably beautiful, the wind, blowing across Main Street, across the Great South Bay, across the Atlantic, blowing her hair, her blonde filaments flying across her perfectly constructed cheekbones. She walks along the thick concrete sidewalk in front of the store. She walks, with her friend, to a red Nissan Sentra. She opens the passenger side door. Gets in the car.

The brownhaired girl, gripping a styrofoam cup, gets in the car.

I sit in the sputtering Toyota. I watch the Sentra. I watch the Sentra, very carefully, like an animal biologist watching the movements of a rare, perhaps endangered, jungle cat. The car starts up, the motor grinds, the tailpipe breathes whitish fumes. The lights flash on. The car moves, slowly, in reverse. The front wheels turn, the Sentra angles into the middle of the lot. Then stops. Then moves forward.

I turn, bend my neck, look through the side window. I can see the Sentra. But I can no longer see the blonde, can no longer discern her extraordinary silhouette.

The Sentra edges onto Main Street. The left directional blinks.

I back out of my spot.

I'm going to follow her. I've got to. There are certain things you've got to do. There are certain laws you've got to obey. If you don't, if you disregard them, you die, you perish. What it comes down to is, I can't let her go. I can't let her dissolve.

The Sentra turns onto Main Street.

I rotate the steering wheel, point the Toyota toward Main Street. For a short moment, I hold my foot against the brake, I let the Sentra roll forward, a bit further. Then I drive onto Main.

I follow the Sentra. I trail the boxy red car, down Main Street, eastward, through Bayview. I stay close, but not too close, to the Sentra's rear bumper. Keep my vision fixed to the taillights. Study the red lights, try to memorize their shape, their pattern.

I follow the Sentra through several towns. Copiague. Lindenhurst. West Babylon. I drive with one hand on the wheel, one hand clutching a can of beer. I slug the beer at intervals. I listen to the radio, to a succession of oldies. "This Guy's in Love with You" by Herb Alpert. "Wouldn't It Be Nice" by the Beach Boys. "This Diamond Ring" by Gary Lewis and the Playboys.

I follow the Sentra, tactically, tactfully. I've certainly watched enough television detective shows to know what I'm doing. I've learned, over the years, that there are a few fundamental rules that you want to observe. You don't want to get too close to your quarry. You want to stay at least five or six car lengths behind. You want to try to maneuver your vehicle as inconspicuously as possible.

In an effort to keep the Toyota concealed, I execute a couple of clever moves.

As I come to Franklin Road, I slow down and let another car, a boaty Chrysler, fit itself into the space between the Sentra's taillights and my headlights. I'm hoping, of course, that the Chrysler will prevent the brownhaired girl from noticing my shitbox. I don't want her, when she looks in her rearview mirror, to suddenly realize that the same car, my car, has been behind her, right behind her, for miles.

The Chrysler turns. But as I cross Marbleton Road I touch the brake and allow another vehicle, a Pontiac Grand Am, to turn from Marbleton and slide into the gap between the Sentra and my vehicle. I perform this maneuver, I perform all these maneuvers, with a certain proficiency, a certain easy skill. All those hours watching *Mannix* and *The Rockford Files* finally paying off.

About a quarter mile past Route 122, the Sentra slows. The left directional flashes. The Sentra pauses, slices across Main, rolls into the parking lot next to a bar, a lowslung concrete structure, a sort of rectangular box, covered with thin white paint, riddled with neon beer signs, a place called The Heavy Dog.

I drive a short distance past the bar. Then pull to the curb. I unhook my seatbelt. Twist around. Crane my neck. Look toward the vehicle-crammed parking lot. I can't see her. I can't see anything except the lot, the field of sleeping cars cloaked in sketchy darkness. Then I see her. I see the blonde. Laurie. I see her walking through the lot with the tall brownhaired girl. I see just her head, bobbing above the car roofs, her blonde strands vacillating in the February breeze. Then I see her completely. She emerges from the maze of cars, attired in her modest blue frock.

She is astonishing.

She changes everything.

She sanctifies the night, the unimaginative, ungodly suburban night.

She's the girl.

She treads along the concrete in front of The Heavy Dog, accompanied by her brownhaired friend. Then she goes through a wooden door, into the unspectacular looking tavern.

I stifle the engine. Let the radio play. A Simon and Garfunkel song, "Homeward Bound," splitters, tinny, staticky.

I open another beer.

I figure I'll wait awhile before I go into the bar. I figure I'll sit in the car and drink a beer, or a couple of beers, and then I'll go in....

I figure I should give the blonde some time...I figure I should give her some time to get her bearings, to acclimate herself to her new surroundings...I figure I should let her get settled, take off her coat, get herself a drink, before I go up to her, before I attempt to make contact with her....

Of course, the primary reason why I feel like I should wait is that I don't feel like I'm ready, I don't feel like I'm ready to go into The Heavy Dog, I don't feel like I'm ready to approach her, to walk up to her, to say hello, to initiate a conversation, to say some interesting things, to say at least a few witty things, I don't feel like I'm ready to say anything in anything akin to a confident, confidently effortless manner, I don't feel like I'm ready to act....

I remove a cigarette from the pack in my jacket pocket. Light it. Crack down the window, a fraction.

I drag, deliberately, pensive. Blow smoke out the window, into the frigid night air.

It gets cold inside the car. It gets fucking cold. Shivering, I begin to think that maybe I should start the engine, get the heater going. The only problem with starting the engine is, I haven't got much gas. I've got just three-eighths of a tank. Then again, I think, perhaps this isn't such a problem. Perhaps, I think, this is the solution I'm looking for, perhaps this is how I should rid myself of the Toyota. Perhaps, I think, I should try, actively try, to use up this meager quotient of fuel, perhaps I should deplete the tank, and then just leave the car wherever I happen to be when the last drop of petrol is spent....

I don't start the engine, however. I decide not to.

I finish my cigarette. Flip the butt onto the street. Turn up the window.

I tear open the pack of baseball cards. I go through the cards. I flick on the interior light, and I look closely at each card. I gaze at the pictures. I examine the statistics and biographical information on the back of each card.

But when I'm through, I feel disappointed. I feel terrifically disappointed.

I feel a powerful, disproportionate disappointment. It lodges itself in the center of my chest, like a rock stuck between my ribs.

I'm disappointed partly, I suppose, because I haven't been graced with very good cards. No, unfortunately the ballplayers pictured and portrayed on these cards comprise a rather unremarkable lot. I'm not familiar with any of these erstwhile major leaguers, I haven't heard of any of them, but from what I can tell, from the data on the back of the cards, each of these players, without exception, is a minor talent, a career benchwarmer, a fringe character. To put it bluntly, to put it the way we used to put it, each of these players is a stiff. Each one of them is a bum.

But, I think, probably the biggest reason why I'm disappointed is that I haven't been bestowed with any Yankees. I haven't received a single Yankee card. What I'd been hoping, more than anything else, I think, when I opened this pack of cards, was that I'd find at least one card that depicted a player wearing the sacred Yankee pinstripes, at least one card with a picture on the front of somebody with a cap inscribed with the classic NY perched atop his ballplayer's skull. I hadn't been hoping, necessarily, that I'd unearth a card that featured a star player, or even a notably capable player, I'd just been hoping, I think, to discover a Yankee, any Yankee....

I no longer consider myself a Yankee fan. (I renounced my allegiance to the team in the early 1980s, when the Steinbrenner regime became too odious to tolerate, when the game itself stopped being a game, but something else, a media-driven money-hungry beast.) I haven't watched a Yankee game on TV in I-don't-know-how-long. But when I was a kid, particularly when I was a young kid, growing up in Bayview, I had been a huge Yankee fan. I had followed the Yankees religiously. I'd watched the games, whenever I'd been able to, on TV. And I'd listened on the radio. I'd listened to countless Yankee games, every baseball season, on my transistor radio. I'd often gone to extremes in order to be able to listen to those games, there'd been many summer nights, for instance, when I'd listened in bed, when I was supposed to be sleeping, I'd curled beneath the sheets, in my bedroom in the house on Jefferson Street, my brother, Eddie, asleep in the other bed, the radio earplug jammed in my ear, and I'd listened to the late night broadcasts from midwest cities, when the Yankees played teams like the Minnesota Twins and the Kansas City A's. In those days, I'd been able to recite the entire Yankee roster, the names and numbers of each of the twenty-five players. I'd been able to tell you something about each player, some statistical information, and, in most cases, some personal information, where the player lived in the off-season, his wife's first name, etc.

When I was a kid, seven, eight, nine years old, if I had bought a pack of cards that included a Yankee, a Tom Tresh or a Joe Pepitone, I was ecstatic. It was a truly joyful moment.

Goddam! How I had loved those Yankee players, the players from those great Yankee teams of the early 1960s. They had been my heroes. Particularly Mantle. But they'd all commanded a place in my heart. And, I guess, they still do. Their names still ring, exhilaratingly, triumphantly, for me, their names still flow, breathtakingly, like lines of the purest poetry. Mantle. Maris. Ford. Boyer. Tresh. Richardson. Kubek. Skowron. Howard. Pepitone. Berra. Downing. Stottlemyre. Bouton. Terry. Stafford. Sheldon. Hamilton. Lopez. Blanchard. Linz.

Sometimes Willy Smithberger and I would play baseball, just the two of us, on the street in front of his house or my house. Whoever was batting would hold the bat in one hand, toss the ball in the air, attempt to hit it somewhere. And whoever was playing the field would position himself near second base, and he would try to catch fly balls and pick up grounders and throw the ball at the tree that served as first base.

We'd represent our favorite teams. Willy'd be the Mets. And, of course, I'd be the Yankees. We'd go right through the lineups. If I was up I'd say something like, "Batting in the leadoff position, for the Yankees, the shortstop, number ten, Tony Kubek." I'd throw up the ball, maybe I'd smack it, maybe the ball would skid along the grey pavement, deflect off Willy's glove. I'd run to first, touch the big tree. Then I'd walk back to the plate. Pick up the bat. And I'd say, "Kubek is on first. Nobody out. Now up for the Yankees, the second baseman, number one, Bobby Richardson. On deck, Mickey Mantle."

And we'd go on like that, for hours, until we'd played nine innings.

A simple, beautiful game.

I knock down two Budweisers.

Then I get ready to go into the bar.

I remove my leatherjacket, contorting my body inside the Toyota. I yank off the blazer. I'd look strange, I think, wearing the blazer in a place like The Heavy Dog. I lay the worldweary sportsjacket on the backseat. Then put my leatherjacket back on. Zip it.

I get out of the car.

I stand on Main Street, next to the Toyota. The cars flooding by. The breeze cutting in, across.

The traffic separates.

I jog across the street.

I go into the bar.

The Heavy Dog is extraordinarily typical. It's dark, smoky. It's crowded, its inhabitants are what you'd expect, young, white, suburban. A long four-sided bar takes up the center of the floor, like a wooden island, and a large number of men and women, boys and girls, are congregated at, or near, the bar.

I move through the bodies, the thick air, the garble of voices, Top 40 jukebox music.

I move past the rectangular bar. I scrutinize the bar, the brown wood, the half-filled glasses, beer bottles, buttridden ashtrays, handbags, crunkled bills. And the bartenders, two virile males moving like karate experts. And behind the bartenders, the rows of bottles, the rows of glinting liquor bottles. And amongst these bottles, a half gallon of my scotch, my beloved Johnny Walker Red.

I let my vision rest, for a moment, on the bottle of Johnny Walker. The half gallon bottle stands there, impressively, majestically. Like a museum-worthy sculpture.

Needless to say, if I had any money I'd go straight to the bar, I'd push my way through the barriers of flesh, summon one of the bartenders, ask for a Johnny Walker on the rocks....

I'd like, needless to say, to be able to suck down two or three, or four, or five, glasses of scotch before I try to approach the blonde....

I'd like to be able to, but, of course, I'm not going to be able to...because, of course, I don't have any cash, I don't have a goddam dollar....

I continue through, past the bar. I weave through the bodies, the clamor. I look for her. I glance around, obliquely circumspect. I peer into the thickets of men and women, boys and girls. Try to catch sight of her.

I move toward the back of The Heavy Dog, toward an area that contains tables and chairs, a pool table, video games. I survey the clusters of people, the different, but not very different, suburbans, milling, drinking, gathered at the tables, playing games.

And then I see her.

She's standing against the rear wall. She's wearing a dark blue sweater, jeans. She's holding a drink. She's talking to the tall brownhaired girl. She angles her head, slightly upwards, toward her friend. Her blonde hair, dropping unerringly, nearly brushing her shoulders, glimmers.

She is beautiful.

In the darkness of this place, in the darkness of this suburb, this life, she is an irrefutable spoke of light. She's the beam, from a lone searchlight, driven by a portable generator, illuminating a landscape paralyzed by blackout.

I move, I snake, surreptitiously, through the drifts of human forms, toward the recesses of the bar. Position myself in a dark neglected corner, next to a brokendown pinball machine. I lean my ass against the pinball machine. I can see the blonde. I can see her fairly clearly. But I'm pretty sure she can't see me. I've situated myself strategically. I've obscured myself behind several thick screens of male and female bodies, hair, flesh, fabric. She'd have to twist her neck, strain, go through a series of awkward machinations to see me. And even then I don't know that she'd be able to see me.

The thing is, I've got a definite knack, a skill, if you will, for finding these sorts of spots, these inconspicuous corners. It's a skill I've developed over the course of many years, during countless nights, in countless bars and other similarly dim places.

I learned different skills, you see, than the skills that some writers learn. I didn't go to writing school. I didn't get a master's degree in fucking creative writing from Cornell or Bennington. I didn't acquire all the fancy moves, all the smooth techniques, that you supposedly learn in those institutions, in those breeding grounds for standout writers. I bypassed, completely shirked, the kind of learning that apparently transpires in those ivy covered buildings on those rustic campuses in the middle of fucking nowhere. I missed out on the sort of education gained by many of the so-called successful writers of my generation.

I learned different things.

I lean against the pinball machine. Drag on a cigarette.

A woman, a girl, with a dense mop of red hair stands in front of me. She's short. But she's unusually, joltingly voluptuous. She's got gigantic knockers and a big behind that's bursting, exploding through her jeans. She's got a body that would ignite a lustful reaction in almost any heterosexual male. Perhaps the best way to put it is, she's juicy. You get the feeling that if you'd touch her, you'd get a hint of moisture on your fingers.

Four or five young men, boys, surround the redhead. They've all got scrubbed white faces, neatly parted hair, they're all wearing the same thing, golf shirts, khakis. They might be coming, you might think, from a meeting for the committee to re-elect the local Republican congressman, a reprehensible character, no doubt (to be honest, I have no idea who the local representative might be). They lean in, toward the redhead, leering, drooling, like starving dogs waiting in an alley for the butcher to throw out the unwanted meat.

I look through the spaces between the redhead and her horny suitors. I see the blonde. Laurie.

I stare at her, through the hazy interstices, the flux of bodies. She speaks to her friend. She smiles.

And I know.

I know. I know that I could live with her forever. I could marry her. I could have kids with her. I could reside with her, and our offspring, in some bucolic setting, in Connecticut or something, in some big frame house, with some booklined room, where I'd pass my days writing my quixotic novels, before joining her when the sun'd begin to drop, when we'd walk in the grass, Whitman's grass, and everyday'd be like that…until we were both grey and ancient, a pair of feeble oldsters with little else to do but hold our bony hands and catalog our memories….

I drag on a Marlboro. The redhead's disappeared. The Young Republicans stand there, staring into indefinite space, like suburban Cub Scouts, lost, off the trail, in a thickly wooded state park. The jukebox belches an archaic Bee Gees tune.

I look through the gaps, the changing separations. Glimpse the blonde.

She tilts her glass to her mouth, presses the glass to her mouth, holds the glass for a short moment to her lips.

I'd like to be able to approach her. I'd like to be able to stride over to her, confidently. I'd like to be able to speak to her, tell her, know her, move her, touch her, some way, find a way, in, to her. I'd like to be able to. I realize, however, that I'm not going to be able to, I'm not going to be able to approach her unless I receive some assistance, I'm not going to be able to make any move, any move toward her, unless I get some help.

I'm going to need help.

I'm going to need a push.

I'm going to need a boost, a significant boost, a boost as significant, as powerful, as the boost provided by the Atlas rocket that propelled John Glenn's capsule into orbit, back when I was a kid, in those days when the space program and things like that meant so much to me.

I know the score.

I know that I don't have what it takes to go over to her and start a conversation with her. I know that I'm going to need something, some unfurling energy, some power, something alot stronger than I am, to intervene, to get behind me, to shove me, to thrust me in her direction....

I drag on my cigarette. Drag fitfully. I smoke the Marlboro down, not quite to the filter. Smudge the glowing ash against the pinball machine. Drop the butt. Crush, grind it with my sneaker. Kick it under the pinball machine, into the same area where I've already kicked five, or six, similarly mashed butts.

I'm going to go to the car, I decide.

I've still got three cans of beer lying in the plastic bag under the front seat. I'll knock down these beers. I'll guzzle them. And then I'll go back into the bar. And if the beers provide a sufficient boost, I'll approach her....

I'm certainly not convinced that the three Budweisers will supply me with an adequate boost, with the sort of boost that I'm going to require...the truth is, I doubt they will...but I figure I should make the attempt...since I can't think of any other strategy, any other way that I might acquire a boost, and since it doesn't seem like I'm going to be receiving a push anytime soon from any sort of as-yet-unseen source, any sort of unexpected source, I figure I might as well give it a try....

I scuffle across Main Street. Get in the bone-cold car. Open a beer. Pour the contents down my throat. Like I'm pouring transmission fluid into the Toyota.

I open another can. Chug it.

I open the last can. I take a long slug. Then pause. Hold the can between my shivering thighs. Stare through the windshield. The cars trammeling down Main. Should I follow these cars? Should I take off? Forget about going back into the bar? Forget about trying to approach her? Let her go? Let her dissolve?

Should I face the facts? The truth? The truth being, of course, that I'm not going to be able to approach her.

Probably.

Probably I should.

Probably I should start the engine, and go, head down Main, into the February night, into the inexplicableness.

I lift the can, touch the aluminum rim to my partlynumb mouth. Take another long slug.

I hold the can between my legs. Stare.

I probably should just go.

But I don't feel ready.

I don't feel ready to go, don't feel ready to give her up, let her burn and fade.

I'm not quite ready.

Not yet.

I lean against the pinball machine. I lean my alcohol-paralyzed ass against the pinball machine. I drag on a cigarette. Exhale gently curved sluices of smoke that vanish quickly into The Heavy Dog's darkspaces.

I check her.

I study her. Standing against the wall. Her hair. Her shoulders. Her blue sweater. Her slender poised body.

I know. I know, if I didn't know it before, that I'm not going to be able to approach her. I'm not going to try. I know, like I know the taste of scotch, the grip I take when I jerk off, the grey in the winter sky, wind, cold. I know.

I understand.

I'm going to let her go. I'm going to relinquish her.

I know. I know that she's going to go and that I'm never going to see her again.

But, for the moment, I feel buoyed. I feel buoyed. Because I've been reminded. I've been reminded that somebody like her does, in fact, exist.

I've been shown that possibility endures, in spite of everything.

And, for the moment, I feel this sureness. Simple as the wind, slicing, chronic, across the suburban pavement.

I know that someday I'll have the thing I'm looking for.

I know.

I watch her go.

I drag on my cigarette, another Marlboro, and I watch her go.

She puts on her coat. She fixes her collar, manipulates the blue cloth, her sensitive, thin sensitive, fingers. Her hair plummets, ever-downward, shimmers, in the dull bar light, the non-light.

And then she goes.

She moves toward the front of the bar, followed by the tall brownhaired girl.

She walks through the tables and chairs, through the bodies. She walks past the rectangle-shaped bar. Unimpeded. Frictionless. Everybody bangs, bumps, detours. But she walks through, effortlessly, as though constructed from different materials.

I lose her, sight of her. Then glimpse her, once more, before she goes through the door. I glimpse a blonde shank, shifting, shimmering.

And then she's gone.

I scurry across Main Street like a depraved raccoon heading for a spilt trashcan. I get in the Toyota, and, wrenching my back, and smacking my hip, drop onto the cold vinyl.

I reach under the seat, grab the plastic bag filled with depleted beer cans. Shake each can, check for any residue, for any small amount of beer that might've slid down the inside of the can and settled on the bottom. Find a can that might have something in it. Hold it to my mouth, upside down. Suck on it. Suck hungrily. But there's hardly any beer. There's just a trickle, an infinitesimal trickle. Not enough to coat my tongue.

I start the car.

I stare. Cars tridding, up, down. Again, and again. Into the hampered perspective. The drain of night.

I lurch.

My cells howl. Membranes tear.

The thing is, *I want*. I want. I want her. I want to write. I want to live, some kind of joyful life.

I want.

I don't want status quo life. I don't want to follow the road designed by society's shortsighted architects, built with the usual contingent of tractors, bulldozers, the same goddam highway that everybody travels. I don't want to go along with the crowd, the numb herd. I don't want to simply go through the motions. *No.* I want to hurl myself. I want to fly.

I want something joyful.

Can't you identify? Don't you ever feel like this? Or have you resigned yourself to your small cabined life? Your joyless life?

323

I'm asking you something and I want answers! I want answers, truly honest answers! Do you hear me?! Do you comprehend my longing?! Do you ever feel this sort of longing?! This longing in the pit of your soul, this voice, this voice pleading for more, for more life, more joy?! Don't you ever hear this voice?!

Or have you silenced it? Killed it off?

I drive.

I drive down Main Street. I drive eastward, for no reason other than that that was the direction the Toyota was pointed in when I pulled away from The Heavy Dog.

I drive. I just drive.

I don't know where. I don't know where I'm going.

I don't know.

I don't know anything. I've never known anything, but now I know less than I've ever known.

I espy a sign for the Sagtikos Parkway, decide I'll get on the Sagtikos. I don't have any idea what my destination is, I decide to take the Sagtikos simply because I realize that I'm not going to be able to keep going in the direction I'm going, I realize that if I continue eastward I'm eventually going to run out of road, I'm eventually going to hit Montauk Point, and I'm going to have nothing in front of me except the ocean, the black Atlantic.

I get on the Sagtikos.

I drive, north. 50, 55 mph. The road narrow, trees, random lamps. A few cars, buzzing, north, south.

I drive past signs for the Southern State Parkway, decide I'll get off the Sagtikos, get on the Southern State. I still don't know my destination. I still don't have the slightest idea what it is. I know, simply, that I'm not going to be able to drive forever on a northward path, I'm eventually going to hit an indisputable deadend,

I'm eventually going to be rebuffed by another large body of water, the Long Island Sound.

I get on the Southern State.

I drive down the Southern State, headed west, toward the city, toward the rest of America. The parkway is rife with fastmoving cars. The cars shoot down the concrete, change lanes furiously, jockey, in, out. I don't feel at all comfortable driving on the manic parkway. I'm afraid that, in my blotted drunken condition, I might not be able to maneuver the Toyota as skillfully as I need to. I'm afraid that I might stray, that I might veer. I cling to the right lane, keep my eyes fixed, for the most part, to the white lines.

I drive down the parkway.

I still don't know where I'm going. I just drive.

I drive.

Precipitation begins to hit the windshield. A mixture of snow and freezing rain. Spatters the glass. Streams down, squiggly rivulets. I flick on the wipers. Clean the glass, to some extent. Turn off the wipers. There isn't that much coming down. But there's some. It mars the glass. Caked icy pieces, soggy flakes. Splatches. Puddles. I flick on the wipers, flick them off. Repeat the procedure, several times.

I keep driving.

I pass the Clark Blvd exit, an exit you can take if you're going to Bayview. And then I pass the Route 140 exit, another exit you can take if you want to go someplace in Bayview.

I see the sign for the Jerusalem Avenue exit. This, of course, is an exit that brings the driver into the center of Bayview. I pass the sign. I near the exit. And, without thinking about it, I slow down. I edge right. Discern the exit lane. Take the exit. Drive slowly, up the ramp.

I drive down Jerusalem Avenue, past the awkward structures, the glaring fastfood restaurants, gas stations, strip malls.

I drive into the neighborhood, the grid, where I had lived. I drive slowly, past the repetitious scenery, the boxshaped houses, the weak light burning in the windows veiled with frayed curtains. The relentless mystery. The grief. Lawns dead. Trees denuded, icy precipitation angling past dark branches. Cars sitting, dumbly, splattered.

I drive slowly down Jefferson Street, past the house where I had lived.

I drive past Chris Adelkravitich's house. Louie Plunkett's house. Kevin Anderson's house.

I drive around the corner, down Adams Street. I drive slowly past the house where Willy Smithberger had lived when he was a boy.

I drive slowly, under the wheezing streetlamps, crooked trees. The precipitation falling. Wet gobs. Pittering. Splotting. Flick on the wipers, flick them off. I drive to Roosevelt Street, drive past Mark Carroway's house.

Drive a few blocks, to Harrison Street. Drive past Andy Lerman's house.

I drive, slowly, up and down. Looking. Looking for an answer.

I drive past Mickey Fitzland's house. Kenny Pelligrini's house. Bob Filch's house.

Steve Longeran's house. Richard Zoolman's house.

I leave the grid of long straight streets, turn onto Main Street. I drive down Main. Looking for some kind of answer. Looking for a clue, a hint. Anything. An old man wearing a torn coat zagging across the wet road. A bird, weighed with ice, cutting through the air. A hieroglyphic formed by telephone wires and tree branches set against the night sky.

I drive down Main, a half mile. The precipitation increases, falls, down, harder, thicker. Plashes the windshield. I keep the wipers going.

I turn off Main, onto Garfield Street, drive, again, into my old neighborhood.

I turn onto Delaware Avenue.

Turn onto Jefferson Street.

Drive slowly down Jefferson.

Then I get an idea, an inspiration.

I perceive a crack of light.

An opening.

I'll go to Furley School, I think.

I'll go to Furley School. I'll park. I'll get out of the car. I'll climb the chainlink fence. I'll go around the defunct school building, to the schoolyard. And I'll stand in the middle of the schoolyard, under the black sky, amidst the icy, snowy mix, and I will plead. *I will plead.* I will plead for something, for an indication, an answer. I will beg. I will pray, if that's what I've got to do. *I will pray.* I will jam my knees into the moist turf and I will raise my arms to the spitting sky and I will beseech God.

I turn onto Illinois Avenue. I drive, fast, down Illinois. Then I turn onto Van Buren Street, the long straight street that Furley School is situated on. I drive down Van Buren. I drive fast. I push the Toyota. I hunch forward, grasp, strangle, the wheel, press my sneaker, down, aggressively, against the gas pedal.

I drive down Van Buren, past the wet houses, small wet yards, glinty trees. Everything blurring.

The precipitation falls, threads, down, through, onto. The wipers slap away some, if not all, of the frozen combination.

By now, the road is in pretty bad condition. The pavement is covered with a thin glaze of ice.

I drive, fast, faster, I press, down, harder, on the accelerator.

I drive, I streak, down the dark barely-lit street, through the thickening splanting precipitation.

Then I realize.

I realize that my journey down Van Buren Street is going to be jarringly halted, terminated. I get a clear picture of the crash before the crash occurs. Everything is revealed.

Then it happens.

There's something blocking my path. Some sort of construction site. Planks pointing skyward. A big mound of dirt. Concrete cylinders. Fencing.

I stomp the brake.

The Toyota skids. The tires lose their grip. The tires, of course, are badly worn. Two, or three, are just about bald.

There's nothing I can do.

The Toyota crashes through the fencing. Smashes into the big hump of dirt. Makes a loud crunching sound.

I lunge forward. I lunge violently. My seatbelt, fortunately, restrains me. My body bangs against the vinyl seat. My besotted carcass bends, shudders.

Then, there's still.

I find breath.

I'm okay, I think.

I fold my arms on the steering wheel, lay my head between my elbows. My heart's beating madly against my ribs, like the flag in front of Furley School beating the wind on a blustery April morning in 1962.

I look through the wet snowsplotched windshield. The Toyota is flush against, partly embedded in the large pile of brown dirt. Clumps of dirt lay, scattered, on the hood. The car, not surprisingly, has stalled. I try to start it. The engine coughs, gurgles. Then turns over.

I back up. The tires roll over, clatter against, the demolished plastic fencing.

I back up several feet.

Then I get an idea.

I back up a little further. Then, moving forward, I point the car. I aim the car. I aim the front bumper, directly, at one of the concrete cylinders.

I hold my foot against the brake. I look through the windshield, past the clicking wipers, the snowy globs. I analyze the concrete cylinder. It's maybe ten feet high, five feet in diameter. Thick grey concrete. A component for a sewer system, perhaps. A tank, perhaps.

I concentrate on the cylinder. I focus. Choose a specific point. A target. A bull's eye.

I clench the wheel.

Then I lift my sneaker and stamp the gas. I strike the rubber pedal with a moderate amount of force. Like I'm trying to kill a medium-sized cockroach.

The Toyota plunges. Dives ahead. Crashes into the cylinder.

There's an abrasive clashing noise.

I fly out. My seatbelt digs fiercely into my shoulder and chest. My body flaps viciously. My neck snaps. My left arm hits the window. My legs rattle, my knee slams against the underside of the dashboard.

I spasm against the vinyl seat. My body contorts, the length of it, like a fish just caught, a flounder pulled from the Great South Bay, contorting on the floor of a boat, a hook in its tiny mouth.

Then I settle. I lean back against the calloused seat. Just sit there. Do nothing. Try to gain some calm, some balance, a clear sense of the moment.

I unhook my seatbelt. Shift around, carefully. Wiggle my limbs. I don't think I've suffered any serious injuries. I've probably garnered a few bruises, strained a few muscles. But, I think, for the most part, I'm alright. I'm fine.

I peer through the windshield. The Toyota has stalled again, the wipers lay slanted against the glass, the ice, the snow, plock down. I check the car. I can't see much, but, from what I can see, it appears that the Toyota is in bad shape. The nose is bashed in. The entire front end is mangled, like the face of some guy who just got beat to a pulp in a savage bar fight. The hood is buckled. Shards of metal and plastic stick out at crude angles. The radiator is hissing. Steam is roiling, rising. I smell rubber burning.

It certainly seems as if I've accomplished my objective, it certainly seems as though I've incapacitated the Toyota. I can't imagine that the old blue car will ever be driven again, not for another gruesome mile, down these suburban streets, by me, or anyone else.

But I figure I should make sure. I should make sure that the car won't start.

I shift into neutral. I put my fingers on the key. I'm a little apprehensive. I'm a little afraid that the damn thing might start, that it might choose this moment to prove its indefatigableness.

I turn the key.

I get nothing.

Nothing.

The Toyota is dead.

Gone.

I open the door.

I stand on the street, the ice and snow dralling my hair, my leatherjacket. I glance at the Toyota, at the disfigured front end. I make a quick inspection of the not insignificant damage. I take a last look.

Then I start walking, down the icy street, through the freezing pellets.

I get back to the motel. I stand next to the door inside my room, and I pull off my leatherjacket, and I kick off my drenched-through sneakers.

In the adjacent room, a man and a woman are emitting strange primordial noises, they sound like amphibious beasts with big flippers and tails, snorting, flapping their appendages in the mud.

I sit on the bed. I peel off my cold sopping-wet socks. I fall back. Roll. Basically, I collapse.

At some point I have this dream.

I dream that I'm sleeping and that I'm wakened by somebody knocking, rather antagonistically, on the motel room door.

In the dream, I crawl off the bed. I step to the window. I separate the drapes a few inches. Look out.

I see Willy Smithberger. He's rapping his huge fist against the door. Willy is wearing traditional policeman's garb, the blue hat, blue uniform, the badge. Attached to his immodest waist, there's a gun with a big shiny silver handle. Willy is terrifically angry. His bald head is throbbing, red, his eyes are bulging, his mustache is quivering, dripping sweat.

"Cmon Pete!" he screams. Big wads of spit fly from his lips. "Cmon! I know you're in there! You better open up, or I'm gonna knock down this fuckin door!"

He removes his gun.

"Cmon Pete!" He holds the gun against his shoulder.

331

"Cmon!" He raises his leg, his knee nearly touches his chest, his big black boot hangs, dangling, in mid-air. And then, in a fast violent motion, he kicks open the door.

He waddles into the room.

"Why didn't you open the door!" he screams, stepping across the carpeting, toward me.

Clutching his gun with both hands, Willy points the barrel at my chest. His hands are shaking. They're shaking horribly. The gun barrel wavers, jerks, side to side, up and down.

"I invite you to my house, introduce you to my wife, and my kids, have a nice lasagna dinner for you, and you act like an asshole." Willy's voice crumbles, like a donut left in a paper bag, for weeks, in a cohort's patrol car. "We were friends," he says. "You were one of the best friends I ever had. Why did you act like that? You didn't show me any respect, not an ounce of respect. Drank my scotch. Got sloppy drunk. Sneered at me. Why the hell did you do that, Pete?"

"It's over," I say, simply.

"Fuck you!" he bleats. He reverts to a childlike state. "Fuck you! Fuck you for saying that!"

He throws his gun across the room.

And then he starts crying.

He cries like a four year old. Long streams of tears rush from his eyes, fall off his face, off his mustache....

He cries and cries....

Later on, I have another dream.

In this dream, I'm standing at the motel room window.

I'm looking out, toward the parking lot.

It's a summer morning. A resplendently sunny summer morning.

The lot has obviously been recently paved. It's shining. A number of trees, filled with bright leaves, grow from the smooth shiny pavement. Clay pots, overflowing with flowers, decorate the scene.

A young couple walks across the lot. The man, who's probably in his early twenties, is handsome, dapper-looking. He's got slicked back hair, and he's wearing a dark sportsjacket that fits perfectly over his broad shoulders. The young woman, who's also probably in her early twenties, is rather pretty. She's got long brown hair. She's attired, stylishly, in a peach-colored knee-length dress. She sort of resembles a movie star from another era, Rita Hayworth, or somebody. And, although I can't see her that clearly, it seems like she's happy, it seems as though she's just, suddenly, been struck with some form of happiness.

I watch this couple. I watch them raptly.

They walk, hand-in-hand, across the sunny parking lot. They step to a car, a bulky green car, a model from the 1950s, I'd guess. A Studebaker, perhaps.

I watch them, the young man opening the car door for the young woman.

And, suddenly, I realize that they're my parents.

And I realize that what I'm watching is taking place before I was born, months, maybe years, before I was born....

I wake, with the dawn. Morning's first chords of grey light slanting past the motel room drapes.

I slide off the bed. Stagger into the john.

Piss.

Pry open the Tylenol. Swallow two tablets.

I'm hurting. I'm aching in all the places I normally ache, and, as a result of my collisions with the pile of dirt and the concrete cylinder, I'm aching in several different, new places, my neck, my upper back, my right shoulder, my ribcage, my knee, my arm.

And, as usual, I'm shaking. I'm shaking like a rusted TV antenna, affixed to somebody's roof, shaking in the incessant winter wind.

Certainly I could use a drink. A drink would slow things, subdue things, defuse things. But the fact remains. The fact is, I don't have any money. The fact is, I'm not going to be able to procure any alcohol, I'm not going to be able to buy a bottle, I'm not going to be able to buy a single drink, not a single can of beer....

I sit on the bed. Grab the Yellow Pages. Turn to the section that lists alcohol and drug rehabs. I study the ads. I focus on the more elaborate ads, the ads displayed in large rectangular boxes, the ads that delineate some of the rehab's key features, that provide snippets of pertinent information. I notice several ads for places that seem, to me, like they might be reputable establishments, that seem like they might be solid, well-run institutions.

After awhile I select a place. A place called The Pines. It's situated on Long Island, on the eastern part of Long Island, not that far from Bayview. It looks like a decent place. And, probably most importantly, it appears that, in all likelihood, I'd be able to use my health insurance to pay for my stay in the rehab, given that, according to their ad, The Pines accepts "most health insurance plans."

I lay the phone book on the bed, open to the page that includes the ad for The Pines.

It's probably too early to call, I figure. It's not quite 7:30. I'll call at 9:00, I figure, at the start of regular business hours....

I sit on the bed, on the edge of the attenuated mattress. I scan the motel room. The early morning light touching the walls, the bed, the furniture, the carpeting. Gently touching. Gracefully touching.

This is something I haven't noticed before, something I haven't noticed since I set up residence in this motel room. This graceful effect caused by the morning light. Normally, of course, I'm not up this early. In fact, I can't remember the last time I was up at such an early hour. Since I arrived at the South Shore Motel the only times when I've been out of bed before 11am have been when I've wobbled, begrudgingly, into the bathroom, to piss, or to vomit. And on these occasions I haven't bothered to pay attention to things like the morning light.

The truth is, I've never been much of a morning person. Even as a kid, I never much cared for the morning, I always preferred to postpone the moment when I'd have to emerge from bed and step into the unpredictable morning air. And as a so-called adult I've maintained this attitude toward the morning, I've always been predisposed to stay in bed, to put off the morning for as long as possible, I've sought, as a general rule, to avoid the morning hours....

And certainly there's a part of me right now that would like to get back in bed, that would like to burrow beneath the sheets and blankets, that would like to shirk this February morning. That would like to delay it, defer it, forget it.

But I know, somehow I know, somehow I understand, that I'm not going to be able to preempt this morning. I'm not going to be able to ignore it. Somehow I know that I'm not going to have any choice, that I'm not going to be able to do anything except confront this morning. Confront these fresh hours. Confront this start of another day.

But, the funny thing is, I'm alright with it. I sort of already know that it isn't going to be such a bad thing, facing this morning. I sort of already know that it isn't going to be bad at all. In fact, I've got this sense, this pretty damn sure sense, working its way inside me like a bird working its way inside the sky, I've got this sense that I'm going to enjoy this morning. You wouldn't think it possible, considering my diseased condition, considering my life-predicament, but I've got this optimistic feeling. I've got this incorruptibly optimistic feeling. *I know.* I know that I'm going to gain something, something positive, from this morning. I'm going to find joy in it. If only a piece.

I'm already getting signs. I'm already getting indications that this morning is going to evolve favorably, that it's going to be better than any morning, or afternoon, or evening, that I've endured since I checked into this godforsaken motel, that it's going to be better than anything I've gone through in a long time, a long, long time.

For one thing, there's the light, the way it's landing, blessing the room.

And then, there's the silence. *The silence.* The room, I realize, is quiet. For the first time since I set up my last-ditch camp inside these walls, *for the very first time*, I don't hear anything. *I don't hear anything.* I don't hear the usual raunchy, sex-driven noises coming through the feeble plaster, I don't hear what I've heard twenty-four hours a day for the past four months, the exclamations, proclamations, grunts, groans, moans. I hear nothing. *Nothing.* It's as if somebody terminated the sound by hitting a switch, the way you terminate the sound on the TV when you press the mute button.

I stand, on my shaky legs. I listen to the silence. The deep gorgeous silence. It's like the purest music. It's like, I think, the voice of God, or something like that.

I walk across the carpeting, to the window. I walk through the silence, like I'm walking through water, like I'm walking underwater, like I'm walking at the bottom of the ocean.

I pull apart the drapes. I look toward Sunrise. I study the cars, the endless rolling forward, the tires making their yearning revolutions, the headlights burning. The morning is dark, grey. The sky blanketed with grey clouds. Everything swathed in grey mist. On the elevated tracks, a commuter train boring a hole in the mist. Beyond the tracks, the boxshaped houses, stripped trees, standing, vaguely, in the dim light.

Two boys, much too impetuous to walk to the light at the corner of Park Blvd, seize a break in the traffic, run from the far side of Sunrise, across the six-lane thoroughfare, toward the motel. Probably seventh graders, on their way to Bayview Junior High, they're typical adolescent boys, medium-length hair whipping in the breeze, winterblushed faces, skinny frames protected by thick coats, knapsacks attached to their narrow shoulders. They walk quickly past the motel, probably, hopefully, unaware of what kind of sordid businesses are transacted inside these rooms. They're talking excitedly, laughing. Their gloved hands jab the mist. Like I said, they're typical adolescent boys, nothing particularly unusual about them. And I suppose that's why I find them so goddam beguiling, so incontrovertibly, heartbreakingly endearing.

I can't help but watch them, walking down the sidewalk, walking to school, in very much the same manner that Willy Smithberger and I walked to school, hundreds, thousands, of times. I watch them, reverentially. They walk, they run sometimes, down the sidewalk. And then, slowly, they fade. And then disappear, into the grey morning.

This is the kind of stuff I find most beautiful.

Do you know what I'm talking about?

Do you know what I mean?

978-0-595-36597-5
0-595-36597-3

Made in United States
North Haven, CT
23 April 2022

18511969R00192